THE MANDEVILLE CURSE

CALLIE LANGRIDGE

Storm

This is a work of fiction. Names, characters, business, events and incidents are the products of the author's imagination. Any resemblance to actual persons, living or dead, or actual events is purely coincidental.

Copyright © Callie Langridge, 2025

The moral right of the author has been asserted.

All rights reserved. No part of this book may be reproduced or used in any manner without the prior written permission of the copyright owner.

To request permissions, contact the publisher at rights@stormpublishing.co

Ebook ISBN: 978-1-80508-561-4
Paperback ISBN: 978-1-80508-562-1

Cover design by: Tash Webber
Cover images by: Shutterstock

Published by Storm Publishing.
For further information, visit:
www.stormpublishing.co

ALSO BY CALLIE LANGRIDGE

The Mandevilles Series

A Time to Change

The Mandeville Secret

The Mandeville Shadow

For Val
For your never-ending friendship and the loan of your wonderful name x

THE BATTLE OF CABLE STREET
4TH OCTOBER 1936

'Down with the fascists!'

'They shall not pass!'

'Down with the fascists!'

Thousands push this way and that in a sea of people so vast that at times it is impossible to glimpse road or pavement. They crowd the narrow streets of the East End, forced back by police on horseback, truncheons raised against those bold enough to lead the charge.

Shops and homes are boarded. Small children are locked behind closed doors for safety. Women lean from upstairs windows, tipping the contents of chamber pots onto the heads of the police below. 'Just let that Mosley come down here,' a woman shouts, 'and I'll give him this full pot I've saved specially for him.'

A group of older children roll handfuls of marbles along the street, attempting to unbalance the police horses to make them fall.

'Down with the fascists!'

'They shall not pass!'

A young woman sits on the shoulders of a teenage boy who

clings to a lamppost as she holds her camera to her eye. She frames a group of men with hastily made placards and takes the shot. The young woman hates Mosley with a ferocity that matches that of the people she has chosen to live amongst and call her friends. They are the descendants of desperate people who found refuge in this place from persecution and troubles around the world. Now they are fighting for their piece of this land. They welcome the woman's presence here, as they welcomed her and her camera at their meetings in the last week to record the planning for their resistance. They want her to capture the scale of their action and their refusal to back away when the police bring their truncheons down on them.

The woman with the camera is not one of them, but she lives amongst them, in a small flat above a delicatessen with a makeshift studio and a darkroom in a store cupboard. She has been to every rally of Mosley and his fascists to photograph his bile, his anger, the feverish loyalty of his followers who behave more like disciples. In her day job, she takes fashion photographs for magazines. But this is her passion. To capture real life. Real people. Real struggles. To record injustices for the pages of newspapers spread out on breakfast tables, in train carriages and in tea rooms and pubs up and down the country.

'Down with the fascists!'

The woman holds her camera to her eye to capture another group of men. She rapidly winds on the film. Those in government are not simply turning a blind eye to the fascists; they are facilitating their activities. Why have the authorities instructed the police to clear a path for Mosley and his followers through the streets that the residents who belong here call home? Has history taught this society nothing of what happens when men of Mosley's kind seek power? And the terror they will unleash if it is gained? These have been the rallying cries at the meetings around Stepney and Wapping in recent days.

'They shall not pass!'

The woman watches from her vantage point, clinging to the lamppost with the young man holding her in place. These are the streets of the people of the East End. Not streets for Mosley and his pseudo-military Blackshirts to march down to further their ambitions. If the fascists and their supporters are allowed to pass, they will find platforms on which to spout their hatred. And that can't be allowed to happen.

A driver stops his tram at a junction, barricading the way. A roar goes up from the crowd. The tide continues to push forward, forcing the police back.

'They shall not pass!'

The boy beneath the woman is buffeted by the crowd. The woman loses her balance and her grip on the lamppost. She sees the scene unfold as though in slow speed. She has not put the strap of the camera around her neck. For a moment she reaches and feels she can catch it. But she can't. The camera crashes to the ground, crushed under so many shoes and boots, the film spilling from its back. She slips from the youth's shoulders. He is tall but slight, the son of the proprietors whose shop she lives above. He shares her love for photography and spends every minute when he is not compelled to work in his parents' shop helping her in her studio and darkroom.

'I'll go and get your other camera,' he shouts over the din.

'I can go,' she shouts back.

'I'll be quicker,' he says.

She nods and watches him begin to push through the crowd. A newspaper editor has already said he will buy the images she captures today. She will make sure the boy is paid handsomely for his help.

She watches until he disappears, swallowed up in the crowd.

She can have no idea that it will be the last time she will see him alive.

ONE

CAMBRIDGE, FEBRUARY 1937

'What are your plans for today?' Hettie's father asked her across the breakfast table.

Hettie pushed a piece of shell from a boiled egg along her plate. 'I don't have any,' she said, staring at the shattered shell. She didn't need to raise her eyes to see the look of concern pass between her mother and father. She had seen it so many times since her return from London to live once again with her parents in Cambridge.

'I'm giving a lecture this morning,' her father tried again. 'And then I plan on spending some time at The Ewart this afternoon. I have a couple of meetings. Why don't you join me there? It will be good for you to get out of the house.'

Hettie sighed. There were only so many times she could refuse these pleas from her parents to do something other than stay in her room. They had been kind and patient with her, but even their patience would wear thin after a while.

'Very well,' she said.

There was a pause before her father spoke, as though her answer had taken him by surprise. 'Splendid!' he said, his voice full of enthusiasm. 'Absolutely splendid. Why don't you meet me at one o'clock? We could have a spot of lunch.'

Hettie looked up and saw her mother reach across the table to touch her husband's arm. 'Perhaps Hettie would rather lunch at home and meet you later,' she said.

Hettie glanced at her mother's face. She was giving her husband a look that seemed to tell him to slow down. After over thirty years of marriage, he was able to read the look instantly.

'Yes... yes, of course,' he said. 'You lunch at home and meet me at two. How does that sound?'

Hettie nodded. 'Very well,' she said.

After breakfast, Hettie retreated to the quiet of her father's study on the ground floor. Her mother worked from her own study on the second floor, from where, for the last year, she had been deep in a project, writing a book about her decade-long research into a particular line of Egyptian royal genealogy. She rarely emerged before it was time for dinner. Generally, the only people Hettie saw during the day were the housekeeper and maids that Mother employed to take care of the large four-storey Victorian house Father had inherited from his father – another Professor Turner. Hettie had heard Mrs Hill, Betty and Martha say more than once that they were just glad they weren't called on to dust the objects and papers in the two studies. A cursory sweep and general dust down, as well as keeping the fires tended, was all that was expected of them in those two rooms. The thought that any of their papers or artefacts might be damaged, misplaced or moved was the kind of thing that would have sent Hettie's parents into a spin.

Hettie took a seat in the armchair before her father's fireplace. She placed the morning newspaper he had handed to her on the small side table. Even without him in it, her father's study smelled of pipe smoke and oiled wood, not unlike the smell of the tweed jackets he always wore. Whether her father was aware of his nickname amongst the undergraduates at Downing College – Tweedy Turner – Hettie wasn't sure. But he wouldn't have minded in the least; he was fond of all the young men and women he took under his wing to share his vast knowledge. And their name for him was a term of endearment. Often, he would invite a group of his students to this very study to consult the books crowding the dark wooden shelves, or to sketch the artefacts. As a young child and when she was home from school for the weekends, Hettie had joined them. She'd enjoyed the company of the enthusiastic young men and women who included her in their discussions and seemed impressed by her knowledge. She had been the only person allowed to touch the papers strewn across Father's desk, as she could be trusted to put each back where she had found it. Father's filing system was one that only he understood. It looked like chaos but if you asked him to locate a particular paper, he was able to put his hand directly on it.

Mother's study was the polar opposite of her husband's. It was neat with books lined up fastidiously on the shelves. Her artefacts were labelled and in a specific order of date. Papers were filed away in a walnut cabinet. Every evening, she carefully shuffled the sheets she had typed that day and placed them in a tray beside her typewriter. And each sheet was annotated with the number of the photograph that could be used by way of illustration – which related to a number in a register of images she kept, with the images in a specific drawer.

There was a soft knock at the door. Betty entered and placed a pot of tea on the table beside the newspaper. Hettie thanked her and Betty closed the door on the way out. With a sigh, Hettie got to her feet and made her way around the room. She stopped at the globe beside her father's desk. Putting her palm to the warm paper surface, she spun it gently so that it showed her all the many pins stuck into the places Father had travelled to as a single man, and with Mother before the arrival of their daughter, and where they had all travelled together.

While her school friends had spent their summer holidays with their families in Cornwall or Devon, she had accompanied her mother and father on their digs and research trips. Father's expertise in Roman England and Wales meant spending rainy days ankle-deep in mud in Welsh fields or rural England. Her mother's field of learning saw Hettie playing in the sand in the vicinity of the Valleys of the Kings and Queens or roaming the noisy street markets of Luxor and Cairo where Mother bartered animatedly for goods to take home. Hettie could still taste the sweets from a particular stall they'd visited once. When her mother had explained that her daughter was named for the Egyptian Queen Hatshepsut, the stallholder had let Hettie have her pick of the treats with no payment required.

Hettie spun the globe again. She rarely corrected the many people who assumed her name was short for Harriet. Telling them her true name was that of one of the greatest Egyptian queens felt too grand. How could she even attempt to live up to it? It was family legend that Father had made a case to have his only child named for his favourite Anglo-Saxon queen. Fortunately for her, Mother had won that particular battle, and a chocolate brown Labrador Father had brought home one day had been given the name instead. That lovely lolloping dog that had been Father's constant companion for over a decade had been Boudica or Bou for short. At least the shortened version of Hatshepsut was an easy name to hide behind, even if her father maintained the position that his daughter was as fierce and magnificent as his favoured queen.

Hettie spun the globe again. There had been times in her life when she had felt magnificent and fierce. All of them when she held a camera. At some points when she had been behind a lens, she had felt almost mighty. Like she could take on the world. After learning her trade over a summer in Paris when she was twenty-one, she had honed it and crafted it until photography had seemed as natural as drawing breath.

The recognition of her talents by fashion houses who were keen for her to photograph their collections saw her earn not inconsiderable sums of money. It had meant she could change direction and turn her attention to photojournalism, which paid significantly less. She earned half of what the male photojournalists did, and had to work twice as hard, and all but force magazine and newspaper editors to consider her for assignments. She stared at the globe as it slowed. She should have stuck to fashion. She should have taken a flat in Kensington rather than the East End. Then she would not have been on that street in Aldgate. She would not have been there to…

Hettie placed her hand on the globe and brought it to a sudden stop. Arrogance. Arrogance and conceit in her abilities had taken her to that point. She distracted her thoughts by looking at the pins sticking from points in the globe. Alongside the pins charting her immediate family's travels, another set of older and more tarnished pins highlighted where her father's father had travelled. When Queen Victoria had been on the throne, her grandfather, Henry, had travelled the world. He had been one of that generation of young men keen to satisfy their sense of adventure after completing university, before settling into whatever they were destined to become. Grandfather Henry had been fortunate that his family had made money in the textile industry and were able to fund his education and then his trips around the globe, heading off on boats to far-flung lands. Not every young man was so lucky.

The sensation Hettie had been attempting to quiet hit her like a battering ram crashing into her chest. It wasn't unexpected. It happened many, many times every day. Even so, each time was never less painful than the last. It never abated. Never diminished. Anything could bring it on. Watching people enjoying themselves in a park. Seeing a young chap walking down the street, whistling to himself. The smell of a meal being prepared in the kitchen. The thought of a young man striking out into his future.

Hettie grasped the edge of the desk, bracing herself. Her thoughts took her to where she feared to go. To the face of a young man who had no future. A young man who would never again enjoy the sun on his face in a park on a summer's day, never whistle a tune as he walked down the street, never knock on her door, insisting that she come downstairs to take dinner with his parents and sisters in the small dining room behind their delicatessen, as she was always too busy to cook a hot meal for herself and his mother and father were worried that she would waste away. Saul had had such plans for his future. More than anything he wanted to become a photographer. He had planned to earn enough so that he could employ someone to help his father in the delicatessen rather than take on the role himself. He always said how much she had inspired him. Not her fashion work – although he was too polite to say as much – but capturing the lives of people on the streets. Real lives. And he had an instinctive talent for it. People trusted him to take their image. He was genuine and could speak to seemingly anyone in a way that made them open up to him. The photographs that he had taken and developed that had hung in her studio had been such joy. He was able to capture the essence of a person. He had inspired her as much as he had said she had inspired him. And now he was gone.

Hettie closed her eyes tight. Seventeen years old. Just seventeen. If he hadn't been with her that day on the corner of Aldgate, he would not have been there when she dropped her camera. He wouldn't have raced away like the Good Samaritan along streets so familiar to him to get her spare camera. And he wouldn't have been mugged and attacked and left to die alone in a dark alleyway. The battering ram crashed into her chest again. How could she have been so stupid not to have put the leather strap around her neck? That was its sole purpose; to stop the camera falling and crashing to the ground. The memory of the camera lying shattered on the pavement came with its constant bedfellows; the look on the faces of Saul's parents who had been so kind to her. The memory of his mother and sisters ripping their blouses after the police constables knocked on the door and told them the terrible news. The memory of them inviting her to sit Shiva with them after his death since she had meant so much to their beloved oldest child and only son. She was a decade older than Saul but had treated him as though he was of value and worth. And for that they were grateful. The memory of their refusal to allow her to take the blame. The only blame lay with whoever had killed their precious son. She had no blood on her hands. They did not bestow forgiveness on her as in their eyes, she was free of blame. But the blame was in her heart.

Hettie balled her hands into fists and pressed them to her forehead. Four months later and the police had made no arrests. They said it was nothing to do with the march or the protest. That Saul had been the victim of an opportunistic crime. That he had been unfortunate to go down the alley when he had. It could have happened to anyone. All they could say was that he had put up one hell of a fight. Which gave his father some comfort.

Hettie dug her fingernails into her palms and opened her eyes. All around was her father's collection of artefacts – shards of pottery, pieces of decorative tiles, smashed bowls and plates. She no longer saw them as treasures. They were dusty old bits of rubbish thrown onto midden piles. Human life was what had value. But, thanks to Saul's friendship with her, he had been thrown onto a midden pile. Someone had treated that dear, sweet boy as though he was rubbish.

TWO

At just after one o'clock, Hettie pulled on her coat and hat ready to go and meet her father. She turned her head away from the mirror as she passed the stand in the hall. Leaving the house, she latched the gate behind her and stepped out onto the path.

A hard February frost had barely melted in the weak winter morning sun and the green opposite their house still wore a crust of ice. A woman pushed a perambulator along the path with a small child skipping beside her, protected from the cold in a balaclava and woollen coat. An older man was taking a turn with his golden Labrador. A young couple walked arm in arm, smiling at each other.

Hettie pulled her knitted hat lower down on her head and secured the button at the collar of her long winter coat. Dressed in slacks, with flat brogues, she was often mistaken for a young man rather than a woman in her late twenties. But she cared nothing for the opinion of others. She would prefer to go through life unnoticed. Unchallenged. Invisible.

She knew that – apart from the people who knew her well – she had often been seen as surly or frosty by those who crossed her path. It seemed that the world was not prepared for a woman who preferred to read or study rather than engage in chit chat or idle gossip. Apparently, she was not considered unattractive. In Paris, her face had interested many of the photographers under whose tutelage she had learned her craft. Her features were defined and definite. Her cheeks deeply dimpled, and her top lip deeply bowed. Her features were considered feminine with a strength that matched her physique and gave her presence. Her hair, which sat just above the base of her neck, had a kink to it, making it interesting to photograph. Thanks to the hair inherited from her father's side and the broad shoulders, height and strength inherited from both her father and her mother – who, as a younger woman, had played competitive field hockey and rowed for Newnham – she had supplemented her income by posing for surrealist photographers intrigued by her looks. Outside her chosen community of artists, others were confused why she chose to dress the way she did. It just didn't make sense. She was an oddity. Some put it down to her parents' professions and her having spent so much time dressed in khakis and desert wear as a child. And she let people believe what they wanted of her.

Hettie had heard people talk behind her back on many occasions. They seemed unable to align the image of the woman in slacks and a man's shirt and jacket with the work of the photographer who travelled the world capturing stunning images of women considered the very model of beauty, wearing clothes by the most celebrated designers. The world didn't know how to take her. And she would rather it left her alone. She wanted to be of interest only for what she captured through the lens of her camera.

If she had learned one thing in her twenty-nine years of life, it was that objectivity was key to understanding a person or situation. She had learned to use objectivity to capture the essence of a person or a subject in her work while in Paris. Paris had also taught her to appreciate the variety of life, which she discovered in the many and varied bars just off the beaten track. One step away from the well-trodden paths of the tourists – down winding alleys and narrow streets of the old city, hidden behind anonymous doors which led to basements or corridors to back rooms – a different world ran in parallel to the world outside. It was in stark contrast to the grey pavements and pale streetlamps. Beyond those doors was colour and personality and life. A world of free dancing and very strong drinks. Where everyone was accepted for themselves; their differences celebrated. The money she made from modelling had even paid for regular trips to Berlin where more of the same kind of clubs and bars existed. As she remembered those places now, she saw walls festooned with silks of pink and orange and red. Intimate seating areas upholstered in velvets and tassels. Bands squeezed into tight corners, playing clarinets and accordions and trumpets. There was dancing. So much dancing, with everyone and anyone. Hot and sticky and deliciously sweaty, with hosts and hostesses weaving expertly across the writhing dancefloor with trays of drinks.

Her favourite club in Berlin had a Moroccan theme. Brass lamps hung from the low ceilings, reminiscent of the markets in the streets of Marrakesh, which was why the bar had been named The Souk. No sign hung outside to announce it, but the clientele knew its name. Spicy incense floated from burners on tables whose tops and legs were decorated with intricate Mother of Pearl patterns. Festooned as it was in red and orange silks it had always felt like a tent. She had felt safe and welcome there, her differences celebrated rather than pointed out to be used against her. She could wear a tailored suit, which seemed at odds with her hair – peroxide blonde back then – and the bright red lipstick she wore. Nobody batted an eyelid.

Hettie stared at a puddle turned to ice in the gutter. Each trip to Berlin had been taken alone on the train, but she had never been alone on arrival. She had come to know many of the other visitors to The Souk and had considered them friends. But only within the confines of the club. There, they were as one, but when they drifted away from the doors in the first light of the early mornings, they waved and embraced warmly before returning to their lives.

Her final trip to Berlin had been over five years ago, two weeks before she had packed up and left Paris to move back to London to pursue her career as a fashion photographer. For a while she had dreamt of returning to The Souk, but the politics of the last half decade had seen that beautiful city alter beyond recognition. In her heart, Hettie knew that the bars and clubs would no longer exist. There was no way that the tyrannical rulers in power would allow a place such as The Souk to breathe life into the world. They had turned that city into a grey place. Devoid of light and colour. They had slammed down the shutters and stolen its soul. And they were of the same ilk as those Blackshirts marching in London. They were despicable brothers in arms. If they had their way, they would march across the whole continent – the entire world – sapping the life from it, seemingly with impunity and with the tacit complicity and acceptance of those in power.

Hettie watched her shoes walk along the path. She shrugged her shoulders to the cold, attempting to drag the pictures in her mind away from the street in Aldgate. But her mind led her down a path to a club in London on a hot August night last year. It had been a pale imitation of The Souk – as many clubs were, gawdy rather than sublime – but it had tried its best. She had agreed to go with someone she had only just met, impressed that they knew of the existence of such clubs. And there on that hot dancefloor, she had allowed her guard to slip. She had allowed a stranger into her life.

Hettie balled her hands into fists inside her coat pockets. He hadn't taken advantage of her. She had been flattered by his attentiveness. How could she have been so stupid? For a month last autumn, he hadn't been able to stay away from her. But since Saul's death he had abandoned her. Had it not been for his treatment of her, she might have stayed on in the flat on the second floor above Besser's Deli. But it held too many memories of what she had allowed him to do to her when she had been a willing participant. Images of them in her bed, far enough away from the Bessers in their rooms on the ground floor that they couldn't be heard, made Hettie dig her hands further into her pockets.

On the day she had moved out, Mother had travelled to London by train to drive Hettie's car back to Cambridge. She had arranged for Hettie's belongings to be packed and moved back to the family home. Her cameras and studio equipment had been placed in her parents' cellar in November and hadn't been touched since. The Bessers had understood the need for her to return to the warmth of her family. But they had insisted that Mother accept a hamper of food from the deli to take home with them and told Hettie that she would always be welcome to return to the flat above their shop. She would always be considered a beloved member of their family.

Hettie kicked at a stone, sending it skittering along the pavement and into the gutter. In all that had happened in those days following the loss of Saul, it had seemed unimportant and selfish to feel the pain of betrayal by the man in whom she had put her trust. But feel it she did. And it had been the final straw that had broken her. Even now, she burned with shame at the memory of how much of herself she had given to him. How vulnerable she had allowed herself to be. How she had trusted the most private part of herself to him. Hettie shook her head. She couldn't bring herself to even think of his name. Because when she did, it came with the recollection of calling it out the first time they had been in her bed together.

THREE

'There she is,' Hettie's father said. He rose from the desk in his office at The Ewart and embraced her. 'Oh, but you are so very cold. Come, sit by the fire. Let me take your coat. That's it.' He fussed over Hettie as she unbuttoned her coat, which he hung on the coat stand. Hettie sat in the chair opposite his, the soft leather warmed by the fire. She held her hands out to the flames. Her father's office at The Ewart was even darker than his study at home. It wasn't quite as full or as seemingly chaotic since the trustees and the curator he employed insisted it was kept in an order they understood.

'I'm having a box of Chelsea buns brought over from Fitzbillies later,' her father said and took his seat. 'I know they have always been your favourite.'

'Thank you,' Hettie said. She would rather not eat anything but didn't want to let her father down. And he seemed happy that he was doing something that used to please her.

Hettie's father smiled. 'It's so good to have you here,' he said. 'It hasn't seemed right your being back in Cambridge and not spending time at The Ewart.' Almost as soon as the words had left his mouth, his face took on a look of mortification.

'That's not to say I don't understand why you haven't felt like leaving the house. You've been through so much. That poor boy and his family. And you being his friend... I'm so sorry, I'm not saying the right things, am I? Your mother says it's probably best not to talk about it. We should let you talk in your own time and only when you are good and ready. And if you never want to talk about it, we should respect that too. But I hate to think of you cooped up in the house feeling glum.'

Hettie reached and took her father's hand. 'Thank you,' she said. 'And you are doing and saying just the right thing.'

He squeezed her hand. 'You are our precious daughter. I just want to see you happy again.'

'Thank you,' Hettie said. She couldn't imagine a time when she would be happy again. But if she could try for anyone, it would be her father and mother. They had never let her down.

There was a knock on the door, and she let her hand slip from her father's.

'Come in,' he called, and stood.

The door opened and a face appeared. 'Would you like me to go to Fitzbillies now, Professor Turner?'

Before her father could reply, his assistant stepped into the room. He was rather short and very slim with thick spectacles and his hair oiled away from his face.

'Miss Turner,' he said warmly. 'It's so good to see you again.'

'Thank you, Robert. And you.'

Robert was the latest in a long line of students who volunteered at The Ewart. They received no payment but gained invaluable experience in managing a collection as well as learning from Professor Turner's vast knowledge of the collection he had inherited from his father. The Ewart had come into being as her grandfather had wanted somewhere to display the many and varied antiques and collectibles he had shipped back from his travels as a young man, when he and his friends had explored the world before settling into their professions. As a professor of archaeology, he had wanted his collection to be used to better understand cultures and histories across the globe. It was well used by academics and students and was also interesting enough that members of the public were willing to pay a small fee to visit, which meant that it had always funded itself. Taxidermized animals – unknown in this country – sat side by side with intricate woodcraft from Asia, tribal masks from South America, jade figurines from China, garments made from the hides of animals in the Arctic Circle and so many more objects. Everything that had piqued Grandfather Henry's interest sat in long glass cases along with more recently discovered treasures brought back from Egypt and dug up in fields across England and Wales.

Hettie's father and Robert exchanged a few words about a talk her father was due to deliver to some interested local businessmen the next week before Robert took his leave.

Hettie's father took the poker from the hearth. 'I hope you don't mind,' he said as he jabbed the coals in the fire, sending a shower of sparks up the chimney, 'but I've invited someone else to join us for tea.'

Hettie shifted in the chair. 'Oh,' she said.

'It's an old friend. You know him. He's asked for a favour and was travelling nearby today. I hoped you won't mind.'

'I…' Hettie started. But any objection she might have made was silenced by a knock at the door. Robert appeared again.

'Professor Turner,' he said. 'Your guest is here.'

Hettie's father placed the poker back on the hearth. 'Show him in, would you,' he said, brushing his hands together. Hettie got to her feet. The door opened wider, and her father stepped forward to shake the hand of the man who entered. 'Edward, old chap. How the devil are you?'

Hettie knew the man instantly. Edward Mandeville. He was the son of a great friend of her grandfather's. Her father and grandfather had taken her to visit the house where Edward

Mandeville and his family lived on many occasions when she was small. It was in the Midlands, set in beautiful grounds with woodland and a fabulous lake that she had been allowed to swim in and boat on with some of the children of the family.

'It's wonderful to see you,' Mr Mandeville said. 'And you too, Hettie.' He took Hettie's hand in his and shook it warmly. 'I hope you're keeping well.'

'Quite well. Thank you,' Hettie said.

It must have been at least fifteen years since she had seen Mr Mandeville. His red hair was a softer shade now, flashed through with white. Age had been kind to him, and he had a friendly sort of face, if the lines were a little deeper now around his eyes. He still had a habit of pushing his round spectacles up the bridge of his nose.

'It has been so long since we last had the pleasure of your company in Cambridge,' Hettie's father said.

'Indeed, it has,' Mr Mandeville said. 'I so enjoyed my time here as a student and I don't get back often enough. Time has a way of getting away from us.'

'It does,' Hettie's father said. 'And again, I'm sorry for your loss. We didn't really have the chance to speak when last I saw you.'

'Thank you,' Mr Mandeville said. 'And thank you for coming to Father's funeral.'

'It was the least I could do, and I was pleased to be there,' Hettie's father said. 'Sir Charles had a good send off. All Saints' in Northampton did him proud.'

'They did,' Mr Mandeville nodded. 'St Mary's just wouldn't have been big enough to accommodate everyone who wanted to attend. But we had a small service there before Father was interred in the family vault.'

Hettie's father nodded and Hettie felt a tightness in her chest. She had no idea that Sir Charles had died. Her father must have kept it from her to protect her from the talk of grief.

She remembered that he had gone away on an unplanned visit at the beginning of January. It must have been for Sir Charles' funeral. Hettie looked to her feet.

'Sir Charles was a wonderful man,' her father said. 'I don't need to tell you how much my father admired him.'

'And you know it was entirely mutual,' Mr Mandeville said. 'My father always considered you father to be his very best friend. I don't think we ever really find friends as close as those we had when we were young and who shared our adventures.'

'Very true,' Hettie's father said. 'Very true. And by rights, we should be calling you Sir Edward now.'

Mr Mandeville smiled, making the lines around his eyes deepen. He pushed his spectacles up his nose. 'Edward will do just fine for me. The new title is going to take a bit of getting used to. They are rather large boots to fill.'

Hettie's father nodded again. 'And how are the family?'

'Bearing up,' Mr Mandeville said. 'You forget how much there is to sort out when someone passes.'

A knock at the door signalled the arrival of Robert bringing tea along with the box of buns from Fitzbillies. The crockery and cutlery were arranged on the small table before the fire and Hettie retook her seat between her father and Mr Mandeville. Hettie's father poured the tea and handed around the cups.

'Now, Hettie,' her father said. 'I told you that Edward has asked for our help with a little matter. Which is why I invited you to take tea with us this afternoon. You might be just the one to help.'

Hettie stopped stirring sugar into her tea and placed the spoon in the saucer. She looked up at her father. 'Me?'

He nodded. 'Sir Charles was as enthusiastic a collector as my father, your grandfather. He amassed quite the collection when they travelled together as young men. But whereas your grandfather opened this wonderful place to house his collection,' he spread his arms out, indicating the building in which they sat, 'Sir Charles' management of the objects amassed on his travels was on an altogether more... casual basis.'

'It's all rather chaotic,' Mr Mandeville added. 'Some of it is in the office in the dower house where he worked when he was in the country. But most of it is housed in one of the little workers' cottages on the estate. Father liked to keep it all together and go to visit it when he was home. He said it gave him great pleasure to be able to spend time alone surrounded by the things in the world that meant so much to him. He loved to research the items to understand them. But I'm afraid he left no notes that we can find that give a clue to what anything is. He kept his passion all in his head. And you see, Hettie, we would so like to understand what is there and what we should do with it. Your father has kindly said that he might look to see what can be housed here so that it can be kept together in my father's memory and in his name. But the curator and trustees want to know what's what before they take it in.'

Hettie's father sighed loudly. 'Honestly, I know that we need them here to keep us all in line, but the bureaucracy can be stifling. And that's where you come in, my dear.'

Both Mr Mandeville and her father looked at Hettie. They watched her expectantly. 'Me?' she said.

'We need to record and then catalogue each object so that we know what we are dealing with,' her father said.

Hettie looked from her father to Mr Mandeville. 'Well,' she said. 'I suppose that would be useful.'

'Your mother and I are too busy now with the university and the publisher's deadline,' her father said. He picked up his cup and saucer and took a sip of his tea. 'And photographs of each item would be jolly handy to help in the identification. You've been around our artefacts and collectibles since you were a babe in arms. You know enough to identify many, and to record the salient details of those that you don't, so that they might be identified separately.'

Hettie knew that there was disbelief in her eyes, because disbelief was all that she felt.

'My family would be so grateful to you,' Mr Mandeville said. 'The loss of my father has been profound, especially to his grandchildren. It's important to the family that we understand his collection and to do right by it. It would show our gratitude for all that he did for us.'

'And the trustees and curator have agreed that they would be content to accept the evidence from you to accession items,' her father said.

'You want me? To record the collection?' Hettie said.

'You would be so welcome at Hill House,' Mr Mandeville said. 'We would be happy to have you as our guest.' He paused and pushed his spectacles up his nose again. He and her father shared a look and for a moment Hettie wondered if he knew of her recent experiences. 'You could treat it as a holiday of sorts with a bit of a project on the side. There are plenty of diversions to be had. And we have a small sum set aside to facilitate the cataloguing.'

'I wouldn't expect payment,' Hettie said suddenly. She hadn't meant at all that she was agreeing to the notion, she was merely pointing out that any such project for a family friend should not be undertaken with payment in mind.

'Wonderful,' her father beamed. 'I knew this was a capital idea. It's just what you need, Hettie, darling.'

'Thank you so much, Hettie,' Mr Mandeville smiled. 'You can't know how much this will mean to everyone in my family.'

Both Hettie's father and Mr Mandeville took a bun from the box. They each took a bite and exclaimed that there was nothing quite like a delicacy from Fitzbillies, which could rival those from even the most celebrated pâtisseries in Paris. Hadn't they all practically lived on them when they were undergraduates? Hettie stared at the two men, happy in each other's company. They were the sons of very good friends who had met at university and in turn had become friends themselves. They were a similar age. And they were both incredibly intelligent. She began to have the feeling that she had been an unwitting pawn in a game of chess, and they had completed a coordinated manoeuvre with her as part of a larger strategy.

Hettie looked from her father to Mr Mandeville. For some reason, she found that she didn't mind as much as she thought she might. Perhaps some time away cataloguing the distant past of Sir Charles' collection would provide a distraction from her own recent past.

FOUR

Bundled in her coat, hat and scarf, Hettie sat behind the wheel of her car and navigated it around the narrow country lanes just north of Bletchley. Pulling onto a verge at the side of the road, she checked her progress against the map Mother had given her with handwritten instructions on the route she should take.

Hettie folded the map and looked out through the windscreen. The grass in the shade beside the road still wore its winter uniform of frost but she was fortunate that the sun had decided to make an appearance, melting the ice from the roads so that her journey so far had been without incident. Removing her gloves, she took a flask from her satchel on the passenger seat. She unscrewed the lid and poured tea into the little cup. She took a sip through the steam, then unwrapped the ham sandwich Mrs Hill had made for her journey and bit into it, relishing Mrs Hill's tangy and spicy homemade piccalilli. She would miss Mrs Hill's afternoon snacks, prepared for her each day. She rarely ate much of them but always enjoyed the piccalilli accompanying a sandwich or slice of cold pie. Mrs Hill had been with her parents since Hettie was small and knew her likes and dislikes. Hettie was sure that's why piccalilli was included on each plate – to entice Hettie to eat since she always refused lunch. And she wouldn't have to miss it for long. This time next week, she would be heading in the other direction, driving back to Cambridge.

Hettie took another bite of the sandwich and watched a bird skim along a field just beyond the shrubs by which she was parked. She still wasn't sure how she had let herself be talked into this venture. On returning home with Father only three days ago, after saying goodbye to Mr Mandeville as he continued his journey to London, Father had told Mother the news. She had seemed just as surprised as Hettie by the turn of events, but she had also seemed delighted that Hettie had agreed. Over dinner that evening her parents had barely been able to hide their grins.

At just after two o'clock, Hettie emerged from a country lane into a small village. She took a left turn, past a small green bordered by a handful of shops and an inviting looking country pub. Wildfowl waddled awkwardly on the frozen duck pond and, since it was a weekday afternoon, there were no school-aged children to be seen, just a few women pushing perambulators along the paths. Some had stopped for a chat and a handful of small children ran in circles around their mothers. Hettie recognised the green and the little post office, where she had been a regular customer when her family visited the Mandevilles so that she could spend some of her holiday pennies on a quarter of sweets.

Hettie glanced at her mother's handwritten instructions balanced on her satchel. She was to continue down this road for half a mile and keep parallel to a brick wall with a row of cottages on the other side. She drove rather slowly and watched the white cottages with small front gardens and trellises around the doors give way to smaller red brick cottages. The further she drove, the more familiar the features of the road became, so that she knew there was going to be a break in the wall which led to the gate and the frontage of the small village church. It was the only interruption in the high wall denoting the boundary of Hill House land until she came to the last few cottages and approached the set of open gates. She came to a stop and craned to look up. High above the gates was a separate panel fashioned in the same wrought iron. On it stood two golden lions, holding a golden globe between them. Instantly, she was taken back to childhood, sitting in the back seat of her parents' car, her mother driving as her father had never been hugely keen on motorcars. On other occasions, she had travelled with just her grandfather to visit his dear friend, Sir Charles Mandeville. As a child, crossing through these gates had always signalled the beginning of a few fun days of swimming or running amongst trees with whichever Mandeville children had lived there at the time, or with cousins visiting from the grand hall across the valley. Hettie had always enjoyed joining her parents on their research trips, but there had rarely been other children to play with on the digs in England and Wales and amongst the desert sand in Egypt. She couldn't complain as, even as a young child, she had known how fortunate she was to gape in wonder at the pyramids and sphinx and to watch as mosaic tiled floors were gradually revealed from beneath century upon century of cold soil.

Hettie started the car engine again. Perhaps it was those early experiences that had made her prefer solitude as an adult. She had spent so much time alone as a child that she had learned to entertain herself and built up a resilience to loneliness. Even now, when she was alone, she didn't feel lonely. She enjoyed the company of others when she wanted it, but didn't crave it. As far as she could tell, the way she had been brought up was neither a good nor a bad way. It was just a bit different to other children.

Accelerating slowly, Hettie passed through the gates and

onto the driveway. In the summer, the trees were full of leaves and the long grass in the parkland bleached to a bright yellow. She remembered how the grass had been taller than her and the other children and it had been wonderful to play hide and seek and to hunt out sheep that had managed to get lost.

Hettie steered around a dip in the surface of the drive. The cold of February gave the land an altogether different feel. The grass was short. It was the afternoon, but a cloak of cold fog covered much of the land. Trees like spindles, stripped of their greenery, were interspersed with the welcome colour of evergreens. But not even the sense that there was less colour in this February world could diminish the sight that lay before her at the end of the drive. Because there, growing larger the closer she drove to it, sat Hill House.

On any day, the fine Palladian mansion sparkled, built as it was from white Portland stone. On their first trip there together, Hettie's grandfather had explained the construction of the house and how the stone had been brought to this point from the south coast. He had explained that it made Hill House a very special house indeed, for all the effort that had been put into building it by a Mandeville a few centuries earlier. As a child Hettie had never fully appreciated its beauty. But somehow the building sitting so proudly yet subtly at the end of its long drive, was just asking to be photographed.

Hettie put her foot on the brake, bringing the car to a sudden stop. That was the first time she'd felt any desire to photograph anything in a long time. For four months, she had not wanted to be anywhere near a camera or a roll of film or trays and bottles of developing fluid. Even now, she could hardly bear to think of the leather bag her father had brought up from the cellar and placed in the boot of the car that morning. It had to be done. She couldn't very well photograph Sir Charles' collection without her cameras. But even knowing that, she had been unable to fetch the bag for herself and had tried to ignore it when she insisted Father place her suitcase on the back seat and the camera bag in the boot.

Hettie took her foot from the brake and drove the car the short distance to the house. She brought the car to a stop and held the steering wheel, taking a deep steadying breath. If it had been an option, she would have turned around and driven back to Cambridge. The only thing that kept her from starting the engine was the thought of her grandfather, Henry. How he had loved this house. He had been dead five years, yet if his presence was somehow still with her, he would want her to help the family of his best friend.

A rapid succession of knocks at her window made Hettie's heart jump into her throat. She turned to see a man's face. He pointed to the door handle as though asking whether he should open it. Hettie didn't know what else to do so she nodded. The man opened the door and held it so that she could step out. Her exit was not quite as smooth as it might have been since she had been sitting for a few hours.

'A good stretch is what you need,' the man said. Hettie recognised the accent. Welsh. A deep Welsh voice like a baritone. She judged him to be some years older than her. He had thick dark hair parted at the side. There were deep creases around his eyes – as though he had spent a great deal of time outdoors. It made him seem older than perhaps he was, which Hettie put at early forties. She had studied so many faces through a lens that making these kinds of assessments seemed second nature. He wore a thick blue sweater in a cable knit with grey slacks and black working boots.

'A stretch, yes,' she said, pulling back her shoulder blades.

'Miss Turner?' he asked.

'Yes,' Hettie said.

'We were told to expect you,' the man said. 'Let me just move this so you can go through.'

The man collected a step ladder that had been resting

against the portico and balanced it on the wall of the house. 'There was some renovation work done on the portico after it was damaged in the strong winds last autumn,' he said. 'I was checking the lead flashing.'

'I see,' Hettie said. She didn't. But it was easier just to make polite conversation.

The man opened the door and let her pass into the vestibule.

'I'll go round back and let them know you're here,' he said.

'You're not coming in this way?' Hettie asked.

He gave her a little smile. 'I'm staff,' he said. 'I use the back entrance.'

'I see,' Hettie said, feeling rather repetitious.

The man closed the front door and Hettie was alone in the vestibule. For a moment she felt unsure what she should do. Did people really live their lives to such old-fashioned rules these days? Mother's staff used the side door at home, but she had always assumed that was because it was closer to the kitchen, and it was where their coat hooks were situated. Hettie felt sure that Mother wouldn't have minded at all if they were to accompany a guest through the front door if they had found them wandering outside.

A cold wind whipped beneath the front door, so Hettie pushed open the double doors leading to the hallway and closed them behind her to keep out the draught.

She turned to look upon the hallway. As with every other time she had entered Hill House, her breath was taken away. A grand staircase ran up the centre of the vast hall, its bannisters decorated with intricately carved birds and fruit and animals, and the newel posts topped with carved pineapples. The steps were covered in a deep scarlet carpet. Above Hettie a glass dome let in daylight, picking out the stylised bronze flower tiles amongst the white mosaic tiles beneath her feet. The walls of the hall were cloaked in blonde wood panelling from which hung many paintings of people, charting the lineage of the family. On pillars in recesses in the panels, white marble statues stood on plinths, including Pan playing his pipes. Many doors led from the hall. Even though they were closed, an image of each presented itself to Hettie as though she had seen them only recently. To her left was the morning room with pink sofas and green curtains. There was a library, a drawing room, a dining room and, her favourite as a child – the billiard room – where she had spent may happy nights trying to pot balls with the other children or dancing to music played on the old gramophone. She remembered that the doors from that room led out to a terrace from where you could run around the entirety of the estate. A door also led to the conservatory where Sir Charles had grown his precious orchids. She recalled that it was as hot as Hades in there in the middle of summer and to be avoided in favour of the refreshing lake beyond the gardens.

At the back of the hall, beside the long-cased clock, a door led to a network of passageways that the staff used to move around the house unseen. It had plain walls and uncarpeted stairs leading to the floors above and stone steps leading down to the kitchen corridor, which was great fun to run up and down if it was raining outside. Another door below the great carved staircase led to a series of rooms where coats and outside games were kept and which led to the estate office. The children had been forbidden from entering that room as it contained all the important papers and ledgers of the estate, which were better off escaping the hands of enthusiastic children full of sugar from the homemade lemonade they drank almost by the bucketful and from the sweet treats the kitchen kept them supplied with. But the greatest room of all was to the right – the ballroom. As a child, it had never occurred to Hettie that it was such a magnificent room to have in a house of this scale. It had seemed right. Like everything at Hill House, it just worked.

Removing her driving gloves, Hettie forced them into the

pockets of her overcoat. She stood before the vast fireplace at the bottom of the staircase where a fire roared in the hearth. Two stone fauns – one playing a flute, the other a lyre – held the mantelshelf on their backs. Above them, standing proud of the stone chimneybreast, was the coat of arms of the Mandevilles. Two lions held aloft a globe, just as they did on the gates at the end of the drive.

Hettie took in the detail of the lions rendered in stone, their manes intricately carved. This wasn't the grandest house she had been inside. As an adult, she had visited any number of royal houses across Europe as locations for fashion shoots. Or mansions in New York and splendid and dazzling hotels anywhere in the world. But none had meant anything to her. Not like Hill House.

Hettie looked at her reflection in the mirror positioned between the mantelshelf and the relief of the coat of arms. She closed her eyes. Placing her hands on the wooden mantelshelf, she felt the warmth seep into her palms. She wasn't one given to flights of fancy, but the moment she had entered Hill House, it felt like a reassuring blanket was placed about her shoulders. As though the years had slipped away, and she was once again a child to be nurtured and cared for and to be allowed to live a carefree life.

'Hello, Hettie,' a voice behind her said.

Hettie spun around. She hadn't recognised the voice. But she did recognise the man who stood before her. The years may have changed him, but there was enough in his features to tell her that he had once been the little boy with a shock of blonde curls who had been one of her playmates. He had been a slender youth the last time she had seen him, who enjoyed wearing sporting clothes and running around the grounds.

'Bertie,' Hettie said.

He smiled and swept his fringe away from his face. The familiar mannerism left no doubt in Hettie's mind that this was the boy, who as he was closest in age to her, had been tasked with introducing her to the grounds around Hill House and all the best areas to play. As she remembered, Bertie's mother had been a lady's maid, still employed by the family during Hettie's childhood visits. Bertie had confided in her that when his father had been killed in the war, the Mandeville family had rallied round to fund his education and to see to it that he was raised as a gentleman should be.

'How was your journey?' Bertie asked.

'Fine, thank you,' Hettie said.

'As I understand it,' Bertie said, 'since we last met, you have become a famous photographer and travelled the world.'

'I wouldn't say I'm famous,' Hettie said. 'It's the models that are famous and the designers and their clothes.'

Bertie seemed to think about her answer for a moment. 'Which is the way it should be, I would imagine. Since you are behind the camera, you should be rather anonymous.'

Hettie's shoulders relaxed a little. It was reassuring to find Bertie as serious and considered as a grown man as he had been as a young man. 'What keeps you here after all these years?' Hettie asked.

'I'm the Estate Manager,' Bertie said. 'I look after Hill House.'

Hettie looked around the hall; at how perfectly it was maintained. 'I can't imagine anyone would care for this house better than you,' she said. She noticed the black armband Bertie wore over the upper sleeve of his tweed jacket.

'Please forgive me,' she said. 'I should have offered my condolences. I remember Sir Charles as a kind man. My grandfather was very fond of him.'

'Thank you,' Bertie said. 'He was such a presence in the family. Everyone is doing their best to come to terms with it. But some in the household are taking his loss very hard.'

There came the sound of the door at the back of the hallway

opening and footsteps crossing the tiles. A woman appeared from around the staircase.

'Hello,' she said.

A smile lit Bertie's face. The woman was about their age, with light brown hair to her shoulders and dressed so very neatly in a grey pleated skirt and pink blouse with a bow at its neck.

'Kate,' he said. 'This is Hettie. Hettie, this is my wife, Kate. Katherine.'

'It's so nice to meet you, Hettie,' Kate said. 'You don't mind if I call you Hettie, do you?'

Hettie shook her head.

'And you must call me Kate,' Kate said as she slipped her arm through Bertie's. 'Since Sir Edward telephoned to say you were coming, Bertie has been telling me all about your visits when you were young. You were great friends, I think.'

'We were,' Hettie said, pleased that Bertie thought of her as fondly as she thought of him. Bertie smiled at Kate and seemed to bask in the love radiating from her. Hettie had photographed enough newly engaged or newly married society couples to know when a smile came from a place of affection rather than the strategic amalgamation of two households.

'Sir Edward and Lady Mandeville are away in London with his mother and aunt,' Kate said. 'They've taken some of the children and Charlotte and her husband Paul have gone too. Bertie's mother is with them to look after Lady Mandeville and Mrs Hart. There are really only a few members of staff here at the moment. And Daphne, Sir Edwards' daughter, and Lula, Charlotte's daughter, are still here so they don't miss out on school. So, there aren't that many people around to get in the way of your work. Otherwise, the children have a habit of running all over the place. Especially Charlie and Oscar!' Kate laughed, clearly relishing the thought of the two young boys. In contrast, a sense of unease left Hettie unable to respond. It might feel to Kate as though the household was depleted but in the past few months, she had grown used to seeing only a few familiar faces each day. Having spent so much time alone recently, she wasn't sure how she would cope with so many new people and so suddenly. She might be able to talk to Bertie with a certain level of ease, but that was because she knew him.

Something touched Hettie's hand. She looked down. Kate had slipped her arm from Berties' and her fingers were on Hettie's. 'Everyone is very kind,' Kate said, softly. 'And there are many places to go if you need some time alone.'

Kate's hand lingered on Hettie's. Her palm was so very warm. Hettie glanced up to find Kate looking on her intently.

'Sir Edward has left instructions with me about what he'd like you to do,' Bertie said. 'Once you're settled in, we can have a chat about it.'

'I don't think I'll take much settling in,' Hettie said. 'I'd like to get straight to work.'

'Let me show you to your room at least,' Kate said gently, removing her hand from Hettie's. 'We can have your luggage brought in.'

'I can bring it in myself,' Hettie said a little sharply.

'Let us do it for you,' Kate smiled. 'You are our guest, and we like to do things properly for guests at Hill House.'

There was something about Kate's calm tone and her gentleness that made it impossible for Hettie to refuse her.

'Very well,' Hettie said. 'My car's just out the front. But I only need the suitcase and satchel from the back seat. Everything else can stay in the car.' Then, remembering herself, she added, 'Thank you.'

After arrangements were made for Hettie's luggage to be taken up to her room and for her car to be moved around to the drive beside the stable yard, Hettie followed Kate upstairs. At home, a well-worn runner ran up the stairs to all the floors, but as she made her way up the grand staircase, running her fingertips over the finely carved animals and fruit and birds, her feet sunk into the thick scarlet carpet.

'It's new,' Kate said over her shoulder. 'Charlotte and Paul came into some money from one of Paul's relatives in America and they insisted on spending a great deal of it on new carpets throughout the house. They've lived here the whole of their married life and want to contribute to its upkeep. Do you know Paul and Charlotte?' she asked.

'Sir Edward's sister and her husband,' Hettie said. 'Yes, I met them when we used to visit.' She let her mind take her back to the summer days and to a very kind and happy couple. Doctor Kenmore had some terrible injuries to his face from when he had been a soldier, but after a while, Hettie hadn't noticed them other than to find the scars intriguing rather than frightening. And she remembered Charlotte as a hilarious woman. Full of fun who always made sure the children had a ball.

'They have a daughter now,' Kate said. 'Lula. As I say, she's still at home as her parents don't want her to miss school. She's quite a bit younger than her cousin, Daphne, but they get along very well, so it was decided that they could both stay home rather than go to London. This way,' she said, coming to the top of the stairs. She pointed left and Hettie followed her. She had only ever turned right on the landing, to the nursery wing where she had stayed in an old-fashioned room decorated with wallpaper adorned with nursery rhymes, even though she had been rather too old for Mother Goose stories.

Hettie followed Kate along a bright corridor with many windows to let in winter sunlight and doors leading away to many rooms. When Kate stopped, Hettie stopped beside her.

'You're in here,' Kate said. Turning the handle, she pushed the door open and stepped aside. Hettie stopped just inside and took in the fine room, with two large windows looking down over the drive, a bed, a chest of drawers and a large wardrobe, all in the same pale wood. The set was completed by matching nightstands and a dressing table between the windows, which were dressed with yellow curtains to match the yellow bedspread.

'The linen and curtains were all new last autumn,' Kate said. 'Another little luxury from Charlotte and Paul. But they are the same fabric as the old ones, which is nice as this has always been a popular room for guests. The bathroom's over there.' She pointed to a door beside the bed and close to one of the windows.

'Thank you,' Hettie said.

'Can I get you some refreshments?' Kate asked. 'Audrey could make you up a tray.'

'Thank you,' Hettie said. 'But I had a sandwich on the way.'

'I hope you don't mind,' Kate said. 'But we'll be eating with Daphne and Lula this evening. We always take our meals with the children if all the parents are away. I hope that won't be a bother.'

Hettie shook her head.

'There's one other thing,' Kate added, almost a little hesitantly. 'We could eat in the dining room – Sir Edward said that perhaps we should as you are here. He said that we should give you the option as you are our guest. But generally, when it's just us and the children, we eat in the kitchen. It's easier for Audrey and Rosemary who prepare the meals. And it means that they can eat with us too. I know that sounds very informal and we are more than happy to serve dinner in the dining room.'

'I would prefer to eat in the kitchen,' Hettie said.

Kate smiled. 'I'll let Audrey know. And we eat at seven, if that suits.'

'It does,' Hettie said. 'But please, don't wait for me. Sometimes I get caught up in my work and may not make it on time.'

'If that happens, we can make up a tray for you,' Kate said. She brushed down her skirt. 'I'll leave you to get settled, then,' she said. 'I wouldn't think Bertie will be too long.'

'Thank you,' Hettie said.

Hettie listened as footsteps retreated along the corridor. Kate had been so perceptive in picking up on how Hettie was feeling and providing reassurance. Ordinarily, she would have whipped her hand away from someone who tried to hold it for too long. It hadn't been necessary for Kate to touch her at all. She was clearly just that type of person. Hettie rubbed her fingers. Kate's hand had felt more than warm. If Hettie could put a name to how it had felt, she would have said that it felt charged with energy.

Hettie let her hands drop. She had been driving for hours, clutching a freezing steering wheel. Cold had leeched through her leather driving gloves so that her hands had been chilled when she entered Hill House. Kate's hands were warm just as Bertie's welcome had been warm.

Hettie looked around. It was a pleasant room, in which many would have been pleased to stay. The yellow upholstery could be considered jolly. The sumptuous curtains held back by swags, refined. She looked into the bathroom. It was just as fine as the bedroom from which it led with a white marble bath and sink and toilet, shot through with dark green lines, with fixtures of a rich dark wood. Bottles and jars of lotions and potions sat on glass shelves above the sink and beside the bath. Even the towels on a rail beneath the window were edged in yellow lace.

Hettie returned to the bedroom. She stared at a crystal dish on the dressing table, no doubt meant for holding pins and clips. Every comfort for a guest had been thought of and yet, she had always preferred something... simpler. Some might say stark. Her bedroom in Cambridge was furnished only with a bed and a wardrobe. The floors were bare wood with a small rug. She had furnished her apartment in Paris from a market two streets away with only what was necessary. She needed only somewhere to store her few clothes and books. A chair to sit on, a table to eat at, and a shelf on which to keep an item or two of crockery and cutlery and something to cook with. Even on assignments, regardless of how glamorous they might have seemed to an outside observer, she had always sought out simple hotels or guest houses in which to stay, over the fine hotels with uniformed doormen. She had always felt the need to be able to leave somewhere at a moment's notice, taking all that was important in a few bags. It possibly came from the fact that once or twice as a child, they had needed to pack and leave somewhere in a hurry, usually when a storm threatened to cut them off or her parents realised that the next aeroplane, ferry or train would be the last one for a week.

As an adult, she had a fear of leaving anything behind that might be precious. Every evening, her cameras and equipment were packed away, should she need to rush anywhere the next day. She had enjoyed the simplicity of the flat above the delicatessen in Leman Street. The single vast room that occupied the whole of the second floor with her furniture pushed back to the very edges. The stark, white-plastered walls beside bare brick and its dark polished floorboards had pleased her. The sparseness made for a perfect backdrop on the occasions she had used it as a studio. The Bessers had offered many times to decorate and furnish it properly. They'd had it renovated and what she was living in was the shell. They had intended to reinstate walls to divide the space into smaller rooms and to paper and paint. They had tried to reduce her rent to account for its unfinished state, but she had always insisted on paying the full amount, since how she lived was her choice. She pictured the small kitchen area, her rail of clothes, the small store cupboard on the landing that she used as a dark room.

And then it came. The battering ram. Because she pictured Saul squeezed into the dark room, diligently learning his trade and smiling when he emerged with a photograph of which he was so proud.

Hettie bent and grasped the edge of the dressing table. She could see his eyes, his smile, the flick of his head when he laughed. She could feel his youthful energy. But it was all just a memory. Lifting her head, Hettie came face to face her reflection in the mirror. What she saw made her turn away and leave the room.

FIVE

Descending the stairs, Hettie found Bertie waiting for her, buttoning up his overcoat. 'It's just a short walk,' he said.

Hettie took the gloves from her pocket, slipped them on, and followed Bertie through the vestibule and out of the front door.

The ladders still rested against the wall beside the portico. The man Hettie had spoken to earlier was at the top, examining the roof.

'How's it looking?' Bertie called up.

'They've done a fine job, from what I can see,' the man said. 'We just need to clear the gutters.'

'Jolly good,' Bertie said.

The wood of the ladder creaked as the man made his way down. His boots crunched in the gravel.

'This is Miss Turner,' Bertie said. 'Hettie, this is Rhys Lewis. Our new groom and groundsman.'

'We met earlier,' the man said. He brushed his palms together before offering his hand to Hettie. She removed a glove, and he took her hand in his.

'It's nice to be properly introduced, Miss Turner,' he said in his deep Welsh accent. Unlike Kate's hands, his were cold, but his handshake was strong and firm.

'Hettie,' she said. 'Please call me, Hettie.'

'Then you must call me Rhys,' he said. He smiled before withdrawing his hand.

Hettie slipped her hand back inside her glove. 'Very well,' she said.

'I'm taking Hettie to the cottage to show her Sir Charles' collection,' Bertie said. 'When I get back, we can go through the plans for repairing the wall in the kitchen garden.'

'As you like,' Rhys said.

Bertie turned once more towards the drive and Rhys made for the ladder. Hettie followed Bertie, walking briskly against the cold. They were a short way down the drive when she said, 'What happened to the old groom? The chap who was always a bit grumpy.'

'Elliot,' Bertie said. 'He's still here. He was getting a bit old to do everything himself. He's worked so hard for the family over so many years and he finally agreed to us getting some extra help in.' Bertie pushed his fringe away from his face. 'It's a good thing as it turns out. Sir Charles' death has hit Elliot incredibly hard. He was Sir Charles' batman in the regiment and Sir Charles gave him this job when he left service. It must have been thirty years ago. He's been here since before I was born. I've never seen him like this before. None of us has. He's devastated.'

Hettie tried not to flinch. She tried not to think of her own loss. 'So, Rhys is here to help Elliot?' she said. It was a benign enough question and would hopefully steer Bertie away from the subject of grief.

'He was in the same regiment as Sir Charles and Elliot. But long after they both left,' he said. 'So, when we were looking for someone to come to work here, it seemed a good fit. He's been here the best part of six months.' They walked through the gates at the end of the drive. 'This way,' Bertie said. They crossed the road and came to a stop at the row of worker's cottages opposite the entrance to Hill House. Bertie pushed open the green painted gate of the cottage at the very end of the row and Hettie followed him up the path. He took a key from his pocket and unlocked the door. 'After you,' he said.

Hettie had barely crossed the threshold when a familiar scent welcomed her inside. It smelled just like her father's study and The Ewart. Paper, wood, and old, old things. Bertie flicked a light switch to reveal a small hallway with bare floorboards and decorated with dark green wallpaper. Two doors led away, one at the end of the short corridor and the other to Hettie's left. To her right, a narrow, steep staircase led up. Coat hooks at the bottom held an overcoat, a jacket and a couple of caps. A walking stick rested against the wall beneath the coats. Next to it was what Hettie recognised as a shooting stick. Her grandfather had owned such a stick when he had grown less mobile. He would take it on his long walks in the countryside around Cambridge and in The Fens. The bamboo handle folded out to make a flat surface of woven wicker. Carefully placing the stick into the ground and balancing on the surface, it made a passable seat on which to take a rest. Hettie had often joined her grandfather on his walks when she was home on holidays. He had enjoyed teaching her how to spot signs left by wildlife in fields and hedgerows. It was on such a trip that she had spoken to him of her desire to pursue a career in photography, even though she had graduated with a degree in English Literature. He had been so supportive. He had paid for her ticket to France and had given her enough to rent an apartment for three months in Paris. He had even smoothed it over with her parents, who had dearly hoped she would follow the family business of academia. Her grandfather had said that she should be allowed to follow her passion, because what else was life for?

'The parlour's just through there.' Bertie said, closing the front door.

Hettie stepped inside the room. The curtains were open, so no electric light was needed. A dark wooden table too large for the space stood in the centre of the room with four chairs tucked beneath its extended leaves. Shelves lined three walls and immediately the source of the familiar smell was clear. Old books with faded and tattered spines filled half the shelves. Ornaments and figurines and vases filled the other half. These were not the items one might find in a department store. They were old. They were different to the collections of her mother and father. They were more akin to the items her grandfather Henry had brought back from his travels and now formed The Ewart. This collection was not the work of a handful of years. This was the result of a lifetime of collecting. A lifetime of devotion.

'Audrey came in and added extra coal to the fire earlier so that it might be warm for you,' Bertie said. 'Sir Edward has her lay a fire each morning. Just like she did when his father was alive.'

The pitch of Bertie's voice altered. He stared into the burning coals. It wasn't really in Hettie's nature to offer physical reassurance but something about the look of sadness in Bertie's eyes made her place her hand on his arm.

'You must miss him very much too,' she said.

'I knew him my whole life,' Bertie said, still staring into the coals. 'He was always so kind to me and my family. The world seems a bit off kilter now.' He swallowed. Turning to her, he seemed to brighten. She knew it was for her benefit. 'Still,' he said. 'He lived a good life. He was respected and loved. And he made a difference to the world. Which is all any of us can ask for in the end.'

'I'm sure he would be pleased to know that you appreciate what he did for you,' Hettie said.

Bertie smiled. There seemed more brightness to it. 'This is quite the room, isn't it,' he said, looking about. 'Sir Charles could bring himself here for hours. As far as we know, he would come and look through his collection or make himself a cup of tea and a meal in the kitchen. He was such a busy man in parliament and around the estate that I think this brought him solace. He rarely let anyone else in, apart from Audrey who he trusted to clean without disturbing anything. He liked to keep it clean and tidy.'

'He has so many interesting things,' Hettie said.

'This isn't the half of it,' Bertie said. 'There's more upstairs. I don't know what any of it is, but it is all very beautiful. I don't think Sir Charles added to the collection in the last decade or so. He simply enjoyed coming to see what he had. Perhaps it reminded him of being a young man. And all his travels. Sir Edward says that some of it might make its way to your family's museum.'

'I'm sure Father and the curator will be delighted to give a home to many of these things,' Hettie said. 'It's rather an eclectic collection, which fits nicely with what my grandfather collected, and my father and mother have added to.'

'It seems fitting somehow that Sir Charles' items should find a home with your grandfather's,' Bertie said. 'They really were the best of friends. Sir Edward says that they went on their first overseas adventure together.'

'Did they?' Hettie said. 'I had no idea.'

'Perhaps some of the items were collected on that trip.'

'From what Sir Edward said, I don't believe Sir Charles kept any records of where he acquired items,' Hettie said.

'Not that we know of,' Bertie said. 'Unless you find anything while you're here.' Bertie rocked back on his heels. 'I should let you get on. I need to go and speak to Rhys before it gets dark. Will you be all right if I leave you on your own?'

'I'll be fine.'

'If I don't see you before, I'll see you for dinner at seven.' Bertie took a key from his pocket and handed it to Hettie. 'The spare,' he said. 'So you can come and go as you please.'

Hettie thanked Bertie and listened to his footsteps on the bare floorboards, the clunk of the lock as he closed the front door and the click of the latch of the garden gate.

Taking off her coat, Hettie placed it over the back of a chair at the table. She took a deep breath, thinking about where to start. She would not begin the cataloguing today. She would treat this like any fashion or journalistic assignment; she would take her time to familiarise herself with the subject first.

She ran her hand over the thick velvet cloth covering the table. When her grandfather was alive, they'd had a similar cloth on the table in the dining room in Cambridge. As they had been such great friends, perhaps Sir Charles had made an exception to his dislike of visitors and welcomed her grandfather into this very room. He would certainly have felt right at home with the heavy wooden furniture, dark curtains and crammed shelves. Perhaps he had sat at this very table with Sir Charles, discussing their collections and their exploits as young men in their Cambridge days, and on that first adventure overseas. She would have to ask her father if his father had ever spoken of that trip. No doubt it was the one charted by the pins in the globe in Father's study.

A coal hissed and slipped through the grate. The clock on the mantelshelf chimed half past two. Its rhythmic pendulum and the crackle of the flames were the only sounds in the room. Hettie turned to warm her back at the fire. She looked along the decorative porcelain items lining the shelves on the wall opposite the hearth. In hues of greens and blues and yellows, they all appeared to be from China. There was a man leading a donkey laden with fruit and vegetables in baskets on its back with a monkey sitting in its saddle. Two men carried a sedan chair with a clearly important person inside. They sat beside an array of vases decorated with mythical creatures. Amongst the statues and vases sat half a dozen creatures – half lion, half dog, with manes and large pointed teeth. Hettie knew them to be dogs of foo, which always came in pairs, and acted as guardians to protect buildings from harmful spirits or people.

Turning to the window, Hettie took in the contents of the desk: an inkwell, a tray of pens, a paperweight. In pride of place sat a chess set, its black and white pieces exquisitely carved and decorated with flowers and foliage. The set was similar in design to one her father had been gifted by a visiting Indian professor who had stayed with them for a month, and which sat on a table in the drawing room at home.

Easing past the table, Hettie looked along the bookshelves running the length of the wall opposite the window. There were publications of all colours and sizes, some with fabric spines, others bound in leather. It seemed that Sir Charles' interests were detailed and expansive, with books ranging from the history of countries and regions, to botanical and geographical histories and those of the peoples who lived within the lands. It would have been the work of a lifetime to consume the knowledge contained within so many pages, especially when Sir Charles had a full-time job of work representing his constituents and overseeing this estate and the livelihood of all who earned a living from his land. Taking a book covered with red fabric from the shelf, its cracked spine fell open at a page detailing the process for felling trees in the province of Ottawa. Hettie turned the book over and read the title on the cover: 'The Logging Industry in Upper Canada'.

After returning the book to the shelf, Hettie went back out into the hallway. She opened the door to the only other room downstairs and stepped into a kitchen with a table in the centre and a sink below the window. Pots and a kettle sat on the range and a fire glowed in the hearth, warming the air. The red stone floor tiles dipped in places from the many feet that had worked their way around this kitchen and who had kept the floor clean and free from dust, just as it was now. On first inspection, it looked just like a kitchen in any house. But similarities to a normal kitchen ended when Hettie saw the items on the dark wooden dresser beside the door. In the place of blue and white patterned dishes passed down through generations were pots that were far, far older. Hettie recognised some as Roman. Others appeared older still, perhaps Iron Age. There were beakers, bowls, jars and jugs. Some dark in colour, others the colour of clay. Some were decorated with patterns scored into the surface. She was sure that a low-sided, beige-coloured dish was a mortarium used to grind spices. A large two-handled amphorae, used to transport wine, looked as though it had been fired mere months ago rather than hundreds of years in the past. Some of its neighbours looked as though they had been taken directly from the kiln and placed on the dresser, rather than having spent centuries in the cold English ground. Hettie thought back to the digs of her childhood in muddy fields. Her father would be thrilled to see these specimens. When he next had a free weekend, she would convince him to let her drive him here so that he could see them for himself.

Hettie opened the door of a corner cupboard beside the sink. Inside, she found an array of everyday items: tea pot; some cutlery and crockery; tins of fish; packages of biscuits; a pot of paste; a bottle of whisky; a tumbler; a neatly folded napkin. Nothing in the cupboard was genteel. Unlike the food and crockery at Hill House, these things would not be found in the food halls of Fortnum and Mason or the china department of Selfridges. These were clearly Sir Charles' refreshments and the crockery he used when he spent time alone at the cottage. What a different life this was to the life he lived at the grand house at the end of the drive.

Hettie closed the cupboard door. The latch clicked and a noise from the front of the house made her stand up straight.

The instant she stepped into the parlour the source of the noise was clear. Crouching, Hettie collected the red-spined book, which lay open on the rug. She couldn't have pushed it far enough onto the shelf and it had fallen open at two pages illustrated by photographs. One showed a large wooden structure sitting beside a body of water. The explanatory caption beneath it read: 'MacGregor's Sawmill, Simpson's Bay'. The second photograph was of a small town viewed from the water's edge with a paddle steamer docked at a jetty. The caption beneath it read: 'Simpson's Bay Settlement'. It seemed to be a small town with dwellings and workshops, all surrounded by trees. Any other detail of the remainder of the town was lost behind the buildings in the foreground. Hettie studied the image. The closest she had got to Canada were her assignments to New York. If the images were to be believed, it looked quite beautiful, with clear waters and lush countryside.

Hettie returned the book to the shelf where it sat beside another book far larger in size than any other on the shelf. It was square and bound in dark brown fabric. She hooked her finger into the top of the spine, pulled it from the shelf and placed it on the table. She knew it not to be a book at all. Her grandfather had owned albums exactly like it, filled with photographs from his travels and photographs of family members and architecture. On many a rainy Sunday afternoon, Hettie had sat beside him in his chair in the drawing room in Cambridge. A fire roared in the hearth, while he turned the pages of his albums, pointing out people and places, attempting to explain his granddaughter's connection to them or the significance of each. Oftentimes, Hettie would drift into sleep to the sound of her grandfather's deep voice and wake with him still turning the pages, still describing the photographs.

Hettie ran her palm over the brown fabric. She had been her grandfather's willing audience, enjoying his company and the closeness to him, as much as she had enjoyed learning about his life and members of their family and his friends that she would never know.

Hettie slid her hand beneath the hard cover and opened the album. On the first page four small photographs were held in place by paper corners. Hettie had to hold in a laugh. Captured in the small images were memories of a day at Hill House many, many years ago. It had been a glorious summer's day, and everyone had taken to the outside. The first photograph was of a picnic on the lawn at the back of the house with a wonderful spread of sandwiches, cold pies, and jugs of lemonade laid out on blankets. The second was of the lake and children playing in a boat and swimming in the water that glimmered in the sunshine. The third and fourth captured games played later in the day on the lawn: a sack race, an egg and spoon race and a three-legged race. In all the photographs, members of the Mandeville family and their household were joined by the soldiers who were being treated at Hill House since that was one of the four summers when Hill House had acted as a hospital for wounded men brought back from France. Those that were able had joined in the games while others sat on deck chairs with Lady Mandeville, Sir Charles' sister, Mrs Hart, and an array of nurses. Hettie turned to the next page and found even more images of that day. She recognised so many of the Mandeville family enjoying the food, swimming in the lake and participating in the games. In amongst them, Hettie spotted Edward and his wife, Alice, and his sister, Charlotte. They all looked impossibly young. Bertie featured in many of the photographs, easily identifiable by his mop of blonde curls and smile. He was so small and slight and couldn't have been more than seven years of age. There were so many children and other adults that Hettie couldn't recall by name, but she knew them to be from the village. They had been invited to enjoy the festivities along with relatives of the Mandevilles from across the valley at Caxton Hall.

In many of the photographs, two older men stood to one side, laughing at the antics. Hettie's heart reached out to them. Sir Charles stood beside a man who had forgone his customary tweeds in favour of linen trousers with a matching waistcoat, crisp cotton shirt and straw boater. Hettie placed her finger beside the photograph of Sir Charles patting her grandfather Henry on the shoulder while they watched the three-legged race. She wished she could dive into the photographs. To relive that happy day almost twenty years ago. Because she had been there. She wasn't in the photographs as she had taken them. It had been her first foray into action photography after her grandfather had given her a Brownie camera the Christmas before.

'Let that camera be your eyes to the world,' he had said, as she sat beneath the Christmas tree, turning the machine around in her hands. 'The world needs bold young women like you so that it might see itself better.'

Closing her eyes, Hettie could feel the boxy camera in her hands as she held it to her stomach and looked down through the viewfinder. Keeping it as still as she was able, she took the photographs. It had felt like she held magic in her hands.

Hettie looked at Sir Charles, with his fulsome moustache that matched her grandfather's. She had only a few vague memories of the man she had met on her family's visits. Like her grandfather, Sir Charles had always felt like an old man. But standing in his parlour, she saw that he was so much more than that. He had been a man with passions that had driven him to amass this collection. She could see why he would want to be left alone to indulge his interest away from the many people and situations that demanded his attention. This cottage was an oasis of calm.

Beside Sir Charles, her grandfather was captured mid-laugh. He must have made this album of photographs to give to his old friend. Hettie smiled at him. It was her grandfather's passion for the life of adventure he had lived – with its thrilling stories of scrapes and escapes, coupled with her travels with her parents as a child – that had fuelled her dreams. Her family had filled her with the notion that the world was hers to take, they had filled her with a wanderlust. And she could trace her love of photography back to the moment her grandfather had placed her first camera in her hands. He had made it all possible.

The clock on the mantelshelf chimed three. Hettie glanced out of the window. The daylight was fading. If cataloguing the collection helped Sir Charles' family, perhaps in some small way, it would also act as thanks to her grandfather, who surely would have wanted her to do this for his friend. She would continue her assessment of Sir Charles' collection in the morning when she could do it properly and give it her full attention.

SIX
APRIL 1876

'How can we be this late?' Henry shouted over his shoulder as he raced along the side of the dock, holding his hat in place, apologising as he pushed through the crowds on the quayside.

'Because Kenmore's always late!' Charles called in reply. 'He'd be late for his own funeral!'

Walter Kenmore was too far behind his friends to hear and too distracted by the bag containing his camera equipment, which he had refused to send in advance and now weighed heavily around his neck. All their other luggage had been sent ahead to be placed in their cabin to await their arrival. Charles glanced over his shoulder to make sure Walter wasn't so far behind that he might miss the ship.

Charles apologised as he followed Henry through the crowds waiting to wave friends and relatives off. If he and his two friends weren't quick, they would be joining those people to wave their handkerchiefs to the departing passengers too. And they would be left to watch the ship slip off into the distance. After the months of planning, arrangements made by their fathers for so many meetings with business contacts, and social activities planned by their mothers that had kept the transatlantic telegraph ringing almost constantly – not to mention their belongings already on board – that would be a catastrophe. Charles glanced over his shoulder again. If anything, Walter had slowed. Unlike Charles and Henry, Walter was not a particularly sporty chap. Charles came to an abrupt stop. He raced back to Walter, shouting his apologies to those kind people who had only just moved aside to make way for him to head to the ship. He wrestled the strap of the bag from Walter and hurriedly placed it around his own neck. 'Go!' he called to his friend. Without the encumbrance of his camera bag, Walter was able to pick up his pace. Even so, he was slow enough for Charles to take hold of the sleeve of his friend's overcoat to pull him along.

'Final tender!' a man called above the din of the crowd. 'Final boarding!'

'That's us,' Charles shouted, getting ahead of Walter and all but dragging his friend behind him.

Charles watched as Henry clambered onto the tender. Men on the quay headed for the ropes. 'Hurry!' Henry called.

With one last yank of Walter's overcoat, Charles managed to get him through the crowd, drag him to the tender, push him up the gangplank and practically fell on top of him as them landed on the deck of the small boat.

'Only just made it there, lads,' a man said, as the gangplank disappeared and the men on shore began to unravel thick ropes holding the tender in place.

Both Charles and Walter struggled to their feet, Henry laughing at them. 'That's a way to make an entrance,' he said.

Charles brushed down his trousers, Walter manhandling the camera bag from him so that he could check his precious cargo was undamaged.

Henry still laughed. 'What was the point in putting up at that hotel last night, so we got here on time, only to just about miss it?'

'I didn't know that we would be getting a tender,' Walter said, still looking in his bag. 'I thought we would be getting straight on the ship. Anyway, it was as much your fault since you wanted a second helping of breakfast.'

While his friends bickered good naturedly over whether it was Henry's insatiable appetite for bacon and eggs or Walter's obsession with his camera that had caused them to be delayed, Charles enjoyed the rumble of the engines beneath his feet as the small tender began to push away from the quay. Save for the crew, they were the only people on board; all the other passengers having left more time to board the ship. 'The Oceanic class are too big to dock at the quay,' Charles said, watching the crowds grow smaller as they began the short crossing. 'That's why they need tenders. And that's why we must wait for the right tide to take us out to sea. They need to clear the sandbank and can only do that when the swell is high enough. Other ships can leave at any time as they don't need the same clearance.' He pushed back the flap of his overcoat and his jacket and removed his watch from the pocket of his waistcoat. He consulted the face. Half past midday. They would likely leave port within the hour.

When his friends failed to reply, Charles turned to look at them. Henry and Walter were leaning against each other, the sides of their heads touching as they feigned sleep. Walter was not a small chap, but Henry was a good half foot taller and almost twice as broad. Henry's height, strength and speed – not to mention skills learned as a pupil at Rugby School – had seen him welcomed to the newly-formed Rugby Football Union Club at Cambridge. But Henry was as big hearted as he was vast in stature. And, like Walter, had a fierce intellect.

Henry yawned and patted his mouth with his hand. 'Do you think Mandeville will ever tire of lecturing us on the ins and outs of the ocean class of ships, Kenmore?' he asked.

'I doubt it,' Walter said. 'And I wouldn't be surprised if he doesn't have a set of blueprints hidden about his person so he can regale us with facts and figures for the whole voyage.'

'Very funny,' Charles said, as Henry and Walter laughed at his expense. He pushed his watch back into his pocket and buttoned his overcoat. Unlike his friends, who had excelled in archaeology and philosophy at Cambridge, Charles' skills lay in the more practical with a particular passion for boats and ships. If he'd had his way, he would have studied engineering and taken a leaf from Brunel's book but, since his future involved following in his father's footsteps, it had made more sense to take a degree in politics. He'd only just scraped through, but it was enough to satisfy his father that the investment in his education had been just about worth it. And his father had the reassurance that his son's upcoming years in the military – not to mention his ability to hold an argument – would be good training for a career on the front benches of the Commons. But that was all some way off and, for now, Charles was simply the butt of his friends' jokes for being so keen on ships when, as a lad from Northamptonshire, his family seat was about as far away as it was possible to be from the English coast.

'You can thank me later, Kenmore, for making sure you got on the tender,' Charles said, pulling down the cuffs of his shirt. 'And it's *Oceanic*, Turner, not *ocean*.'

'I know, I know.' Henry adjusted the brim of his hat. 'And you know very well that I'm only pulling your leg,' he said. He slapped Charles on the shoulder and smiled.

Unable to stay cross with Henry for long, Charles instantly forgot what had irked him.

Henry's conversation turned to what refreshments they might expect when they boarded. Charles already knew. He had requested details of the itinerary along with a deck plan be sent to him from the White Star Line Office in London so that he might familiarise himself with the SS *Baltic*. They could expect a dinner of multiple courses to be served in the middle of the day, as it would be every day of their eight-day voyage to New York. But he decided against telling Henry. He would only make a joke at his expense again for knowing so much. Besides, Henry might rather have the surprise.

After transferring from the tender to the SS *Baltic*, Charles did his best to hold in his excitement as the distinctive fawn-coloured funnel with a black band loomed above them. A flag of a white star on a red background fluttered on the breeze high above the deck. Following a medical check by the ship's doctor to ensure they would be accepted by the authorities in New York, and showing their tickets to the purser, they were free to find their cabin.

'It's a bit pokey,' Henry said, after unlocking the door and stepping inside. 'But it's only for a week. Just you two make sure you don't snore.'

Charles and Walter followed Henry inside. It was indeed a small cabin, made smaller by their luggage waiting for them. It was exactly as Charles had imagined from the descriptions, with bunkbeds on one side and a single berth on the other. A small sink and a dresser unit separated the bunks from the single bed. Charles was to take the top bunk with Walter in the bunk beneath. There was no question that Henry would take the single bed. He even made a joke about how the top bunk was unlikely to take his weight and whoever was beneath might have a rude awakening when they found him crashing down on them in the middle of the night!

Their fathers, who were all members of the same London club, had been at pains to impress upon their sons how much had been spent on their trip. It was a post-graduation gift of sorts, before Charles took up his place at Sandhurst and Henry and Walter returned to Cambridge to further their studies in Archaeology and Philosophy respectively. A career in academia beckoned for Walter and a life of hunting treasures across the globe awaited Henry. Charles was to train to become a captain in the Prince of Wales's Lancers, the regiment of his father and forefathers. But that wasn't until September. And it was a small concession to share a cabin with his friends to reduce the cost of the trip. In truth, they had rarely been out of each other's rooms in Cambridge. And who knew where they might end up staying if they went off the beaten track in the Americas.

They had limited themselves to one suitcase each with the remainder of their luggage kept in the hold of the ship until their arrival. Walter's photographic exploits meant that he had a whole trunk of equipment and potions. He had even managed to arrange for a small cupboard somewhere in the depths of the ship to be set aside should he want to set up his equipment, which required absolute darkness. Walter's paraphernalia aside, with so many social engagements arranged by their mothers, each of them needed a range of appropriate suits. Charles' mother had insisted that he have a dozen starched collars packed in his trunk, along with a fresh necktie to go with each, for evening and everyday use. His mother was nothing if not thorough when it came to the presentation of her son.

From New York State, they would travel cross-country on the railroad to San Francisco and from there they would take a ship south to spend a month exploring Argentina, Mexico, Peru and Colombia, before heading home. Charles couldn't wait to shed the formality of the city for more relaxed attire. But before they could leave New York to head west, Charles would take a trip to the southernmost part of Canada to visit a business in which his cousin had an interest and had been offered the opportunity to invest in a new venture. Even though he was a few years older than Charles and his friends, there had been talk of Jonty joining the trip. Ultimately, he had been advised against it. Since his father had passed suddenly the year before, Jonty had increasingly found that his time as Lord Caxton was consumed by running Caxton Hall, which was so much larger than the estate Charles was to inherit. Instead, Jonty was funding the part of his trip that would take in Canada. With Charles' passion for engineering, Jonty trusted that he would be able to advise on whether the investment was wise or not.

Charles could barely hold in a smile when they jostled to push their cases beneath the beds. This time away was the start of a great adventure. He could feel it in his bones. He had been the instigator of the trip and had managed to convince his friends and all their fathers that it was a good idea. The truth of it was that he wanted to see something of the world. He had been away to school and then to Cambridge so had spent a great deal of his life away from the family home. But his had been a life of duty. He had attended the school his father had. Graduated from the same university. And he would go to Sandhurst to train to join his father's old regiment and then follow his father into politics. It was as it should be. Was as it always had been. As the only son of the family, he had enjoyed a privileged life. And none of that privilege was lost on him. But surely in a lifetime, there should be a time of independence. A time to go out into the world and explore. No doubt as an officer in the Lancers, he would see more of the world, but even then, that would be a life of duty, not only to his family but to the army.

Aside from a few misdemeanours as a young boy, he had tried his very best to live up to his father's and family's expectations. And he had tried to heed his mother's words when she said that he always seemed in such a rush to get to somewhere that if he wasn't careful, one day he would outrun himself and end up lost. Even now, he felt an obligation to justify this trip by making sure he earned his keep by looking after his father's and cousin's business interests. But this felt like a time for him. A time to ride wild horses across plains. A time to meet new and interesting people and to expand his horizons beyond that piece of land in Northampton – as beautiful as it was, as precious as it was to him. And Henry and Walter were willing travelling companions since Henry had ideas of furthering his knowledge of civilizations of the Americas and beginning his collection of artefacts in earnest and Walter was keen to deepen his knowledge of cultures, peoples and their practices.

'Something funny?' Henry asked.

'Pardon?' Charles said, standing up straight.

'You're smiling,' Henry said.

'Am I?' Charles said, knowing full well that he was. 'Hungry?' he added.

'Famished,' Henry said.

'Let's go up to the saloon,' Charles said. 'They'll be serving dinner at one.'

'Our walking encyclopaedia of the White Star Line does have some use after all,' Henry laughed.

Charles caught Henry off guard and pushed his bowler hat from his head. 'Why do you insist on wearing that?' Charles said.

Henry collected the hat from where it had fallen onto his bed. He brushed the brim and turned to look in the mirror, placing the hat back on his head and adjusting it so that it sat straight. 'It lends me an air of... dignity,' he said, still looking in the mirror and adjusting his tie.

Walter stood up and straightened the sleeves of his overcoat. 'It will take more than a hat to do that,' he said.

For a moment there was silence, before Charles and Henry roared with laughter. Walter rarely said anything that wasn't serious and his jibe at Henry's expense was no doubt unintentionally funny.

'Well done, old man,' Henry said, patting his friend on the back. 'You seem to have unearthed a sense of humour.'

Walter smiled, clearly pleased with himself. He was considered handsome by the girls that came into their path. He was rather fair with a bookish air about him that women seemed to find appealing. Charles glanced into the mirror above the sink. He ran his hand over his dark hair in an attempt to straighten the curls that seemed to want to break free from his hair cream. He was fighting a losing battle since the slightest whiff of moisture in the air saw his hair take on a life of its own. He always returned from family trips to the coast at Hunstanton with uncontrollable locks that made his little sister, Leonora, call him Medusa. Since for the next week he was to be surrounded by hundreds of leagues of salty air, he may as well get used to presenting himself as nature intended.

Smiling at his reflection and at the reflection of his friends, Charles said, 'Leave your overcoats on, chaps. We can take a turn on deck and watch our departure from Liverpool. Hand that bag here,' he said to Walter. 'If we hurry, you can set your camera up on deck before we leave port so you can get that photograph you want.'

SEVEN
FEBRUARY 1937

Daylight had all but faded when Hettie pushed open the great front door of Hill House. She paused to warm her hands before the flames in the fireplace in the hallway. Apart from the tick of the long-cased clock, the house was silent. It was the lull following teatime, when people retreated to separate rooms, perhaps to read or pursue a hobby for a few hours before dinner.

Her family's home mightn't be anywhere close to the grandeur of Hill House, but her father insisted they maintain the mealtimes he had known all his life and had been established by his parents. Her father took after his parents; he enjoyed eating and found great pleasure in feeding his household and any guest lucky enough to stay in their home and experience his hospitality. Hettie had broken with the mealtime conventions with which she had grown up when she left home. She was often too busy to sit down to eat and frequently rustled up meals on the small cooker of whatever apartment or flat she rented, eating while standing in breaks in her work. She was just as likely to grab a baguette from a boulangerie in Paris and eat chunks of it while walking. Or buy a penny loaf from a bakery in London. She might go to a restaurant in whichever city she found herself working in. Eating alone was not a prospect that bothered her in the slightest. It wasn't that she didn't enjoy eating – she enjoyed it very much – but she hated the thought of being tied to a time and a place. As often as not, when she was in London, she would not eat but head straight to her darkroom to complete the day's work or go out to meet friends in bars or cafes. If she forgot to eat when she had spent an evening in her darkroom, she would invariably find a cracker or two in the battered silver-coloured tin that went with her wherever she lived. It had been her Grandfather Henry's tin – the tin that he carried sandwiches in whenever they went on one of their walks. He would produce it from the canvas bag he carried over his shoulder and, with great ceremony, remove the lid so that Hettie might take her sandwich first. The sandwiches were always the same – cheese and Mrs Hill's piccalilli. As Hettie settled herself on whichever tree stump her grandfather had found for her to sit on, he would lay out their picnic, while resting against his shooting stick. There would be steaming sweet tea poured from his flask and there was always cake tucked inside another tin.

'Every meal should be a small celebration,' her grandfather would say, when he held up his sandwich for her to tap hers against his as they both called out, 'Cheers!'

It had been Grandfather Henry who had explained to her that people said cheers and smashed their glasses or pint pots together so that some of each drink would slop into the glass of the other person. That way each would know that the other wasn't attempting to poison them. When Hettie had asked him why one person would want to poison another, her grandfather had said that it was wise to always be a little suspicious of a stranger until you got to know them. It was even a good idea to keep an eye on a friend, lest they turn against you.

Hettie smiled. There he was in her mind's eye again – Grandfather Henry – the tall and broad man who, like her father, had worn tweeds and was always so smart, with a freshly pressed handkerchief in his pocket to match his bowtie. Apparently, Hettie's grandmother had picked it out for him each morning when she was alive. But Hettie had no memory of her grandmother who had died before she was born. It was the reason her parents had decided to move into Grandfather Henry's house. They couldn't bear to think of him alone.

Growing up, Hettie couldn't have imagined not living in her grandfather's house and having him around every day. He had spoken to her like she was quite grown up and had explained everything so that his only grandchild might learn. He answered any question she asked of him and if he didn't know the answer, he would take her to his study to consult the books and encyclopaedias on the shelves. Hettie had secretly thought that really, he knew the answer but enjoyed the little performance and enjoyed even more teaching her how to research using resources. It had worked to an extent as she did like to learn, but not in the traditional sense. Even Grandfather Henry's influence hadn't been enough to pull her back to the world of academia – the lure of the arts had been too strong and irresistible.

Hettie smiled again. She had thought about her grandfather more that afternoon than she had in many years. Leaving the warmth of the fire, she took a turn slowly about the hall, the squeak from the leather soles of her boots joining the tick of the clock. She paused to look at the many works of art. The old portraits lining the walls were fine in detail and captured rather stern-looking men in powdered wigs, women in silk dresses and children playing with hoops, many with animals seated beside them or at their feet. Hettie stopped to peer into the face of the statue of Pan positioned in a recess in the panelling. He was carved from the purest white marble, which glittered in the light from the lamps around the hall. He stood proudly on his plinth, forever blowing his pipes. On one of their visits, when Hettie had been eight or nine years of age, her grandfather had explained that to avoid Pan's amorous advances – her grandfather had never shied away from using the correct terminology, believing children should not be spoken to as though they could not understand concepts – the nymph Syrinx had run to the river and begged the river nymphs for assistance. To save her, they had turned her into a reed. Bereft at the loss of Syrinx, Pan was destined to spend eternity playing pipes, replicating the haunting sound of the wind through the reeds, reminding him of his lost love. Hettie had said to her grandfather that Pan sounded like a rather nasty person to have been so determined to have driven Syrinx to turn herself into a reed. And wasn't it rum that it was he who was immortalised rather than Syrinx? Her grandfather had agreed.

'It is often the case that the rotten are remembered,' he had said. 'Often but not always.' That's when he had taken her by the hand and led her to the portrait hung beneath the staircase. It was the largest painting in the hallway and was the life-sized portrait of Thomas Mandeville. He had been Sir Charles' oldest son and had given his life in the war. 'Remember,' her grandfather had said to Hettie. 'In our own lives, we should place laurel wreaths on the heads of our heroes and consign villains to the past. But we must never forget the wrongs the villains have done us.'

Then, as now, Hettie stared up into the eyes of the man in the portrait. Thomas Mandeville had been her grandfather's only godchild. Since she had been her grandfather's only granddaughter, as a young girl she had felt it meant that she had an affinity with that handsome man in the painting, sitting astride his fine horse, in his marvellous blue uniform with golden braid and a red plume blowing from the golden helmet in an unseen breeze. With no brothers, sisters or cousins, in her childish mind, she had decided that Thomas Mandeville was as close she would ever get to a sibling, even if he had been more than two decades older than her.

It was a memory that Hettie hadn't considered in years. The odd familiarity of a man who, when she had known him, had probably been just about old enough to be her own father. Vague memories of Thomas came back to her. She was sure she had ridden on his shoulders when he pretended to be a horse, and she had squealed with delight as he charged around Hill House with his mother telling him off as it might make their little visitor ill. Wouldn't she rather play with the dolls' house instead?

Hettie had foregone the dolls in favour of pretending to be a general. Thomas had always been kind and a fun grown-up to be around. He was full of japes and jokes, as though he was an overgrown little boy. But beyond those memories of charging around on his shoulders, her recollections of Thomas were few and far between. She knew she had spent time with him, as after his passing her grandfather had reminisced often about the times she had taken tea with him and Thomas.

Hettie looked up into the eyes in the painting. When she was small, she had delighted in moving around so that Thomas' eyes always seemed to follow her. They were kind eyes. With a smile in them. As she had grown older, she realised that it was a technique artists had perfected to make it seem that their sitters were looking at the viewer.

Hettie continued to stare into Thomas' eyes. Her grandfather had considered his godson a hero. But in being heroic, his actions had meant that he had died before achieving all that had waited for him in life. Hettie turned away briefly. When she looked back, he was still there. Still looking at her with his kind eyes. If he knew the part she had played in the death of another young man, he would not look on her with such benevolence.

'Miss Turner,' a voice said behind her. It was a deep voice. With a Welsh accent.

Hettie rubbed her hand across her eyes and breathed in deeply before turning around slowly. Rhys stood before her. Watching her. Waiting for a reply.

'Hettie,' she corrected.

Rhys tipped his head to one side. 'It seems rather informal to address you by your Christian name when we've only just met.'

'But you want me to call you Rhys?' she said.

'I work here,' he said. 'So, there's nothing unusual in a guest of the family addressing me by my Christian name.'

'I'm here working. So, we're equal,' Hettie said.

Hettie was sure she saw a smile in Rhys' eyes. He lowered his voice and leant in a little closer. 'I've never received an invitation to stay for dinner. And I've never been offered to stay in the fanciest guest bedroom. So, I think we know who is more equal.'

Hettie had spent so little time around people outside of her family for months that she was at a loss for how to respond. At one time she had been known for her dry wit and comebacks. And she had frequently been asked for her opinions as she took an interest in every subject discussed within the pages of the serious newspapers. When she said something in company, people listened. Now she rarely opened the pages of The Times, and it was even rarer for her to hold a conversation. She was almost tempted to explain that her preferential treatment was only because her grandfather and Sir Charles had been friends. But that might sound like she was attempting to sound grand. Which wasn't her intention. 'I didn't mean to be rude,' she said.

'Oh,' Rhys said. 'I don't think you're rude at all. Straight talking. I admire that.'

He paused. But Hettie had nothing to say.

'Katherine asked me to bring your luggage in,' Rhys said. 'I left it inside your bedroom door.'

A sense of dread welled in Hettie. 'Just the suitcase and satchel,' she said.

'That's right,' Rhys said. 'Only what was on the back seat. Katherine asked me to leave everything else.'

Hettie's dread sank back to where it had come from. She looked to the floor. Rhys' black work boots seemed so large and utilitarian against the fine bronze and white floral tiles. She watched as his stance shifted slightly.

'Is everything all right?' he asked.

Hettie continued to stare at his boots.

'Some might say that I speak out of turn,' Rhys said. 'But if I see someone is not quite right, I must do something. It's the way I'm made.'

Hettie looked up to find Rhys looking at her intently. His eyes were so dark and there seemed such a depth to them that for the briefest moment, she was tempted to say 'no' everything was not all right. But she knew nothing of this man. And her secrets were hers to keep. 'Thank you,' she said. 'For your concern. And for bringing my luggage in.'

'It was no trouble. No trouble at all,' he said.

'I should go,' Hettie said. 'I should unpack.'

Rhys nodded. 'If you need anything during your stay that I can help with, I am always here.'

'Thank you,' she said. Turning from him, she steadied herself briefly on the newel post shaped like a pineapple. When she took the first step on the scarlet carpet and moved her palm to the handrail, she watched as Rhys walked slowly up the hall towards the door at the back. She continued and didn't look down to see whether he was looking up at her.

EIGHT

Hettie made her way along the landing to the guest bedroom. She found her satchel and suitcase just inside the door and after unpacking, sat at the small desk and made some notes in her notebook from her first perusal of Sir Charles' collection, recalling the objects as best she could. After that, she sat in a chair before the fire that someone had kindly made up in the room for her. She hoped she hadn't offended Rhys in some way. Or caused him to feel concerned about her. He must have been confused by her reaction to simple statements and questions. If she was unable to control how she might react, she could not expect anyone – especially a complete stranger – to understand why she had responded as she did. And he seemed decent enough. She would apologise to him when next she saw him. There would be no explanation for why she acted as she did as that would require a revelation. It would be enough to say sorry and leave it at that.

At just before seven o'clock, Hettie took the stairs down into the hallway. It was a relief that Rhys hadn't felt the need to tug his forelock around her. Even if he had baulked at using her Christian name initially, he had spoken to her in what had seemed to be a candid and casual way. He hadn't appeared to feel the need to treat her as though she was better than he was – when she was nothing of the sort. As far as she was concerned, nobody was inherently better than the next person, simply by virtue of their birth or good fortune. A person's worth should be found in their actions, not their breeding. That aside, she would need to be more on her guard. As pleasant as Rhys was, she couldn't allow her composure to slip. The façade she had constructed around herself was all that was holding her together. And she was here to do a job of work, a job from which she must not be distracted by mining her thoughts or feelings.

Hettie recalled enough of the geography of Hill House to know how to find the kitchen. At the back of the hall, she opened the door beside the long-cased clock. The moment she entered the narrow passageway, she shivered. In contrast to the hall she had left behind, this passage was unheated, its walls simply whitewashed and lit by unshaded bulbs. Wrapping her arms around her body against the cold, Hettie walked along the flagged floor. Each step was familiar to her, as this was the network of passages she had run along in frenzied games of hide and seek with the children of the house. She came to the series of bells high up on the wall, each linked to rooms by a series of springs and pulleys, and all labelled to denote the rooms that a member of staff would be summoned to: *Ballroom, Morning Room, Dining Room, Billiard Room*, and any number of other rooms across the three floors. Hettie knew that if she continued, she would come to a staircase leading to all the floors above that gave out onto landings through a series of hidden doors, decorated to mimic the walls in which they stood. There was a similar staircase at the other end of the house leading up from the secret door in the billiard room. If it had been possible for a building to possess the ability to replay events or to soak up a noise to replay, she would be hearing the screeches of children racing to find each other. She would be hiding inside the wardrobe up in the nursery, holding her breath, peering through the gap in the doors, afraid that the seeker might spot her eyeball, and she would lose the game! How free those times had been. How much fun there had always seemed to be with such enthusiastic playmates at Hill House.

Coming to the steps leading down, Hettie paused. The sound of voices floated up to greet her. She made a pyramid of her fingers and placed both forefingers on either side of the bridge of her nose. She pressed her fingertips into the corners of her eyes. In a moment or two, she would be in the familiar kitchen, but it would be filled with unfamiliar people. She would have to sit with them. Eat with them. Converse with them. It couldn't be avoided. To return to her room would be rude. She may be considered brusque by some. Standoffish by others. But she would never intentionally cause offence. Bertie would be there at least. She knew him. Sort of. She knew five-year-old Bertie. Ten-year-old Bertie. Twelve-year-old Bertie. Adult Bertie had been kind to her today. As had Kate. And she couldn't repay that kindness by returning to her room with no explanation.

Hettie covered her face with her hands briefly, before drawing her palms down her cheeks and rubbing her hands together. She was not here to make friends. She was here to work. She could be polite but reserved. If that was the impression she gave, then she would not have shamed herself. Or embarrassed Sir Edward who had invited her here.

Hettie took the few steps down, placing her boots into the grooves worn into the stone by years of footsteps heading this way. She came to the long basement corridor painted in pristine white with flagged floors and doors leading to what she recalled as a variety of storerooms and rooms for preparing food, offices and a parlour. A half-glazed door at the very end led to the outside and to a set of steps heading up to ground level. It was the way staff and tradespeople entered the house. As Rhys had reminded her earlier.

'Hello.' A woman had appeared from the door that Hettie knew led to the kitchen. She wore a dark dress with a white apron around her waist and her dark hair was pulled back in a tight bun, which gave the impression of a woman older than Hettie guessed her to be, which was mid-twenties. She pushed her spectacles up her nose with the side of her hand and said, 'You're a bit early.'

'I can come back later,' Hettie said.

'No, it's all right. The others are always late anyway.' The woman stepped aside. 'Come in,' she said. 'Take a seat.'

Hettie entered the kitchen. Like everything else at Hill House, it was just as she remembered. A huge range ran along the opposite wall with many ovens and hotplates. Gleaming copper pots of all styles, shapes and sizes hung from hooks or sat on the shelves of the vast dresser on the wall beside the door, along with plates, cups, glasses and ceramic tureens and serving vessels. The long sink and draining board to the left ran the entire width of the wall beneath the window, which was high in the wall, since the kitchen was in the basement. The only concessions to the passing years seemed to be a few modern appliances, including a refrigerator.

'Sit anywhere you like, Miss Turner,' the woman said, pointing to the large table that ran down the centre of the kitchen.

'Thank you,' Hettie said. 'But please, call me Hettie. And you are...?'

'She's Audrey,' a voice said from out in the corridor. Another woman appeared behind the first woman. She was similarly dressed for work, but her dark wavy hair was cut shorter and sat to her shoulders, the fringe held back from her face by grips. She held a stack of plates to her stomach. 'And I'm Rosemary. But you can call me Rosie, everyone does.'

The new woman pushed past the first woman to stand before Hettie. 'I was sent to get the better china from the cupboard since there's to be a guest for dinner. And we've got the better linen on the table too.'

Realising that the guest was herself, Hettie said, 'Thank you.' She stopped short of saying there was no need to go to any special trouble on her account as it would be rude to belittle the effort that everyone was going to for her.

'Ignore my sister,' Audrey said with a tut in her voice. 'She has hardly an ounce of sense in that head of hers. It's nice to meet you, Miss Turner.'

Rosemary placed the plates down on the table rather heavily so that they crashed together. 'Hey now,' she said to her sister. 'You being older doesn't mean you should talk to me like that in front of guests.'

'It does when you go crashing the plates down like that. If you break one, I shall dock it from your wages.'

'It's not for you to do that. Mrs Mandeville has never taken money from me if I break something.' Rosemary stared at her sister, her hands on her hips.

'I'm the housekeeper now until the new one can start. So I shall dock your wages as I see fit. And it's Lady Mandeville now, not Mrs Mandeville.'

'I can't wait for you to start working in the gardens,' Rosemary said. She began placing the plates around the table, again rather heavily.

'Neither can I.' Audrey turned to Hettie. 'Please excuse us. Rosemary is so used to the family being relaxed with us that she can forget herself when we have guests.'

'There's no need to apologise,' Hettie said. She looked from the stern sister with neat hair to the sister with wavy hair that was muttering under her breath.

Audrey smoothed out the crisp white tablecloth. 'Won't you

take a seat,' she said to Hettie. 'You could sit in the housekeeper's parlour if you'd prefer,'

'Oh no, this is fine,' Hettie said. 'Can I help at all?'

'I wouldn't hear of it,' Audrey said, looking at Hettie over the rim of her spectacles. 'Rosemary and I do for the family, and we will do for you too.'

Not wanting to disturb the sisters any further, Hettie took a seat at the far end of the table, watching as they laid out seven places. Audrey turned to the range every so often to tend pots of steaming food. Hettie's stomach rumbled as though in reply to the rattling pan lids and the smell of food cooking.

Rosemary took water glasses down from the dresser and placed them to the top right of each plate. Dining with her parents in Cambridge was always a formal affair. This reminded Hettie more of the meals she had taken in the back room of the delicatessen in Leman Street. The Bessers had insisted she join them for dinner at least a couple of times each month. The family crowded around the table full of food that Mrs Besser had prepared with the help of her four daughters. Hettie had always been mystified at how so much food could be produced in such a small kitchen. Each meal was like a feast with meats and vegetables, bread fresh from the oven, pickles and cheese. Their table was round, and they constantly nudged the elbow of the person beside them when they cut into food or raised their forks to their mouths. Mrs Besser nudged Hettie to put food onto her plate if she ever tried to pass a dish around the table without taking something from it. Mr Besser carved whatever meat had been cooked and heaped it onto the serving plate. And always to Hettie's right had been Saul. It was he who passed each dish to her, always with a smile. He said that his family's hospitality where she was concerned was their way of repaying her for all the trouble she was taking in teaching him the art of photography. That, and they liked her.

Hettie felt a stab of pain as she thought of Saul. To distract herself she looked down at the pattern of vines around the rim of one of the serving dishes. Green tendrils curling and swirling in a continuous loop.

'Hello again, Hettie.'

Hettie snapped into the moment. She stood up abruptly. 'Hello,' she said as Kate smiled at her.

Bertie stood beside his wife. 'How did it go this afternoon?' he asked.

'Well... Good... thank you,' Hettie said.

'No sign of the girls yet?' Kate asked.

Audrey shook her head. 'I've not seen hide nor hair of them all afternoon, since they got back from school and went upstairs with a plate of our Rosie's Madeira cake.'

Bertie lifted his sleeve and looked at his watch. 'I'll go and give them a nudge,' he said.

Kate set about helping the sisters. Hettie wanted to offer her help but was sure it would be refused again. Sitting down, she watched the sisters and Kate, listening to their chatter. They spoke about housework and the laundry that would be collected in the morning. About meals that would be prepared over the next few days. Kate helped the sisters transfer food from pans and trays into the serving dishes. Rosemary filled two jugs with water from the tap and placed them on the table. They all worked around each other as though it were a choreographed dance. Each knew their role and their steps and what had to be done. There was a beauty in their actions. There was as much grace and skill in how these women moved and worked around one another as there was on any stage graced by any ballet company in London. But here was real life, not a manufactured story to thrill and delight a paying audience.

There was an honesty in it that compelled Hettie to watch. As she did, she saw each of the three women as though framing them through a lens. Audrey looked into a huge saucepan, her spectacles hazed from the steam but her hair in its bun neat and precise. Rosemary flitted around deftly, collecting items, placing them on the table, arranging napkins and cutlery with a precision that belied the speed and seeming effortlessness with which she went about her tasks. She was almost a blur of activity. Kate, on the other hand, oversaw. Her attention was on Audrey and Rosemary while delivering her own task of placing bread rolls neatly into a bowl. She carried out her role as a conductor would lead an orchestra, using her own skills and talent while overseeing that of the others around her.

In another lifetime, Hettie would have worked out how best to frame each element and then the entirety of this scene. She would have pitched it to an editor as a piece on the continuing role of women in a large country house. She would have observed and worked out how best to tell the truth of each woman. She would have been compelled to capture this moment to tell its story. Now, all she could do was observe. She was a voyeur with no purpose, either in helping with the task or capturing it. She thought of her car and the bag her father had placed in the boot that morning. She had put her suitcase and satchel on the back seat, much to the surprise of her father who had said the boot was almost empty save for the heavy square leather bag with rigid sides and compartments. The battered leather bag that at one point she had never wanted to let out of her sight. So much so that she had always slept with it where she could see it, should a telephone call in the middle of the night from her editor see her leap from bed and head out on an assignment. Until the day she had moved back into her parents' house when it had been placed down in the basement along with the two trunks containing her studio and dark room equipment.

'Hello,' an unfamiliar voice said. It was light and so very bright.

Hettie released the tablecloth that she hadn't realised she had grasped and got quickly to her feet. 'Hello,' she said.

Two young girls had entered, followed by Bertie. Hettie guessed that it was the older girl who had spoken. She was tall, with beautiful long auburn hair, plaited and pinned up in a style reminiscent of those favoured in alpine countries. Her skin was pale and speckled with light-coloured freckles across her nose. Her lips rose in a smile. She was stunning to look at and appeared older than her years. She would not have looked out of place in a painting by Rosetti. The younger girl beside her was clearly attempting to mimic her older cousin, with her blonde hair similarly styled in plaits that crossed over her crown. She was a good foot shorter and her face rounder and flushed with rude health. In some ways, she reminded Hettie of the little girl she had once been. Jolly and fresh. The girls both wore grey school pinafores and grey cardigans over white blouses.

Bertie stepped forward. 'Hettie,' he said, 'this is Daphne – Sir Edward and Lady Mandeville's daughter. And this is Lula – Paul and Charlotte's daughter.'

'Hello,' Hettie said, smoothing out the wrinkle she had left in the tablecloth.

'Hello,' the girls said in unison, which made them laugh.

Kate called for the girls to sit down. Since Hettie sat at the end of the table closest to the dresser, Daphne sat beside her. Lula took the chair opposite Hettie. Both girls looked at Hettie. All she could do was try to smile at them.

'Are you sure I can't help?' Hettie asked the other adults.

'You relax,' Kate said. 'We'll be ready to eat in no more than five minutes. Daphne, would you pour the water please?'

Daphne took up the jug closest to her. Hettie thanked her when she filled her glass. She took a sip, looking over the rim of her glass. The two girls still looked at her. Still smiled.

After filling the other glasses, Daphne placed the jug down on the table. 'I believe we've met,' she said to Hettie.

Hettie swallowed a mouthful of water. 'We have?' she said.

'I don't remember it,' Daphne said with a laugh in her voice.

'Auntie Alice said that Daphne was still a very little baby when you met,' Lula chimed.

'I see,' Hettie said. There had been so many Mandeville babies, and babies from Caxton Hall across the valley – all dressed in frilly white outfits and pushed around in perambulators – that she would have been hard-pressed to remember meeting any of them. Since she would have been about fourteen or fifteen the last time they had visited, any baby would have held no interest for her whatsoever. 'Well,' Hettie said, taking another mouthful of water. 'It's nice to meet you again.'

'I like your clothes,' Lula said. 'They remind me of how Mummy dresses. Don't they remind you of how my mummy dresses, Daphne?'

The older girl looked Hettie up and down with her green eyes. 'They do, rather. Aunt Charlotte always says that she will jolly well dress as she likes rather than how society would have her dress.' She looked over Hettie again. 'Your clothes seem so very stylish. Is that what they wear in London these days?'

Hettie glanced down at her brown slacks, brown boots, white shirt with a brown tie at her collar and orange sweater. She had no idea how they dressed in London these days and wouldn't have cared what anyone thought of her clothes.

'It's what I wear,' Hettie said.

Daphne nodded, giving her an approving look. 'It's much better than a dull school uniform,' she said. 'Perhaps while you're here I can get some advice from you on the latest styles. I shall be going to university in just two years and want to start wearing the latest fashions. Perhaps we could go into Northampton, and you could help me pick out an outfit.'

'Or perhaps not,' Kate said from across the kitchen. 'I don't think your mother had that in mind when she left you in my care.'

'But I have my allowance, which I could spend.' Daphne protested.

'And you can save it until your mother is here to take you into Northampton,' Kate said. 'We are under strict instructions that you go to school and then come home. If you want to go anywhere outside of that, we will need to telephone your mother and father to get their permission.'

Daphne sighed and folded her arms across her chest. She didn't seem like a girl who would put up an argument or make a fuss. From what Hettie could see, she seemed a rather gentle and compliant soul.

'Uncle Edward says your real name is Hatshepsut?' Lula said suddenly. 'Is that true?'

Hettie turned her attention from Daphne to the younger girl across the table. 'It is,' she said.

The little girl smiled. 'Fascinating!' she said. 'Daphne and I looked your name up in a book in the library. You are named for an Egyptian queen, did you know that?'

'I did.'

'And she was the most magnificent queen according to the book,' Lula said. 'I should like to have been named for an Egyptian queen. How simply marvellous that would be. Instead, I am named for someone called Louisa, who I've never even met. She's an old friend of my mother's. But everyone calls me Lula, as Mummy says that we should all have an identity to call our own, even if our names honour those who have gone before.'

'That's enough now, girls,' Bertie said, placing a gravy boat on the table.

'Yes,' Kate added. 'Give Hettie a minute's peace, won't you?'

The two girls did as they were told and stopped asking questions. Instead, they made an agreement to play a board game in the billiard room after dinner. They invited Hettie to join them, but she declined. More dishes were added to the table and eventually the other adults took their places. Rosemary sat beside Daphne with Audrey on her other side and closest to the range. Kate took the chair beside Lula, and Bertie sat beside his wife. Hettie noticed that nobody took the chairs at either end of the table. Her parents always sat at either end of their dining table for meals with her at a chair on the side with her back to the fire.

'Here you are, Hettie.'

A plate had appeared before Hettie. 'Thank you,' she said to Daphne.

'You're welcome,' Daphne said.

With a plate before each person, they took up their napkins, shook them out, and placed them in their laps. Hettie followed, glad for the familiar communal action. The plate before her held a very generous slice of pie. Serving dishes were handed around the table and Hettie felt that she had to take a scoop of mashed potato, followed by a spoonful of peas and a spoonful of carrots. When the gravy was handed to her, she poured some over her food.

She took up her knife and fork and stared at the meal that was larger than any she had eaten in so long. Chatter came from around the table as cutlery chinked, and Kate asked the girls about their days at school. Rosemary chipped in often. Bertie didn't say much; neither did Audrey. Of the group, they appeared the most serious. Rosemary laughed uproariously at something Lula said. She might be staff, but it didn't appear that her voice was any less welcome or valued than anyone's around the table.

With the prongs of her fork, Hettie broke the crust of the pie. Come to think of it, Kate and Bertie were just as much staff as Audrey and Rosemary, yet Daphne and Lula had been left in their care. For Sir Edward and his sister to have left their daughters with these four adults showed the great trust placed in them. Which was no doubt why Kate was keeping such a close eye on Daphne. As much as she seemed quite a compliant girl, at sixteen, she was really a young woman. Whether she wanted to or not, Daphne would find the impulse to test and challenge too great to resist. And Hettie could see why Kate would not want that to be done on her watch.

Hettie pushed some of the meat and pastry onto the back of her fork. As she lifted it to her mouth, the smell reminded her of how hungry she had been on entering the kitchen. She closed her lips around the fork and eased the food into her mouth. The moment it met her tongue, she closed her eyes. The pastry crumbled and tasted of butter. The steak and kidney in its rich sauce simply melted in her mouth. She chewed slowly, savouring the flavours. As she swallowed, she opened her eyes.

'Good, isn't it?' Kate said.

'Very good,' Hettie said, the flavours dancing across her tongue.

'We shall miss Audrey's cooking when she goes out into the garden come spring,' Kate said.

'I've taught our Rosie everything I know,' Audrey said. 'She's as good a cook as me. And with the new housekeeper and maid starting, there'll be more help around the house.'

Hettie had taken another mouthful of the sublime pie. It would seem rude if she didn't further the conversation since she had been brought into it. 'You'll be going into the gardens?' she asked.

'Yes,' Audrey said. 'I've been learning from the Caxton Hall gardeners this past two years. Lady Mandeville says they need someone permanent to run the gardens here and has asked me to do it.'

'Audrey has a way with plants,' Bertie said. 'Particularly vegetables. She's taken to it like a natural. The head gardener at Caxton Hall has said he's never seen anyone learn so quickly.'

'And the courgettes we got last summer,' Kate said. 'You should have seen them, Hettie! There was a mountain. Rosie found an old recipe in a cookbook, and we turned them into courgette jam.'

'It's a bit like marmalade,' Daphne added. 'And quite delicious. You should have it on your toast in the morning, Hettie.'

If it was anywhere near as good as the pie she was eating, Hettie would not be shy in sampling Audrey's courgette marmalade. 'I might just do that,' she said.

'Can everyone eat up, please,' Audrey said. 'Before it goes cold.' She looked down at the food on her plate when she spoke rather than at the people around the table. She was clearly trying to steer the conversation away from herself. From what Hettie could tell, Audery was either shy or reticent. Either way, she saw in Audrey a kindred soul. 'Would there be any more gravy?' she asked.

Audrey picked up the gravy boat and it was passed along the table to Hettie. She poured another steaming glug onto her potatoes.

The moment of speaking about Audrey had passed. While Lula updated them all on a costume she needed to make for an upcoming school production, Hettie glanced along the table. Audrey had returned to her food and appeared more comfortable with the glare of the spotlight taken from her.

Lula kept everyone entertained with a discussion around making her costume, which Kate said she would be happy to help with. Rosemary was particularly animated, offering to make some pom poms should they be needed for decoration. Since everyone was busy, Hettie was able to return to her dinner. With every mouthful, her tastebuds and stomach demanded more. Almost before she knew it, she was pushing the last piece of pie onto her fork with the final smattering of potato. She passed her empty plate along the table and was glad to receive a bowl of apple crumble to take its place. She all but smothered it in the custard from the jug that Daphne handed to her before passing the jug across the table to Lula. She was glad that the discussions between the others at the table continued without the need of contribution from her, outside of polite nods and smiles. It meant she could savour the sweet apples and crumble and the creamy custard without interruption. And enjoy the second serving Audrey helped her to.

'Do you make your own clothes, Hettie?' Lula asked.

Hettie placed her spoon in her empty bowl. 'No,' she said. 'I go to a seamstress or a tailor.'

'A tailor?' Lula said, a little shock in her voice.

'Yes,' Hettie said. 'I find tailors cut trousers and jackets more to my liking.'

'It's London, Lula,' Daphne said. 'They do things differently there. I find it fascinating. Father wants me to go to Cambridge as it's family tradition,' she said, raising her eyebrows. 'But I might just look at universities in London.'

There came the noise of the feet of a chair scraping across the tiles. 'You've plenty of time to think on that,' Kate said, getting to her feet. 'For now, you can help clear the table. And you, Lula, come along. Collect the glasses, please.'

Hettie stood and began to help with clearing the table. This time, nobody thought to stop her as she was a guest, and they thanked her for her help. But they stopped short of letting her help with the washing up.

'I'll see to that with our Rosemary,' Audrey said.

'May we be excused to go and start our game?' Daphne asked.

Kate looked at her wristwatch. 'Yes, you have an hour before bedtime.'

Without waiting to ask a second time, Daphne and Lula hurried from the room. The sound of their chatter carried along the corridor and disappeared up the stairs.

Bertie excused himself, saying that he would do a round of the house to make sure the doors were secure. He would take coffee in the office.

As he left, steam escaped the pot of coffee Kate had put the stove. She removed it from the hotplate. 'You'll join us for coffee, Hettie, won't you?' she said. 'While the girls are upstairs having their game and Bertie's doing his rounds.'

Hettie looked about the people in the kitchen. 'Thank you,' she said. 'If nobody minds.'

'Why would we mind?' Rosemary said, drying a plate and placing it on the side. She paused with the towel still in her hands and rested against the sink. 'It'll be nice to have someone else to talk to. I bet there's lots of exciting things you could tell us about London. I should like to visit one day. Miss Daphne says I might be her lady's maid when she is grown up and go to do for her and—'

'That's enough,' Audrey said to her sister. She swiped some crumbs away from the tablecloth. 'Miss Turner doesn't need to be bothered by your silliness and daydreams.'

'It's all right,' Hettie said.

'See—' Rosemary started. But she was silenced by a sharp look from her sister and an instruction to get the milk from the refrigerator and the coffee cups from the dresser. When Rosemary left with a tray to take coffee up to Bertie, Kate took a seat beside Hettie. Audrey sat opposite them.

'If it's not out of turn, Miss Turner, I should like to apologise for my sister. We've been here so long, and the family treats us kindly, so that she forgets herself in front of visitors.'

'Really,' Hettie said. 'There's no need to apologise. I'm working here too, so I'm not a guest as such.'

'That's as maybe,' Audrey said. 'But our Rosemary should know her place. And she needs to remember to mind her manners. It's best she remembers now. Otherwise, she shall have a surprise when the new housekeeper starts. They might not put up with so much from her.'

'How long is it that you and Rosemary have been here?' Kate asked, pouring the coffee.

Audrey peered at Kate over the top of her spectacles. 'I'm sure you know.'

'I don't remember precisely. And I thought Hettie might be interested in how you came to be here.'

'We've been here off and on for the past twelve or so years,' Audrey said, still looking at Kate over the rim of her spectacles with what Hettie took to be a little suspicion for having to answer a question which Kate obviously knew the answer to. 'Lady Mandeville had us come for training when we were still in the orphanage and then a few years later she brought us here permanently.'

'You know the new Lady Mandeville, don't you, Hettie?' Kate said, handing a cup to her. 'Alice as was.'

Hettie thanked Kate. 'I met her a few times when I came here as a child.'

'She's a marvellous employer,' Kate said, passing a cup of coffee across the table to Audrey. 'I know she was always going to become Lady Mandeville, but it's so much for her to take on. Especially since the previous Lady Mandeville is still with us. I wonder how they're all getting on in London.'

Audrey stirred sugar into her coffee. 'Have you got all the paperwork done for Mrs Kenmore?' she asked.

'Almost,' Kate said. 'I've a few more letters to type and then I've to stuff two hundred envelopes with the letters and pamphlets. They should be arriving in the morning.'

Audrey took a sip of her drink. 'Our Rosemary and I can give you a hand if it's needed.'

Hettie watched Kate pinch the handle of the small cup and turn it a quarter circle in its saucer. She detected a little uncertainty in Kate's voice when she said, 'I don't want to drag you away from everything you've to do. There's already so much.'

'You've no call to feel guilty, Katherine,' Audrey said. 'I've told you already that me and our Rosemary can cope with the housework. We did it before you came, and we can do it again. Your skills are needed now for Mrs Kenmore.'

Hettie looked up from her coffee cup. She had got lost somewhere in their conversation.

'I've only been here just over a year,' Kate explained. 'I started as a maid but at the moment I'm helping with some of the administration around Charlotte's campaign for the by-election.'

'By-election?' Hettie said.

'To replace Sir Charles as MP.' Kate took up the pot and refilled their cups. 'The tradition would be for Sir Edward to stand for the seat. But he's just not made for politics. He and Charlotte have agreed that she will stand. It's rather marvellous. I'm sure she will win. She has huge support in the area. It's why many of the family have gone down to London. Charlotte has lots of meetings in Westminster.'

'I had no idea,' Hettie said.

'She's down to earth and a decent person.' Audrey poured milk into her cup. 'She has time for everyone. It's an honour for me and Rosemary to help do Kate's old chores. Makes us feel like we are helping Mrs Kenmore's campaign in some way.'

Hettie let Kate and Audrey's words sink in, while they continued to discuss the plans to prepare and then post the letters and pamphlets as part of the campaign. She too had known Mrs Kenmore as Charlotte. She was terrific fun, with a way of never making a child feel as though they were a nuisance. And she had such energy and enthusiasm for everything. As did her husband, Paul. If Charlotte put that energy and enthusiasm into her politics, then her constituents would be lucky to have her.

Rosemary returned and sat down heavily in the chair beside Audrey.

'What's to do?' Audrey asked.

'It's the girls,' Rosemary said. The earlier playfulness had vanished from her voice. 'After I took the coffee to Bertie, I stuck my head into the billiard room to check on them.' She stared at a point on the tablecloth before her. 'Lula was crying. Daphne was comforting her. I asked if there was anything I could do but Daphne said it would be all right.'

A silence fell across the table. Kate leant a little closer to Hettie. 'Lula has taken her grandfather's death very hard,' she said. 'She was his particular favourite, although he would never have admitted he had one. Daphne's very good with her. She consoles her and takes care of her when she gets sad. I remember how it was when my father died a couple of years ago...'

Silence fell again. Until Rosemary sniffed and wiped her eyes with the cuff of her dress. Audrey reached to touch her sister's hand.

'I've never known anyone die before,' Rosemary said, still staring at the same spot on the tablecloth. 'I mean, not that I remember.'

'I know,' Audrey said. Her voice was softer than it had been in her earlier exchanges with her sister. 'Would you like a cocoa?'

Rosemary nodded.

Audrey gave her sister's hand a pat before leaving her seat. She filled a small pan with milk and put it on the range to warm.

Hettie looked from Kate to Rosemary to Audrey. It seemed that each was lost somewhere. Kate breathed in deeply. When she breathed out, she smiled. It was a smile that appeared painted on. 'Well,' she said brightly. 'It will be good for Hettie to let us know all about Sir Charles' collection. That will bring relief to the family.'

'I'm simply photographing the items,' Hettie said. 'My parents and their friends will assess what they are.'

Undeterred by Hettie's explanation, Kate still spoke

brightly. 'You'll take breakfast with us before you go to the cottage tomorrow, won't you?'

Hettie was about to say that she wasn't sure, when the opportunity to speak was taken away from her.

'The cottage?' Rosemary said, an odd tone to her voice. She looked up from the spot on the tablecloth and stared at Hettie.

There came the sound of a wooden spoon dropping into milk. 'Now you can stop what it is you're about to say,' Audrey said. 'Miss Turner doesn't want to hear any of your nonsense.'

'But the cottage,' Rosemary said. Again, there was a strange tone to her voice when she said the simple words. If Hettie could put a name to it, it would be fear. A fear that was matched by the look in Rosemary's eyes when she turned her attention from Hettie to Audrey. 'Has anyone warned her?' she said.

'Stop it, Rosemary,' Audrey said.

But Rosemary's eyes widened still further. 'She should be told.'

Milk sizzled on the hotplate as Audrey dropped the spoon into the pan again. '*I said*, stop it.'

'What if the girls come down and should hear you,' Kate said.

'But the curse,' Rosemary persisted.

It was Hettie's turn now to look around the room.

'There is no curse,' Audrey said, taking up the spoon again. 'It's just a lot of silly nonsense.'

'So why won't anyone go there?' Rosemary said.

'Sir Charles didn't want anyone in his cottage. He didn't want prying eyes or hands playing with his collection and perhaps breaking or damaging something.'

'No, it's because nobody will step foot in there. Except you. You're braver than me, going there every day to clean and set the fires.'

'Other people go when needed. Bertie, Katherine, Rhys and Elliot. It's just you and the children that talk that silliness. And

I'm not brave. I just don't believe in the nonsense stories you all tell.' Audrey stirred the milk rather aggressively. 'And that's why Sir Charles had me do for him there.'

'Why are you still going every day when you don't have to?'

'So Miss Turner can be comfortable when she is working there.'

'But it's been over a month since Sir Charles passed. And you've been going every day. To an empty house.'

Hettie noticed Audrey glance at Kate.

'A house needs to be kept warm otherwise it will get damp,' Kate said.

'And does a house need fresh flowers cut from the conservatory every day to be put in vases in an empty house?'

Audrey's response was to pour the milk into a cup and stir it vigorously.

Rosemary turned back to Hettie, her eyes still wide. 'You'll be there alone,' she said.

Hettie wanted to ask what on earth Rosemary was talking about, but Audrey's clenched jaw signalled that she was in no mood to hear anything further from her sister.

'Here,' Audrey said abruptly. 'Take your cocoa through to the parlour. Miss Turner and Kate have business to discuss and don't want you disturbing them.'

'But—' Rosemary started.

'But nothing,' Audrey said. She forced the cup and saucer onto her sister so that Rosemary had no choice but to take it. She got slowly to her feet, still looking at Hettie. And she looked at her all the while she walked from the room with Audrey behind her. The sound of footsteps disappeared along the basement corridor. It was followed by the groan of a door opening and then closing so that the only noise left in the kitchen was the murmur of voices from that other room.

The chair beside Hettie creaked as Kate adjusted her position. 'I'm sorry about that,' Kate said. 'Please don't take any notice of Rosemary. She's as bad as the children when it comes to tall tales and fairy stories.'

Hettie shrugged, waiting for Kate to continue.

Kate let out a sigh. 'It's a story that was brewed up years ago as I understand. Long before the current children were born. Apparently two children snuck into the cottage against Sir Charles' specific instructions to steer clear. Something happened and they got a fright. From there, they convinced themselves there was a curse on the building that would scare and chase away anyone who entered. I don't think Sir Charles ever tried to talk them out of it. I suppose it suited him to keep everyone away.'

Hettie pictured the shelves of collectables and antiques and books. She wouldn't care for anyone poking about through her private and precious things either.

Kate gave Hettie a rather tight smile. 'Audrey can't seem to break the habit of cleaning and laying the fires every day. She misses Sir Charles. We all do. He was a very decent man. And it's true that Bertie says it's best to keep the cottage warm otherwise damp might set in. We're staying here while everyone is away, but we usually live in the cottage next door to Sir Charles' cottage, so we try to keep the shared walls warm.' She took a sip of her coffee. 'The children have scared each other so much through the years that none of them will step foot inside. And Rosemary is still rather like a young girl in many ways.' Kate held up the coffee pot.

Hettie shook her head. 'I think I'll turn in,' she said.

Kate placed the pot down on the table. 'I hope what Rosemary said hasn't disturbed you.'

'It will take more than tall tales of curses to worry me,' Hettie said. 'Thank you, Kate. For making me welcome today. And for dinner. Will you pass on my thanks to Audrey and Rosemary?'

'Of course,' Kate said. 'Rest well. I'll see you tomorrow.'

. . .

Back in the guest room, Hettie undressed in the bathroom and pulled on her pyjamas. She draped her clothes over the chair at the dressing table in the bedroom and turned out the light. The fire had died to just embers and with the curtains still open, she crawled under the covers. She preferred to sleep without curtains blocking the view of the dark night sky.

The clock down in the hallway chimed half past eight. It was unheard of for her to go to bed so early. Apart from the drive from Cambridge, she had barely done anything all day. But what she had done had tired her more than a day's work.

Looking out at the stars, her thoughts turned back across the day. It had been so long since she had been in the presence of so many people and even longer since she had met so many new people in a single day. She might not have spoken much but had listened and taken in every word. Which in itself was tiring, especially when added to visiting Sir Charles' cottage to make a first pass of his collection. She took her work seriously and was often exhausted at the end of the day. But the one thing from her first day on this assignment that she could not take seriously was the suggestion of a cursed object somewhere in Sir Charles' artefacts. What a clever man he had been to allow that rumour to persist. It had no doubt saved his objects from sticky fingers and the clumsiness of those who would not have understood the value of the items lining the shelves. Hettie thought of the look of horror in Rosemary's eyes and could barely contain a smile. The sisters were only slightly younger than her, but with her old fashioned and severe ways, Audrey seemed so much older, while Rosemary seemed so much younger.

Hettie pulled the blankets to her chin, enjoying the warmth. It had been charming to share dinner with Audrey and Rosemary as well as Bertie and Kate and the girls. As much as there were traditions at Hill House which seemed to belong to another century, there was an informality to the way they lived. It was rather touching that they Audrey still cleaned the cottage and took fresh flowers each day. And it had been touching to see how the staff wanted to comfort and support Daphne and Lula through the loss of their grandfather.

Hettie closed her eyes. It had been pleasant to think of her own grandfather so much across the day. To sit where he might have sat with his great friend Sir Charles, to look on the objects in his friend's collection, to pass through the great doors of Hill House as he had done on so many occasions, with and without her. Hettie pictured the door with its impressive portico, its great pillars, a gravel drive. And she pictured a ladder leaning against the wall.

NINE
APRIL 1876

After stopping at Queenstown where the tenders brought a hundred or so new passengers to join the ship, the SS *Baltic* navigated the southern coast of Ireland before heading out to the wide and empty Atlantic Ocean.

Charles stood on deck until the very last glimmer of the Celtic coast disappeared from view. It would be at least another seven days before they saw land again when they reached the northeast coast of America.

Closing his eyes, Charles held his face into the breeze. His fringe blew back from his forehead and speckles of seawater dampened his cheeks. He breathed in deeply, taking in a lungful of the fresh salty air. Gulls cawed as they rose and fell on the mild spring breeze. Every so often a bell rang out, punctuating the call of the birds, the creek of the rigging and the gentle shush of the waves against the *Baltic*'s hull.

Never, in his whole twenty-one years on the planet, had Charles ever felt the size and scale of the Earth more. And never, in his twenty-one years, had he ever felt freer. It had become his habit to stand on deck whenever possible while his fellow travellers spent their time promenading the covered boat deck, sitting in lounging chairs, reading books and periodicals borrowed from the library on board, socialising, playing cards or enjoying the bar in the saloon. Charles preferred the bow of the ship or the stern, so that the sounds of the other passengers were a distant murmur, almost lost by the sounds of nature and the ship.

Charles imagined the depth of the ocean below them. The further they sailed out to sea, the deeper it would become. How many fish and sea creatures might be under his feet at that very moment? It was a thrilling thought to be surrounded by so much life. Aside from swimming in the lake at home, family visits to the seaside in Hunstanton, a spot of rowing at school, and the occasional day spent punting on the Cam, he realised that he had been landlocked. His life had revolved around the family estate, school, university and accompanying his father to London to watch from the public gallery as he made speeches in the Commons and then accompanying his father to his club to sit in high backed chairs, the leather grown soft from the behinds of all the men who had warmed themselves before the fire while discussing politics and considering how fine this or that whisky was. Before that moment, he had been surrounded by... things. People, buildings, horses, carts, shops, trees, fences – all hemming and penning both land and people. Everything divided by a boundary of some sort. But here... Here, he was free.

A shout came from above. Charles opened his eyes, shielding them from the bright spring sunshine. Steam escaped from the funnel high above and, for the first time, he saw so many men up in the rigging. He watched as they set about the business of unfurling the sails and listened to the thwack as the reems of fabric tumbled down before the sails were secured to catch the wind and harness its power as they headed further out to sea.

Charles could barely contain his excitement. He had particularly wanted to travel on the *Baltic* since it had won the Blue Ribband for the quickest crossing between New York and Queenstown. Another ship held it now, but the *Baltic* was still the epitome of modernity and all that was new and good with the world. But even modernity was aided by nature. Which was the way it should be – man and his developments working hand in hand with the natural world, harnessing the power of nature for good.

Charles closed his eyes again and listened to the thwack of the sails in the wind. The movement of the ship beneath his feet felt different now, as though it was being pulled along. It had a new impetus, a fresh power.

'There he is,' a familiar voice called.

Before he could turn around, Charles felt a large hand pat him square between his shoulders. The owner of the voice took up position beside Charles and leant against the rails.

'What are we looking at?' Henry asked.

'The power of nature,' Charles said.

'The power of nature?' Henry said. 'Looks more like mile after mile of water to me!'

'It's not measured in standard miles,' Charles said. 'It's nautical miles.'

Still holding onto the rails, Henry leant back and laughed. 'You are nothing if not precise, Mandeville. Now, old chap,' he said. 'It's time for dinner.'

'Already? It feels like we've only just eaten breakfast.'

'That was four hours ago,' Henry said. 'And I'm famished. Come on,' he said, releasing the rail. 'Kenmore's going to meet us in the saloon.'

Charles walked along the deck beside Henry, who updated him on how he and Walter had passed the hours since breakfast. They had taken a turn around the boat deck, each read a little from magazines in the library and enjoyed a fine mid-morning pot of coffee. They had got into conversation with a few chaps travelling to Boston for business who had invited them for drinks and a game of cards that evening. Every time they passed a woman, Henry raised his hat. There were so many women that he had to do it often, but didn't fail on any occasion. He might appear like a bit of an oaf, but Charles knew his friend to have impeccable manners and to be the most honourable of men. Charles looked up at Henry as he tipped his hat to a couple of older women seated on lounging chairs.

'I'm so glad that we are taking this adventure together,' Charles said as Henry replaced his hat. 'I consider you and Walter to be about the best pals a chap could have.'

Henry paused. He looked down at Charles with a quizzical expression. 'What brought that on?' he asked.

'I think sometimes in life, things just need to be said,' Charles said.

Henry laughed. 'You'll have me blushing, Mandeville,' he said. But from the way he nudged Charles with his elbow and smiled, Charles knew that Henry felt the same.

The dinner was as fine as on the previous day and as plentiful as Henry had hoped for. Unlike on shore, their main meal was taken in the middle of the day, for a reason that Charles couldn't fathom. Course after course was delivered to their table. Soup, fish, white meats, roasted meats, vegetables, fruit and cheese. Charles shared a bottle of claret with Henry and Walter. A band played throughout the meal, a variety of polkas and waltzes, which made the passengers tap their feet in time with the music. The atmosphere in the saloon was light and jolly with chatter and the chinking of glasses and cutlery against fine china. Waiters weaved between the tables, refreshing glasses and serving the dishes. The movement of the ship in the ocean was only noticeable in the gentle sway of water and wine in glasses.

Following the meal, Henry and Charles decided that they would sit out on deck to make the most of the afternoon's sun while Walter decided that he would retreat to the bowels of the ship to work on the photographs he had taken.

Out on deck, the sun warmed Charles' face. In the lounging chair beside him, Henry had placed a magazine over his face. He was snoring softly, making the pages flutter on each exhale. The waves glimmered. The gulls – the constant travelling companions of the ship – coasted the breezes that were making the sails billow to push the ship along. The creek of the rigging and the masts was joined by the chatter of the passengers walking around the deck. Charles sat forward and looked past Henry. Men were asleep in all the chairs for as far as he could see. They had clearly enjoyed portions of dinner the same size as those enjoyed by Henry. Charles scratched the side of his nose. Dozing was all well and good but there was so much to see, and he didn't want to miss a second of it.

Getting carefully to his feet so as not to disturb Henry, Charles left his friend and made his way to the back of the ship. It hadn't taken long to grow acclimatised to walking with the movement of the ship as it cut through the swell of the ocean, rather than against it. There had been a few pale and peaky looking passengers who hadn't quite mastered how to be on a ship and Charles was quite proud of himself that he had found his sea legs from almost the moment they had set foot on the *Baltic*.

Leaning against the rail, he looked out over the waves. Somewhere far out of sight, lay the coast of Ireland. Charles peered into the distance, across the waves dancing silvery in the sunshine. It was quite thrilling to be so far from safety. That wasn't to say that he didn't feel secure on the ship – accidents happened but statistics showed that they were few and far between and generally not with a huge loss of life. An accident could just as easily befall him on land.

Charles lent further over the metal rail. There seemed little point in dwelling on the vagaries of chance or misfortune. Life was for living. For soaking up every experience and making the most of every opportunity. It was what he had always felt. Even when, as a small boy, his belief in exploring had seen many a gashed knee as he stumbled in pursuit of adventure. Or bumps on the head when he had fallen from too great a height – the top branches of a tree on Hill House land or the roof of the dormitories at school, which were very much out of bounds for the boys.

Closing his eyes, Charles saw the brightness of the sun through his eyelids. He may fall or stumble or sometimes take the wrong path, but he would bounce back. Better to have an experience and enjoy it or learn from it than plod along a path out of reluctance or fear.

Still with his eyes closed, Charles smiled. Gulls cawed in the air. Men up in the rigging called to each other. The fabric of the sails thwacked in the wind. With the change in seasons, the cold of winter had begun to give way to the warmth of spring. There may be a chill in the air, but that's what an overcoat and scarf were for.

Taking in a deep lungful of air, Charles opened his eyes. His intention had been to return to Henry to see whether his friend thought it about the right time to take a glass of ale in the saloon. But any thought of beer disappeared at the sight that met him. Out on the sea, the sun still shimmered, picking out the peak of each wave as it formed then swelled before breaking. But there was more than that. Charles looked harder. There was a different movement in the deep blue green, travelling swiftly below the surface. It appeared to be riding the wake created by the ship. Charles hung further over the rail. As he stared harder into the waves, the object he had been tracking broke the surface. Charles laughed and then rocked back on his heels, one hand on the rails, the other clutching his head. There, leaping and riding the waves was a beautiful blue-silver dolphin. It kept in time with the ship, practically dancing and skimming along the surface. Charles leant further over the rails again.

'Hullo,' he called and waved wildly.

Still the dolphin pursued as though in a game.

Charles could do nothing but stare at the creature. He had only ever seen this mammal who lived in the world of fish in the pages of books. And the sketches did nothing to convey its beauty. It seemed perfectly designed for its environment with smooth skin that helped it slip easily through the water. At some points only its fin was visible, and it swam so swiftly that at others, it seemed it might slip down the side of the ship to overtake the vessel. When the dolphin broke the surface, its face was visible. In its playfulness, it remined Charles of all the puppies there had been at Hill House that had liked to chase a stick for no other reason than the sheer joy it brought.

Once more the creature disappeared beneath the waves. But this time as it surfaced, it seemed to rock back a little and let out a call. The sound was like nothing Charles had ever heard. The dolphin seemed to chortle. And as it opened its mouth to make the sound, the dolphin appeared to smile!

Charles laughed out loud. If he had been wearing a hat, he would have thrown it into the air. This was about the most thrilling thing he had ever witnessed. 'Hullo!' he called again, and again the dolphin broke the surface of the sea. Charles waved and the dolphin seemed to rock a little as though it too was enjoying this chance encounter. But as quickly as their meeting had begun, it came to an end. The dolphin fell back. It still broke the waves, but it seemed like its destination lay in a different direction. Charles gave the creature a final wave as it dipped below the surface and disappeared.

Charles knitted his fingers together in his hair. He looked around. He was all alone. He laughed again, making the gulls above him caw in reply. Nobody else had witnessed his meeting with the dolphin. They had all been dozing or sitting in cabins or promenading further forward on the ship. He had been right to go and look for adventure. Only by looking – by being open to possibilities – could anyone make sure they were ready and waiting for what the world had to offer. And surely it had to be a good omen. Nature he had never known had made itself known to him. What more experiences were awaiting him on this adventure to the Americas?

'I went looking for you,' Henry said, sitting back in his chair in the saloon. There were two glasses of ale on the table. He pushed one towards Charles who took the seat opposite him.

'You'd fallen asleep,' he said to his friend. 'After that vast lunch. Three helpings of roast beef is beyond even me. And I'm told I have a good appetite.'

'Lies!' Henry said with a smile. 'All lies. It was a mere snack. And anyway, I wasn't sleeping. I was just resting my eyes.'

'If you say so,' Charles smiled back at his friend as he collected his glass. 'Cheers,' he said and held up his glass. Henry slammed his ale to Charles' and for a moment Charles was afraid that the glasses may shatter. Henry never did anything in life by halves, including toasting a drink. They both took a long sip.

Henry let out a contended sigh. 'The first beer of the day is always the best,' he said.

Charles nodded, staring at the dark liquid in his glass.

'What's tickled you?' Henry asked and took another sip of his beer.

'I'm sure I don't know what you mean,' Charles said.

'You look like the cat that got the cream,' Henry said.

'Do I?' Charles said. He tried to hide his smile behind his glass. He knew that Henry was just about the most curious chap on earth and would want to know the cause of his pleasure. But he had already decided against saying anything about his encounter with the dolphin. It had felt like a magical moment that he wanted to keep only for himself.

'I wouldn't be surprised if he's got his eye on a filly!'

The voice came from the next table where three men were seated.

There were only a few tables occupied since it was early afternoon, and exclusively by men since the women had retreated to the separate lounge towards the bow that was solely for their use. They were the men Charles and his friends had spoken to the previous evening after the evening meal and with whom they had shared a few drams of a fine whisky the barkeeper kept behind the bar. They were British and travelling to America to scope out investments in oil wells. Like Charles, Henry and Walter, they were travelling without female company. But unlike the three young men, these chaps were all past their thirtieth year, married and seemingly very wealthy. Initially they had attempted to get the boys interested in investment but when they realised the coffers were not overflowing, resorted to conversations about sport and schools and people they may know through their fathers' clubs in London. Their names were Bailey, Hardman, and Swire, although, for the life of him, Charles couldn't remember which was which. They were friendly enough and it had been pleasant to pass the evening in their company, talking and then playing cards into the early hours. They hadn't even seemed to mind that the boys suggest they play for matchsticks rather than cash.

'What's that about a filly?' Henry asked.

'A woman,' another of the chaps said. 'Bet he's spotted one he likes the look of.'

Charles laughed and took another sip of his beer. He hoped the laugh hid his discomfort and the beer might take any colour from his cheeks. 'Nothing could be further from the truth,' he said.

'Me think he doth protest too much!' the third chap said.

The first chap got to his feet. He made his way to Charles and Henry's table and stood between them. 'I wager you've been sent by your families to bag a Yankee heiress a-piece.'

'I beg your pardon?' Henry said.

The man placed one hand on Henry's shoulder and the other on Charles'. 'To swell the family coffers,' he said. 'Isn't that what all your class are up to these days?' Clearly reading their bewilderment in Charles and Henry's faces, he let out a roar of laughter. 'You may look like grown men, but you are as innocent as lambs in the way of the world. It's a good job we played for broken matchsticks rather than cash last night. We'd have taken you to the cleaners!'

His laugh was good natured rather than mocking. When Henry laughed, Charles joined him.

'Too much of the world to see, old man,' Henry said, 'to be bothered with the fairer sex.'

'Quite right,' the man said. 'There's enough time to get bogged down in the mire of marriage and domesticity when you have a few more notches on the tally stick. Although, you will succumb to their charms soon enough. Take it from those who know.' He looked towards his friends, and they agreed wholeheartedly. 'Sow your wild oats while you can,' he said. 'Before the shackles of matrimony are clamped to your ankles!' The man slapped both Charles and Henry on their backs. 'Cards after supper?' he said. 'If you're up for it, we might push the bet to a round of drinks rather than matchsticks.'

'I'm sure we can extend to that,' Henry said. He reached and shook the man's hand. Charles watched. Henry seemed always to know the best way to manage a situation. He never seemed flustered or in any way out of his depth. Businessman, bar man, future baronet, Henry knew how best to talk to them, and, without exception, everyone seemed to like him.

Henry exchanged a few further words with the man before

he took his leave and returned to his friends. A few more passengers arrived and took seats. Again, Henry exchanged a few words with them and a joke or two before returning to his beer. Charles watched his friend as one might watch a tutor.

'How do you do it?' Charles said.

'What's that?' Henry asked. He had just taken a large draught of his beer and wiped his damp moustache with his palm.

'You seem comfortable in the company of everyone.'

'There's no call to be embarrassed about what that chap said about women. He was simply ragging us.'

'I know.' Charles shrugged. He shifted in his chair. 'Actually, no I don't. What bothers me seems water off a duck's back to you.'

Henry placed his glass down on the table. He paused for a moment. 'I've had to learn how to read people,' he said. 'You haven't had to. Not in the same way.'

'I'm not sure I follow,' Charles said.

'You were born to this life,' Henry said and stroked the edges of his moustache with his forefinger and thumb. 'Naturally, you belong in it. I am new to it, or rather my family is. New money, old chap. Just two generations ago, my family was living in tiny worker's cottages with ne're two pennies to rub together. I'm fortunate that they were grafters. I sit here before you the result of my forebears who climbed the rungs of society with sweat on their brows and muck on their hands. It was thanks to their industry that I had a good schooling and am free to do what we are doing now. Don't think that for one minute I take it for granted. I am indebted to them. And that's why it's my life's work to fit in. To be a part of the society that they so wanted to be a part of. I mould myself, if you like, to situations.' Henry paused. He took a sip of his beer and wiped his damp moustache again. 'But it's for a purpose. Assimilation. And then change from within, my friend. I have my sights set on a life of academia. My passion is archaeology. Always has been. And it's my responsibility to make sure I can be the best in my field. To do that I have to fit in. I have to be accepted and make sure I am not caught out. That nobody takes me for a fraud. If some of the dons realised my lineage, their prejudice would mean they would discount me. It's a double-edged sword, you see. I am proud of who I am and my background, yet I must make sure that it doesn't cause me to be singled out and kicked to the gutter.'

'Your father is accepted,' Charles said. 'He's more than accepted at our fathers' club.'

Henry smiled. 'Money will open many doors. But not all.' He tapped the table before Charles. 'But you. You were born to it. You are authentic. And yet you are not as confident in your boots as I appear to be in mine. I have a theory,' he said. 'If you'd like to hear it.'

Charles nodded.

'I have the blood of a brawler. You have the blood of refined gentlemen. Each of us is a product of the history of our own families. You can stay younger for a while longer than I. I have had to be a bit wilier throughout life. A bit more vigilant.'

'Are you saying I'm wet behind the ears?' Charles asked.

'It's not a criticism,' Henry said. 'Merely an observation. The military is where your class go to be made into men. Mine are more likely to do it in a makeshift ring covered in sawdust. And that is why I am as I am. Reading people and situations and assimilating.' He turned his profile to Charles. 'I wasn't made for brawling. Imagine depriving womankind of this straight and true nose by having it broken in a fight. I am doing not only a service to myself by fitting in but a service to all women who like a handsome chap.'

Charles laughed. 'If you say so.'

Henry turned to him. In feigned surprise, he said. 'Are you mocking me?'

Charles shook his head. Henry raised his finger and asked the bartender for two more glasses of ale. He held his glass up for Charles to chink his against and they finished their remaining ale in one sip each.

Henry let out a long sigh. 'Do you think it's true?' he said, nodding to the table behind them. 'Do you think your mother has sent you out to America to find a wealthy heiress to make your bride?'

Charles puffed out his cheeks. 'She's wasting her time if she has. I plan on seeing something of the world before Sandhurst. I don't intend on going home with anything other than memories and souvenirs!'

Henry thanked the waiter when he delivered two more beers. 'It wouldn't be outside the realms of possibility that she's in cahoots with your cousin Caxton's mother to have that as an ulterior reason for your trip to America.'

Charles thought for a moment as he tapped his glass to Henry's. 'Come to think of it,' he said. 'She did insist on my packing *many* suits and three boxes of collars.'

Henry raised his eyebrows. 'Didn't you know,' he said. 'Many a maiden has been entranced by a crisply starched collar!'

Charles laughed and took a large mouthful of beer.

'Hello.'

Charles and Henry looked up from their drinks. They both rose from their chairs at the sight of Walter standing beside the table. Unusually for him, he was not wearing his jacket but had it across his arm. He placed it on the back of his chair so that he was only in his shirt sleeves. He took his seat and Charles and Henry joined him. Henry raised his finger and the waited knew instantly that another beer was required.

'Productive morning?' Charles asked Walter.

'Very,' Walter said.

'So, when are we going to see some of these photographs you've taken so far?' Henry asked.

The waiter delivered the third beer. Walter took a large draught – larger than was normal for him since he wasn't much of a drinker – and wiped his mouth on the back of his hand. 'I needed that,' he said. 'It's fiercely hot down below the waterline. I reckon the captain has given me that little storeroom to use as it's so close to the furnaces that nobody else will want to use it!' He took a handkerchief from his pocket and wiped sweat from his brow.

'Well?' Henry said.

Walter paused with the glass halfway to his lips. 'Well, what?' he said.

'When are we to see some of these photographs?' Henry repeated. 'Or has the makeshift nature of the set up in Hades scuppered the quality of your output?'

'Not at all,' Walter said. He finished his beer with his third mouthful and raised his finger for the waiter to bring another. He looked at Henry and Charles' glasses, but they shook their heads. 'Just the one,' Walter mouthed to the waiter. 'All things considered, they've come out pretty well. I'm saving most of my plates for when we get to America. I know I can buy more in New York, but I don't want to run out. I shall show you the photographs of Liverpool over dinner.'

'Looking forward to it,' Henry said. 'I have to say, I admire your dedication to your craft. It's still like alchemy to me, the fact that you can take a box, and a glass plate covered in Lord only knows what substances and transform them into an image to be kept forever!'

'With any luck the images will stay fast to the paper,' Walter said. He thanked the waiter as he took away his empty glass. 'But you can't tell how long for. It is such a new science that one can't say whether they will last fifty years. One hundred years. Or perhaps more.'

Henry rocked back in his chair. 'You know,' he said, 'I've thought for a while now that the worlds of photography and archaeology would make happy bed fellows. I've already seen the possibilities in photographs sent back from travels abroad. One can now see the pyramids while still sitting in one's parlour. Or imagine oneself amongst the relics of ancient Aztec civilizations over toast and marmalade at the breakfast table.'

'You don't see a contradiction in that?' Charles asked, watching the liquid in his glass sway slightly in time with the movement of the ship. 'One being so ancient and the other a recent development.'

'On the contrary,' Henry said, 'It's marvellous. I think of it like this. They are all the epitome of modernity. Take the pyramids. When they were constructed, they used the latest equipment and methods. We still don't really understand how it was achieved with the most rudimentary of machinery. And here we have cameras and photography. Most of us don't really understand the science behind how they work. And yet they do. Chaps like Kenmore here are our modern-day magicians! As the civilizations of the pharaohs were to theirs. And I can see how the two will work together nicely. Very nicely indeed. In fact,' Henry leant forward, as was his way when he got excited. 'If I buy – what was it you called them 'plates'?'

Walter nodded.

'Then perhaps, we can go into a partnership while we are in South America. You could photograph anything of interest I find. I've a mind for a study of South American ancient architecture for my thesis and the photographs would help no end.'

'It would be my pleasure,' Walter said.

'Splendid!' Henry said.

The remainder of the afternoon passed in enthusiastic conversation and planning. Charles was happy to involve himself in the talk of what was to come over the following weeks. Upon arrival in New York, they would travel further north to visit and socialise at some rather grand houses belonging to wealthy American types, as arranged by their mothers, necessitating the many suits in their trunks. They decided that they would enjoy the hospitality even if that was the part of the trip they were looking forward to least. From the banks of the Hudson River, Charles would travel alone to visit the logging town in Canada for his cousin Caxton. It would be a short stop from where he would retrace his steps back to New York. After a further week there, the group would board a train to cross the huge expanse of North America to San Francisco, from where they would board a ship down to Mexico and then the many countries of South America. The tasks each had been set by their fathers were really at the bottom of the highlights of the trip. Henry was full of the joys of what he would see, Walter of what he would learn and Charles, well, he was just full of the thrill of it all. Listening to his friends only filled him with more delight. Over the rim of his glass, he smiled at Henry and Walter. He really couldn't imagine making this trip with anyone but these two fine chaps.

But the words of their fellow passenger replayed in his mind. He knew that he was a bit wet behind the ears. In truth, he knew himself to be rather shy. It seemed an effort to be in company. He much preferred the close friendship and conversation of a small group rather than many people. He had always been the same. Even as a small child, he had stolen away to sit with the horses in the stables when the house was full of people. He enjoyed the company of animals as much as he enjoyed the company of a select group of friends. He felt at peace amongst the many dogs belonging to those who worked around the house and the stable of horses his father kept. And he was never more at home than when on horseback. Which was a good thing, since, as a cavalry officer he would be spending at least the next seven years of his life on a horse. That part of his future filled him with joy. But it was mixed with trepidation. He would be called upon to lead men. They would look up to him. They would look to him not just for orders, but they would entrust him with their safety. It was this thought that had occupied his mind in the wee small hours of many a morning. Was he up to the role?

His father had seemed a natural leader of men. He held court in any room. Men gravitated to him. They looked to him in conversation and for his opinion. He had never been unkind to his only son. But he had never instructed Charles on how he should behave. All Charles could do was watch and attempt to learn. His father simply expected that his son would be the same type of man as him. Seemingly it was assumed that the blood flowing through his father's veins and that had passed to his son, would be sufficient to make Charles into the man he needed to be – into an officer and then a member of parliament. But it seemed to Charles that he was a different sort of man to his father. Somehow that blood hadn't done the job intended. Try as hard as he might to live up to expectations and his name, he was afraid he was unequal to the challenges awaiting him.

Charles looked at Henry. Everything about him appeared older than Charles. His stature. His composure. Even the moustache that he liked to pinch between his thumb and forefinger. Henry seemed so assured. He was so clever and yet generous with his time and patience and friendship. Walter matched Henry in all these qualities and he was so sincere and earnest. Where Henry was quick to joke and laugh, Walter would be considered and mull over another person's words.

'Got an itch?' Henry asked.

'Beg pardon?' Charles said.

'You were scratching the corners of your mouth,' Walter explained.

'And you were miles away!' Henry said.

Charles took his hand from his mouth. 'I was just wondering whether I should grow a moustache,' he said.

'I can recommend it,' Henry said. 'In cold weather, it's like a little overcoat on your top lip!'

'I took the liberty,' a voice said. The waiter stood beside them. He placed a plate of sandwiches on the table.

'I say,' Henry said. 'They look wonderful. That'll just about see us through to supper.' He took a coin from his pocket and handed it to the waiter, who seemed delighted. Charles joined his friends in tucking into the cold roast beef sandwiches with hot horseradish sauce. As they ate, Henry compelled Walter to instruct them in the art of photography and Charles sat back and looked at his friends. If there were lessons for him in how to be a good man – and how to be the man he needed to be – he could do no better than look to these two chaps as his guides. He had a suspicion that the men at the other table might have been right in thinking their mothers had an eye on future wives for their sons on the shores of the Americas. But he was sure too that Henry and Walter felt as he did – that the world was too wide and broad with too much to explore to let romance get in the way of their adventures. There would be plenty of time for marriage and settling down at some point in the future.

TEN

FEBRUARY 1937

Hettie rose early – so early that the night had barely turned to day – and she bathed while it was still dark outside. She couldn't assume that Audrey would have been to lay the fires in the cottage at such an early hour, so she dressed in a heavy cotton shirt, red knitted sweater, and woollen slacks over thick woollen socks. She pulled on her leather boots and shrugged on her overcoat with the first glimmer of daylight. Tugging her satchel onto her shoulder, she let herself out of the room, closing the door gently behind her.

Down in the hall, the fire blazed in the hearth beneath the Mandeville coat of arms. It was as quiet as it had been when she returned from the cottage yesterday. Only the deep tock of the long-cased clock at the back of the hall punctuated the crackle of the dry bark on the logs in the fire.

Pushing back the sleeve of her overcoat, Hettie glanced at her wristwatch. Ten to eight. It was likely that everyone was downstairs in the kitchen, taking their breakfast. She didn't want to appear rude by not joining them, but she wouldn't be good company. There was something she had to do that couldn't be put off any longer and which made her feel sick to her stomach every time she thought of it.

Taking her hat from her pocket Hettie pulled it over her hair. She slipped on her gloves. She pulled her scarf from her satchel and wrapped it about her neck, tying it over the front of her sweater, before buttoning up her overcoat. Securing the two buckles on her satchel, she crossed the hall, passed into the vestibule, unlatched the great front door and stepped outside. After closing the door behind her, Hettie stood in the gravel beneath the portico and tied her scarf even tighter against the sharp cold.

A cloak of morning mist obscured the land so that the gate at the end of the drive was lost to the white haze. Digging her hands into the pockets of her overcoat, Hettie turned from the drive and crunched through the gravel around the side of the house to where her car was parked in the space between Hill House and the wall of the stable yard. Easing down the side of the car, she stood before the boot, looking down at the silver-coloured handle. She reached out to turn it. Then pulled her hand away. She stared at the black metal of the boot. It was as simple as turning the handle. That's all she had to do. She reached her hand out again and as she pulled it away, she felt something nudge her ankle. It was sudden and unexpected. She looked down. A Jack Russell stood beside her, one of its front paws raised and its tail wagging wildly. Hettie sunk to her haunches, she stroked the dog's head, which made its tail wag even more rapidly.

'What are you doing here all alone?' she said to the dog.

'He can't hear you,' a man said. 'He's deaf.'

Hettie got to her feet.

The man gave some kind of command using a hand signal and the dog ran to him and sat at his feet. The man looked a lot older than Hettie remembered him, but he wore the same type of clothes he always had. Tweeds and a flat cap. 'Elliot?' she said.

His expression was a blank.

'I used to come here when I was small,' Hettie said. 'You won't recognise me.'

'I know who you are,' he said. 'Professor Turner was your grandfather.'

Hettie had forgotten that Elliot was from Yorkshire. There was no mistaking it when he spoke in such a broad accent. But even though he spoke, his words were hollow, matching the expression on his gaunt face. It was natural that he would look older for fifteen years had passed. But he didn't just look as though the sands of time had passed, he looked as though he was ailing. His skin had a greyish pallor. His cheeks were drawn and the skin around his eyes dark, as though he had not slept soundly in a very long time.

Elliot touched the peak of his cap. He turned and walked away along the path, his shoulders hunched. He had always seemed old to Hettie but now he was barely a shadow of the slender yet strong man who had once carried a small wooden boat he had repaired above his head down to the lake on a scolding summer's day so that the children might play in the water.

Hettie watched Elliot disappear into the stable yard with his dog close at his heels. She watched for longer than was necessary, listening to footsteps cross the cobbles and a door creak as it was opened and then closed. She was putting off what needed to be done. But she could delay no longer.

Turning back to her car, Hettie took hold of the handle on the boot. She turned it and slowly lifted the lid, making the metal hinges groan. Placing the heels of both hands to the lip of the boot, she lifted it higher and looked inside. The sight of the single item sitting in the small space behind the back seats sent an icy chill through her blood. What had once been so familiar to her was now alien. The large square bag that had sat beside her bed every night for years seemed like it belonged to another life. The life where she had been unafraid to run towards danger or into whatever fray was occurring and needed her to capture it so that it could be shared and understood. She grasped the lid of the boot, the cold from the metal seeping through her gloves. What had once thrilled and excited her and was her reason to leap from bed each day, now filled her with a dread she could hardly bear. She had not touched that square leather bag in over four months. Not touched it and not looked at it. And now it sat there, waiting for her.

Still holding the boot open, Hettie turned away and shook her head. That bag was an inanimate object. It held no significance other than it was a receptacle holding the tools of her trade, with which she was supposed to be helping the Mandevilles. It was the sole reason for her visit to Hill House. She had already accepted the hospitality of the residents and must repay that hospitality with her labour. She shook her head again. The equipment in her car was not responsible for what had happened, for the events that had brought her to this point.

Grabbing the strap, Hettie pulled the bag onto her shoulder before slamming the boot shut. She immediately began walking, her boots crunching in the gravel as she made her way down the side of the car and along the driveway. There was something so familiar about the weight of the rigid bag on one side and her satchel on the other. There was a balance to it. Many was the time she had sprinted through the streets of London to get to a political rally or attend the scene of a disturbance, the bag bouncing from her hip on one side, her satchel on the other.

She walked rapidly between the trees on either side of the drive, her breath clouding the cold morning air. The gates stood open. She passed through, crossed the road and pushed open the small wooden gate of the cottage. Fishing in her overcoat pocket, she pulled out the key and opened the front door.

Crossing the threshold, Hettie found the lamp on the small table in the hall had been turned on. In the parlour, a fire glowed warm in the hearth and fresh pink flowers had been arranged in vases on the mantelshelf and in the window.

Hettie placed her large bag and satchel on the floor beside the desk. Removing her hat, gloves and scarf, she laid them on the blue velvet covered table. Audrey must have been in at an incredibly early hour to have done all this.

Hettie held her hands out to the fire before shrugging off her overcoat and taking it back out into the hall to hang on the hooks at the bottom of the stairs. She looked into the kitchen. A fire blazed in the hearth there too and another bunch of fresh flowers sat in a vase on the windowsill above the sink.

Back in the parlour, Hettie slid her notebook from her satchel and took her pen from the front pocket. It had been a gift from her grandfather on her eighteenth birthday, since he believed that everyone should have a quality pen with which to write. She had used it to write the letters and postcards she sent to her grandfather from her travels in France. Once or twice, she had been tempted to send him a postcard from Berlin but had never had the chance as each trip had been a whirlwind. She paused at the memory of The Souk. How incongruous it was to think of that vibrant and decadent place in this staid parlour. For a moment she was back there in the music and the heat, surrounded by perfume and cologne and incense, watching a cabaret show on the tiny stage, drinking the strongest cocktails of unidentifiable liquor and dancing to the music of the band, dancing, dancing, dancing. Her body and mind recalled the joy she had experienced there – the freedom, the sense of being light, the sense of finding herself.

A coal spat in the fireplace. A thud on the ceiling directly above her head made her look up. Going out into the hall, she held onto the bannisters and looked up the stairs. 'Hello?' she called.

No response.

'Hello,' she tried again. 'Audrey, are you still here?'

No response.

Hettie took the first step onto the carpet runner up the stairs. The old wood creaked beneath her foot. She took the second and the third step and was soon at the top. The stairs gave out onto a very small landing, with a door directly before her and a second door to her left. Both were closed. Hettie opened the door to the room directly above the parlour, since that was the source of the bump on the ceiling below.

As with the rooms downstairs, a fire blazed in the hearth warming the air. A heavily decorated rug in reds and blacks covered all except the very edges of the floorboards but, as far as Hettie could see, there was nothing obvious on the floor that might have made the thud. She shrugged. She had lived in enough flats, with many floors above and below, to have experience of noise travelling in unexpected ways. It was just as likely that the thud had come from a neighbouring property as within this cottage.

She looked about the room. Since she was upstairs, it made sense to make an initial assessment of Sir Charles' collection on the first floor. Unlike in the parlour and kitchen, there were no open shelves in this room. No books. No ornaments. Instead, a series of drawers and cupboards lined the walls. A desk sat in the window with a functional chair tucked neatly beneath. It was free of anything, apart from a blotter and an inkwell. The only other item of furniture was a comfortable looking armchair beside the fireplace with a plump cushion and a tapestry footstool by its side. As with downstairs, the room was fastidiously clean with a vase of fresh flowers in the window.

Enjoying the subtle perfume of the pink flowers, Hettie crossed the room to the drawers closest to the door. The furniture along each wall appeared to have been purpose built to fit the room. It was dark wood, chest height and consisted either of a run of shallow drawers, eight deep, or a cupboard. Taking hold of the handle for the top drawer, Hettie pulled it open. Inside, the drawer was split into compartments. Each compartment held a nest of thin paper. Carefully, Hettie pulled back the paper in the bottom left corner. She couldn't help but let out a small gasp at the item revealed. It was gold, such a rich deep gold, and fashioned into a small figure with tiny red jewels suspended from its outstretched arms. It was rather crude in its execution but quite beautiful. Hettie peeled back the paper from the next compartment to reveal a square in silver with a many-armed figurine in relief. The next was a blue stone set in a band of gold with another band around its middle, the next was a sort of cross that Hettie recognised from her mother's books. It looked like it might be made from bone, with tiny hieroglyphs carved into its surface. Next came an exquisite filigree bird, studded with soapy green stones. From its design, it seemed to Hettie to be Egyptian too. The next compartment held a gold and green scarab beetle, most certainly Egyptian.

She continued to push back the paper until she had revealed twelve tiny works of art, many taking the shape of animals and people. To Hettie's untrained eye, they appeared to be charms. Perhaps talismans or amulets. If she had to guess, she would say they were tokens to provide protection.

Hettie rewrapped each item with great care. Her mother would be best placed to assess this part of the collection.

Moving to the next drawer, Hettie expected to find more amulets. What was revealed as she pulled out the drawer could not have surprised her more. In place of the compartments of precious metals and jewels was a single item. A dazzling wood block print. In a palette of various shades of intense blue, it depicted three women sitting beneath a tree blooming with cherry blossom. They wore traditional Japanese dress, each decorated with a different pattern. Their hair, again in blue, was held in perfect style and adorned with what seemed to be feathers. A series of Japanese characters ran down the side of the print, but Hettie had no clue what any of them meant.

Closing the drawer softly, Hettie opened the next. It contained another Japanese print. But this shone with colour. It depicted a boat afloat on a beautiful blue sea. The boat, whose many-decked hull was a deep red, had details picked out in yellow, and was decorated with flags billowing in the breeze – red and white banners, blue and white banners, ribboned festoons in many bright colours. On an open deck below a canopy, a host of people stood watching the sun set behind a grey mountain rising from the sea. Their dress was not distinct as the figures were small, but from the shape and appearance, Hettie knew it to be traditional in style. A red block in the sky of the print held a number of Japanese characters. A second – fashioned in the shape of a lantern over the waves – held even more. But again, Hettie could not read their meaning. She closed the drawer and pulled out another to reveal the depiction of two men being served tea before a mountain in the distance; the next drawer held a print of another mountain with a parade of people before it – some on horseback – with two women in the foreground, in full Japanese regalia, consulting what looked like a painting; the next was the print of a cherry tree before a mountain range, its bountiful blossom-laden branches reflected in a lake. And so it went. Each drawer revealed another print in dazzling colour palettes.

When she closed the final drawer, Hettie stood back and looked about the room. There seemed no rhyme nor reason to what Sir Charles had collected. From Asian ceramics to Roman pottery, Egyptian amulets and charms to delicate and stunning Japanese wood block prints. It was an eclectic mix. Perhaps he had collected simply what had taken his fancy at any given time. Or perhaps there was a logic lost on her. Anyway, she was not here to understand what any of it meant, she was here to capture an image of each item so that experts who had spent decades learning their speciality might evaluate them for inclusion at The Ewart.

Considering how best she might utilise the light in the parlour, Hettie went back out onto the landing and pushed open the door to the final room. She stepped inside. And stopped short.

A bed stood beneath the window looking out over a small back yard. Pale green curtains with a pattern of delicate white flowers matched the pale green blanket over the white linen on the bed. Hettie stepped further into the room. Aside from the bed, there was a small chest of drawers, an armchair in the corner below the window, three shelves of collectibles and a highly decorated box on legs. Prints of flowers lined the walls but appeared to be modern and decorative to match the curtains and bed linen, rather than part of the collection.

Hettie looked along the shelves. Everything in this room appeared natural in design. An exquisite incense burner took the shape of a dome of pale coloured flowers, adorned with ceramic butterflies. It sat beside a small musical bird in a cage fashioned from tiny blue and green feathers. An old relative of Hettie's had owned a similar novelty musical box so she knew there would be a mechanism somewhere that when turned would cause the bird to twist on the perch and flap its wings while it warbled its high pitched and jolly song. Alongside the incense burner and the bird was a collection of tiny boxes of varying shapes and sizes. They were decorated so finely that Hettie felt they would not look out of place in the grandest houses in the land. Some had hinges and framework that seemed to be gold. They were decorated with tiny paintings of creatures – rabbits, squirrels, deer in a forest, a dog or two. Others were decorated with scenes from nature – trees, flowers, mountain ranges, streams running through glades. On the shelf above were some of the most beautiful earthenware items Hettie had ever seen – a bowl, a slim necked vase, and a two-handled jar with a lip. The top half of each of the coarse earthenware was glazed in a brilliant turquoise decorated with a series of concentric circles. The lower part of each was the colour of sand. As she studied them, Hettie noticed the daylight catch the glaze so that it became iridescent in patches. They brought to mind pieces from her grandfather's collection that, as she remembered, he had collected on his trips to Turkey.

Hettie stepped back to take in the entirety of the pieces in the room. In many ways, it shouldn't have worked. Fine bone china trinket boxes beside musical novelties and earthenware. But each piece in this room shared a common trait – it was exquisite and beautiful. The other rooms in the cottage were heavy with dark furniture, sombre colours on the walls and thick drapes, whereas this room felt... feminine.

Leaving the shelves, Hettie crossed the room to examine the final piece. She stopped at the chest on legs – which sat beside the bed and below the window – and crouched on her haunches to better see the detail. With her face on a level with the bed, she could smell the lavender radiating from the fresh linen. Perhaps Sir Charles had been in the habit of sleeping in this room as a respite from the noise of Hill House with the many children, or the dower house at Caxton Hall that he shared with his wife and sister. Hettie had vague recollections of Lady Mandeville and Mrs Hart and knew them to both enjoy talking. And bickering. Here, Sir Charles would have been alone, to enjoy the solace and the peace of his collection. As with the rest of the cottage, Audrey no doubt changed the sheets regularly as she would have done when Sir Charles was alive.

Hettie let her eyes travel over the detail of the dark wooden chest, the main body of which took the form of a deep box held up on exquisitely carved legs. It was inlayed with what looked like Mother of Pearl. The luminescent inlay shone from the dark wood in which it was set. Swirls covered the entire surface of the box, extending from the lid down the sides. Each piece was tiny – no larger than the smallest shell found on a beach – and intricately placed. At a guess, Hettie would have said it was Spanish or at least influenced by Spain. Perhaps it was South American. Wherever it had originated, the craftspeople responsible for its construction and decoration had been highly skilled. Hettie looked around the piece. There were no drawers or extra compartments, simply the one lidded box supported by legs. She placed the heel of her hand to the lip of the box but the moment she tried to lift the lid and found it would not move, a cacophony of sudden and terrific noise made her spring to her feet.

Her heart battering her insides, Hettie ran from the room while someone pounded at the front door. She must have left something in a precarious position in the other bedroom so that it had smashed to the floor. She reached the landing and a blur of white launched itself towards her. Hettie shrieked as the blur cried and fled back into the front bedroom. She bent forward and rested her hands on her thighs, catching her breath. It was a cat. Just a cat. It must have been the source of the earlier noise when she was in the parlour. The pounding continued. Hettie raced downstairs and opened the front door.

'Morning,' Rhys said. He was holding a tray covered in a cloth. He smiled and lifted the tray higher as though by way of offering.

'Good morning,' Hettie said, her hand still on the door handle, still slightly out of breath.

'Did I disturb you?' Rhys asked.

'What?' Hettie said. 'No. No, it's fine.'

'Sorry about the commotion,' Rhys said. He looked down to his heavy work boots. 'I had my hands full, so I only had my feet free with which to knock.' He held the tray up again. 'Kate had Audrey make it up for you. I said I'd bring it over since I was planning on checking round the cottage this morning to see all was in order. Should I put it in the parlour for you?'

'Yes. All right,' Hettie said. She released her hold on the door and stepped aside.

Rhys wiped his boots vigorously on the boot scraper outside the door and again on the mat before he stepped inside. Hettie followed him into the parlour. If he felt the February cold, he didn't show it as he wore no overcoat over his blue sweater, shirt and work trousers. Placing the tray down on the table, Rhys nodded to the fire.

'Shall I add more coals?' he asked.

'Thank you,' Hettie said.

Rhys removed the guard before picking up the scuttle and shaking a healthy heap of coals into the hearth. With his back to Hettie, he collected the poker and set about arranging the fire. This was not her cottage, but she already felt used to having it to herself. The sudden presence of another person felt unusual. Especially when coupled with the shock of the cat making an unexpected appearance upstairs.

Balancing the poker against the tiles, Rhys placed the guard before the fire and turned back to Hettie. 'If you wouldn't mind,' he said, 'I'll go and wash my hands in the kitchen.'

'I don't mind,' Hettie said. This was not her house, and she had no more right over it than anyone else. She had less right to it than Rhys, since the Hill House estate was his place of work and his home.

Hettie listened to the water from the tap in the kitchen and soon Rhys returned to stand in the doorway to the parlour. 'I'll put the kettle on, if you don't mind?' he said. 'Kate asked me to make tea to go along with the bits of food on the tray.'

'I can manage,' Hettie said.

'I've no doubt you can,' Rhys said with a gentle smile. 'But I have my orders. If you don't mind, that is.'

'No,' Hettie said, 'I don't mind.'

Rhys disappeared once again into the kitchen. Hettie stared at the parlour door. This all felt a bit off. Rhys was not her staff that he should be doing these things for her. Even if he was following instructions, she couldn't simply stand by for him to wait on her when his job was as a groundsman, not a maid or a cook. Stepping out into the hall, she watched Rhys through the open kitchen door. He moved around the room as though it were second nature to him. He opened the cupboard in the corner and removed a teapot, which he placed on the table. He took out a cup and saucer, as well as a caddy of tea, before closing the cupboard door.

Hettie took a step closer to the kitchen. 'Can I help?' she asked.

Rhys turned to her. 'All in hand,' he said. He removed the lid of the caddy and measured out a spoonful of black tea leaves, which he tipped into the brown glazed teapot. He looked up at Hettie, the spoon hovering over the caddy. 'Would you like company?' he asked. 'I won't be offended if you'd rather I left.'

Hettie thought quickly. On any given day, she would much rather be alone. But she couldn't exactly turn Rhys away when he had been kind enough to bring a tray to her. It would be uncharitable, unkind and rude. And it might appear that she thought herself above taking tea with a groundsman.

'Please,' she said. 'Add another spoon to the pot.'

Rhys smiled. It seemed that he smiled easily. Hettie had seen enough faces through her lens to know when an expression was genuine or pasted on by the sitter for her benefit or the intended audience of the photograph. She thought about the bag in the parlour. She had yet to open it. Yet to face what was inside.

'Would you mind if we took our tea in here?' she asked.

Rhys shook his head. 'Not at all. I'll go and get the tray.'

Left alone, Hettie took a deep breath. She focused on the warmth from the fire in the grate and the water bubbling in the kettle on the range. Rhys soon returned and placed the tray on the table. 'Why don't you take a seat?' he said.

Hettie pulled out the chair closest to the fire and sat down. Rhys placed a cup and saucer before her. He took another cup and saucer from the cupboard.

'I should be helping,' Hettie said.

'Not at all,' Rhys said, placing some cutlery on the table. 'If I can't lay a table and make a pot of tea then what am I good for?'

'Sorry,' Hettie said. 'I meant no offence.'

'None taken,' Rhys said. He smiled again. His dark eyes shone a little in the light from the fire. He pushed his fringe back from his face and Hettie watched as he arranged the things on the table. He would have made an interesting study. His features were strong, like his frame. His hair thick. He was a solid man. And yet he moved around the table with dexterity and familiarity. It shouldn't have surprised her, but it did. And she knew of editors who would have relished the chance to publish a piece on this apparent contradiction of a man so at ease in a kitchen when his place in the household was to be outdoors using his strength to keep the house and grounds in order. Especially when the man in the pictures to accompany the story was what many would consider handsome. But Rhys was not an oddity to be poured over. He was not a specimen to be examined as entertainment in the pages of a magazine over a morning coffee. From what she had seen of him, he was a genuine and kind man. From his behaviour, it seemed that there was a depth to him that others might have thought at odds with his status.

The kettle whistled as it came to the boil and Rhys poured the boiling water onto the leaves in the pot before returning the kettle to the range. He removed the cloth from the tray to reveal a series of plates and dishes. There were slices of bread, cold sausages, two hard boiled eggs already shelled, a dish of what looked like marmalade but was probably Audrey's courgette jam, a jug of milk and a bowl of sugar. Rhys removed each item and placed them on the table between himself and Hettie.

'Thank you,' she said, taking a freshly poured cup of tea from him. She added a splash of milk from the jug and stirred it.

Rhys stirred his own tea and placed the spoon in the saucer.

Hettie put her hands around her cup, feeling the warmth seep through to her fingers.

'I've missed this,' Rhys said.

Hettie looked up to find him looking around the room.

'I'd take tea in here sometimes with Sir Charles,' he said. 'Always in the kitchen. Never the parlour. He may have had grand titles, but he was a down to earth man. I'm sure it would please him to see people sitting at his table again. He was very fond of this cottage.'

There was real affection in Rhys' voice. Perhaps it was the way in all houses for the groundsman to take tea with his master, but Hettie doubted it. 'Was that to talk about your work?' she asked.

Rhys' expression was soft, as though he was reliving past times in this kitchen. 'Sometimes,' Rhys said. He took a sip of his tea. 'But most of the time, he liked to share anecdotes of his time in the military. And hear mine. We were in the same regiment.'

'He was your officer?' Hettie asked, testing her rudimentary knowledge of how the army worked.

Rhys laughed softly and shook his head. 'No. I enlisted long after he left. But Elliot was in the regiment with him. That's how he came to be here. That's how I came to be here really. My connection through the regiment.'

Hettie shifted in her seat. She twisted her cup in its saucer. 'I saw him, this morning,' she said. 'Elliot. I remember him from the visits when I was a child. He seemed...' she thought to the sullen face as he had begrudgingly remembered her. The sadness that seemed to leech from his rolled shoulders. 'Sorry,' she added, looking into her tea. 'It's none of my business.'

There was a short pause before Rhys spoke softly again. 'Grief takes us all in different ways. There's no rhyme nor reason to it. And neither should there be. Elliot had known and served Sir Charles most of his adult life. We are all just human. Sir Charles might have been his officer, then his employer, but there was a bond. They were friends. We might shy away from acknowledging affection but when it's there, a loss is keenly felt. Regardless of whether one person sits in robes and ermine in the highest house in the land and the other sweeps the hay from his cobbles.' Rhys paused. He took his cup from its saucer and replaced it again. 'Elliot is a man of few words. But he is a good man. It's my honour to be able to help with his tasks so that he has time to grieve. We all of us need a helping hand at times in our lives.'

Hettie wanted to reply. She didn't want to appear rude. But she was afraid of what her grief might make her say.

'Would you mind if I helped myself to one of these sausages?' Rhys said. His tone was brighter, his words light.

Hettie shook her head. Rhys took up a fork. He transferred one of the sausages onto his plate and cut it into pieces. He added a little salt and pepper. 'Audrey is always generous with food,' he said after chewing and swallowing a mouthful of the sausage. 'And she's a fine cook.' He ate another mouthful of sausage. 'If you don't fancy any of this now,' he said. 'We could cover it up. You might want it for lunch. Although, you would be welcome to help yourself to anything in the cupboards. Audrey keeps them stocked and I'm sure Sir Charles wouldn't mind if he was still here.'

Hettie stared into her tea. Rhys spoke about Sir Charles as though he had simply taken a trip into town rather than died. He was interred in the vault in the church across the road. He was not taking a turn down the high street. This cottage and how it was tended could make anyone believe that the occupant was still alive. It felt lived in. Like a home. Even though it had never been that – it was simply a place where Sir Charles had stored his collection.

'It would please him to know his things are being admired,' Rhys said. 'I'm afraid most of us wouldn't know a collectable from something that was only good for the bring and buy sale at the church. Is your assessment of his things going well?'

Hettie clutched her teacup. 'I'm not assessing as such,' she said. 'I'm not an expert. I've been sent to make notes on each item so my parents and their colleagues might make an assessment.'

'And to take photographs?' Rhys said.

Hettie gripped her cup tighter. 'Yes,' she said.

'If I can be of any help with that,' Rhys said, 'you just have to say. As I understand it, you need good light for cameras.'

Hettie nodded. 'You do,' she said.

Rhys could have no idea that he was taking the conversation into an area she did not want to go. She raised her cup to her lips and took a sip of the hot tea. But she would have to tread that path sooner rather than later. Her only reason for being here was to catalogue Sir Charles' collection. Without photographs, her parents and their colleagues would be reliant on the written descriptions in her notebook.

Hettie released her grasp on the cup. 'Thank you,' she said. 'I'll let you know if I need anything.'

'I'd be glad to help,' Rhys said. He took the final mouthful of sausage and another sip of tea.

'Would you like anything else?' Hettie asked.

'Thank you, no.' Rhys said. 'That did me just well.'

Hettie shook out the cloth and placed it over the tray of food.

'Well,' Rhys said. Picking up his cup, he drained the tea. 'I should let you get back to your day.' He stood and made to take his plate and cup to the sink.

'I'll do that,' Hettie said. 'I'm sure that you have things you need to be getting on with.'

'Thank you,' Rhys said. 'If you do need me, I'll likely be in the walled garden. There's no permanent gardener at the moment so I make use of one of the outbuildings that has a fire. It's very comfortable. Otherwise, I'll be about the estate, but you can leave me a note with whatever you need. There's a workbench in the outbuilding and I keep a pad and pencil in there.'

Hettie took up the teapot. 'There was one thing,' she said. 'Should I feed the cat? There doesn't appear to be any food left out for it.'

'The cat?' Rhys said, his eyebrows raised.

'It was upstairs earlier. We gave each other a fright on the landing.'

Rhys laughed. 'I'm not surprised. There should be no cat here. It must have snuck in when the door was open. Would you like me to go and find it and put it outside?'

'No,' Hettie said. 'No, it's all right. I'll find it later and put it out.'

'As you like,' Rhys said. He smiled again. 'Thank you for the company. I'll see myself out.'

'Thank you,' Hettie said. 'For the company. And for bringing the food.'

Rhys nodded before turning and leaving the kitchen. Hettie watched his progress through the hall. He opened the front door and a chill breeze briefly whipped about her ankles as he pulled the door closed behind him.

Hettie stared at the front door for a few seconds before turning to place the teapot in the sink. She pushed in the plug and poured the still warm water from the kettle into the sink. She washed and dried the crockery and cutlery and placed them back in the cupboard, then tucked the cloth tighter around the leftover food so that it wouldn't spoil. She was tempted to retake her seat and warm herself at the fire but the ancient pots on the dresser reminded her what she was there to do. Closing her eyes, she breathed in deeply and then exhaled.

Without allowing herself a moment to change her mind, Hettie left the kitchen, walked the short distance down the hall and stepped inside the parlour. Heading directly for the desk, she collected her bag from where she had left it on the floor and placed it on the table. She released the buckles and pushed the rigid lid back so that the contents were exposed. She looked inside. Everything was... as it should be.

Hettie felt her shoulders go slack. What had she been expecting? The bag and its contents had sat safe and sound on a shelf in her parents' cellar for months. It was a dry environment that her father kept heated, so anything stored down there was kept in good order. She looked in the various compartments. Two cameras. Lenses. A cubby with a clip for films. She let her eyes travel over the familiar equipment before reaching to take one of the cameras from its compartment. She turned it over and examined the silver levers and mechanisms. The weight of metal in her hands felt so familiar. It felt right to hold it. The cameras she used in studios might have made her more money but the cameras in this hamper-like bag were what fuelled her passion. Although there was no hiding from the empty compartment. Knowing what had happened to the camera that she usually stored in that empty space, and how she would have felt about seeing it, her parents would have removed it. They would have placed it somewhere to return to her when she was ready.

Hettie gripped her camera tighter. She couldn't imagine a time when she would be able to look at that other camera. A time when she would be able to touch it without being reminded what its smashed state meant.

The daily battle to hold the grief at bay faltered. She was winded as though she had taken a punch to the stomach. Life filled Hill House. With the two young cousins, the sisters in the kitchen, the wonderful married couple acting as temporary custodians and the two loyal ex-servicemen in the outbuildings. But that vibrant life was tempered by grief. Last night, over dinner, family and staff alike had expressed their sadness at the loss of a benevolent head of the household and beloved grandfather. Yet they were still able to function as human beings. To go about their life and business and to wear their sadness as a mark of their love. Her grief felt more like Elliot's grief, paralysed as he was by the loss of the man who had been his officer and had brought him into this household.

Rhys' words came back to her. Grief takes people in different ways. What it did to her was render her powerless to function as the human she had once been. And it made time stand still in moments. In the moment she had watched Saul disappear into the crowd. In the moment the Bessers had opened the door to the police inspector and two constables. In the moment the inspector broke the news of Saul's death. In the moment his mother and sisters tore their blouses. In the moment his father collapsed against the wall. In the moment she had worn black lace over her head as she took a low chair in the Besser's dining room to sit Shiva for Saul's soul.

Hettie clutched the camera tighter still. This was who she had been. When she had held that first Brownie, it had felt right. As though it was an extension of her. It had affected her in a way touching the ancient artefacts of her parents and grandfather never had. Her first forays into photography had mainly involved her father's dog, Bou, and posing her parents and grandfather in costumes. They had always humoured her. Her father had taken the films to a man at the university who turned them into photographs that the family would laugh over, enjoying seeing themselves in jolly or quite ridiculous costumes from Hettie's dressing up box. How innocent it had all been. If only she had kept photography as a hobby rather than enlisting her grandfather's support to pursue it as a passion. And then a career.

Had she followed the family business of academia, she would not have gone to Paris to study, returning to plaudits from the fashion industry, which had turned her head. She should have drawn a line under it there and then. She should have taken up a more sensible job. But she had been so in demand that she listened to the praise. She had earned good money. She was never out of work and had more commissions than she could accept so that she had to take on the services of an assistant to manage the telephone calls and correspondence. Anyone else would have been satisfied with that level of success and admiration, but not her. Oh no, Hettie Turner would not let her ambitions lie unfulfilled.

She had worked so hard to get the editors of newspapers and magazines to take her seriously as a photojournalist. If anything, her success and reputation for capturing 'women in frocks' had made it harder. So, for four years, the money she earned from fashion had subsidised her photojournalism. She had lived a double life capturing the most privileged in society and those that society would keep down at heel. She had followed the hunger marchers from northern towns to rallies in Hyde Park to protest the government's lack of help after the closure of so much heavy industry that saw them destitute. She had photographed them protesting starvation and degradation. She had captured the images of people who had walked hundreds of miles from Scotland, Tyneside, Burnley and Liverpool, sleeping in mission halls and living off food handed out to them along the way by others who could ill afford to give it but wanted to show their support for the marchers so that the government would hear their calls. And it was those photographs that had become her calling card to editors who started to take her seriously and grant her admission to their offices.

Finally, an editor had seen something in her and had paid her to follow the men and women launching counter demonstrations at the rallies of the British Union of Fascists. She had been accepted by the protestors who had willingly let her follow them to their meetings so that through her, the world might hear their calls to smash the fascist bigots. She had begun to make a nuisance of herself as far as Mosley's followers were concerned. She doubted their leader knew of her existence, but many of his thugs certainly did. She had been chased away from many BUF meetings. At one of their rallies in Hyde Park, she had captured images of a lone protestor heckling the fascists until the police stepped in, as much to protect him as to supress him. Suspecting they would take him to Albany Street Police Station to the east of the park, Hettie had run through the streets to be there before them and had captured an image of the man being taken into the station and declaring himself a communist who was not afraid to stand up to Mosley and his thugs! She had applauded him for his fearlessness. Those fascists were aligned with other such groups across Europe, including those who had taken power in Germany.

Berlin.

As always, when Hettie thought of Berlin, the memories of those colourful and, some might say, hedonistic nights at The Souk down that back alley with its spiced incense and silks and music and cocktails came flooding back. What had become of the people she knew then? They had wanted nothing more than to find likeminded people with whom to spend their evenings. They had done nobody any harm. Yet their lives would have been deemed debauched by the new authorities in Germany. Anything different was something to be quelled and quashed. If her old friends had not been fortunate enough to go into hiding, their fate was something she could barely comprehend. Who could have so much hate in their hearts that they lived to inflict pain and to wipe out parts of society. When there was an option to relish differences and learn from the experiences of others, why choose to silence them? Or worse.

Even in this country, Mosley had managed to brainwash thousands of seemingly normal people into joining him and his cause. They could have no idea that he treated them with the same disdain with which he treated the people of the East End who he had been attempting to push out and eradicate with his marches and spewing of bile.

Had it not been for the fascists' hatred of their fellow humans, there would have been no march in Aldgate. She would not have been holding on to a lamppost to take photographs. Saul would not have pushed through the crowds to get one of her spare cameras after she had smashed the one she was using. He would not have been mugged and murdered just a few short streets from his home. He'd had nothing of interest on him. No wallet. No valuables. Even the few coins in his pocket had been of no interest to his killer. They had been returned to his family along with his cleanly-pressed handkerchief and the spare camera film Hettie never knew he carried but which his parents said he took everywhere when he was with her in case she needed it.

Hettie clutched her camera tighter. She had done her best to comfort the Bessers, to console them and help them memorialise their son. But she had felt alone in her grief. Alone because – despite what the Bessers had said – she felt guilt weigh her down. She had nobody to turn to. Nobody would accept that it was her fault. Not the Bessers and not her parents.

The one person she should have been able to talk to had abandoned her.

Gray.

For the first time in so long, she allowed herself to think of him. They had known each other only a month before the events in Aldgate, but she had trusted him with so much of her. He had betrayed that trust. Images flashed in her mind of the club in London where she'd first danced with him. It had been hot, and she had been drenched in sweat on the crowded dance floor, her body pressed so close to Gray's that they may as well have been naked and in bed together. Which, later that same night, they had been.

Hettie placed the camera down on the table. She covered her face with her hands. It was always this way. When she let one memory in, it was followed by another and another until it felt she was careering out of control on a helter-skelter, memories and images rushing by and dragging her on a terrifying ride with no end. But these were all separate. Her job. The Souk. Berlin. Saul. Gray. These were separate parts of her life, yet the thought of one always led to the thought of the other and then the next. Somehow, in her mind, they were all connected. The only way she could explain it to herself was that in her darkest moments, her brain wanted to drag her somewhere darker still, to the places where her guilt, her shame and her pain lived.

The muscles in Hettie's hands tensed and she found herself digging her fingertips into the delicate flesh around her eyes and the soft skin of her cheeks. Her body might be in the parlour of a cottage outside the gates of Hill House but there was no escape from the twisting, never-ending ride that was her mind. Or her rage.

Opening her eyes, Hettie pulled a chair from beneath the table. She had so much anger inside her. Anger at Mosley and his fascists. Anger at the fascists across Europe. Anger at whoever had killed Saul. Anger at Gray for abandoning her. But more than anything else, anger at herself.

Digging her hands into her hair, Hettie clutched her scalp. This was why she tried not to think. It always ended like this. Thoughts with no resolution and no end. She had no control over any of this. No power. She dragged her palms down her face. The only thing she had any control over was the task she had been sent here to do.

Looking down at her camera, she placed one hand on the cold metal. If comfort was to be found anywhere, she would find it in the thing that felt most familiar to her. She put her other hand on the camera and held it. She would need to make some preparations before she could begin photographing Sir Charles' collection. The light in the parlour was passable but what she really needed was a studio in miniature on the table in which she could place each item against a plain background so that her parents and their colleagues would not be distracted by the features of the room in the photographs and could better focus on the detail of each object.

Getting to her feet, Hettie went through to the kitchen. She opened drawers and cupboards in the hope of finding some table linen that might do as a backdrop. But the only linen was patterned so of no use. A movement close to the fire made her turn around. Expecting it to be a coal slipping through the grate, she made to collect the poker when she realised it had not been a coal at all. Sitting on the chair beside the fire, looking as though it had every right to be there, was the cat, white with a patch of black on its back and one ginger and one black ear. It was licking its paw and using it to clean its ears.

'Hello,' she said. 'What are you doing in here? This isn't your home.'

The cat paused in its ablutions. Tipping its head to one side, it stared at her. Hettie smiled. 'Are you hungry?' she asked.

The cat leapt lightly from the chair and began to circle Hettie's legs. She bent and stroked its ears. The cat responded by closing its eyes and lifting its face to her. She laughed softly and obliged the cat by running her hand over its head again.

'You must belong to someone,' she said. 'You're very friendly.'

The cat shadowed Hettie across the room as she took a tin of sardines from the cupboard. Using the metal key, she peeled back the lid of the tin and tipped the contents onto a saucer. Into another saucer, she poured milk from the jug on the tray.

She placed the impromptu meal down on the tiles and the cat instantly fell on its lunch.

Hettie rested against the sink. Folding her arms across her chest, she watched the cat move from the sardines to lapping the milk with a flick of its little pink tongue. Not for the first time in her life, she wondered how it could be that a scrap of life could provide so much pleasure. The cat could have no clue that its ancestors were hailed as higher beings by ancient Egyptian civilisation, honoured in hieroglyphs and in statuary. They were given their elevated status as they were considered protectors from vermin and attackers. They were so highly regarded and deified that mummified cats were placed in the tombs of the pharaohs. But this domesticated cat probably wanted nothing more than a warm lap on which to sit, a daily meal and the occasional treat of a bowl of cream. Hettie was thinking of the regal examples of Mafdet and Bastet which stood on the shelves in her mother's study when the cat suddenly stopped drinking. In one instant, the fur spiked down its spine and its attention turned to the back door. It hissed and bared its sharp, pointed teeth.

'What is it puss?' Hettie said.

The cat let out a guttural growl. It glared at the back door. When it hissed again, Hettie pushed herself away from the sink. She slid the bolts from the top and bottom of the door and turned the key in the lock, opening the door with the intention of showing the cat either there was nothing to make a fuss over or to let it out.

'See,' Hettie said. 'There's nothing there.'

The cat did not move. If anything, its hackles rose higher as it hissed and then growled, staring at the spot where the door had been. Hettie opened the door further and looked outside to a small yard with an outside privy and a gate beside it. The gate stood open, swinging back and forth slightly as though someone had just left. Looking down, Hettie saw a disturbance in the frost covering the cobbles. Footprints. Heading towards the back door and heading away. They were large. Could they belong to Rhys? He had said he was checking on the cottage. But why would he have left the gate open? And why would he have seemingly left at the sound of her turning the key in the lock? Hettie stepped out into the yard. Crossing the cobbles she looked out through the open gate. It led to a small alleyway running along the length of the back of the row of cottages. It was in shade and the footprints on the cobbles were more pronounced. They seemed spaced far apart as though someone had been running. Hettie considered following them but whoever had made them was most likely gone and she didn't want to leave Sir Charles' cottage and its collection unsecured. Returning to the yard, she closed the gate. In the kitchen she bolted and locked the door. She pulled the curtain back from the window above the sink and looked out. All was still and peaceful. Letting the curtain fall, she knelt down to the cat who had given up its alarm and was licking its paws and cleaning its ears.

'Clever puss,' she said. 'Thank you for the warning. I shall go to ask Rhys if it was him in the yard.' She collected the empty saucers and washed them in the sink. The cat followed her into the hall and sat on the mat while she pulled on her coat. When she opened the door, it followed her outside. 'Are you off then?' she asked, giving the cat's head another stroke. Hettie watched it trot away down the path around the side of the cottage, its tail held proudly in the air.

ELEVEN

It was late morning tipping into afternoon, but Hill House and its land was still cloaked in a shroud of icy fog. It was only when Hettie was halfway up the drive that the features of the house began to emerge, its white Portland stone appearing ethereally from the white fog. The first specific detail to reveal itself was the great portico but, unlike the day before, there was no ladder leaning against the wall.

Taking a right outside the house, Hettie followed the path past the stable yard and along to the gates of the walled garden. She stepped through and pulled her coat closer around her. Freezing fog hovered over the bare beds of soil, which stood in hard peaks, waiting for the warmth of spring when they would once again be planted with new life. Twisted branches trained on wires around the walls had not a bud between them. Like the soil, they were waiting for the warmth of the sun to help them burst from their hibernation.

Hettie was pleased to see the benches still dotted along the paths. On many a day, when she had tired of playing with the other children, she had snuck into the garden to lie on one of the benches, looking up at the endless blue, listening to birdsong, imagining the endless possibilities of life.

'Hello there.'

The sound of the voice came as a surprise. Hettie spun around. 'Hello,' she said.

'I didn't mean to startle you,' Rhys said. 'I thought you would have heard my boots on the gravel. There's nothing subtle about me.' He smiled. 'You looked deep in thought,' he said.

'I was,' Hettie said. 'I was just... thinking about the times I spent here as a child.'

'Good times?' Rhys asked.

'Mmmm,' Hettie said. 'Very good.'

'Was it me you were looking for?' Rhys asked.

Hettie nodded.

'Well, it's a good thing you have found me,' he said. 'Come on then, let's get you inside and out of the cold.'

Hettie followed Rhys towards the back of the garden. He still wore no coat but appeared impervious to the cold. His breath misted the air as did hers, like small clouds melting into the larger cloud of frosted air. Rhys turned right onto a path and as he did, Hettie detected the smell of a coal fire. Soon, an orange smudge of light became visible through the gloom. Rhys stopped at a brick built shed running along the back wall of the garden with a window through which the orange light glowed.

'It's just through here,' Rhys said, opening a door.

Hettie stepped inside and warmth wrapped around her. The wall opposite the door was made entirely of exposed brick with a fireplace that seemed out of proportion with the room. A series of industrial large black metal doors were arranged in the brickwork. An old-fashioned black range sat in the fireplace. A shallow shelf beside it held a few items of crockery and cutlery. A small table and chair sat on one side of the fire, an armchair on the other. Running the entire length of the room beneath the window was a sturdy looking workbench with tools placed neatly at the far end and a series of boxes and crates.

'I had no idea this was here,' Hettie said as Rhys followed her inside and closed the door behind them.

'That's the idea,' Rhys said. 'It's made of brick so that it blends in with the wall of the garden rather than standing out. In the summer the outside is covered in climbing roses and a plum tree is trained over it so that it becomes almost invisible.'

Hettie looked about the brick room. 'What is this place?' she asked.

Rhys dug his hands into the pockets of his trousers. 'Back in the days when there were a lot of gardeners, this was the room that heated the glasshouses next door, just behind that wall with the fire. It is intentionally hot to help the flowers grow in the glasshouses. It hasn't been used for many years. Sir Charles had a conservatory built onto the house with modern heating, so this stood empty. Once upon a time there would have been a lad in here all day and night to keep the fires stoked. There's a small bed at the back end there,' he nodded to the end of the room beyond the armchair. 'That's where the lad would have slept so he could keep an eye on the fires. I've been known to bunk down there myself sometimes if I'm working late and don't fancy going back to the house. It's rather cosy and does me well.'

Hettie looked to the end of the room. A checked blanket was just visible. She pictured Rhys sitting before the fire on a cold evening. Kettle boiling in the hearth. Something cooking in a pan on the range. Sleeping in the bed beyond the armchair. She turned back to Rhys. He was looking at her.

'Sorry,' she said, shaking her head.

'For what?' Rhys asked.

'Nothing,' she said. She shouldn't be thinking about the sleeping arrangements of this man. And she shouldn't be intruding on his privacy. Searching her mind for something sensible to say, she said, 'Is there electricity here?'

Rhys paused a second before replying. He seemed a little amused by her. 'No,' he said, 'there's no electricity. But I have lots of candles for the evenings. When I grew up – about a thousand years ago – we lived by candlelight, so I'm familiar with it and content with it.' His eyes still smiled. 'Was there something in particular you wanted me for?' he asked.

'Yes... yes, sorry... my brain is all over the place.'

'No rush,' he said. 'Would you like tea?' He pointed to the kettle on the range.

'Thank you, but no,' Hettie said. 'I have a lot of work to be getting on with. Which is rather why I am here.'

'Oh?' Rhys leant back against the workbench and folded his arms across his chest.

'I'd like to construct a small backdrop on the table in the parlour in the cottage. I wondered if you might have a square of muslin or something that I could use? Another piece of white fabric would do. I can suspend it from some books as a sort of temporary frame.'

'How big would it need to be?'

'A couple of feet square?' Hettie said, indicating the approximate size with her hands.

'Leave it with me,' Rhys said. 'I'll have something to you later today. Would that suit?'

'It would,' Hettie said. 'Thank you.' She paused. 'I have something else to ask you.'

'Go on,' Rhys said.

'Did you come back to the cottage after you left this morning?'

'Why do you ask?'

'The back gate was open. And there were footprints in the ice in the yard and in the alley. As though someone had been in and run out.'

Rhys pushed himself away from the workbench. Any smile disappeared from his eyes. 'Did you see anyone?'

'No. It's possible that it was an opportunist looking for an open door. But I wanted to let you know. Some of Sir Charles' collection is valuable.'

'I've said to Bertie we should put a bolt on the back gate. I'll do it today,' Rhys said. 'Were you concerned at all?'

'Only for the collection.'

Rhys nodded. 'Good. That's good. And you're sure you won't have a tea before you go back to the cottage?'

'No, I'm fine thank you. I have everything I need there.'

Again, there was no sign of a smile in Rhys' eyes or amusement in his voice, when he said, 'As I say, I'll be over later today to fit that bolt. If you see anything else untoward, you will let me know.'

'Of course,' Hettie said. 'I should imagine it was just a child.'

Rhys nodded but didn't reply.

TWELVE
APRIL 1876

It was a glorious early spring morning when the SS *Baltic* docked in New Jersey. Charles was on deck to witness their arrival as he had been present on deck every day of the voyage. They had to transfer to a smaller boat to take them across to Manhattan Island from where they would catch a train to take them to the house where they would spend their first night.

'Look!' Charles said, hanging over the rails of the boat as the buildings of New York came into view, stacked up, crowded together, and built as high as engineering would allow.

'I see it,' Henry said, a little boredom creeping into his voice.

'Aren't you excited?' Charles asked.

Henry shrugged. 'A modern building is a modern building. Give me a pyramid and you might just pique my interest.'

'I wish I could get my camera out to take a photograph,' Walter said.

'No time,' Charles said. 'We'll be there in ten minutes.' He closed his eyes and felt the breeze on his face.

. . .

Arriving on the docks on Manhattan was like arriving on a different planet. Charles looked around in wonder at the sheer number of people thronging the quayside. He had thought Liverpool busy but there had to be double, if not triple, the amount of people here. So many porters vied to carry passengers' luggage on their trollies. Vendors sold goods from carts: baked goods, coffee, lemonade, fudge, hot pork sandwiches, newspapers, magazines, neckties and scarves. A chap offered to clean boots and shoes for a couple of cents. So many languages were spoken. Charles understood a little of the French and German, but the other tongues were a mystery to him.

While Walter went to secure a carriage, Charles waited with their luggage, the tallest buildings he had ever seen on one side of him and a sea of masts and funnels on the other. He was nudged from behind and turned around.

'Want one?' Henry said, offering him a paper bag. 'It's called "Taffy",' he said.

Charles peered into the bag at the small sweets wrapped in waxed paper. 'No thank you,' he said. 'I value my teeth too much.'

Henry shrugged. 'All the more for me then,' he said, popping another of the sweets into his mouth and chewing vigorously.

Charles spotted Walter waving to them through the crowd and called on two porters to load their luggage onto their trollies.

Craning out of the window of the carriage, Charles tried to take in all the buildings they passed. It was rather like London – the streets filled with horses and carriages and people, so many people – but it was bigger and newer, and everyone spoke so loudly, as though they were afraid they would not be heard.

They were soon delivered to a station where the carriage driver arranged for two porters to take their luggage to the train. Walter stopped briefly to buy a newspaper before rejoining the little procession. Henry handed some coins to the porters after they loaded the luggage and they seemed very happy with the bit extra he gave in excess of their fee.

As the train pulled out of the station, the landscape of grey buildings stretched out around them. Low buildings, tall buildings, factories, shops and blocks of dwellings, many with intricate metal landings and ladders attached to the outside. The further they travelled from the centre of Manhattan the more industrial the landscape became. Huge buildings with external machinery of pulleys and conveyer belts, facades blackened by smoke billowing from chimneys that dwarfed the chimneys Charles had seen on trips to the industrial north of England with his father. The bitter smoke from the chimneys mixed with the steam from the train.

'Might we close the windows?' Walter asked. 'I don't think my lungs can take much more of this smoke.'

'I second that,' Henry said. 'We don't want to turn up at our host's house stinking of smuts!'

Reluctantly, Charles pulled the window up. He settled for looking out while Walter retreated to his newspaper and handed Henry the middle pages to read. Charles watched as the train travelled alongside the Hudson River, the great expanse of water they would run alongside until they reached their destination – Tarrytown – which lay twenty-five miles from the centre of Manhattan. Charles knew this as he had studied the relevant rail timetables and maps.

Pressing his forehead to the glass, Charles watched the water and the strip of land separating it from the track. If it was up to him, he would stay on this train to the station where he could catch the connection to Montreal. He would be boarding that train the very next day to start his trip to Canada and had pointed out on many occasions that it seemed a waste of time for him to break the trip when he could travel straight to Montreal. But his mother had convinced him that he should accept at least one night's hospitality on arrival. His father's contact in New York would expect it. She was appalled that he was breaking the trip with five days on the Canadian visit while Henry and Walter stayed on with their hosts. But she had been relieved that on his return, her son would be immersed in New York society for a week before he had his friends boarded a different train to begin their trip across the continent. Charles frowned at his reflection. He was beginning to wonder whether his mother might be hoping that he meet an American heiress after all, even if it was very much not his on his list of things to do.

When the train pulled into the station at Tarrytown, Charles stood ready with Henry and Walter to unload their cases and trunks. But as they stepped down from the train, they were greeted by a man in a blue uniform with gold braid and buttons. Behind him stood five more men in blue uniforms. 'Mr Mandeville, Mr Turner and Mr Kenmore, follow me this way, if you please,' the man said. 'Your luggage will be transported to Anderson House.'

Henry looked at Charles and raised his eyebrows as they followed the man away from the platform.

At the front of the station, another man in blue uniform stood before the largest carriage Charles had ever seen. It was jet black and every part of the wood and metal construction was waxed and varnished so that it gleamed just as the four black horses gleamed at the front of the carriage. The man stood to attention beside a set of wooden steps leading up to the carriage door.

'Is this really for us?' Walter said, leaning into Charles and Henry.

'I hope so,' Henry said, 'unless the local bandits have upped their game and intend to let us enjoy a spot of luxury before they rob us of all our worldly goods!'

Charles followed Walter and Henry into the carriage. The look of wonder on their faces surely matched the look that must have been on his face. As splendid as the exterior of the carriage was, it came nowhere close to the interior. Every part of it was decorated in gold. The fabric of the vast cushioned seats, the fabric lining the walls and doors. The curtains, the handles, the mechanism for opening the windows.

The man who had been standing sentry took the steps away and the first man, who had greeted them, informed them that they would be at Anderson House in around ten minutes. They thanked him then waited for the doors to close before they spoke.

'Bloody hell,' Henry said. 'Do you think they've mistaken us for royalty?'

Charles looked around as the horses started up. Inside the carriage, they barely moved. The suspension on the carriage was like nothing he had ever known. He sunk back into the seat.

'If this is what the carriage is like, imagine what the house is like!' Walter said.

They didn't have long to wait to find out as soon the carriage slowed to navigate through a huge set of gates and began to climb a drive. The grass surrounding the drive was perfectly green and so neat that Charles felt it could have been cut with manicure scissors. Spring blossoms at seemingly regimented distances apart lined the entirety of the drive, which was shorter than those he knew at home. But, whereas at Hill House, one would expect to see at least some working land from a drive, here it seemed that it was gardened and manicured just for show.

The carriage stopped and the door was opened by another man in a blue uniform who waited with another set of steps.

Charles followed his friends down to find the sun shining over a vast house at least three stories high, built in what looked like granite. Everything about its construction appeared solid, from the stone walls to the huge portico and front door. It reminded Charles of the houses he had seen in Scotland on his visits with his mother to one of her friends. But it was the backdrop to the house that struck him dumb. The grass and flowers and lines of trees rolled down to the Hudson River which glittered in the early afternoon sunshine. A man of about Charles' father's age, and another man about their own age, came through the vast front door and beneath the portico.

The older man held out his hand. 'Well, what a great pleasure it is to see you gentleman,' he said as though he had known them all his life. He shook the hand of each of them warmly, patting them on their shoulders. 'Howard Anderson,' he said, introducing himself. 'Now,' he said, 'you will have to tell me who is who.'

Henry, Walter and Charles each introduced themselves and Mr Anderson introduced them to the younger chap with him as his son, Daniel. Daniel shook hands with Charles and his friends. He didn't appear as loud as his father but like his father, there was a confidence about him. And they both seemed... polished... it was the only word Charles could think of to describe them. They were as smart and clean and as manicured as the lawns surrounding their house.

Mr Anderson ushered the party inside where an older woman and two younger women waited to greet them. 'It's a pleasure to have you in our summer home,' Mrs Anderson said and introduced her daughters as Elizabeth and Emily. 'We don't usually use it until later in the year, but this spring has been so mild that we just had to open it up for your visit. The views are much more appealing than the town house. And I prefer it for entertaining.'

Charles looked around at the hallway, hardly able to contain his surprise. This was their summer house! His father had told him they had a house in the grandest part of the city that dwarfed even the house in Tarrytown. Mr Anderson had made his fortune from the railroads, and it seemed that he liked to spend it. Charles and his friends were taken on a tour around the house by the family. The huge hallway, with a grand staircase that was about twice the size of the staircase at Hill House, led to a series of interconnecting rooms. Charles had never seen a home decorated with so much gold leaf. It was used everywhere from the doorframes to the skirting boards. Moving through the rooms, their hosts explained the use of each. A music room, the dining room the drawing room, the morning room. Mrs Anderson explained that any of the rooms could be closed off with partition doors. 'But we wanted to make the most of the views, so it seemed sensible to have this run of rooms. It gets the very best of the daylight.'

Mr Anderson pointed out that his study, the billiard room, and the smoking room were on the other side of the house. 'Away from the womenfolk!' he said and roared with laughter.

The daughters were asked to explain the artwork on the walls and the fine furnishings – many of which had come from Paris – before the party took tea on the veranda looking out over the Hudson.

Charles sipped his tea. He was glad of Henry and his love of talking. He spoke animatedly to Mr and Mrs Anderson, Daniel and Elizabeth, while Mrs Anderson insisted he have more cake and more sandwiches. Walter seemed rather taken with the younger of the daughter's – Emily – and was deep in conversation with her about what apparently was a shared passion for photography.

Charles looked out over the river. The Andersons seemed nice enough, if a little loud. But this opulence just wasn't him. Hill House was a working home, with farmland and gardens and tenants. The money that kept his father's house going was honestly made and bolstered by judicious investments. There was nothing wrong with the way the Anderson's had made their fortune, but it seemed so vast that Charles couldn't comprehend it.

When talk turned to the engagements planned for the next week, Charles excused himself. He had added so little to conversations that nobody seemed to mind his going to stretch his legs.

He walked around the entire outside of the house, admiring the architectural features. At the very far end, he found a great glasshouse attached to the main building. He stopped to look inside.

'Good afternoon, sir,' the gardener said. 'Won't you step inside?'

'Thank you,' Charles said. He joined the gardener at a raised bed with the most spectacular red flowers he had ever seen on a plant with waxy dark green leaves.

'They're orchids,' the gardener explained. 'Mr Anderson has a passion for them.'

'Are they difficult to grow?' Charles asked, looking around at the other examples with lilac and yellow and pink flowers.

'Not if you get the conditions right,' the gardener said. He went on to tell Charles more about each plant as he gave him a tour of the glasshouse.

Thanking the gardener for his time, Charles walked down to the river's edge. He could hear the lively chatter from the veranda but felt no need to return to join in. He would play no part in the social engagements for the next few days so there was little point becoming embroiled in the details.

Picking up a stone, he skimmed it across the water. Orchids. He would like to learn more about the cultivation of those plants.

Closing his eyes, Charles held his face up to the sun and

listened to the shush of the waves of the river and the call of birds on the opposite bank. This was when he felt most alive. Out in nature.

THIRTEEN
FEBRUARY 1937

On her walk back down the drive, Hettie wrapped her arms across her front against the cold. She thought of Rhys' reaction to what she had told him. His bearing had altered the moment she mentioned the open back gate and the footprints in the ice. He had tried to keep his concern from her, but she had read it in the way he had gone from relaxing against the workbench to standing up straight at the suggestion that someone was lurking about the cottage.

A welcoming cloud of smoke rose from the chimney of the cottage and as Hettie got closer, she saw something waiting on the mat on the front step. She smiled. She had already decided against telling anybody else about the cat. For all anyone knew, it had been Sir Charles' pet. He had been keen to keep people away, so it wasn't beyond the realms of possibility that he had a pet he hadn't told anyone about. And the cat did seem very at home in the cottage.

Hettie pushed open the gate. Removing her gloves, she bent down. 'Hello, puss,' she said, stroking the cat's ears, enjoying the soft fur as the cat closed its eyes and leant into her. Standing up,

Hettie took the key from her pocket. The instant she opened the door, the cat slipped inside.

Hettie shrugged off her coat and placed it on a hook. Removing her hat and gloves, she left them on the stand in the hall before following the cat into the kitchen. She ruffled her hair and checked her watch. 'It's almost one. Shall we have a spot of lunch?' she said. The cat looked from her to the table. 'I'll take that as a "yes",' she said. After shaking some more coals onto the fire, she filled the kettle and placed it on the range.

Removing the cloth from the tray, she looked over the leftovers from breakfast. Sausages, bread, boiled eggs, courgette jam. 'It's a feast,' she said to the cat who was looking up expectantly. Hettie took two saucers from the cupboard. She cut a sausage and one of the eggs into small pieces and placed them into a saucer. Into the other, she poured a helping of milk. The cat followed her to the sink where she put the saucers on the floor. 'I've never had a cat,' she said. 'Sorry, I don't know if this will be to your taste.'

She stepped back and watched the cat sniff at the saucers. It took up a piece of the sausage and began to chew it at the side of its mouth so that its sharp pin-like teeth showed. Content that her little guest was enjoying its meal, Hettie set about preparing her own. When the kettle came to the boil, she made a pot of tea. She sat down at the table to a lunch of sausages and boiled eggs with bread and jam. The only sound was the cat chewing and then lapping at the milk. Every so often, as Hettie ate, she looked out of the window. The gate was still closed and as the cat seemed relaxed, she felt happy to put thoughts of an intruder to one side.

After washing their lunch dishes, Hettie went through to the parlour. The cat followed her and sat on the rug before the fire. Hettie fed the hearth with more coal and the cat curled into a contented ball and closed its eyes.

Everything was as Hettie had left it. Her camera sat on the

table. Her leather bag was open on the floor beside the desk. Flipping open her satchel, she took out her notebook and pen. She placed the notebook on the table, removed the lid from her pen and looked over the first item on the shelf. One of the pairs of dogs of foo. She recorded its colour and approximate height. Lifting each of the dogs gently, she made a note of the marks on the bases. Moving along the shelf, she made similar notes on each item and gave each a number to correspond with the photograph she would take. She left a space beneath each description where she would attach the photograph when she returned to Cambridge. She looked about the room; to the comical ceramic monkey sitting on the donkey's back, the chess set on the desk, the rows of books on the shelves. For the first time in so long, she had something to fill the hours in a day. She knelt down and stroked the cat. Its fur was warm from the fire, and it barely moved. She had even found a purpose in feeding this little creature.

Taking a seat at the table, Hettie smoothed out the pages of her notebook. She read through what she had written and added a few notes until she was satisfied with the details she had recorded. She turned to the next blank page. The fire warmed her back. She closed her eyes briefly. Opening them again, she tried to focus on the pristine white page before her. She looked to the shelf of ceramics and began writing. But her eyes closed again. She felt her head fall and she snapped back to attention. She tried to focus on the page as she wrote more words. But the fire was so very warm. She felt comfortable and... She was wrapped in warmth on a long hot summer night in the back streets of Berlin. She walked from the light that one streetlamp cast on the pavement to the light of the next. Light came from windows of apartments above shops long closed for the evening and from restaurants full of customers spilling out onto tables on the pavements. She felt such lightness, such freedom, as she turned into the alleyway and saw the small queue outside the vast door of the industrial building. She greeted the familiar faces and was greeted in return. They marvelled at her new suit. She had found it in a second-hand shop in Paris and she'd had the men's trousers, jacket and waistcoat tailored to fit her. It was cream linen, which she wore over a pale blue shirt with a blue necktie. Her brown brogues gleamed from their fresh polish and her hair was the palest blonde it had ever been after a visit to a hairdresser in a side street in Montmartre only two days earlier.

Through the door she went and down the dark narrow steps. She dipped to avoid hitting her head on the low part of the staircase that always took newcomers by surprise so that they entered the club rubbing a bump on their head. Music floated up to greet her. Clarinet, trumpet, piano, drums, accordion. Voices. So many voices, raised in laughter and chatter, melding so that it seemed a single voice welcomed her into the room of red and orange silks. Dark wood furniture. Candles and brass incense burners. Cigarette smoke clouded the air along with perfumes. A drink was handed to her. She tasted it and laughed at its strength. All the faces she knew. All smiles. Some in suits. Others in extravagant and wonderful dresses. Others with not many clothes at all. Anyone and everyone was welcome as long as they welcomed all others.

She was soon pulled onto the dancefloor, laughing as she spilled the drink she had just held to her lips. So many people. The band playing lively and loudly. Such a small space that everyone on the dancefloor was pressed against someone else. They danced how they wanted. A tango. A waltz. A foxtrot. Or no known dance at all, simply moves that pleased. Nobody was on show, and everyone was on show. In the outside world, they did their best not to be noticed. At The Souk, they did their best to be seen and accepted. For who they were. For what they were. Hettie's damp hair clung to her face as she laughed and danced, shrugging off her jacket and placing it over the back of a chair.

A female singer in a dark suit with hair swept back took to the small stage and they danced joyfully to her songs that would have seemed scandalous to the world beyond these four walls. Another dance. Another strong drink. Hettie twirled around; her arms raised in the air. But when she completed her twirl, she was no longer in a world of orange and scarlet and brass and incense.

The clientele was similar but rougher somehow, with less panache. They were similar to the people of The Souk but not the same. Someone pressed themselves against her. And she did not stop them. They kissed her. She did not stop them. They kissed her again and pulled her so close that she could feel all of them on her. It had never been like this at The Souk. It had been gentler. This person was not her usual type. He was slender but strong. Sort of handsome but with a rough edge. He felt dangerous. Unpredictable. And she found she wanted it. Wanted this person, whose hands were in her hair. Down her back. Feeling inside her waistcoat so that she arched her back when he bit her lip. The smell of him was there. The cologne. The imported cocktail cigarettes he smoked. His tight and taut body. In bed. No. No. She didn't want this. Not him. Not here. Not now. Not anymore.

Hettie opened her eyes. Her breath came in thick gasps. She looked around. She was in the parlour of the cottage at Hill House. She was safe. And yet... she could still smell the thick familiar smoke. She jumped to her feet and looked around. The room was empty. The cat was gone. She ran through to the kitchen. But all was as she had left it. She ran up the stairs two at a time. The front room was empty. The back room was calm and peaceful. She ran down the stairs again and into the kitchen. She tried the back door – still locked. She went to the sink and took one of the teacups from the draining board. Filling it from the tap, she drank the ice-cold water. She filled the cup again and drained it again. She paused for a second, clasping her forehead.

This was ridiculous. It was a dream. She had dreamt of The Souk which led to a dream of Gray. She had been warm before the fire and drifted away. She could not control her dreams. If she had been able to, they would not have included him. Never. She grasped the edge of the table. Her subconscious was working things through. That was all. She breathed in deeply. She looked around the kitchen. It was as it should be. Domestic pottery mixed with shelves of ancient pottery. A fire in the grate. She looked to the mat before the fireplace. No cat there or in the parlour. It had clearly taken fright at her sudden and unexpected awakening and darted for safety somewhere in the cottage.

Collecting the saucer from the draining board, Hettie filled it with milk from the jug on the tray and placed it on the floor before the sink. She wanted to stand but had no energy. She sank to her knees and held her head in her hands. Images rushed at her. Images of them together in dark alleyways, shop doorways, parks that had been closed for the night and whose gates they had to climb over to gain access. Grasping at each other. Images of them stumbling through the back door on Leman Street that led directly to her flat. Stopping on the stairs. Her slamming her hand across his mouth so that he didn't make any noise and wake anyone. Tumbling through the door of her flat. Sometimes making it to the bed. Sometimes only just making it inside. On the floor. Against the door.

Hettie shook her head but still the images came.

It had always been frenzied. Like they were attacking each other. Often her under things were ripped. She had never stopped him. She had never wanted to stop him. Almost every night for a month throughout that warm autumn, they had met. And on the nights they hadn't, she had wanted him so badly.

Hettie held her head tighter. There had been no tenderness. When they kissed their teeth crashed. They clawed at each other. He had rarely stayed in bed long after. Just long enough to drink a whisky and smoke a cigarette. He was busy, he had said. He had a job as a driver for a rich duke who lived on Eaton Square. He had to be available at a moment's notice. The time he spent with her was snatched while the duke was at dinner or entertaining. When they were able to meet at the club, it was on his nights off. There was no telephone number where she could reach him as he lived above the garage. He would let her know when he could come. He would knock on her door downstairs. There had been evenings where she waited in, cancelling social engagements with friends only for no knock to come. Sometimes she went downstairs and waited behind the door, worried that she might miss it.

But after the events of that day in November where she had smashed her camera, she had not seen him again. He never knocked at her door again. It might have been the shop downstairs swathed in black for mourning that put him off. He may have heard the wailing from behind the closed doors. All she had wanted was his body. To feel something other than the pain of Saul's loss. In her desperation she had taken the Underground to Victoria and wandered the alleyways and mews houses behind Eaton Square where once horses had been stabled but were now the haunt of chauffeurs and cars. She had hidden herself and watched the chauffeurs play cards on upturned crates, smoking cigarettes and waiting to be summoned by their masters and mistresses. But she had not seen Gray. When one of the chauffeurs left the group to buy cigarettes, she had asked him if he knew where Gray worked. But he said that he had never heard of anyone called Gray. She had gone to the basement club and to the restaurant where she first met him. But he was not there. He had disappeared from her life as abruptly as he had entered it. He left no trace that he had ever been there apart from the memories pressed into her flesh and seared into her brain. She had given herself so easily to him and in so many ways.

Shame. It was all she could feel. That she had given herself to him so willingly when she usually kept most of herself closed from anyone. She had enthusiastically and eagerly participated in the exploration of their bodies. When Saul had died, she wanted to feel Gray's body on her. It had become like a hunger. She had wanted that release. But she had been so stupid. She had no idea who he was. She had been reckless in a way she had never been before. She had told none of her friends of him. She had wanted all of him for herself. He had no doubt moved on to the next willing participant having exhausted all he wanted from her. He wanted danger. He wanted excitement. Not her.

'You're stupid. You are so, so stupid,' Hettie whispered to herself. She couldn't blame her behaviour on naivety. She had taken lovers before Gray. Some had been casual; others had been for longer and had more meaning. But before Gray, she had known what each person wanted from her, what she was prepared to give, and what she wanted from them. She hated him. Hated him for what he had done to her. But in the same breath, she couldn't be sure that she wouldn't take him again if he knocked on her door. That she wouldn't press herself to him. And she hated herself all over again for even thinking of letting him into her life. The thought of him disgusted her. But it was more the thought of how she might respond that made her want to rip all memory of him from her life and burn it.

Hettie let her hands fall to her sides. She rubbed her fingertips across the rough stone floor. Gently, she became aware of something touching her. Looking down, she found the cat rubbing its face against her hand. She breathed in deeply. 'Hello, puss,' she said. She stroked the cat's head. Gradually her breathing slowed. She got to her feet, which seemed to be a sign for the cat to go to its saucer and lap at the milk.

After finishing its drink, the cat retreated to the mat before the fire. Hettie had just topped up the milk in the saucer when a knock came at the front door. She wiped her hands and went through to the hall. Opening the door, she was greeted by a welcome face. But when Rhys saw her, a frown creased his brow.

'Has something happened?' he said.

Hettie was unsure how to respond. 'No,' she said. 'Why?'

'You're very pale.'

'I'm tired,' she said. It was the truth. The unwanted flood of memories had drained her of any energy.

'I can come back later,' Rhys said. 'If this is an inconvenient time.'

Hettie opened the door wider. 'It's fine.'

Rhys stepped inside, carrying a toolbox in one hand and a sort of wooden frame in the other. Closing the door, Hettie followed him through to the parlour where he placed the box on the floor and the frame on the table. He stood the frame up. It had a central portion made from four thin pieces of wood to form a square with an empty middle, like a picture frame without the picture. Two further sections in the same construction were hinged to the central part. Rhys opened them and the construction stood independently on the table in an empty triptych. From his pocket, he pulled a large piece of white fabric, which he unfolded and secured to the wood with a series of clips on the back of the frame. Pushing the sides out further pulled the fabric taut so it was free of any creases.

'Will that do?' he asked.

'You went to all that trouble for me?' Hettie said.

'It was no trouble,' Rhys said. 'I had all I needed in the shed, and it was the work of less than an hour.' He took up his toolbox. 'Would it be a convenient time for me to see to the bolt on that back gate?'

Hettie nodded. 'Thank you.'

She heard his boots on the wooden floor in the hall and then on the stone flags in the kitchen. She heard him slide the top and bottom bolts across the back door and turn the key in the lock. It was soon followed by hammering. Hettie stared at the construction on the table. The craftsmanship was beautiful. So much care had been taken over the frame's construction, with the tiny hinges placed precisely to secure the sides and the clips at regular intervals to hold the fabric. She would be able to stand an object in front of it and it would provide the perfect backdrop, like a studio in miniature. It was portable so she could take it upstairs to photograph items in the front room to make the best of the light in there too. It was perfect.

Soon the hammering stopped. The backdoor was closed, and footsteps came back through the house.

'Thank you so much,' Hettie said, turning to the door. 'It really is perfect for what I need.'

'I'm always glad when I can make something of use,' Rhys said. He paused, placing his toolbox on the floor. 'Have you been out the back at all since we spoke this morning?'

Hettie shook her head. 'Why?'

'It's just that the gate was open.' He paused again, seeming to consider his thoughts for a moment. 'You're probably right in what you said earlier. Children are letting themselves into and out of yards. The new bolt will put a stop to that.' He paused again. 'As I understand it, there have been some problems with intruders over the years at Hill House. Sir Charles and now Sir Edward have instructed me to always be on the lookout and report anything to them. Would you let me know if you see anyone or feel there's anything untoward.'

'Of course,' Hettie said. 'Who were the intruders?'

'I'm not sure,' Rhys said. 'Most likely criminals looking for easy things to steal. I'm sure that any big property such as Hill House is a target.'

'I'll make sure I lock up well before I leave the cottage each night,' Hettie said.

'It would be as well to do that,' Rhys said. He looked to the frame. 'I should let you get on with your work then before you lose the light for the day.' He glanced at Hettie's notebook. 'There's lots of notes there.'

'It's a start,' Hettie said.

'A good one from what I can see,' Rhys said. 'You'll let me know if there's anything else you need from me, won't you?'

'There is one thing,' Hettie said. 'Would you mind letting Kate know I won't be joining them for dinner this evening. I have lots of work to do and I can finish what was on the tray if I'm hungry.'

'As you like,' Rhys said.

'Will I see you out?' Hettie asked.

'No,' Rhys smiled. 'You've enough to be getting on with.' He collected his toolbox from the floor. But he once again paused in the doorway. 'I can see you have company here,' he said.

'Sorry?' Hettie said.

'The saucer of milk on the floor.'

Hettie laughed. 'The cat does seem rather at home. I don't have the heart to put it out.'

Rhys nodded. 'We all of us need companionship,' he said. 'When I was in the military, there was a lot that I saw – a lot I had to live through. I didn't always talk about it. We don't, do we? Everyone here is friendly. If someone needs to talk, there's always someone that will listen.' Rhys smiled again. 'As I say, just let me know if there's anything you need from me.'

'I will, thank you,' Hettie said. She watched Rhys leave and listened to the door open and then close. Through the window, she watched him pass through the gate and disappear behind the bushes separating the small front garden from the pavement.

Once Rhys was gone from sight, Hettie returned to the miniature studio. It was so much more than she could have asked for. And since Rhys had gone to so much trouble, she was eager to test it out. Collecting the sturdy leather bag, she placed it on the table and lifted the lid. She paused only briefly before reaching inside to remove her tripod. Extending the legs, she placed it on the rug before the table and adjusted the feet. She took a roll of film from a compartment and opened the back of the camera still on the table. Removing the film from its box, she rolled it onto the spools. She positioned the camera on the tripod. Making the adjustments to ensure it was secure felt like second nature. As did every other interaction with the camera and equipment. There was no thought behind any of her actions. It came as easily as putting one foot in front of the other to walk.

With preparations complete, Hettie positioned the floor lamp behind her and switched it on. She set about positioning the fabric-covered frame. As she touched the wooden frame, she imagined Rhys touching it, nailing the batons together and screwing in the hinges. He had done this all for her in the name of kindness. There was no expectation of payment or trade of any kind. He was paid to be the groundsman, but he was not paid to make things for visitors to Hill House.

Hettie adjusted the hinges on one side. Rhys certainly had a reassuring presence. He was calm and measured. Perhaps it came from his military training and experience. The need to keep a level head and work hard. It was refreshing to find a decent man who wanted nothing more than to help. And refreshing to be in the presence of a man so different to the one who had plagued her dreams before his arrival. She paused and felt her fist clench. That man didn't deserve to inhabit the same space in her brain as the man who had more honour in his little finger than the other man had in his entire body.

Hettie directed her effort into making sure her equipment was ready and stable before carefully removing the first items from the shelf. She placed a pair of dogs of foo on the table before Rhys' frame. After adjusting the light behind her to best illuminate them, she stood behind her tripod and lifted the view finder mechanism. She hesitated for a moment. Since the day in Aldgate, she had only seen the world though her own eyes. She breathed in and bent to look through the piece of glass on the top of the camera, manoeuvring the level of the tripod so that it was the correct height. She adjusted the shutter speed and the level of the camera until the ceramics were perfectly framed. Taking her hands from the body of the camara, she looked through the viewfinder and placed her finger on the small silver button. With one click, the shutter closed. She took the handle to wind the film on. And that was it. The first photograph of the project had been taken. It was simple. Instinctive. It hadn't been monumental. It had felt... natural.

Hettie took up the dogs of foo and placed them back on the shelf. She took down a vase with a blue dragon wrapped around it like a tendril. Placing it within the frame, she looked through the viewfinder and with another press of the silver button, she had her second photograph. She wound the film on again. The process felt more normal than unusual. As though a very good friend who had been away for years had returned and she had arranged to have drinks with them. At first the conversation was tenuous and stilted. Distance had bred unfamiliarity. But sitting down, face to face, the friendship and closeness came rushing back.

Hettie placed the vase back on the shelf and took down another ceramic and then another and another, until she had photographed seven items. After the eighth, she would need to change the film. She placed the vase with a mythical serpent-like creature back on the shelf and took down another dog of foo. She took down the second and placed it with its partner before the white backdrop. Looking through the viewfinder, she left the camera to reposition them to better see their features. If these regal protectors of Chinese temples had any of their promised power, then this little cottage in Northamptonshire must surely be a safe place, since Sir Charles' collection contained so many. Hettie had just captured the image when she felt something rub against her leg.

'This is becoming a habit,' she said to the cat. 'You keep sneaking up on me.' She bent to stroke the cat's ears, and it leant into her hand. 'Are you sure it's not you who is the intruder?' She looked up to the lion like creatures in the miniature studio. 'Or perhaps you are protecting the place, like them.' The cat leant into her even further. 'You are certainly a good alarm for anyone sneaking into the yard. But we don't have to worry about that. Not now that Rhys has put that new bolt on the gate.' Hettie smiled. With this little guard, along with the new bolt on the gate, and Sir Charles' many dogs of foo, the cottage surely had all the protection it needed.

Hettie looked at her watch. It was almost three o'clock. Standing up, she raised her hands above her head, knitted her fingers together in the air above her, and swayed from side to side. Through the window, she saw that the best of the daylight had gone. She would need to continue her project in the new light of the next day. It would probably be a good idea to retake the photographs of the last two items, just in case she had been over ambitious with the waning light.

Hettie set about winding on the film in the camera so she could remove it. She slipped the rolled film into its cardboard box and placed it in a compartment in the leather bag. She left the frame on the table and the camera mounted on the tripod but placed the leather bag on the table.

'You've got the right idea,' she said to the cat, which had

taken up position on the rug before the fire. Hettie removed the fire screen and added more coals to the grate, working around the cat and trying her best not to disturb it. She sat down in the armchair. She hadn't done much of anything today – at least not even a fraction of what she would have done in her normal working life – but all she wanted was to close her eyes. She yawned. It was more than she had done in a long time and much more than she was used to. As much as she had managed to get on with her work during the afternoon, the residue of the dream of Gray was still inside her. She curled her hands into fists. He didn't deserve a place in her memories. He had earned no place in her life at all. She glanced down at the cat. It was warm and secure, its little chest rising and falling. She glanced at the miniature studio again. People had to earn their place in another person's life.

Hettie closed her eyes. The fire warmed her cheeks and eyelids. Silence. Perfect silence. Apart from the noises of the fire and the occasional sigh from the cat as it slept. Forgoing a meal up at Hill House was a small price to pay for this chance to be alone. She breathed in deeply. In all that had been so unfamiliar in the last few days there was something so familiar in the smell of books and old objects. It had become such an everyday occurrence to be troubled by thoughts she would rather keep buried and these moments when her mind found peace were precious. Thoughts of the cat and of the frame specially made for her had managed to stem the tide of the thoughts of that disastrous lover, dragged into the daylight by the dream over which she had no control.

Lover.

It was a ridiculous word to describe what he had been to her.

There had been no love.

FOURTEEN
APRIL 1876

At just after ten o'clock the next morning, Charles changed trains at the connecting station for the train that would take him to Montreal. Mrs Anderson had wanted the carriage to take him to the connecting station, but Charles insisted that he get the train from Tarrytown. He travelled light, with only one small suitcase so the change would be no hardship. In truth, he didn't want any more fuss than was necessary.

He placed his suitcase on the overhead rack and took his seat as the train pulled out of the station. He had already experienced enough of the Anderson's hospitality to keep him going for months. He thought back to the night before. He had been asked to dress in tails, which his mother had packed for him. What his mother had failed to tell him was that a ball had been planned for their arrival. On finishing tea, he had been shown to his bedroom at the back of the house, with the most splendid view of the river. He had passed a few hours reading a book before bathing and dressing for what he thought was to be a formal dinner.

Henry knocked on his door at just before eight o'clock. 'I always feel like a bloody penguin in this thing,' Henry said, pulling at his stiff collar. 'Come on then, old boy, ready for the party?'

'The what?' Charles said.

'The party,' Henry repeated. 'That's being thrown in our honour. If you'd hung about at tea this afternoon, you would have heard all about it.' He put his arm around Charles' shoulders. 'Come on then, into the lion's den we go. We'll pick Kenmore up on the way!'

What had ensued was a party the likes of which Charles had not seen, even in the ballroom at Hill House. The whole of the downstairs had been transformed. Furniture in the morning room and drawing room had been removed to make a dancefloor. A ten-piece band sat at the front end of the house and at the end closest to the river was a vast buffet. Along with Henry and Walter, he was introduced to every guest at the party which must have been at least one hundred, possibly more. Henry was in his element, talking easily to anyone and everyone. Walter seemed even more taken with Miss Anderson than earlier and at every opportunity, excused himself from dancing to stand and talk earnestly with her. Charles ate some of the buffet in between dancing with what seemed to be every woman in attendance. He enjoyed dancing well enough but by ten o'clock his feet burned, and he took solace in the billiard room where Mr Anderson had opened a fine bottle of malt. He joined in the men's conversation for a while before retreating unseen to the glasshouse where he spent half an hour wandering through the orchids in darkness with only the moonlight for company.

Charles breathed out heavily. There would be more of the same to come when he returned to New York State in less than a week. He would need that time to recover and steal himself for the social engagements at the next house that was lined up on their itinerary. How lucky he had been to have this trip planned for Jonty so that he could get out into the wilds.

Charles had a compartment to himself. With no companions to object, he slid the window open to smell the air and steam as he watched the view roll past. From what he had read, he knew that the scenery would be spectacular, but he hadn't expected it to be awe inspiring. The further north the train travelled the more any signs of human habitation began to thin until only a smattering of small towns, villages and farms peppered the landscape. All around were meadows and trees and mile after mile of open countryside. It was vast, so very vast, and the sky seemed so much larger than it did at home. The train crossed bridges over great bodies of water and soon they were travelling through mountains. Charles craned to see the sheer scale of them. He smiled to himself. What a treat this was.

After taking lunch in the restaurant car, he returned to his carriage and found that he was still alone. Closing his eyes, he fell asleep to the sway of the train and the scent of the steam mixed with nature.

When Charles woke, the scenery had changed still further. The temperature outside must have dropped as snow covered the higher ground and sheets of ice floated on the water over which they passed. He knew that the spring arrived later in Canada and had packed accordingly with a thick sweater, his overcoat and a scarf and gloves.

He watched out of the window until daylight turned to night, when he went to take dinner in the restaurant car. On returning to his carriage, he read his book. This was what he enjoyed. Time alone. Time to think. It seemed a rare thing somehow.

The train pulled into Montreal in the early hours of the morning and Charles was directed to the hotel he had booked for the night. After only a few hours' sleep, he ate a quick breakfast and was on his way again, boarding a train to Ottawa. It seemed a shame that he had seen nothing of Montreal apart from the station and the inside of his hotel room, but he had a schedule to stick to.

It was still dark when the train pulled out of the station. Charles could just make out the outlines of buildings which began to thin and give way to countryside. It was becoming a theme of his trip, this balance of man and nature. In this huge continent, nature most definitely had the upper hand. There was something visceral about it that appealed to Charles. Something wild.

As the day dawned pink on the horizon, Charles was treated to another spectacle. Trees. Thousands upon thousands of trees. Perhaps even millions. As far as the eye could see there were snow-covered trees. It was no wonder that logging had become such a lucrative business in this land. The resources were everywhere. He stared at mile after mile of trees and frozen land. He had truly entered a different climate to that which he had left behind on the banks of the Hudson.

Sooner than he anticipated, signs of human habitation began to appear. Villages and small towns, turning into a city. The train pulled into Ottawa station and as with Montreal, Charles had no time to explore the capital of the country, but from what he saw the architecture was not dissimilar to New York. Outside the station, he hailed a carriage to take him to the river from where he would take his final mode of transport.

Showing his ticket, Charles boarded the steamboat. They set off along the Ottawa River and Charles was the only passenger to stay on deck. He was glad of his overcoat and scarf and gloves as he wanted to stay outside to see everything. He lent against the rails, his warm breath clouding the icy air. Once the city was out of sight, the only thing on the banks of the river was trees. As far as Charles could see were trees. He breathed in deeply, feeling the cold on his cheeks and filling his lungs with the oily scent of pine. It smelled fresh and clean.

Taking pity on him, a member of crew brought a mug of

coffee outside for which Charles thanked him. His time was too precious to spend inside at the refreshment bar.

The boat stopped at a few small inlets to let a handful of passengers on or off. But it was when he heard the announcement that they were approaching Simpson's Bay that Charles felt a wave of excitement. Within minutes, the trees on one side of the river began to thin. First a few houses were visible, small and made of timber, surrounded by what looked like farms. A few chickens pecked about the snow and Charles heard cows mooing from inside barns. Soon more buildings appeared, more barns and outbuildings and houses, their chimneys billowing smoke into the air. There were more people too, walking along paths, working on the land surrounding the buildings. But it was when they turned a slight bend in the river that Simpson's Bay truly made itself known. A whole town was set back from the water's edge of the bay. There were many wooden buildings, but there were also many constructed from brick. From what Charles could see, there were many businesses around the landing area and the steeple of a church rose behind. But the building that dwarfed all others sat a little further along from the landing: MacGregor's Sawmill. Constructed from wood, the building was vast with a series of ramps and pulleys. Huge piles of logs were stacked on one side, and some sat in the water before the building, which had its own jetty. Even from a little distance away, Charles could hear the activity of the mill, the sound of mechanical saws cutting through timber, men calling to each other. The sound of industry.

The water lapped around the steamboat as it pulled alongside the landing and Charles left the boat, along with many of the other passengers. Carrying his small suitcase, he made his way towards the businesses which clustered about the bay. He shared the path with many other people; women with shopping baskets over their arms, gentleman in smart clothes and gentlemen in working clothes. The roads were busy with carriages and carts. Charles passed a livery stable with the tang of leather coming from within, a blacksmith with the red glow of a furnace and the metallic chink of metal against metal, a cabinet maker with many items of furniture outside. A little further along, the shops became less industrial. There was a dressmaker's shop with many fine items hanging in the window, a shoemaker's where the man inside seemed to be working the sole of a boot, a general store with barrels outside filled with produce and jars and tins displayed in pyramids in the window. There was even a shop specialising in selling brooms and another selling wool and textiles.

Charles came to a square enclosed by decorative railings. The buildings around the square were exclusively brick built and housed a physician, a lawyer and many other serious looking businesses, along with the church. Stopping a passerby to asked after the hotel in which he was due to spend the next three nights, Charles followed their directions back to the street with the shops. Taking a turn in another direction, he came to Harvey's Hotel beside Mallory's Tavern. Charles checked into his room that was small and clean and perfect for his needs. The hotel was owned by an older couple who both welcomed him and were very interested in his life in England and the reason for his stay.

'I worked at MacGregor's for twenty years until we set this place up,' Mr Harvey said. 'Just ask me if there's anything you want to know.'

Charles thanked Mr and Mrs Harvey and asked where he might buy some food. Mrs Harvey directed him to a restaurant and a bakery on the other side of the square. Charles found the bakery and bought a hot mutton pie straight from the oven. Out on the street, he took the pie from its paper bag and ate while he walked, blowing on the hot filling. He smiled to himself, what would his mother say if she saw him eating while walking along the street?

His plan had been to head directly to the mill but as he finished his pie, he realised that he had left the list of questions Jonty wanted him to ask in his suitcase.

Retracing his steps, he returned to the hotel.

He rang the bell on the desk in the small, neat lobby, but the person who came through the door behind the desk was unfamiliar. Charles felt his breath catch in his chest. The young woman who stood before him had the greenest eyes he had ever seen. Her dark hair and pale skin left him unable to do anything but stare.

'Can I help you?' she said.

Charles struggled to find his words. 'You're not Mr or Mrs Harvey,' he said.

'You are very perceptive,' the young woman said. 'Can I help you?' she repeated.

'Do you work here?' he asked.

The young woman looked up to the ceiling before looking back at him. 'If I were to ask you why you thought I was standing behind this desk if I wasn't working here, would you think me rude?'

Charles couldn't help but laugh. That wasn't the type of response he would normally expect from someone working on the reception of a hotel. 'Not really,' he said, still laughing. 'I suppose it was a stupid question.'

The woman opened her eyes wider as though agreeing that it was indeed a stupid question. 'I'll repeat the question,' she said. 'Can I help you?'

'My key,' Charles said. 'I'd like the key to my room.'

The young woman nodded. 'You're the Englishman come to visit MacGregor's,' she said. 'My daddy said you would be coming.'

'Oh?' Charles said.

'My daddy is the foreman at MacGregor's. You'll come to realise that it's a small town,' the woman said. 'Everyone knows everyone's business. It's probably not like that in England.' She took a key from a hook on the board and handed it to Charles. When her warm fingers briefly met his cold hand, he felt something shift inside him. He stared at his hand for a moment.

'Was there anything else?' the woman asked.

'No... no, thank you,' Charles said.

The woman nodded and turned from him. Charles watched her push through the door. He watched her dark hair held back in a single plait, her slim shoulders in a black working dress, the crisp white apron tied in a bow in the dip at the base of her back. He watched the closed door long after she had disappeared.

Charles returned to his room to collect Jonty's list of questions. He was all fingers and thumbs when he tried to open his suitcase, and he saw that his hands trembled a little. It must be the cold. He looked to the fire burning in the hearth.

After tucking the sheet of paper into his pocket, he ran down the stairs. He stopped at the desk in the lobby and eagerly rang the bell. But the person who came through the door at the back didn't have the greenest eyes he had ever seen.

Mrs Harvey took his key. He wanted to ask the name of the young woman but surely that would be too forward. He thanked Mrs Harvey, and she bid him a good day.

FIFTEEN

When Hettie came to, it was dark outside. The coals in the fire glowed red with no flame. The light from the floor lamp she had used earlier gave the room a warm glow. The cat still slept on the rug. Hettie's photography equipment sat on the table.

'Are you hungry?' she said to her little companion. The cat barely moved. 'I'll have to give you a name,' she said. 'I can't keep calling you "cat" or "puss".' She looked around the room. And then out through the open curtains to the stars in the dark night sky. 'How about Stella?' she asked. The cat moved slightly. 'Stella it is,' she said.

Getting to her feet, Hettie pulled the curtains in the parlour before going through to the dark kitchen. The coals in the hearth had all but gone out but provided what little light there was in the room. There was no point adding more to make up the fire since at some point soon, she would need to return to the main house. She peered through the window into the yard. The gate was still closed. No sign of anyone. Closing the curtains, she switched on the light, and the shaded bulb glowed overhead. She lifted the cloth from the tray. All that was left from breakfast was a drizzle of milk in the jug, a solitary sausage, a slice of bread, a little dish of butter and another of jam. Wrapping the bread in the cloth she covered it with an upturned bowl. The butter and marmalade, she covered with another bowl. She cut up the sausage and placed it in the saucer on the floor and poured the drizzle of milk into the other. After washing up, she dried her hands on a clean tea towel and placed the crockery belonging to Hill House back on the tray. She would need to make sure that it got back safely.

Turning out the light, she returned to the parlour. She crouched on her haunches before the rug and stroked Stella's ears. 'I think I may need to put you out for the night,' she said. 'I'm not sure you're supposed to stay here.' The cat didn't move. 'All right,' she said. 'Ten minutes while I plan what I need to do tomorrow and then I'm afraid it's out into the cold night air for both of us.'

Getting to her feet, Hettie looked at the clock on the mantelshelf. She had slept for longer than she thought. It was after seven o'clock. Aside from the clock, the only other item on the mantelshelf was a brass ashtray. The fireplace was high in its design so it would be possible to miss such a small and shallow item. On only the briefest of inspections, it was clear that it was a functional modern item and not a part of Sir Charles' collection. Hettie picked it up to see whether there might be a mark on it before she could discount it completely and was surprised to find a cigarette stub in the shallow bowl. With how fastidious Audrey was in cleaning the cottage, it seemed odd that she would leave an old cigarette to fester with its ash. Hettie picked it out, thinking to throw it into the fire but stopped. Perhaps it had been intentionally left. Perhaps it was sentimental in some way. Perhaps it had been Sir Charles' final cigarette. But it felt so soft and so fresh and there was still so much of it left unsmoked. A cigarette smoked months ago would have dried out; the tobacco turning to brittle fibres. The gold band around the top of this cigarette still had a lustre as did the printed word on the paper:

Astine

Hettie dropped the cigarette into the ashtray and placed it back on the mantelshelf. She took a step away. It was a coincidence. There would be thousands of people smoking that brand of cocktail cigarette. It was surely sold in hundreds of tobacconists across the country. Holding her hand to her face, she smelled her fingertips that had touched the cigarette. It was Gray's fragrance. Rather exotic and feminine, when he had been neither of those things. It was the fragrance that had lingered on his neck. On his mouth. On his fingers when he put them to her mouth. It was the taste of his lips.

No. No. It was just a smell. He was not here.

Hettie took another step away. She crashed into the chair closest to the hearth. The chair she had sat in to make her notes before the frame had arrived so that she could take photographs. Straightening the chair beneath the table, she saw there was writing in the notebook. A couple of sentences. It was not in her hand. Yet she had been the only person in the cottage. Hadn't she? Rhys had been here, but he had not been alone in the parlour and would have had no opportunity to write in her notebook. And why would he? And if he had, why would he have written those words on an otherwise blank sheet of white?

Thomas knew
Gray is not a stranger

Hettie scrabbled to turn the page back to find the last of the notes she had made for the day. She knew for a fact that after making them, she had turned over to a fresh, blank page. Her heart began to race. What was this? She looked around. Had she written these words while she had slept? Had she risen from the comfortable chair before the fire, taken up her pen and scrawled these words all why she had been still asleep? The hand was so unfamiliar. And what did the words mean? Why would she have written about Thomas? And Gray.

A crash came from the room above. It was the same as the crash she had heard earlier in the day. Hettie spun around. Stella was still asleep on the rug. The noise earlier had not been Stella, and it was not Stella now.

Hettie tried to slow her breath but, try as hard as she could, the pace of her breathing would not slow. She put her hand to her chest. It rose and fell at an alarming rate, propelling her thoughts at the same breakneck speed. Images of the footprints in the ice. The swinging gate. As her mind raced, a presence almost made her stumble back, an overwhelming sense that someone was in the room. She spun around. She was all alone. The hairs on her arms sprung to life.

'Who...?' she said. The word tumbled from her mouth. She was speaking to the room and to nobody. The presence seemed to retreat and was then on her again. She couldn't... this was so... she grabbed her satchel and slung it over her shoulder. She stooped and collected Stella from the rug. The cat seemed surprised but didn't resist. Hettie ran out into the hall, grabbed her coat and managed to shrug it on while still holding onto Stella and grabbing her hat and gloves. All the while she sensed the presence in the entrance to the parlour. She unlatched the door and ran out into the cold night air, still with Stella tucked beneath her arm.

Only once she was standing on the other side of the gate did she pause to look back at the cottage. And when she did, she knew that the presence had moved and was watching her through the window of the parlour.

SIXTEEN

With her satchel bouncing against her hip, Hettie hurried as quickly as she could along the drive without running. She was rushing from something that was not there. But still her mind wouldn't be still. It was dark, so very dark, in a way it never was in the city. She clutched Stella to her and was glad of the cat's warmth nestled as it was beneath her coat, and glad that it did not seem to mind. It didn't even seem alarmed by the constant narrative she kept up on their progress.

'See,' she said, glancing into the darkness of the woods bordering the drive, 'trees. They are just trees.' She knew it to be true even if all she could make out were twisted dark shapes. At least the moon was out. Guiding their way. And in the distance, the lights of Hill House shone like a guiding North Star.

The gravel crunched beneath the soles of her boots. 'Nothing to worry about,' she said, her voice growing increasingly heavy with breath. 'Nothing at all.' An owl called in the distance and Hettie shrank from it, holding Stella tighter. She picked up her pace and Hill House grew in size as they approached.

When they reached the portico, Hettie paused to catch her breath. She looked back down the drive. It was in darkness. She couldn't even make out the gates at the end.

'We're here,' she whispered to Stella. She took hold of the handle, turned it, and let out a sigh when the door opened. Stepping into the vestibule, she closed the door behind them.

Lights and lamps shone around the hall. A fire roared below the mantelshelf held up by the fauns playing their musical instruments. The long-cased clock ticked at the back of the hall. The pale wooden panelling glowed a honey colour. The bronze floor tiles glittered slightly and the faces in all the paintings and of all the statues on plinths in recesses seemed at once familiar and friendly. She was even pleased to see Pan with his pipes.

It was only once they were inside that Hettie realised Stella might not be welcome in Hill House. She tickled the cat's ears. 'I'm sorry,' she whispered. 'But I think I might have to put you out.'

Stepping once again into the vestibule, she opened the front door. She placed Stella down on the step outside. Rather than try to sneak past Hettie's legs to get back into the house, Stella paused briefly to clean her ears before slinking away and disappearing around the side of the house.

Hettie hung her coat on a hook in the vestibule and returned to the hall. At least Stella hadn't seemed bothered by being put outside. If anything, she had seemed completely at ease. Hettie had just closed the door to the vestibule when a voice called out.

'Hello there, Hettie.'

Kate crossed the hall from the doorway leading down to the kitchen.

'Evening,' Hettie said.

Kate paused at the door to the billiard room. 'The girls wanted us all to join them for a game of cards this evening,' she said. 'They finished their homework early and I didn't have the heart to refuse them. Do you want to join us? Bertie has put an extra log on the fire and Rosemary's made some lovely shortbread as a treat. Audrey and Rosemary are coming up too.'

Hettie thought to the guest bedroom upstairs. If she went up there, she would be alone. She thought immediately of the crash from the room above the parlour and the sense of a presence following her around the cottage and watching her from the window.

'If you wouldn't mind?' she said.

Kate smiled. 'We'd be delighted to have your company. Especially Daphne. She can't stop talking about you. She is rather taken with you and thinks you'll be able school her in the ways of being a grown-up in London. I apologise in advance if she is a bit much. She has started to get rather excitable of late. I think it's her age.'

'I don't mind at all,' Hettie said.

Kate held the door to the billiard room open. 'After you,' she said.

The billiard room had always been one of Hettie's favourite rooms in Hill House. It had only one purpose. Fun. As a child, she had enjoyed playing billiards, listening to music on the gramophone, playing cards sitting on the rug before the hearth, playing games on the folding green baize card table that was brought out every night. There had always been pitchers of fresh lemonade on the sideboard and sweet treats from the kitchen. The doors led directly onto the terrace at the back of the house and as they had generally visited during the summer months, she had spent many long, balmy evenings running in and out of the doors with the children of the family while the grown-ups drank cocktails, seated at a long table set up on the lawn, to the sound of crickets chirping down in the long grass of the meadow.

The room Hettie stepped into was still very much as she remembered it, although the doors to the terrace were closed and a log blazed in the hearth. The green baize table was open in the middle of the room beside the billiard table with chairs arranged around it.

Hettie placed her satchel on the floor beside the sideboard. She wandered through the room and brushed her fingertips along the edge of the billiard table, the wood warm to the touch. She stopped at the set of doors at the far end of the room. Cupping her hands around her eyes, she pressed the sides of her palms to the glass and peered inside. There was just enough moonlight to see the outline of Sir Charles' collection of flowers. As she remembered it, orchids had been his favourite. He had a gardener who grew them for him. The children of the household had been under strict instruction that they were not to venture into the conservatory unless in the company of an adult. The blooms were so very delicate and precious that Sir Charles hadn't wanted any damage done to them, especially as despite it being unintentional and without malice, it would nevertheless have upset everyone involved. The outline of the plants brought a memory rushing back to Hettie from somewhere deep in her mind.

There had been a day when she was very small that she had been admitted to the conservatory. She had been in the care of her grandfather. Sir Charles had wanted to show him the latest orchid he was growing. She couldn't have been more than four or five years old. And as she remembered, she saw her grandfather ahead, gently cupping a bloom to better take in its detail and scent. But she had not been alone. Her hands had been occupied. On one side of her was Sir Charles, holding her hand. And on the other was Thomas. The Mandeville men had been so very tall as she looked up at them, their hands so very warm and reassuring. So many years later, she could still feel the kindness of those two tall men, who, like her grandfather, had terrific moustaches. She smiled to herself. No doubt Sir

Charles and Thomas were holding her hands to keep them occupied and away from mischief, such as the temptation to pull at a stem or pick a flower or two. Even so, the memory was a happy one.

Taking her hands from the glass, Hettie pressed her palms together. That was surely why she had written Thomas' name in her notebook. Memories buried deep inside her were being woken by her presence at Hill House. Because it must have been her that had written those two strange lines. It couldn't have been anyone else. She had walked in her sleep. She had left the chair before the fire, taken up her pen and written the notes on the page. Of course the writing had been unfamiliar. She had been asleep when she had written it. Perhaps she had walked in her sleep before. She would not have known if she had. And she had obviously written about two men who had been in her thoughts at points during the day. One through fondness and the other who plagued her.

Shapes of blooms inside the greenhouse became clearer as Hettie's eyes adjusted to the dark. Tendrils trailed up to the glass ceiling and pots lined the waist high planters. She may not have thought of Thomas Mandeville in years, but as she thought of him now, she realised that he been a bigger presence in her life than she had remembered. It was the way of things. What was important in childhood so often slips from memory with the passing of time. Once-cherished dollies or stuffed animals which a child could not go a minute without for fear of bawling as their heart broke, with the passing of time became just another plaything abandoned on a shelf or in a trunk. The love for them forgotten. Or simply pushed away for new loves or interests.

'Hettie!' a voice called with glee.

Even before she turned around, Hettie smiled. 'Daphne,' she replied.

Daphne crossed the room in a hurry. She stood before

Hettie and looked her up and down. 'Is that what they wear in London this winter?' Daphne asked.

'It's what I wear,' Hettie said.

Daphne was soon joined by Lula. Both girls wore their hair down rather than up, with a single plait fashioned from the front section and pinned back. Daphne's hair fell in auburn waves whereas Lula's blonde hair sat straight just past her shoulders.

'Good evening, Hatshepsut,' Lula said. 'Do you mind if I call you Hatshepsut? It's such a marvellous name and I like how it sounds.'

'It's my name,' Hettie said. 'And no, I don't mind at all.'

'Have you been at our grandfather's cottage today?' Daphne asked.

'I have,' Hettie said.

'Good,' Daphne said. 'That's very good.' She paused and looked down at her cousin. 'Lula and I had a chat earlier. We've decided that we want to be a bit braver when we talk about Grandpapa. It won't do to cry so very much. And I'm sure he wouldn't have wanted us to get so upset when we talk about him. He always wanted us to be happy.'

'It's only natural to be sad after someone has passed,' Hettie said. 'It's a sign that we miss them.'

Lula studied her intently. She was an earnest little thing. 'Has your grandfather died?' she asked.

Hettie nodded. 'He has.'

'And he was a great friend of Grandpapa's?'

'He was,' Hettie said.

'And do you still miss him?'

No sooner had the words left Lula's mouth than her older cousin nudged her. 'Lula,' Daphne said and shook her head.

'It's all right, Daphne, I'm happy to answer Lula's question,' Hettie said. 'My grandfather, Henry, died quite a few years ago.

I still miss him but when I remember him now, it makes me smile.'

'Henry?' Lula said. 'And Hettie. They are very similar. And are you similar to your grandfather?'

'I hope so,' Hettie said.

'Now, girls,' Kate said entering the room with a tray. 'I hope you're not bothering Hettie.'

'They're not,' Hettie said. 'It's a pleasure to talk to Daphne and Lula.'

Kate called the girls over to help her lay out treats on the sideboard. Hettie watched them. Both girls were so compliant and seemingly pleased to be so. They had been brought up well and clearly knew how to treat people. They were a credit to their parents. And she had meant what she said. It had been a pleasure to speak to them. There was something about the girls that endeared them to her, and she could say that about very few people. She smiled when Lula explained to Kate that since their grandfather had been such good friends with Hettie's grandfather it was only right that they too should be friends.

'That's as maybe,' Kate said. 'But as Hettie is a grown-up, see that you mind your manners.' Kate ushered the girls to seats at the card table. 'Would you like to join us?' she asked Hettie.

'Would you mind if I sit the game out?' Hettie said.

'Not at all,' Kate said.

'Daphne is a terrible cheat, Hatshepsut,' Lula said. 'So, I don't blame you for not wanting to play.'

'It was just the once!' Daphne objected. 'And I told you, I dropped the card, I didn't hide it down the side of the chair.'

'A likely story,' Lula laughed.

Soon, Audrey and Rosemary appeared, Rosemary carrying another tray of sweet treats. They wore normal clothes – sweaters and neat skirts – not their work uniforms. Kate asked after Bertie.

'He said for us to start,' Audrey explained laying out the

treats on the sideboard. 'He's got a bit of business he needs to sort out.'

Hettie accepted Kate's offer of a cup of tea and a shortbread. 'We could find something stronger, if you'd prefer,' Kate said. 'Sir Edward keeps the cabinet stocked. A whisky or a brandy perhaps?'

'Tea is fine, thank you,' Hettie said. Collecting a cup from the sideboard and balancing a piece of shortbread in the saucer, she took a seat on the comfortable sofa before the fire.

A rowdy game of Happy Families started at the green baize table, punctuated by pauses to refresh cups and replenish plates with shortbread and other treats. Lula was particularly enthusiastic, and Hettie had the very real feeling that she was being allowed to win. Hettie drank her tea and ate her biscuit, watching the bark curl away from a log in the hearth. She could ask Audrey about the stub of the cigarette in the ashtray on the mantelshelf at the cottage. But the thought of it seemed ridiculous now. If Audrey said that it had been left there as a reminder of Sir Charles, it would likely upset everyone and spoil their evening. If Audrey said that she wasn't aware of the cigarette and ash in the tray, she might have thought Hettie was calling into question how fastidious she had been in keeping the cottage clean. Either way, Hettie couldn't win. It would be best all-around for her to say nothing. As with the writing she had scrawled while walking in her sleep, there would be a logical explanation for the presence of the Astine in the ashtray.

When Lula excused herself for a few minutes and the women fell into a conversation about the list for the grocery delivery later in the week, Daphne left the table and joined Hettie on the sofa.

'I'll have to be quick,' Daphne said, glancing over her shoulder. 'I adore Lula but it's rather like having a shadow. She must know everything I'm doing and...' She glanced over her shoulder again before turning back to Hettie. 'I should like your opinion on a dress that I have ordered,' she said, lowering her voice. 'I want to know if you think it suitable for an... an event I'm attending. I would value your opinion over all others as you know about London and fashion and what is the very best thing to wear.'

'I'm not so sure about that,' Hettie said.

'I think you do,' Daphne said. 'At least you will know better than anyone else in the house.' She looked over her shoulder again. 'Might I show you tomorrow afternoon? Lula will be at her Brownie group at the church hall and Katherine will walk her there and back. She often stays to help with the activities. I could come to your room at five o'clock. If that would suit?'

There was a look of such pleading in Daphne's eyes, that Hettie didn't have the heart to refuse. 'Five o'clock tomorrow is fine,' she said.

Daphne's face broke into a wide smile. 'Thank you,' she said. 'I knew you would help.'

The door to the billiard room opened and Lula returned.

'I should get back to the game,' Daphne said. She smiled at Hettie as though they had just shared a secret. Hettie watched Daphne retake her seat at the table. She wasn't sure what help she could be to Daphne. Her job was to photograph the designs and creations of others. She was able to style their fashions to please readers of magazines. But her own style was just that; her own. But since Daphne seemed so desperate for her opinion, she could hardly refuse. She remembered something of what it was like to be sixteen years old and wanting so much to join the world of adults most of the time while the world wanted to keep you a child for just a while longer.

Audrey rose from the table offering to refresh their cups. She picked up a jug from the sideboard. 'We're out of milk,' she said.

Hettie placed her cup and saucer on a small side table. 'Let me,' she said. 'You're busy with your game.'

SEVENTEEN

Hettie crossed the hall, clasping the jug, followed by voices raised in fun coming from the billiard room. She paused to look at the portrait of Thomas Mandeville. On his fine black horse and in his dress uniform with a gold helmet and braid, he looked so grand. But the man she remembered was far more down to earth. Thinking of him while looking into the dark conservatory seemed to have opened some sort of channel in her mind. Thoughts of him that had rested quietly for many years made themselves known again. Thomas may have been two decades older than her, but he had treated her as she imagined a much older brother might. He had been close to her grandfather and looked up to him and turned to him for advice. She now remembered visits to the house in Cambridge where Thomas would take dinner with her parents and grandfather. And visits to take tea when she had been very small. How had she forgotten that? Thomas seemed always to make a point of spending time with his godfather's granddaughter. He would join her in the nursery where she introduced him to all her toys, or in the garden to picnic with her dollies and stuffed animals. And he would gallop through the house with her on his shoulders just as he did at Hill House. She would insist he go faster and faster until her father and mother laughed loudly and brought a halt to the galloping lest she get too excited to sleep.

The kind blue eyes looking down at her from the portrait were the eyes she remembered smiling at her. He liked to joke and had always seemed so enthusiastic about life. She had spent so much time alone as a child that she had been rather self-sufficient, and it had been a novelty for a grown-up to take an interest in her games.

'Sorry that I forgot how kind you were to me,' she whispered to the portrait. 'Thank you.'

She felt a little silly saying the words out loud but something inside her wanted to acknowledge Thomas Mandeville and his importance to her family. And to her.

As ever, when she turned from the portrait, she felt as though Thomas' eyes were watching her, following her progress across the hall until she passed through the door at the end. But as ever, she knew it simply to be the result of a talented artist, able to capture a person in paint and make each aspect of them appear realistic to the viewer.

Hettie was already halfway down the stone steps into the basement when she heard voices coming from a room further along the kitchen corridor. A door stood slightly ajar, and she could make out Bertie's voice. In response, she heard Rhys' voice. Audrey had said that they were discussing business, which was of no concern to her and eavesdropping was not something she had ever been keen on. But when she was about to enter the kitchen, she stopped short.

'And Hettie wasn't too alarmed?' she heard Bertie say.

She hovered in the doorway. Could it be considered eavesdropping if she was simply listening in on a conversation that included her? While she was struggling with her conscience,

Hettie heard Rhys say, 'Not overly, I don't think. The gate is secure now.' He paused. 'I know I'm to be on the lookout for intruders. Elliot was very clear about that from the day I arrived. But neither you nor Elliot has ever explained why. It would be useful to be fully informed, so I know what to be alert to.'

Bertie sighed. 'A few years ago, we had a nasty incident. There was a break in, and a police constable was attacked. As well as Elliot.'

'I had no idea,' Rhys said. 'Elliot has never said anything about that.'

'I'm sure you know what a private man Elliot is. He was rather embarrassed that he allowed the intruder to get the better of him. And you know how protective he is of this house and family.'

'And were the intruders caught?'

Another pause. Bertie seemed to lower his voice when he said. 'They were. Or rather the man behind it was.'

Hettie had to take a step closer to the room as Bertie's voice was growing increasingly quiet. 'It was a member of the family. A cousin. George Caxton.'

'From Caxton Hall?'

Hettie assumed Bertie nodded when he said, 'It's been going on for decades. He has always hated this branch of his family. He's made it his business to try to... to try to do away with the family.' A chair creaked. 'He kidnapped Sir Edward's oldest son – Tommy – when he was still a small boy. About ten years ago. In the process, he stabbed a police inspector. It was only thanks to the quick thinking of a visitor – Nell Potter – and Doctor Kenmore that Inspector Painter survived. If it hadn't been for Nell and Doctor Kenmore, George Caxton would have hung rather than festering in that prison in Scotland for the last ten years. And then there was a further incident the year before last with Tommy.'

There was a pause before Rhys spoke. 'I'm afraid you've lost me,' he said. 'How can this George Caxton be the intruder now if he has been in prison for a decade?'

Bertie coughed. 'I need to speak to Elliot,' he said. 'Would you mind going to get him for me.'

'I'll certainly try,' Rhys said. 'But you know how stubborn he has been of late about leaving the stables other than to walk his dog.'

'Tell him I need to speak to him about Caxton. He'll come.'

'As you like,' Rhys said.

Hettie heard the feet of a chair scrape across the floor. She opened the door to the kitchen and closed it gently behind her. She heard the door to the outside at the end of the basement open and then close. She looked down into the empty jug she was still clutching. She was supposed to be replenishing the supply of milk for the billiard room, not listening in on other peoples' conversations. She should fill the jug, return to the company of the women and girls and leave whatever this business was to Bertie and the other men of the house. The thought made Hettie grasp the handle of the jug tighter. Why must she feel the need to return to the women when she had not been playing the card game with them? If anything, she was more involved in the conversation taking place in the room just along the corridor. Her name had been mentioned. And wasn't she the person who had reported the possibility of an intruder? So why should she not hear what had to be said on that matter?

As justified as she was in that thought, if she tried to involve herself in the conversation between Bertie, Rhys and Elliot, then they would likely change the subject until they could find a time when she was not around to continue their conversation. To be fair to Rhys, it seemed that Bertie was excluding him from some of the background, since he wanted only to talk to Elliot.

Opening the refrigerator door, Hettie filled the jug from the bottle of milk. She carried it back through to the basement corridor and up the stone steps to the billiard room. The women and girls still played their game, oblivious to the conversation taking place downstairs. When they asked her to join them again, she made her excuses and went back down to the kitchen. She stood just inside the room, with the door still open. While she waited, she thought continually that she should just go and ask Bertie what was happening and why he seemed so concerned about a man who was in prison hundreds of miles away, so couldn't possibly have been in the back yard of the cottage, leaving the gate open as he fled down the alleyway, his footprints imprinted on the ice.

At the sound of the door opening at the end of the corridor, Hettie briefly retreated further into the kitchen. There was the sound of two sets of footsteps in the corridor accompanied by the lighter tap of dog's claws on the tiles.

'Elliot,' Hettie heard Bertie say. 'Thank you for coming.'

'He's up to it again, isn't he?' Elliot said gruffly.

Bertie coughed. 'Rhys,' he said. 'Would you mind going around the ground floor and checking that the doors are locked, and the windows are secure?'

'As you like,' Rhys said. His voice didn't alter from its usual calm pace. As a man used to taking orders, it was likely that he would not challenge an instruction given by the man overseeing his work.

Hettie retreated further into the kitchen at the sound of footsteps in the corridor. This felt wrong. But as much as she wanted to leave, something told her to stay.

'Is he doing it again? Still, from his prison cell?' Hettie heard Bertie say. She moved closer to the door and opened it slightly wider.

There was silence.

'Then what is happening here?' Bertie said. After a few seconds, he said. 'Who, is it if it isn't him? I sense something but I can't be sure what.'

Hettie could only presume that Elliot was responding by gestures rather than in words as Bertie spoke again. 'Is it Hettie?' he said.

Almost on instinct Hettie placed her hand across her mouth.

'It's not her,' Elliot said. He spoke so quietly that Hettie had to strain to hear.

'But is it her presence here?' Bertie said.

'I can't be sure. Those things once clear to me, I can no longer see.'

Hettie heard a sigh. 'I know how hard you are feeling his loss,' Bertie said softly. 'But it is our duty to protect his family.'

The sudden scrape of the feet of a chair across tiles made Hettie take a step back.

'I don't need you to tell me what my duty is,' Elliot said. His voice was louder. His tone sharper and full of anger.

'I'm sorry,' Bertie said quickly. 'I chose my words unwisely. You know our duty better than anyone. You were by his side before any of us. Please,' he said. 'Take a seat.'

There came the sound of feet scraping across the floor again. 'It's me who should apologise,' Elliot said. 'I'm no use to man nor beast at the moment.'

'Yes, you are,' Bertie said gently. 'I know you don't want to speak about it and we all respect that. But you are allowed to grieve. I wouldn't have asked Rhys to bring you here if I didn't think it was important. Can I get you a glass of something?'

'Only if you join me,' Elliot said.

'It would be my pleasure.'

There was the pop of a stopper removed from a decanter. The chink of glass against glass and the glug of liquid. The chink of glass to glass.

'Thank you,' Elliot said.

'It's always a pleasure to share a glass with you,' Bertie said.

He paused and it sounded like both men took a drink. 'Do you think Rhys suspects anything?' Bertie asked.

'What would he suspect?' Elliot said. 'All you've told him is to be alert for intruders?'

'It is,' Bertie said.

There was the click of a lighter. The sound of someone inhaling. 'Rhys is a straightforward man,' Elliot said on what sounded like a breath of smoke. 'And good at following instructions. I doubt he'll suspect anything other than what you tell him. If you've asked him to be on the lookout for intruders, you can be sure that he will find out any that there are.'

'That's good. That's very good,' Bertie said.

The conversation paused so that Hettie couldn't be sure what was taking place in the room next door. The smell of cigarette smoke wound down the corridor to her. It was straightforward tobacco. With none of the spice or floridity of a cocktail cigarette. She closed her eyes. Not now. Not now.

After a few moments more, Elliot spoke. 'When events such as the events of the last few months occur in a house then things can... awaken. Restless souls make themselves known. As I say, I see nothing. It doesn't mean it's not him, but I don't feel that.'

Bertie sighed. Hettie could imagine him scooping his fringe away from his face. 'Thank you,' he said softly. 'I'm sure it takes effort to speak of such things at the present time. But with Hettie here, we need to be sure what we are dealing with. Why does it always happen when we have a guest?'

'You know why,' Elliot says. 'With everything that has been happening in her life, she's likely brought her own souls with her.'

'Sir Edward asked that we make sure that her time here is peaceful so that she can recuperate,' Bertie said. 'Her parents have been very worried about her. This was supposed to provide a break and a chance to be productive and to bring her out of herself. I don't feel that she needs us in the way previous visitors have. There has been no... pull in that way. And Tommy hasn't returned as he ordinarily would if he were needed.'

'The lass is all right,' Elliot said. 'I remember her when she was a young 'un. Spirited then. And spirited now. And she has inherited her presence from her grandfather. He was such a good friend to Sir Charles. You won't remember this, but the professor was the man who advised him when he faced near ruin. Even when he knew that he could bring ruin on himself by intervening with the plans of that... that bastard Caxton. Any man who is such a friend to Sir Charles can be trusted. Was a friend.' He seemed to stumble over the name of his deceased employer. His voice cracked.

'Another?' Bertie asked.

Hettie could only assume that Elliot had nodded since there came the chink of decanter to glass again.

'What will we say to Rhys?' Bertie asked. 'To explain.'

'He will see through a lie,' Elliot said. 'So don't even try to fool him. Give him orders and he will follow them. But he is not a sheep. He doesn't do it blindly. He is clever. And sharp. It's why he made a success in the military. We've had intruders here. That is the truth. What kind of intruders is for thee and me to know.'

'Thank you,' Bertie said. 'I know the last month has been difficult for you. But I'm grateful you agreed to come tonight. There's nobody else I can talk to. Kate would understand but I don't want to burden her... not at the moment.'

'Some things are more important than a man's grief,' Elliot said. The feet of the chair scraped against tiles again. 'If there's nothing else, I'll take my leave.'

'No, nothing,' Bertie said. 'But thank you.'

Hettie heard footsteps and the tap of claws head towards the outside door before it opened and then closed. Then came a click of the light switch in the next room followed by footsteps along the corridor towards the stone steps leading to the passageways. When they passed the kitchen, Hettie peered through the gap between the door and the frame. Bertie looked down to his feet as he walked.

Once his footsteps disappeared, Hettie leant back heavily against the sink. What on earth had just happened? She tried to recall as much of the conversation as she could but there was so much to take in, to process the meaning behind it all. That her parents had volunteered her services by way of distraction came as no surprise whatsoever. Bertie and Elliot's kind words about her were welcome too. But how could this Caxton cousin be the intruder if he was in prison? Although Elliot had seemed unsure that he was involved this time. And why couldn't they tell Rhys? All the questions bumped around in her brain. Even thinking of her grandfather didn't quiet them – it added to them. She had no idea that Sir Charles had once faced near ruin – and why would she? The affairs of a baronet were not hers to know. It most likely took place before she was even born. But what service had her grandfather performed that was so worthy of merit? From what Elliot had said, it was beyond the simple fact that he had been a friend to Sir Charles. He had put himself in some sort of danger to help his friend. That sounded just like him. But neither her grandfather nor Sir Charles had been ruined, so all was good. Still, the question of how and why this George Caxton may be involved played in her mind. And if he wasn't the intruder, who was?

Hettie took a glass from the dresser and filled it at the tap. She took a long draught of the freezing water. She drained the glass and refilled it. Turning out the kitchen light, she made her way up the stone steps. Instead of turning right in the passageway, she turned left and took the staff stairs up to the first floor, emerging onto the landing through the secret door at the head of the grand staircase. The voices of the women and girls rose from the billiard room. Laughing and having a jolly time. But all

Hettie could think about was being alone. There was no space in her thoughts to chat or even observe others playing a game.

Once back in her room, she closed the door and placed the glass of water on the nightstand. Without switching on the overhead light or either of the lamps, she stood in the window and looked down at the drive.

Memories from the day came to her along with the voices from the room beside the kitchen. The threat of an intruder was a very real danger, and it was only natural that the Mandeville household wanted to counter it. Bertie and Elliot clearly had a culprit in mind. But how could he be in prison and running away down a back alley behind a row of cottages at the same time? George Caxton couldn't possibly be their man if he was in a cell in Scotland. And why would they feel the need to keep their conversations from Rhys? Surely Rhys would be better placed to help if he had all the facts. None of it made sense.

Hettie stared out at the drive. A frost had already begun to settle. It glittered on the gravel and the grass. At the end of that drive and through the gates was Sir Charles' cottage. But it was out of sight, cloaked by darkness. Hettie rested her palms on the windowsill. Something about that cottage felt different from when she had arrived. And it was a difference that was affecting her. The unexplained crashes from empty rooms. The smell of smoke from a cigarette long since stubbed out. Writing opaque statements in her notebook while she slept. What had Elliot said in the basement? That she had brought souls with her? She shook her head. The long dead and the recent dead had been her constant companions since her arrival at Hill House. But they resided in her thoughts. They were not driving the activity around her.

Prising her hands from the windowsill, Hettie went through to the bathroom to brush her teeth before bed.

EIGHTEEN
APRIL 1876

The first meeting at MacGregor's went exactly as Charles had hoped. Mr MacGregor shook his hand warmly when he arrived. In his office over a rather fine coffee, he gave Charles a potted history of the mill and how it had been established by his father who had come over from Scotland. With the passing of his father, he now owned and managed the mill.

'We run a tight ship here,' Mr MacGregor said. 'Every man is professional to the last. You can be sure of that.'

Charles nodded. He knew Mr MacGregor was trying to impress him and from what he had seen there was nothing to doubt Mr MacGregor's words. After the meeting, Charles was passed into the care of the son of the family, Ewan, who was roughly the same age as Charles. He proudly gave the tour of the mill, often having to shout over the noise of the machinery.

'It's a vertical saw,' he said pointing to a saw moving up and down, through which the lumber was passed. 'My father is keen that we have the very latest and very best machinery. The old way was to have two men with a long two-handed saw, one down in a pit and the other above. This is far more efficient. And the saw is powered by water. My father and grandfather dammed a stream of the river and redirected the water to the mill to turn the wheel, which powers the saw. That's why this is a perfect location. The logs are driven down here after they are felled, and we have all the water we need to power the machinery.' He took Charles to see the giant waterwheel in action, the water thundering and cascading over it as it forced it around. 'We produce almost eight hundred feet of board in a working day and there's never a shortage of customers. It's needed for building and barrels and furniture – just about anything you can think of needs timber in its construction.'

Returning to the office, Charles was treated to another cup of the delicious coffee. He had just added sugar when the door opened, so that the din of the machinery grew louder until the door was closed. Mr MacGregor and Ewan stood, so Charles stood with them. 'I'd like to introduce you to our foreman, Bryn Bennett,' Mr MacGregor said.

Charles turned to see a man just about as broad and tall as Henry. The man held out his hand and shook Charles' warmly.

'I hear you're think of investing in the mill,' Bryn said. Charles noted that he had an English rather than a Canadian accent. He would have said it was Yorkshire, since he'd had a friend at school who spoke in a similar way.

'Not me exactly,' Charles said. 'But my cousin.'

Mr MacGregor laughed. 'Don't mind Bryn's directness. He's known for it. Come,' he said to Bryn, 'join us for coffee.'

Charles tried to focus on the facts the three men shared. But his mind kept drifting to the girl at the hotel with green eyes. The man sitting before him was her father. And his daughter had inherited her father's directness.

When Bryn stood, the other men stood. 'I've to be back to my work,' he said. 'But you'll join me and my daughter, Monica, for dinner tomorrow evening?' he said to Charles. It seemed a statement rather than an invitation to be accepted or declined.

'Thank you,' Charles said. 'It would be my pleasure.'

He watched Bryn leave.

Monica. The girl with green eyes was called Monica.

At half past six, Charles stood before a house on one of the roads leading from the town's green. It was brick built and double fronted, with a veranda of sorts running along its full length. Many similar grand houses lined the wide road, all with slightly different features. Charles pushed open the white painted gate onto a path, swept clear of snow. He climbed the steps up onto the veranda and knocked at the door. While he waited, he looked around. Everything was so fresh and clean and new. Pristine, some might say. Unlike Hill House which had been added to over more than a century, making it slightly hotchpotch in design and rougher about its edges. But that added character so far as Charles could see and was all the better for it.

The door was opened by a maid. She curtseyed, took Charles' coat and gloves, and led him through to a drawing room. He didn't have the chance to tell her that there was no need to curtsey for him as Mr MacGregor waited to greet him with Mrs MacGregor, Ewan and a younger son, William.

'Welcome, welcome,' Mr MacGregor said, shaking Charles' hand enthusiastically. After introducing Charles to each member of his family, Mrs MacGregor handed him a glass of sherry.

'Thank you,' Charles said. 'You have a wonderful home.' It was one of the compliments his mother had advised him to use if he couldn't think of anything else to say to a host or hostess, as everyone liked to have their home appreciated.

'Why, thank you, Charles,' Mrs MacGregor said. 'We had it built just two years ago.' She offered him a seat and sat beside him. There followed a rather lengthy explanation from Mr MacGregor of how the land had been purchased in the best part of town, how they had always lived on this road but this was a far larger plot, how they had decided on the number of rooms and the layout of the house, how they'd had the new furnishings shipped from the finest stores in Ottawa or made locally from the timber from their mill. Charles sipped his sherry. He nodded and attempted to ask polite questions. He was glad when Mrs MacGregor said to Mr MacGregor that perhaps Charles didn't need to see the plans for the house when he offered to bring them from his study.

Ewan and William stayed rather quiet throughout the conversation and Charles felt sure they must have heard this story many times when guests were entertained at the house.

When dinner was called, Mrs MacGregor escorted Charles through to the dining room with pristine white walls decorated with swags of gold and gold-coloured cushions to the chairs and curtains at the huge window. Charles was seated beside William with Ewan opposite. Mr and Mrs MacGregor sat at either end of the table. The meal they were served was very fine, with a shrimp salad, roasted guinea fowl and a selection of jellies and fruit. The MacGregors were pleasant enough, but it was the conversation after they had exhausted the subject of their home that Charles enjoyed.

'It's quite a thing to behold,' Mr MacGregor said, instructing Charles on the business of logging. 'Hundreds of men living further north to fell the trees in the winter when the sap is frozen and then driving them down the rivers. Some stay in camps on the banks, some construct rudimentary living accommodation on the logs. They set off in the spring when the weather is warmer, and the ice begins to melt. When you see them coming round the bend in the river it is indeed a sight to behold. Mile after mile of felled timber.' He turned to his son. 'You are planning on joining a raft next year, Ewan, are you not?'

'I am, Father,' Ewan said.

'But it is so dangerous,' Mrs MacGregor said. 'Can Ewan not continue to work at the mill?'

'He can,' Mr MacGregor said. 'Once he gets to know all areas of the trade. I went north for a season when I was a young man and Ewan will too. He will have the best team of men with him. And he will be a better manager when he has experienced all we do.' Mr MacGregor turned to Charles. 'It's something we pride ourselves on; knowing all areas of our business.'

Charles smiled. 'That sounds like a sensible idea.' He knew that Mr McGregor was selling the benefits of the mill and the investment again and it was only to be expected since he knew Charles would report all that was discussed to Jonty.

The dinner concluded with a coffee and some chocolate bonbons. 'Well, Charles,' Mr MacGregor said, after taking his final sip of coffee. 'Ordinarily I would invite a guest to take port in the drawing room after dinner. But since you are a young man, I thought you might prefer to go to the tavern with Ewan. I remember some of what it was to be a young buck and I'm sure you will enjoy it more.'

'Thank you,' Charles said. 'That is very thoughtful.' He considered saying that he would be happy to stay for a port but really, he would prefer to get out into the fresh air.

After thanking his hosts for their hospitality and for a very fine meal, Charles joined Ewan in leaving the house and heading towards the green. It was a crisp night, and they walked briskly.

'I'm sorry about that,' Ewan said. 'My parents do like to talk about the house. You were lucky my mother stopped my father bringing out the plans. You might have been there all night.'

Charles laughed. 'There's no call to apologise. Your parents are generous hosts. That was a very fine meal.'

'My mother will be pleased you enjoyed it.' He turned to Charles. 'My father tells me that you are going on a great adventure with your friends from university when you leave us. That sounds marvellous.'

'Joining the raft sounds wonderful too,' Charles said. 'It will certainly be an adventure.'

'I'm looking forward to it,' Ewan said. 'It can be dangerous, but my father is right in what he says, that I will be joining the most experienced of teams. When I come back next spring, my father has said that I may enrol at university. I'll be the first person from our family to go and my father is very keen for me to study engineering and return to the mill with the very latest ideas and knowledge.'

'That's wonderful,' Charles said. 'I should have preferred to study engineering, but my family business is the military followed by politics. It made more sense to study politics, so I have at least a clue of what I'm doing.'

Ewan laughed. 'I guess we are all products of the expectations of our fathers,' he said.

'I guess we are,' Charles said.

When they entered the tavern beside the Harvey Hotel, they were met with a thick fug of cigarette smoke, the sound of loud conversations and the smell of beer. Ewan showed Charles to a table before going to the bar to order two beers. Charles removed his overcoat and placed it over the back of the chair. All around, groups of men talked, drank and played table skittles, cards or dominoes. Those that won and those that lost, shouted just as loudly.

Ewan returned with the drinks and took a seat.

'This place is lively,' Charles said.

'It certainly can be,' Ewan said.

After saying cheers, they continued their conversation about the army and South America and engineering. It seemed they had a great deal in common and Charles was pleased to talk to another chap who shared so many of his interests. It also provided a distraction. Charles couldn't help but look out of the window regularly on the off chance that Monica was passing on her way to or from work.

When they finished their first drinks, Ewan insisted on buying the second. 'My father gave me some money before we left. It would be rude not to spend it,' he said.

Over the second beer, they made a loose agreement that Ewan should visit England to stay at Hill House. When that beer was finished, Charles insisted that it was his turn to buy the drinks. Before Ewan could object, he collected their empty glasses, took them to the bar and ordered two large whiskys from the bartender. While he waited, he took the chance to look out of the window again. When he turned back to the bar, he felt someone watching him. A man was leaning against the bar, staring at him. Charles smiled. But the man frowned. He said something that Charles presumed was directed at him but couldn't hear over the noise.

'I'm sorry,' Charles said. 'I can't hear you.' He moved a little closer.

'I said, are you the English?' the man said.

'I'm English, yes,' Charles said.

The man turned and spat on the floor.

'That's enough, Fergus,' the bartender said when he placed two glasses on the bar. He turned to Charles. 'He doesn't care for strangers,' he said. 'Best you ignore him and take your drinks.'

'Do you know that man at the bar?' Charles asked Ewan as he sat down.

'Fergus?' Ewan said. 'If he's said anything, ignore him. He lets his mouth run away with him when he's in drink.'

They picked up their conversation but every so often Charles glanced at the man sitting at the bar. Sometimes he glared at him. Sometimes he did not.

Charles and Ewan had just finished their second whisky when a shout came from the bar. 'There she is!' Fergus said. 'The daughter of that English.' He spat on the floor again. Charles looked to the window and saw Monica walk past in the direction of the hotel. He pushed his chair back, the feet scraping along the floor.

'What did you say?' Charles said.

Fergus looked at him. Ewan placed his hand on Charles' arm. 'He's not worth it.'

Fergus took a few unsteady steps from the bar to the table. 'I said, there is the daughter of the English.' He rested with his knuckles on table, staring at Charles. 'What of it?'

'I'm English,' Charles said.

Fergus looked him up and down before turning to spit on the floor again. When he turned back to Charles, he said, 'Are you sweet on the little witch?'

'What did you say?' Charles said. He could feel the anger rising in his body.

'Her mother was a witch. Did you know that? And she married that English. And now that one goes around thinking she is better than us.'

Charles felt Ewan get to his feet beside him. 'That's enough, Fergus,' Ewan said. 'We all know you've tried, and she won't have anything to do with you.'

Fergus looked from Ewan to Charles. 'Little bitch,' he said.

Something took hold of Charles, and he could bear it no longer. He grabbed Fergus by his collar. 'Say that again,' Charles said, 'and I will make you very, very sorry.'

Before Fergus could respond the bartender ran from behind the bar. He took hold of the back of Fergus' shirt and pulled him away from Charles.

'You've had enough for one night,' the bartender said, pushing Fergus towards the door. 'Come back here again tonight and I'll make sure you're not served for another month.'

'All right, all right, I'm going,' Fergus said. The bartender released his grasp and held the door open for him. Before he left, Fergus spat on the floor again and glared at Charles.

The momentary distraction from the commotion came to an end and the men all returned to their drinks or games.

'Sorry about that,' the bartender said. He reached over the bar and collected the half full bottle of whisky. He placed it on the table where Charles and Ewan sat. 'On the house,' he said. 'For the inconvenience.'

Charles felt himself shake as he sat down.

'I'm so sorry,' Ewan said. He picked up the bottle and poured large slugs into each of their glasses. 'He doesn't know what he's saying. He's a terrible drunk.'

Charles picked up his glass and knocked the whisky back in one. 'It's not your fault,' he said. 'You don't need to apologise for such a vile man as him.'

Ewan refilled their glasses and with each sip Charles took he felt the edge ease off his anger a little.

It wasn't more than an hour later that Ewan stood with his arm around Charles at the door of the hotel. Charles braced himself against the doorframe.

'Do you have a key?' Ewan asked.

Charles felt his legs give way slightly. He shook his head. 'Inside,' he said. He watched Ewan knock gently on the door. A bolt slid across. A key turned in the lock.

'Thank heavens it's you,' Ewan said.

Charles turned to see who Ewan was talking to. He tried to stand up straight. 'Good evening, Monica,' he said.

'What are you two doing?' she said quietly. 'If the Harveys see him like this they will likely chuck him out.'

'Are they in?' Ewan asked.

'They're in bed. I'm looking after reception until all the guests return.'

Charles looked at Monica. He blinked, trying to focus.

'Come in,' she said quietly. 'I'll help you.'

Charles felt himself helped up the stairs. When he made to speak, he was told to be quiet. A door opened and he felt himself placed on a bed. He sank back into the eiderdown.

'What do you think you were doing letting him get like that?' Charles heard Monica say.

'It wasn't me,' Ewan said, 'There was a bit of a scene, and the bartender gave us a bottle of whisky to finish by way of apology. My father will kill me if anything happens to him.'

'You had better go,' Monica whispered. 'Let yourself out of the front door. I'll see to him. It's better you are not here, or you might get caught.'

Charles heard a door close. He felt himself pulled up and his jacket removed. Then his shoes were removed. He opened his eyes. He was sitting on the edge of the bed and somebody knelt before him.

'Monica,' he said, smiling.

'Yes,' she said. 'I'm Monica. I've hung your coat and jacket and waistcoat up so they are ready for you in the morning.'

Charles nodded. 'Are you a witch?' he said.

'I beg your pardon,' Monica said.

Charles pointed in the direction of the tavern. 'The man. He said. Fergus.'

'Oh,' she said, with a raised eyebrow. 'Yes, I should imagine he did. In any case, I've had worse and less accurate things said about me.'

Charles closed his eyes and opened them again. The room around Monica looked as though it was underwater. 'I saw a dolphin,' he said. 'On the ship.'

'That's nice,' Monica said.

Charles nodded. 'Can you do magic?'

He watched Monica smile. 'If by magic, you mean can I make you sober, then the answer is no. Only time will do that.'

'The things he said about you,' Charles said. 'I wanted to punch him in the face.'

Monica laughed softly again. 'It's probably best that you didn't. Otherwise you'd be in the cells now rather than on this comfortable bed.'

'It is rather comfortable,' Charles said. He looked into her face again. 'And you have beautiful eyes.' He closed his eyes and nodded.

He felt himself pushed by the shoulders and found his head on the pillow.

'I'll bring some water up for you,' Monica said. 'And I'll see you tomorrow for dinner. Now go to sleep.'

NINETEEN
FEBRUARY 1937

Hettie rose early again. It was still dark outside, and she washed and dressed using the faint light coming through the window. It was just enough for her to see to tie a necktie at the collar of her linen shirt before pulling on a brown woollen cardigan. After fastening the buttons on her grey slacks, she laced up her brogues. She opened the door and only just stopped herself tripping over something directly outside her bedroom. It moved. It didn't just move, it stretched. Hettie smiled and sunk to her haunches.

'Stella,' she whispered. 'What are you doing here? How did you get back inside?'

She stroked the cat's ears, and it rubbed its chin against her hand.

Hettie smiled again. 'Have you been out here all night?'

The cat rubbed its chin to her hand again. Scooping Stella into her arms, Hettie held the cat close and got to her feet. 'We'll have to put you outside,' she whispered quietly. 'We don't want you – or me – getting into bother for letting you in.'

Creeping along the landing, Hettie held Stella close, without any sort of complaint from the cat. At the head of the stairs, she found that there were two pools of light on the floor of the hallway, one from the open door of the morning room and the other, the dining room. The fire in the great fireplace glowed brightly, illuminating Hettie's way as she picked her way carefully down the stairs. She paused beside the faun playing a lyre holding up the mantelshelf. Movement crossed the light from the open morning room door. There was no possible way to let the cat out the front without being seen, so Hettie stayed close to the bannisters as she made her way along the hallway, past Thomas' ever watchful eyes, and through the door at the back. She paused just inside the staff passageways and below the room bells high on the wall.

'If you do belong in here,' she whispered to Stella, 'then I am going to great lengths to conceal your presence for absolutely no reason.' She stroked the cat's ears again.

Lights lit the long basement corridor, and Hettie descended the stone steps as though she was a cat-burglar in a dreadful film at the picture house. She crept past the kitchen and the smell of bacon and sausages floating out into the corridor. Opening the door to the outside, she placed Stella down on the bottom step. 'I'll see you later,' she whispered and smiled as she stroked the cat's ears. Stella began to climb the steps up to the grounds and Hettie was about to close the door when she saw something on the flags just outside. Crouching, she picked it up. It was a book of matches. And it was empty, each match having been torn from the inside. Hettie turned it over. The cover was mainly burned away. Perhaps a member of staff who worked in the grounds had lit a cigarette and tossed it down into the stairwell. Or it had fallen from somebody's pocket. Hettie closed the door softly and looked down at what was left of the cover. All that remained was a fragment of charred card with the final letters of the name of the establishment from which they had been handed out: '—ni's'. It was in an elaborate script – navy blue on a white background – and it seemed familiar somehow. But any number of bars and restaurants used an elaborate script in their signs and menus and books of matches. Hettie pushed the matchbook into her pocket. She would put it in the rubbish when she got the chance.

In the kitchen, Hettie found Audrey tending the many pans. Reluctantly, it seemed, Audrey accepted Hettie's offer of help, and she set to, taking plates and cutlery from the dresser. She was laying the places at the table when Rosemary appeared. She made directly for the sink, where she washed coal dust from her hands with a stiff nailbrush and a bar of carbolic.

'Daphne showed me a picture of a new frock she has ordered,' she said over her shoulder to Audrey. 'You should see it! When she wears it, she'll look like the proper grown-up woman she can't wait to be!'

'That's enough,' Audrey said, turning from the pans to look at her sister at the sink. 'Miss Turner doesn't want to be hearing your gossip.'

Hettie laid a fork down beside a plate. 'It's all right, honestly,' she said. 'Please, just go about your business. Imagine I'm not here.'

Rosemary cocked her to one side as though she had just won a little victory. 'Well,' she said. '*Hettie* will know all about it this evening. Daphne is beside herself to get the opinion of someone who knows London fashions.'

'That's as maybe,' Audrey said, leaving Hettie no time to respond to Rosemary. 'But it is none of your business, so wind your neck in.' She wiped her hands vigorously on her apron. 'Now show me those hands,' she said. 'I want to see that they are good and clean before you touch a thing of breakfast.'

While Audrey took hold of her sister's hands and checked first the palms, then the backs, paying particular attention to each fingernail, Hettie returned to laying out crockery and cutlery. She could see why Audrey wanted everything just so, but Rosemary was a grown woman. She felt sure that if someone spoke to her in such a way, she would have something to say about it. But perhaps that was how sisters behaved with one another.

Soon Kate arrived in the kitchen along with Daphne and Lula. The girls had their hair styled in long pigtails that had been curled overnight in rags. After a series of "good mornings" and helping with placing serving dishes on the table, everyone took their seats.

'No Bertie this morning?' Audrey asked, passing a plate of sausages to Daphne, who sat beside her.

'He's down in the stables,' Kate said, taking a slice of toast from the rack. 'He wanted to see Elliot and Rhys this morning.'

'Elliot?' Audrey said. Her normally deadpan voice brightened a little. 'Does that mean he's feeling better?'

'He must be if he's seeing visitors and speaking to people,' Rosemary said, taking a bite of bacon. 'Last week he nearly bit my head off when I went to see if he wanted some of our leftover supper.'

'Bertie said he's a little brighter,' Kate said. She looked to the girls who, with sad faces, were hanging on every word. 'It was a fun night, last night, wasn't it, girls?' Kate said, plainly attempting to divert their thoughts. Her tactic worked, and the girls soon began chatting about the games. Kate, Audrey and Rosemary joined them. It sounded like their jolly evening had continued long after Hettie left them.

Hettie took the plate Lula offered to her. After taking a sausage and putting it on her plate, she passed it to Kate. In many ways, she wished she had stayed with them to play games rather than lurking behind the kitchen door listening in on the conversation of Bertie, Elliot and Rhys. Curiosity had done her no favours since she was in possession of information relating to the possible intruder and their motivations, but only partial information. And it was clear that the men were discussing it down at the stables. But what were they discussing? Last night, Bertie had intentionally kept things from his groundsman and there was information that only he and Elliot shared. If she spoke to Rhys of it, she might let something slip that she wasn't supposed to know. And she would give away her eavesdropping.

Hettie jabbed the sausage on her plate and cut into it. She put a chunk in her mouth and chewed slowly. As difficult as it was, and as much as it was against her nature, she would not give anything away about what she had heard Bertie and Elliot discuss. Since she had no clue of the totality of their conversations, it was best not to think of them at all, other than to recall the kind words they had shared about herself and her grandfather, and how she had been invited to Hill House through the kindness of the Mandevilles and her parents. Her payment for the kindness was to catalogue Sir Charles' collection. Anything else to do with this house was none of her business.

Breakfast concluded when Kate looked at the clock on the wall and chivvied the girls along. Daphne would need to leave to catch her bus to school from the village green in less than ten minutes. Lula took a final sip of tea and followed Daphne from the table after a round of "thank yous" and "have a nice day". Daphne paused at the door. She looked back at Hettie and smiled. 'See you later,' she mouthed when none of the adults could see her, before running off down the basement corridor, calling after her cousin.

Hettie began collecting crockery and cutlery and taking them to the sink where Rosemary was up to her elbows in warm water. Hettie scraped some bacon rind into the food bin. She remembered how secretive girls of Daphne's age could be, even when there was nothing to be secretive about. Which was clearly why she wasn't announcing the fact that she had asked Hettie to look at her new dress. It was only natural that girls turning into young women wanted to begin to keep part of themselves from their family.

When Hettie offered to do more to help the sisters, they refused. 'We have our routines and way of doing things,' Audrey said, placing the butter back into the refrigerator.

Hettie thanked the sisters again for breakfast before making her way out into the basement corridor, up the stone steps, through the passageways, and into the back of the hall. Lights still shone from lamps, but through the great glass dome above her head, the first signs of daylight were beginning to break through the gloom of night.

Hettie collected her satchel from the billiard room and paused to warm her hands at the fire in the hall. She looked up at the stone relief of the coat of arms of the Mandevilles. Just what had her grandfather done to help Sir Charles and his family? It sounded like it was more than would be expected of the actions of friendship. It also seemed unlikely that anyone living would know. Whatever it had been was now lost in the mists of time.

Hettie took her hat from her satchel. In the mirror above the fire, she watched as she placed it on her head and adjusted it to sit just so on her hair. That woman in the reflection was the sum total of her grandfather, Henry. She was the only daughter of his only son. The continuation of his line rested on her shoulders. All that kindness, warmth, intelligence and good humour had come to sit with her. And it was a weighty responsibility to bear. She tucked a strand of hair inside the hat. On the passing of Sir Charles, there were many Mandevilles to carry on his name, even after the tragic passing of Thomas. The Bessers had daughters who would carry the bloodline to the next generation. But who was there to carry the torch for her grandfather?

Hettie sighed deeply. It was a thought that had weighed on her in recent years. And there seemed something about Hill House that was intent on bringing her grandfather to mind, and with him came thoughts of the obligation – no, the duty – to honour him. But there had never been anyone with whom she had wanted to settle down. Her lifestyle was such that relationships were transitory. Passionate – yes. Sometimes so deep that she felt her soul rested in the hands of the other person. But those feeling always passed in time.

Except for Gray – she shuddered at the very thought of his name – her relationships had ended amicably. Some had even turned into long term friendships. But a partner for life? The thought was alien to her. She valued her independence and her autonomy too highly to hand part of herself to another person.

Hettie shook her head at her reflection. This was too weighty a subject to even consider so early in the morning and there was no answer to be found in standing in the hallway of Hill House, staring at herself.

Collecting her coat from the vestibule, Hettie closed the front door behind her. She took a lungful of the sharp winter air. Darkness still clung to the ground below the trees and in the shadow of walls and buildings. Freezing fog hovered low over the land. But the morning was dawning pink on the horizon.

She looked down the long drive. There would not be enough light to begin her day's work for some time. A walk in the grounds would clear her head before going once again to the cottage. Buttoning her overcoat, she took the path running to her left and away from the house.

In the wee small hours of the night when her thoughts had disturbed her sleep, she had turned the events of the previous evening over in her mind. What a ridiculous sight she must have cut running up the driveway, clutching a stray cat. Noises in an old house, a cigarette discarded in an ashtray, some scribbled writing she had scrawled when she had been half asleep and incoherent. These things were explainable. There had been no call to run from them. And the conversation she had overheard between Bertie and Elliot was simply that – a conversation. She had spent so much time alone in recent months that she had got out of the habit of the ebb and flow of conversations. The shorthand between people who knew each other well. And things that were said that would make no sense to anyone else. She felt sure she could read something odd into the most innocent of conversations. Or events. When she returned to the cottage later in the morning, she would put her sensible head on. She smiled at the phrase her father had always used when she was small and in anyway afraid of anything he considered to be illogical.

Hettie walked briskly, building up warmth beneath her coat, following a cloud of her own breath past the cobbled yard of the stables. Was Bertie still inside with Elliot and Rhys? If he was, was he instructing them on how to deal with the potential intruder? Now that she had her sensible head on, she would look out for anything unusual when she was at her work and report it back to them.

Hettie soon left the stables behind. Coming to the gates of the walled garden, she paused to look inside. As with the land outside the garden, icy mist hovered above the paths and the bare earth in the empty beds. But at the very back of the garden, a small patch of light shone. Hettie smiled to herself. It meant that Rhys was there or close by. She pushed back her sleeve and looked at her watch. It was only just after eight o'clock. The best of the daylight wouldn't be for a few more hours. After hesitating for a moment more, she stepped through the gates, her shoes crunching along the path. She raised her hand but before she could knock, the latch clicked. The door opened and Rhys looked down at her. 'Kettle's on,' he said.

'How did you know I was here?' Hettie asked.

'I wouldn't be much good as a look out for intruders if I hadn't heard the gravel or seen movement on the path.' Rhys stepped aside and nodded into the room.

Hettie looked to the floor briefly. 'Thank you,' she said, and stepped inside.

Rhys closed the door behind her. 'You can hang your coat on there,' he said, pointing to a hook beside the door where a coat already hung.

'That's a surprise,' Hettie said.

'What's that?' Rhys asked.

'I thought you were hardy.'

Rhys raised his eyebrows.

'You never seem to wear a coat,' Hettie said. 'So I thought you mustn't feel the cold.'

Rhys laughed softly. 'I am not without sensation and sensibilities. Tea?' he asked.

'Please,' Hettie said. She placed her satchel on the flagged floor and unbuttoned her coat. She hesitated briefly before lifting it and placing it over Rhys' grey overcoat. As she placed the inside collar of her coat over the back of his collar, she realised that she was pleased that he had laughed at her gentle jibe about his hardiness. Or lack of.

'Sugar?' Rhys asked.

Hettie turned around slowly. Rhys stood before the fireplace, his hand on a tin on the mantelshelf. She nodded. Rhys pulled out the single chair at the small table. 'Take a pew,' he said.

Hettie took a seat. She removed her hat, gloves and scarf and tucked them inside her satchel. She tried not to notice that Rhys wore just a shirt with no jumper. It was thick cotton with a check, the sleeves turned back and pushed up to his elbows, the collar open. His forearms were bare as was the base of his neck and the dip where his collar bones met.

Rhys placed two mugs on the table. He took the tin and a teapot from the mantelshelf and placed them on the table. He took a jug from a shelf beside the door. Removing the cover, he placed it on the table. 'No refrigerator here,' he said. 'But the milk stays good for a while at least.'

Hettie realised that she hadn't responded for a few moments. She had been staring at the soft, dark hair on his forearms. 'People managed without refrigerators for thousands of years,' she said.

'Indeed, they did,' Rhys said. He took up a cloth and doubled it over, placing it on the handle of a kettle coming to the boil on the oversized range.

Hettie stared at a knot in the wood of the tabletop. She usually avoided making small talk. If she spoke, she had always believed her words should matter. All she could picture was the skin at the base of Rhys' neck.

The tea leaves in the pot fizzed when Rhys poured on steaming water.

'Can I help at all?' Hettie asked quickly.

'I have it all in hand,' Rhys said. He put the kettle back on the range and took a crate from beside the hearth. Turning it on its end, he placed it at the table.

'I'm sorry,' Hettie said. 'I've taken your seat.'

'No bother,' Rhys said. He sat on the crate. It creaked and he grimaced a little through a smile, making Hettie smile.

'I wouldn't make any unnecessary movements,' she said.

'I think you're right,' Rhys said. He stirred the tea in the pot. 'So,' he said. 'To what do I owe the pleasure of your company this morning?'

Hettie looked at the knot in the tabletop again. She didn't have an answer for why she had come to the shed at the back of the garden, other than she had thought of him and how pleasant his company was. And that wasn't an admission she wanted to make. Especially as she hardly knew him, and he might think her odd. Unlike her, not everyone acted on impulse when they felt comfortable with another person. Not everyone was as impetuous. Some people preferred a more formal introduction.

'I saw the light was on,' she said. 'I was taking a walk around the grounds. It's too early to take photographs. The light's not good enough.' Every word she said was the truth.

Rhys nodded. 'I can see why you would need good light. I read up about photography. There's a book in the library that I borrowed.'

'You did?' Hettie said. She could hear the smile in her voice but wasn't sure why it was there.

It was Rhys' turn to leave the question without an answer. He picked up the tea strainer. Placing it over the first mug, he poured the tea. Hettie removed the spoon from the second mug so that he could pour tea in that mug too. 'It piqued my interest,' he said. 'Knowing that there was a famous photographer coming to stay, I wanted to have an idea what you do. In case it was useful in conversation.'

'I'm really not famous,' Hettie said. She placed the strainer back on its saucer. Taking up the jug, she poured milk into each mug.

'You are well known, at least,' Rhys said.

'In some circles,' she said.

'But being behind the camera makes you somewhat anonymous,' Rhys said. He looked at Hettie intently, his dark eyes searching her face. It seemed that he was genuinely trying to understand her trade.

'It's why I enjoy it,' Hettie said. 'I can be creative, but I can let the images I capture take centre stage.'

Rhys offered her the tin of sugar. She took a spoonful and stirred it into her tea.

'Do you find this a little difficult then?' Rhys said. 'Being the centre of attention since your arrival here.'

Hettie clasped her mug. 'I mind it less than I normally would,' she said. 'I've known this house and the Mandevilles most of my life. Being here has reminded me how important they were to me in my early years. And I'm happy to be able to do what I can for the family. Especially if it helps them come to terms with the loss of Sir Charles.'

'Your grandfather was a great friend to Sir Charles,' Rhys said. 'So, being a friend to the Mandevilles runs in your family.' He took a sip of his hot tea.

'Do you believe in that type of thing? Hettie asked. 'That traits can live on in a family. That we can been affected by what those who have been before us experienced?'

Rhys placed his mug down. He rested his elbows on the table and pressed his fingertips together. 'We are the sum total of our forebears,' he said. 'Their blood runs through our veins. All that they were, we are.'

Hettie looked into his dark eyes. His attention did not waiver from her.

'I know you have been through difficult times of late,' Rhys said, his voice soft. 'I hope you feel you might be able to talk to me. Should you feel the need.'

For a few moments they sat in silence. The fire crackled in the grate. They sipped their tea. But Hettie did not feel the need to fill the silence with words. On the contrary, she felt a calm she had not felt in ever such a long time. She closed her eyes briefly and breathed in the sensation. 'My grandfather was Thomas Mandeville's godfather,' she said. Opening her eyes, she looked into her mug. 'Not the current Thomas; Sir Charles' son, Thomas. I have no siblings and often thought of him as a much older brother. Being here has reminded me of that.'

'A better older brother you couldn't hope to find,' Rhys said.

Hettie looked up. 'You knew him?'

It was Rhys' turn to look into his mug. He nodded. 'Captain Thomas Mandeville was a great man.' He paused as though in reflection. 'I was still wet behind the ears when I enlisted at eighteen into his regiment. I was a skinny thing from Port Talbot. All my family before me had worked in the iron works or down the pit or in the steelworks. But I was good with horses, you see. I worked in the stables for a brewery. But one day, I decided that I wanted to see more of the world. I set my heart on enlisting in the Prince of Wales's Lancers, the combination of riding for a living and serving for a regiment with Wales in its name had me hooked. I didn't think they would take me.' He laughed. 'But the recruiting officer must have seen something in me that I didn't see in the mirror each morning when I shaved when as of then there was barely anything to shave.'

He threaded his fingers through the handle of his mug. Hettie said nothing, not wanting to disturb him. Wanting to hear more.

'I'd been in only six months when war was declared. I was on the ship to France before I knew what was happening. Some of the older privates took me under their wing. We had coffee and pâtisserie on the harbour when we landed, we shared a tent, we held each other's places in the queue in the grub tent each day, we even shaved each other's hair with horse clippers.' Rhys laughed gently. 'It felt like some kind of dream. Some kind of holiday. I was in France. With pals. Eighteen years old and off on adventure. Until...'

He stared into his mug. 'A week we had been there. Just a week. The weather was glorious and there had been a lot of laying in the sunshine. Drinking wine in villages. Playing cricket. Whatever was happening was further north than we were. It might have been a million miles away for all we knew. So, when some locals reported that they had seen enemy soldiers in an orchard, the two troops of us sent to look for them thought it was a wild goose chase. And... well, it was anything but that. There were enemy soldiers. Many more than we expected.' Rhys paused. He ran his fingers through his thick fringe. 'Captain Mandeville was the bravest man I have ever seen. I was in the military for fourteen years – all through the war and after – and I never saw a man so determined to save his men. A man with so much courage.'

Rhys' eyes fixed on the tabletop. Hettie found herself fighting an overwhelming urge to reach across the table to touch his arm.

'I'm sorry,' she said quietly. 'I didn't mean to raise difficult memories for you.'

Rhys ran his fingers through his fringe again. He smiled a little sadly. 'You have nothing to apologise for,' he said. 'The memories are there. The passing years have made them less difficult to recall. I will never – and should never – forget the man who gave himself to save the life of me and the men under his command. I came to Hill House after the war. I had a need to speak to Captain Mandeville's family of the events of that day. To make sure they knew what their son had done. That's when Sir Charles said that if I was ever in need of a job, I should come to see him. So, you see, as difficult as it is to remember the circumstances of Captain Mandeville's passing, it is he who brought me here. To this point. Sitting at this table. Opposite you. And I shall be forever grateful to him for that.'

Hettie realised that Rhys was looking at her once again.

'I'm glad,' she said. 'That you are here.'

'As am I,' Rhys said. 'Tell me,' he said. 'Who do you have taking care of you?'

'Taking care of me?' Hettie asked.

'Like this,' Rhys said. 'Sitting down and talking about what is in your head. And in your heart?'

'No one,' Hettie said.

'No beau?' Rhys asked.

'No,' Hettie said. 'No beau.'

Something in the atmosphere seemed to shift. Hettie could not bring herself to turn away from Rhys' dark eyes. She could explain that her solitary nature meant she chose to spend time alone. But she wanted to leave her declaration there on the table. She had no beau. Their hands were so close. Rhys' finger moved as though he may touch hers. Instead, he placed his palm on the side of the teapot.

'This wants refreshing,' he said. The crate creaked as he rose to take the pot to the range. He placed it on a trivet and removed the lid, before pouring in steaming water from the kettle. Hettie watched him all the while. The way the light from the fire picked out his features. All around them the room was in darkness since the day was still to break through the window. Hettie watched his every movement. She watched the light pick out the muscles moving in his hands. His hair falling forward as he placed the kettle back on the range. The strength of his body. His slim waist and strong shoulders. It hit her. A sensation she had not experienced in so long. The sudden and overwhelming desire for another person. It felt like the attractions she'd had in Berlin. More recent infatuations hadn't been this instant or arriving with such power. A rush of energy travelled through her body in an instant, awakening every nerve. Her mouth was dry. Her pulse quickened with each second she watched him. And when he turned back to the table, she could not look away. He placed the teapot down and took something from a shelf.

'You might be interested in this,' he said, sitting once again on the crate so that it creaked. He held out his hand and a small object sat in his palm. It was clear that he wanted her to take it. Her fingers touched his as she took the small item from him. His hand was warm, and Hettie hoped that he could not sense what was in her mind.

'Sir Charles gave it to me,' Rhys said. 'I always admired it so he said I should have it. Apparently, it's a pinch pot. Made at least one thousand years ago. Look,' he pointed to marks on the pot. In doing so, he brushed Hettie's fingers. His touch sent a thrill through her. 'You can see the fingerprints of the person who made it pressed into its surface.' Rhys lowered his voice. 'It's as though the artist is reaching through time to talk to us. Imagine leaving such an impression on something. Or someone.'

Hettie swallowed. 'Imagine.'

'If you could leave an impression on the world for future generations to see,' Rhys said, 'what would it be?'

It was a question that Hettie didn't have to think about. And she was relieved to be once again on safe ground. 'My journalism,' she said. 'My photojournalism.'

'That is what you take most pride in?' Rhys said.

'It is,' Hettie said. She shook her head. 'Some might think it silly, but it's an idea that my grandfather planted in my head when I was small girl. When he gave me my first camera and said I should use it to help the world to see itself.'

'I don't think that silly at all,' Rhys said. 'Your grandfather sounds like an intelligent man. I can see why he and Sir Charles were friends. I should like to have met him.'

'He was a good man,' Hettie said. She turned the pot over in her hands to see the fingerprints.

'We are fortunate if we are able to leave our mark on the world for others to learn from,' Rhys said.

Hettie nodded. Then remembering herself, said, 'It's beautiful.' She placed the pot down on the tabletop to avoid Rhys touching her again. Not because she didn't want him to. But because she wanted to feel his touch. Very much.

'I should probably go,' she said. 'I can begin cataloguing again and take photographs later.'

For a moment Rhys looked disappointed. 'I should go to see Elliot,' he said. 'See what he needs me to do for the day.'

Hettie had almost forgotten that Bertie had met with Elliot and Rhys that morning. The conversations in the basement corridor the night before and any conversations that might have taken place that morning seemed so far away, flooded as she was by so many sensations. All finding their home in the man sitting across the table from her. He collected the pinch pot and turned it around in his hands. The firm set of his jaw. The bow of his lips. The curl of the hair at his collar. All of these things made

Hettie bite her lip to keep from saying what she wanted to. In the clubs of Paris and Berlin, she would have said exactly what she felt to anyone who took her fancy, with no need for a filter or to check herself. And if she had said what she felt, she would have said that she wanted him.

Over Rhys' shoulder, she saw the small bed in the shadows. 'I should let you get on with your day,' she said. Pushing back the chair she got to her feet. 'Thank you for the tea. And your company.'

Rhys stood and placed the pinch pot back on the shelf beside the range. 'It was my pleasure,' he said. Before she knew what was happening, he had placed his hand on her arm. Not in a possessive or predatory way, but in a way that spoke of reassurance. 'I might feel overwhelmed if I was in your position,' he said. 'So many people wanting so much from me when I might have spent so much time alone recently. Know that I am here, should you want to talk. Or to just sit in silence for a while in the company of another.'

Hettie looked at Rhys' fingers on the sleeve of her jumper. 'Thank you,' she said.

Reaching past, Rhys took her coat from the hook. He held it out, and Hettie slipped her arms inside. With her back to him, she fastened the buttons and collected her satchel from where she had left it on the floor.

Rhys opened the door. 'I hope your day is productive,' he said.

She barely glanced at him when she said, 'So do I,' and stepped out into the February frost.

TWENTY

Why? Why here? Why now?

The questions played over and over in Hettie's mind as she strode down the driveway. Of all the times for an attraction to strike, this was possibly the most inconvenient. And the least appropriate. Two days. She had known the man barely two days and yet the desire to be with him hit her like a hammer blow to the chest.

Hettie forced her hands deeper inside the pockets of her overcoat. He had not asked for this. He was not complicit in the way she lived her life. In her lifestyle. The impulsivity and acting on it. Would he be shocked if he knew? Possibly. She was unconventional and there was safety in following her lust when it was directed towards people like her, people who stepped outside the norms of society. He had been a soldier, for god's sake. He was a groundsman in a great house. He was about as traditional and conformist as it was possible to be. And yet... there he was in her mind. His dark curls. His physique. His dark eyes that she would have look at her and never turn away. All she could picture was his strong hands on that pinch pot.

She would have those hands on her. Touching her. Knowing her.

Hettie put her head down and increased her pace. There was something wrong with her. Clearly. To imagine such things with an unsuspecting man. All he had done was show her kindness. To offer to listen if she wanted to talk to him. Was that all it took these days? Rather than meeting someone and having a loud conversation to make themselves heard over the sound of the band in a club, or admiring how they moved on the dancefloor, all she now needed was someone to be kind to her. And Rhys had been just that.

Rhys.

It took all her effort not to turn on her heels and run back up the drive to the brick shed at the end of the walled garden. And that little bed. To those dark curls, dark eyes and strong hands. The soft Welsh voice.

Hettie shook her head and carried on, her breath coming faster as she increased her pace. It wasn't until she was almost at the end of the drive that she considered where she was going. And not until she was at the gates of the cottage that she looked at the window. There was no presence standing watching her as she had imagined there to be last night when she had been in a semi delirious state after waking suddenly and finding she had scrawled words onto the page of her notebook. The only presence making her delirious now was the presence she had just left behind.

Hettie placed both hands on the wooden top beam of the gate. It was impulsivity that had led her to Gray last year. She could feel her lip curl away from her teeth at the thought of his name. Why was he plaguing her thoughts so in recent days? The more she tried not to think about him, the more he seemed to be there. Perhaps this sudden and impetuous attraction to Rhys had been percolating and had resurrected what had happened with Gray. He had been the only lover she'd had that left her feeling... dirty. Dirty and ashamed. He had fooled her. She wouldn't have cared what they had done in bed if he had been honest with her. If he'd said that all he wanted was a brief fling involving sex. At least that would have been honest. Instead, she felt like a dirty rag, used and discarded on the floor. He had lied to her. And if he had lied to her about the job as a driver to a duke, what else had he lied to her about?

Honesty. That was the thing she had always insisted on in her lovers. But she had failed to lay out the usual ground rules with Gray when first they met. She had been having dinner with two friends at Pagani's on Great Portland Street. He had been eating alone and had approached their table. He had flirted outrageously and when her two friends had said they needed to head off, she had agreed to go to a club with him. She had found him attractive, if a little rough in his manners. But that hadn't stopped her. It hadn't bothered her. If anything, it had made him more appealing. Which was why, later that same night, they had ended up in her bed. She had let herself get carried away without establishing the rules of engagement. Did that make it her fault? Was she somehow responsible for how he had treated her and how he had disappeared from the face of the Earth? Everything he had told her about himself had been a lie and she had fallen for it. A man more different to the man in the shed in the walled garden it would be impossible to find.

Hettie kicked the bottom of the gate. In her mind, one man seemed to lead to the other although there were no similarities at all. Not even physically since Gray was tall and slender and, one might say, rakish, where there was a solidity to Rhys. A strength of presence. She didn't want to think of Gray and yet appeared unable to do anything but think of him. She made to kick the bottom of the gate again but stopped suddenly.

She sunk to her haunches, her overcoat pooling on the pavement around her. 'Am I glad to see you,' she said to Stella. She stroked the cat's ears. 'Come on,' then, she said. 'Let's get you inside.'

Once in the hall, Hettie took off her coat. Stella slunk past her legs and made directly for the kitchen. 'You'll have to wait for something to eat, I'm afraid,' Hettie called after the cat, hanging her coat and satchel on the hook at the bottom of the stairs. 'I've work to do first.' Over breakfast, she had said to Audrey that she would make up the fires in the cottage. It would be no trouble at all. Of course, Audrey had objected but had finally been talked around by Kate, who had said that the cottage could go without a clean for a single day since it was best for Hettie to be able to get on with her project undisturbed.

Hettie stopped at the door to the parlour. That would be the natural room to make up first, but enough of a residue of the events of the previous evening played in her memory that she continued to the kitchen, where she made up the fire in the range. Stella rubbed around her ankles. 'You shan't get round me that way,' Hettie said. 'You'll have to wait a few minutes longer.'

Climbing the stairs, Hettie went first to the bedroom at the front of the cottage. She added coals and twists of paper to the fireplace. Striking a match from the pot on the mantelshelf, she lit the paper and stood back, watching as the flames licked around the coals. When the fire took, she replaced the guard and stepped back. As she looked around the room, the scale of her task began to dawn on her. At the rate she was photographing the items in Sir Charles' collection she would be here for months rather than a week. Especially as Bertie had said there was even more to Sir Charles' collection over in the dower house at Caxton Hall.

Hettie pictured the face in the brick shed that morning. Perhaps an extended stay at Hill House might be no bad thing. A thrill ran through her body. There was nothing like the rush of attraction. The sensation of natural chemicals coursing through her veins and finding their way to every nerve ending was beyond the effect of any manmade stimulant. They were still pumping through her when she opened the door to the second bedroom.

Crouching before the fireplace, she added a shovelful of coal. After lighting the paper, she waited for it to take and looked around the room. Ordinarily, an overtly feminine room would not have appealed to her, but there was something so relaxing about the decoration in this room, as though it had been chosen to create a sense of calm. From the feminine ceramics lining the shelves to the delicate bedlinen, it was easy to imagine a person sitting in the chair before the hearth reading a romantic novel or daydreaming an afternoon away.

Standing up, Hettie checked for water in the jug on the washstand. Audrey, she thought with a smile. Hettie poured some of the water into the bowl in which the jug sat. She placed her hands in the cold water and watched it darken with the coal dust.

After drying her hands on the fresh towel hanging from the rail beside the stand, she took her favourite object down from the shelf. The incense burner decorated with exquisite butterflies was so delicate and beautiful. The workmanship that had gone into creating the dozens of tiny pastel creatures was beyond any skill she could imagine.

Just to her left and between the bed and the washstand, sat the dark wooden chest on legs. Hettie placed the incense burner back on the shelf. She ran her fingertips over the luminescent Mother of Pearl inlays. As with everything in the room, the chest felt feminine, with its carved legs and pattern of swirls across the top and down the sides. Hettie ran her fingers down the sides and along the bottom of the chest, feeling for any drawer or hidden mechanism that might unlock the lid. She found none. Each surface was flat and without indentation of any kind. She ran her fingers beneath the lip of the lid, hoping to find a catch or a latch and was surprised when the lid moved with no effort from her. It hadn't moved at all when she had tried it before. Thinking that perhaps Audrey had unlocked the chest to clean inside, Hettie lifted the lid and pushed it back so that it rested against the wall.

Protected as it had been from the effects of sunlight, the interior of the chest was so much darker than the exterior, so dark that it seemed to shine. A single item sat inside. A bottle of sorts lay on a small red fabric cushion. Hettie leant in closer to get a better look. The bottle was on its side with a cork sealing the neck. From what she could see, it was old-fashioned, made from incredibly thick glass with a green hue. It appeared to contain some dried foliage and perhaps a pressed flower or two, along with some small twigs and seeds and what looked to be a lock of hair secured with twine. Hettie looked closer still. The lock seemed to contain the hair of two different people, half was reddish wavy short hair and the other perfectly straight, far longer and much darker. She had never seen anything like this bottle or its contents in her parents' collections. It seemed to be more of a keepsake than an antique or collectible. As though someone had assembled some mementos and pushed them inside the bottle for safe-keeping.

Hettie tucked a strand of hair behind her ear and peered at a tiny, pressed flower. It still had much of its colour, no doubt as it had been saved the effects of sunlight by being kept in the box. There was still colour to the small twigs and other plant matter, and the two strands of hair secured by twine still had a lustre to them. Of all the items in Sir Charles' collection, this was the only one afforded such protection. It was unlikely to have any monetary value, but it had clearly meant a great deal to Sir Charles.

Hettie was reluctant to move the bottle in case she dislodged any of the contents. But she had been sent to examine the collection, so examine it she must. With great care, she eased her fingers between the cushion and the bottle.

The instant her fingers touched the green glass, she felt a shock charge her body. An image flashed before her eyes. Two small boys. In this room. They wore shirts with starched collars and short trousers. The fashions of the end of the last century. One boy had what looked like a crowbar, which he was using to try to prise open the lid of the chest. The other boy stood beside him, holding his arm, desperately trying to pull him away. The second boy was taller and seemed older, but he was unable to stop the younger boy who had something terrifying in his eyes. A look of determination and... evil.

Hettie pulled her fingers away from the bottle. She clutched her hands together. She was breathing heavily. She looked hastily about the room. All seemed as it should be. The only thing out of place was what was in her mind. Something inside her told her to close the lid and go downstairs to make up the fire as she had planned. But a louder voice told her to touch the bottle again. If she touched it and nothing happened, then she could put it down to being tired and imaging things. If she touched it and saw something, then... well, she would have to deal with that. Taking a steadying breath, she reached out her hand, letting it hover over the bottle for a second before lowering it. The moment her fingertips touched the glass, she felt a jolt and the boys were there again. Only now, the smaller boy had managed to open the lid. He was reaching inside. The older boy was yelling at him to stop. But there was that awful look in the younger boy's eyes again. The older boy was determined to pull him away, but the younger boy was just as determined to get to his quarry. The moment it seemed the older boy had won, the younger boy lurched forwards. He grabbed the bottle and snatched it from its cushion. A loud crash made both boys spin around and look in the direction of the fireplace. They had seen something. Absolute terror flashed in their eyes. The younger boy screamed. It was so loud and so alarming. He dropped the bottle and ran for the door. The older boy had the wherewithal to collect the bottle from the rug and place it back on its cushion before sprinting for the door.

Hettie snatched her hands away again. Again, her breath came thick and fast as though she had been running. She spun around and looked at the fireplace. Whatever the boys had seen was not visible to her. Instead, when she had touched the bottle, she was aware of ... a presence. She tried to regain control of her breathing. It felt like the same presence that had been with her in the parlour last night and that had watched her from the window. It was more the sensation of a presence, like a shadow. It had no form or substance. Hettie turned back and looked down at the bottle. It appeared so innocent, so benign, sitting on its cushion. It was an oddity that she couldn't name, the like of which she had never seen before. But those boys in her dream – or whatever it had been – were familiar to her. At least the older boy was, although she couldn't place him. What she recognised of the younger boy was the look in his eyes. She was sure she had seen it somewhere before. Sure she had been the subject of its intensity. But she couldn't have been. She would never have known those boys who would have been so much older than her.

A gust of wind brushed Hettie's ankles. She looked to the window for its source. But the window was closed, the curtains still. She looked to the hearth. The flames stood upright; they were not guttering in a breeze. And yet she felt it, around her ankles again. She looked to the bottle. It sat there as though nothing had happened. As though nothing was happening. She sensed something in the doorway and spun around.

Putting her hand to her chest, she let out a nervous laugh. 'It's just you,' she said.

Stella stood for a moment and then turned and headed for the stairs.

Hettie took a final look at the bottle before closing the lid of the chest then closing the door to the room when she was out on the landing.

In the kitchen, Hettie put the kettle on to boil. She opened a tin of sardines from the larder and placed them on a saucer on the floor for Stella. She took the kettle off the heat when it came to the boil and poured the water into the teapot before realising she hadn't put tea leaves in the pot. She poured the water away, placed the teapot on the draining board and looked out through the window. The gate was firmly locked. No intruder would be able to get into the yard unless they climbed over the wall. Had there really been an intruder or had she imagined it, like she had imagined so many things since arriving at Hill House?

She looked out at the icy yard and pictured the bottle on its cushion with its odd contents sealed inside. She pictured the two boys and their tussle over the bottle and their fear at what she had sensed as a presence in the room, but which they had clearly seen. Was this the curse that Rosemary had spoken of? Was it possible that this cottage had the power to make visitors believe in strange events?

Hettie stooped to stroke Stella, who was licking her paws after finishing her meal. 'Am I going mad?' she said to the cat. 'I must be if I am looking to you for answers. I think all I need to put an end to these ridiculous dreams is a solid night's sleep.'

As she headed down the short hall, she conjured images of what she might find. More writing in her notepad? A presence hovering in the corner? Items missing from her camera bag?

Pushing the door open, she stepped into the parlour. Everything was just as she had left it. The makeshift studio and notepad on the table beside the photograph album of a long-ago Hill House summer. Her camera bag on the floor beside the desk. Nothing out of place. Nothing unexpected.

Hettie removed the guard and set the fire. She turned the page with her ridiculous scrawls in her notebook to a clean page. From when she had been a small child, if she had ever felt confused or in need of reassurance when she was away at school or abroad, she had written a letter home. Her parents and grandfather had always been ready with sage advice or words of encouragement to buoy her spirits. Her parents still enjoyed receiving letters or telegrams from her to update them on where she was and what she was doing. That her notes were often scribbled on whatever paper she could find – sometimes even a paper napkin from a café – seemed to add to her parents' enjoyment of receiving them. Perhaps it reminded them of some of the more chaotic trips they had shared when Hettie was young.

Pulling out a chair, Hettie sat at the table. She tore a page from her notebook and took her pen from her satchel. Since there was now no doubt that her mother and father had engineered this trip to Hill House, they would be keen to hear how she was getting on. Taking the lid from the pen, she began to write. Her missives home were only ever a few paragraphs, but there was something about putting pen to paper to her parents that brought with it a sense of normality in all the strangeness. Their work may involve the study of ancient civilisations with superstitions and religious practices, but her parents were nothing if not pragmatic. With a smile, Hettie wrote the lines that she thought would please them. She thanked them for arranging the trip, she recounted some of the happy memories it had awakened from her childhood and how she had thought of Grandfather Henry a great deal since her arrival. That would particularly please her father, who spoke of his father often, as though saying his name kept a part of him alive. Hettie looked down at her silver pen and smiled. Whenever she wrote, she was holding a memory of her grandfather.

Signing off with her love to her parents, she folded the page

THE MANDEVILLE CURSE

and put it to one side. She would find an envelope from somewhere and take a walk to the little post office in the village later.

Since there was enough sunlight coming through the window to begin her day's work, Hettie got to her feet. She took a film from her bag and as she was loading it into her camera, Stella slunk into the parlour, jumped onto the armchair beside the fire and immediately curled into a tight ball. Hettie rolled the film onto the spools. The presence of that little life was reassuring in all the ridiculousness. Daydreams, writing when she was asleep, imagining things. Perhaps her brain had become overwhelmed with so many new people and events. Perhaps its way of processing all the new information was to generate sleeping and waking dreams. Dreams rarely made any sense at the best of times. As Rhys had said, there were so many people wanting her attention or her help that her brain was likely overwhelmed and sorting new events and information out in the only way it knew how – farfetched and nonsensical fantasies. She smiled as she allowed herself to think of Rhys, enjoying the warmth radiating through her. At least the sensations of an attraction were familiar to her. The infatuation would come to nothing but there was no harm in basking in the glow of it. For now, at least.

Once she had set the camera on the tripod, Hettie began taking ceramics from the shelves. She positioned them inside the three-sided backdrop and took photographs, making notes in her book.

When it got to midday, there was a knock at the front door and Rosemary delivered a tray of food to her. Hettie invited her in.

'No fear,' Rosemary said with a look of horror on her face. 'I didn't even want to step through the gate, but Aud said I must bring this to you.'

Hettie took the tray and placed it on the bottom step of the staircase. 'What exactly is it that you are scared of?' she asked.

'The curse,' Rosemary said.

'But what do you understand that to be?' Hettie asked.

Rosemary looked over Hettie's shoulder into the cottage then looked away, folding her arms over her tightly buttoned coat. 'I don't know, but strange things happen in there. That's all I know.'

Hettie thanked Rosemary for bringing her lunch. She watched Rosemary walk back down the path as quickly as she could without breaking into a trot. Rosemary took a final look back before shaking her head and disappearing behind the bush.

Hettie closed the door and took the tray through to the kitchen, where Stella joined her. Stella shared the two hard boiled eggs and the filling of the beef sandwich but left Hettie to eat the bread and slice of seedcake. Hettie made a cup of tea and once Stella had had a bowl of the fresh milk Rosemary had brought over, she returned to the parlour. Hettie joined her after washing up and set about photographing the collection again.

The light began to wane after two o'clock, so Hettie packed away her equipment. She was tempted to sit down beside Stella but while she had been working, she had made a promise to herself that she would face her fear as soon as the light failed.

With everything packed away, Hettie left Stella and climbed the stairs to the first floor. With no hesitation, she opened the door to the back bedroom. It was as peaceful and as calm as it had been each time she had been in before. Making directly for the chest, she lifted the lid. It offered no resistance, and Hettie held it up to look down at its contents laying on the cushion. With a little more hesitation than she had entered the room, she reached out her hand to touch the bottle. Nothing. She felt nothing except cold, hard glass. No boys bickering. No presence lurking beside the fireplace. And despite her earlier roughness with the bottle, the contents appeared not to have been disturbed.

Down in the hall, Hettie pulled on her coat. She returned to the parlour to collect her satchel and took the note from the table. There wasn't enough time to return to Hill House to ask for an envelope and get to the post office in time to buy a stamp before it closed for the day. She looked to the desk. She opened the single drawer. A box of pen nibs, a bottle of ink, some sheets of notepaper, but no envelopes. Opening the door to one of the two cupboards either side of the knee hole, Hettie said, 'Bingo!' She took an envelope from a neatly stacked pile on the top shelf. Slipping the note inside the envelope, she licked the gum and grimaced at the taste. After sealing the flap, she bent to get a better look at two items on the bottom shelf. They appeared to be albums, leatherbound, rather than bound in the fabric of the photograph album. It was possible that they held some clues to the origins of Sir Charles' collection and any purchases he had made. They could be ledgers. Hettie glanced at her wristwatch. They would still be here tomorrow, but the Post Office would close in ten minutes. She really did want to get the letter off to her parents. Closing the cupboard, she stopped to scribble her parents' address onto the envelope. She turned out the lamp and collected Stella from the chair before the fire. 'Sorry, little one,' she said. 'But it's time for us to go.' With a final look back at the parlour to check everything was in order, Hettie held the cat to her and let them both out of the cottage.

TWENTY-ONE
APRIL 1876

On his second day in Simpson's Bay, Charles woke early. It was an effort to lift his head from the pillow. He licked his lips. He took up a glass from the nightstand and drained the water. He refilled it from the jug and drained that glass too. Pushing back the eiderdown he placed his feet on the floor. He rested his elbows on his knees and let his head hang loose. Whatever had possessed him to drink so much whisky? He licked his dry lips again and looked down at himself. Whatever had possessed him to go to bed in his shirt and not his nightshirt? And why hadn't he removed his socks and sock suspenders?

Fragments of the previous evening came back. A fine dinner at the MacGregors'. An interesting conversation about the logging business. A suggestion that Ewan might like to take Charles to the tavern since they were young men. Bar billiards. Whisky. An odious chap saying wicked things about Monica. Monica! She had helped Ewan bring him up to his room. She had hung up his jacket and... and... Charles groaned and fell back onto his pillow. He hoped it was Ewan who had helped him out of his trousers. Otherwise, how would he ever look Monica in the eye again?

Somehow, Charles managed to wash and shave and dress. Leaving his key on the reception desk, he pushed out into the cold air of the early morning. He made his way to the restaurant near the green and ordered coffee and plain toast. The thought of bacon and eggs made him want to run from the building. After sipping two coffees and eating the toast, he ordered two sausages, which he managed to eat. Thankfully the day had been left free for him to explore the town, with another day at the mill planned for tomorrow. Stopping to buy two buns and a pie from the bakery, Charles returned to the hotel.

'You're up early,' Mrs Harvey said when she handed him his key.

Charles nodded. 'I wanted to start the day,' he said. 'I thought I might work in my room today. If that won't be a bother.'

'No bother at all.' Mrs Harvey smiled. 'Can I bring anything to your room? Coffee, perhaps.'

'Thank you,' Charles said. 'And perhaps a jug of water.'

'I'll bring them right up,' Mrs Harvey replied.

In his room, Charles placed his bags of food on the chest of drawers. He waited for Mrs Harvey to bring up his drinks and place them on the nightstand. When she left, he drank the coffee and another glass of water, undressed and collapsed back into bed.

At six o'clock, Charles stood at the gate of a small house on the edge of town. It backed onto the forest and thick snow lay all around. It was a modest house constructed from timber with a window on either side of the door and a single window above. Much of the land was fenced in and Charles could hear the noise of livestock in a couple of small outbuildings.

Charles looked down at his clothes. He felt refreshed at least, after his sleep. He had woken late morning to eat his food and had even managed to dress and take a walk around town to clear his head. He had washed again in a bowl of water in his room and parted his hair neatly, so he was presentable. He thought back to the scene in his bedroom the night before and held in a groan. All he could remember was talking to Monica. But he remembered none of what he said and none of what she said. No matter how hard he tried.

Taking a deep breath, Charles knocked on the door. From inside came the sound of footsteps on floorboards. The door opened.

'Mr Mandeville,' Bryn said. 'Please, come in.'

'Charles, please,' Charles said, stepping across the threshold. 'Call me Charles.'

'Charles it is,' Bryn said.

The room Charles entered seemed to take up the entirety of the downstairs of the property. And it appeared that all domestic activity occurred in this one large room. A huge fireplace ran the length of one wall and a log burned brightly in its hearth. A black stove was positioned within the fireplace and pans bubbled on the heat on the top. Along the opposite wall ran a dresser with crockery and a few ornaments, along with some books and jars of preserved fruit and vegetables. There were many small jars, which had been repurposed to display an array of dried flowers and foliage. The room was fashioned from huge logs which were exposed on two walls, the other two having been rendered had some framed pictures hanging from hooks. It was a warm, homely room and smelled deliciously of food. Two armchairs sat before the fireplace and a table sat between the armchairs and the dresser. There were four chairs at the table, but only three places were set. Charles' heart sank. Perhaps Monica had declined the invitation – knowing what a buffoon he had made of himself, and he was joining just Mr and Mrs Bennett for dinner.

A door opened at the back of the room, letting in the cold.

But the sight that met Charles warmed his heart. Monica rushed inside bringing a flurry of snow with her. She shook the snow from her hair and clasped her arms about her. 'I know animals need feeding,' she said. 'But that new cow has taken a dislike to me, and she tries to push me up against the wall any chance she gets.'

Bryn laughed. 'I understand you've already met my daughter,' he said as Monica went to the small table beside the fire and washed her hands in some water from a bowl. 'So you may have experienced her directness.'

'Directness isn't anything to be ashamed of,' she said, drying her hands on a towel and placing it back down beside the bowl. 'If you are direct, everyone knows where they stand.'

Bryn turned to Charles and lifted his eyebrows.

Monica stood before Charles. 'Good evening, Mr Mandeville,' she said.

'Charles, please.' It was about all he could say now that those green eyes were looking at him again. He thrust out the small paper bag he had carried from the hotel after making a purchase at the general store. It was rather crumpled. 'For you,' he said.

Monica looked into the bag. 'Taffy,' she said. 'Thank you.'

'I didn't want to come empty handed,' he said. 'Sorry the bag's a bit crumpled. It's just a small token.'

'And it is very welcome,' Bryn said. 'Come, sit at the table with me.'

Bryn offered Charles the chair with its back to the fireplace. He poured Charles a glass of beer. 'Unless you don't feel up to it,' Bryn said.

'I beg your pardon?' Charles said.

Bryn looked to his daughter and smiled. 'I hear you enjoyed an evening in the tavern with Ewan last night and Monica had to help you back to your room.'

'Sorry,' Charles said.

Bryn slapped him on the back. 'No apology needed.' He smiled at Charles. 'So, beer or no beer?'

'Beer, please,' Charles said.

'I'm surprised you can stomach it,' Monica said, a laugh in her voice.

'Take no notice of my daughter,' Bryn said 'And good for you, Charles. There's nothing like a hair of the dog.'

Bryn pushed the glass of beer across the table to Charles. He began to talk about the mill. Much of what he said went over the same subjects that Ewan had covered. The history of the mill and the machinery. The details were such that Charles didn't think it mattered too much that he was taking hardly any of them in. Because all he could think about was the woman behind him who was working at the stove, preparing the meal. The temptation to turn around to look at her was almost too much to bear.

'Ah, there it is,' Bryn said.

Monica approached from behind Charles. She placed a steaming pot on the table.

'Our Monica is a wonderful cook,' Bryn said. 'What have we tonight, my dear?'

'Pork and bean stew,' she said. Untying her apron, Monica folded it and placed it on the dresser. She sat opposite Charles. He noted that she wore a purple dress with a black pinafore over the top. She began to slice a loaf of bread that sat on a board on the table. She glanced at Charles and he immediately looked down at his beer. Taking a sip, he said. 'This is delicious.'

'If you're free tomorrow evening,' Bryn said. 'Perhaps you'd like to take a jar or two at the tavern with me.'

'Thank you,' Charles said. 'That's very kind.'

Monica took up a ladle. She collected Charles' bowl, filled it with stew, and placed it before him.

'Thank you,' he said, looking up at her.

'You're welcome,' Monica said.

'I was fortunate that Monica's mother passed on all her recipes to her before she died,' Bryn said.

'I'm sorry,' Charles said. 'I didn't realise.'

'It was a long time ago now,' Monica said, adding a ladle of stew to her father's bowl. 'You don't need to worry that you will upset us. We should talk of the dead often. By saying their names, we are keeping them alive.'

It was the most she had said that wasn't in relation to her job, or the response to something stupid Charles had said. He wanted her to continue but Bryn spoke next.

'My wife was Irish,' he said to Charles. 'Fell in with me when I was over there working on helping set up a farm. She had a lot of the superstitions and mystics about her, which our Monica has inherited.'

'It's not mystics or superstitions, Daddy. It's a way of living,'

'See,' Bryn said. 'She even calls me "Daddy", like a good Irish girl should. He patted his daughter's hand before she spooned stew into her own bowl.

'How did you come to be in Canada?' Charles asked. He had already decided that he would not mention what the odious man at the bar had said the night before. He was simply spewing bile as Monica had rejected him.

'Looking for a better life,' Bryn said. 'Like so many, we thought to better our position. But my wife died of a tumour six years ago. It would have happened anywhere so we can't blame the move over here. Our Monica was just thirteen years old, but she started keeping house, looking after the animals like her mother did, tending the vegetables and now she works a few shifts a week at the hotel. I am a lucky man to have such a daughter.'

Monica pushed the board of bread to her father. 'That's silly talk,' she said. 'Anyone would have done it. What were we to do? Starve and live in an unclean house? Now have some bread.'

Bryn took a chunk of bread and placed it on a plate beside his bowl. 'Always embarrassed to be the centre of attention, this one,' he said and patted his daughter's cheek. She shook her head and offered the bread to Charles.

'Mr Mandeville,' she said.

'Charles, please,' he said.

'All right, Charles it is. But when I see you at the hotel it will be Mr Mandeville.'

Charles smiled as he took a slice of bread. This was a conversation. He and Monica were having a conversation. And she expected to see him at the hotel. He smiled again and followed Bryn's lead by tearing off a piece of the bread and dipping it into his stew. He listened to Bryn talk more about the mill and the town and nodded politely as he ate the delicious meal. It was no doubt why he had been invited: so that Bryn could promote the sale of the mill as a good investment. From what he had seen already, Charles had decided to recommend the investment to Jonty, but he was under strict instructions not to give anything away as there would be a negotiation to be had. All the while Bryn talked, Charles was aware of Monica opposite him. He may have been looking at her father but from the corner of his eye, all he saw was her. How she brushed a strand of hair back from her face when it escaped her plait. How she tore off pieces of bread and added a little butter. How she raised the spoon to her lips. Her lips.

'It's marvellous!' Charles said suddenly. 'That the work of the mills is all down to nature.'

Bryn paused with his spoon to his mouth. 'How's that?' he said.

'Without the water there would be no way for the wheel to spin. And the mill would still rely on two men with a saw to cut the timber, which is incredibly inefficient.'

Bryn smiled. 'Ah, but it was man who dammed the stream to force the water to turn the wheel.'

'But is it not also the power of water that brings the lumber down the river when it has been felled? Were it not for the water, then it would only be possible to mill timber felled locally.'

'But it is men who felled the timber,' Bryn said. It was clear from the amusement in his voice that he was enjoying the to and fro of the conversation.

'So, it is the perfect partnership of man and nature,' Charles smiled.

'So it is,' Bryn said. He held up his glass and Charles tapped his against it. They both drank a mouthful of beer.

'You and my daughter seem to be of one mind,' Bryn said. 'She prefers the natural world over the mechanical. She would be outside working the land or walking amongst trees, given half the chance.'

'And what is wrong in that?' Monica asked.

'Nothing.' Bryn smiled. 'But you are surely your mother's daughter.'

She shook her head again. 'Charles,' she said, 'can I offer you some more stew?'

Charles felt he might fall off the chair at the sound of his name coming from Monica's mouth. From her lips. He swallowed. 'Please.' It was all he could say.

Bryn began to tell Charles more about the mill. But all Charles could think was that he wished Henry was there so he might talk to him about these sudden overwhelming feelings for that young woman sitting across the table from him. He'd had infatuations before, but nothing like this. And Henry was more a man of the world when it came to women.

Monica cleared the table and served an apple pie. As they ate, Charles glanced at her every so often. She looked back at him. She did not turn away or avoid his gaze and he felt sure that she smiled each time, just as he did.

. . .

It was almost nine o'clock when Charles stood at the door of the house, buttoning up his coat. For the third time he thanked Bryn for his hospitality.

'It's my pleasure to have you in my home,' Bryn said. 'Regardless of this deal with your cousin and the mill. It was good to have someone to debate with. You are a canny young man.'

'Thank you,' Charles said. 'And thank you, Monica, for the delicious meal.'

'You are very welcome, Charles,' she said. She was standing behind her father and the light from the fire lit her face.

'I'll say goodnight then,' Charles said when Bryn opened the door to let him out.

Charles walked just a few steps away from the house. When he was out of sight of the windows, he leant against the trunk of a tree. He held his face up to the stars in the dark sky. Snow gently began to fall. He felt something touch his hand and looked down. He had heard the expression about one's heart leaping into one's mouth but had not truly experienced it until that moment.

'I told my father that I was coming out to feed the scraps to the animals,' Monica said, her hand touching Charles'. 'It's not a lie. I will feed the scraps to the animals.'

'What are you doing out here?' Charles said. 'You will freeze.'

'I'm used to it,' Monica said. 'I live half of each year in the winter.'

Charles looked down at her and she looked up at him. Only the moon lit her face. 'You didn't answer my question,' Charles said quietly. 'What are you doing out here?'

'I wanted to say sorry,' she said. 'For being so brusque with you yesterday at the hotel. It's just my way.'

'I should apologise,' Charles said. 'For the state I got into last night. I want to thank you for helping me. And you don't need to apologise for anything.'

'I do,' Monica said. 'My mother always taught me to leave nothing unsaid. No apology ungiven and no feelings unknown.'

Charles swallowed. 'I see.'

Monica smiled at him. It seemed a genuine smile. 'I'll say good night then. Charles,' she said.

'Good night, then. Monica.'

She smiled at him again and he watched her run through the snow to the side of the house where she collected a bowl. She disappeared inside one of the outbuildings without looking back at him.

TWENTY-TWO
FEBRUARY 1937

Stella followed Hettie part of the way down the street, but when she started to run, the cat gave up and headed back towards the cottage. Hettie pulled up the sleeve of her overcoat to look at her watch. She picked up her pace and was soon sprinting. When she got to the post office, she pushed the door with such force that the bell swung rapidly above her head. The postmistress looked up from the counter and reassured Hettie that she still had five minutes to spare. Hettie thanked her and paid for a postage stamp, which she affixed to the envelope. She looked along the display of chocolate bars on the counter and the jars of sweets lined up on the shelves. She thought of Daphne and Lula.

'May I take two bars of Fry's chocolate?' she said. And then she thought of herself. 'And a quarter of barley sugar, please... oh, and a quarter of coconut ice.'

Slipping the chocolate and bags of sweets into her satchel, she thanked the postmistress. The bell above her head rang again as she left the shop to post her letter in the post box outside.

. . .

'Good afternoon, Hatshepsut,' Lula said when Hettie pushed through the doors of Hill House. It was shortly after three o'clock and Lula was standing at the bottom of the stairs.

'Good afternoon, Lula,' Hettie said. 'Good day at school?' She stopped at the fire and removed her gloves to warm her hands.

Lula wrinkled her nose. 'It was a bit dull. One of the boys kept interrupting the English class when I was trying to write my story,' she said. 'Just because he doesn't like the composition class, I think he jolly well shouldn't interrupt those of us who do.'

Hettie had to stifle a laugh at Lula's indignance. 'I jolly well think so too,' she said. 'Did you tell your teacher?'

Lula sighed. 'Yes, she tried to stop him, but he wouldn't be told. Aren't boys simply awful?'

This time Hettie couldn't help but smile. 'They certainly can be,' she said. She took a step towards Lula and lifted the flap of her satchel to remove one of the bars of chocolate. 'Perhaps this will make you feel better,' she said, handing the chocolate to Lula.

Lula looked down at the bar in her hands and then up at Hettie. 'Thank you,' she said, a grin lighting her face. 'Is this all for me.'

'Every last piece,' Hettie said.

Kate entered the hallway through the door beside the clock. 'Hello, Hettie,' she said. 'Have you had a productive day?'

'Thank you, yes,' Hettie said. 'I was hoping to continue it here since the light at the cottage has given up for the day. I might look through the library to see whether there are any reference books I can use in my research.'

'You won't be short of books in there!' Kate said.

'Look, Katherine,' Lula said. 'Look what Hettie gave to me.' She held out the bar of chocolate.

'Well, isn't that kind,' Kate said. 'Did you say thank you to Hettie?'

Lula nodded. 'Might I have a piece before dinner?' she asked.

'I don't see why not.' Kate smiled. 'Now, young lady, come along to the kitchen. There's a glass of milk and a slice of seed cake waiting for you. You must let Hettie get on with her work without disturbance.'

'But I was waiting for Daphne,' Lula said. 'She said she had some exciting news today and I wanted to hear what it is. Although she seems not to want to talk to me about everything anymore.'

Kate smiled at Lula. 'That's because Daphne is a big girl now,' she said. 'And sometimes big girls want to keep things to themselves a bit more. In any case, the bus won't be arriving for another half an hour, and you can't wait here that long.'

'Why do big girls want to keep things to themselves?' Lula asked.

'It's just the way it is,' Kate said. 'You'll be the same when you're a big girl.'

'I don't think I shall be a big girl if you have to become secretive,' Lula said.

'I don't think any of us have much choice in that matter,' Kate said. 'We all grow up some time. And Daphne is just excited as her parents have given her permission to visit her friend for tea tomorrow.' Kate reached past Lula and took an envelope from the post tray on hall stand. 'This came for you in the second post,' she said, handing the envelope to Hettie. 'We should leave you to enjoy your letter,' Kate said, with a smile. 'We'll see you at dinner. Now, come along, Lula.' She placed her arm around the little girl's shoulders and Lula let herself be guided towards the back of the hallway.

'Thank you again for the chocolate, Hatshepsut,' Lula called, as they disappeared through the door beside the clock.

Hettie stayed in the hall for a moment longer. She looked down at the handwriting on the envelope and smiled.

In the library, she removed her coat and draped it over her satchel, which she placed on the floor. She took a seat in a chair before the fire and felt immediately at home, surrounded as she was by so many books of varying sizes, from tomes at least a foot tall to tiny books of poetry with spines of so many colours. As with any room of so many books, it had a specific scent: reassuringly musty and papery.

Hettie turned the envelope over and smiled at her name and the address on the front. She would have known who it was from even without seeing the familiar handwriting. Her parents used a very particular brand of notepaper and envelopes, which they bought from the stationer's shop beside The Ewart.

Hettie slid her finger beneath the flap and pulled out the letter. She unfolded it and smiled again. As with every letter she had ever received from her parents, it was two pages long; one written by her mother, the other by her father. As with her own letters home, each sheet contained just a few paragraphs. Her father's page began: 'My dearest daughter, Hettie.' Her mother's began: "My darling, Hatshepsut."

Each page updated her on how her parents had spent the day after she had left for Hill House. Father had been at The Ewart for a meeting with the curator, which was dull but necessary. Her mother had spent the day in her study. She'd had an exciting development on a line of one branch of an Egyptian royal family that everyone had assumed had come to an end. She would share with Hettie what she had found when she arrived home, which her mother hoped wouldn't be too soon as she hoped Hettie was having a lovely time with the Mandevilles. Her father's page had a similar paragraph, saying what a wonderful thing it was that Hettie was helping Sir Edward. He was so proud of her lending her excellent talent in photography to help the family of her grandfather's dearest friend. And what a gift she had. He ended his letter saying that he and Mother were writing together after dinner and hoped to get the letter in the post to arrive with her at the earliest opportunity. They both signed off with their love to her.

Hettie reread both pages. She could picture her mother and father sitting in the drawing room, each taking a turn at the little writing desk beside the fire as they shared a glass or two of port. Every mealtime since she had returned to live at home had been something of an effort, followed as it was by drinks in the drawing room. She rarely made conversation, but her parents never seemed to stop talking. If they attempted to bring her gently into their conversations and she refused, they seemed never to be offended, but filled the gap left by her silence.

Folding the letter, Hettie pushed it back inside the envelope, which she slipped into her satchel. It had been worth the sprint to the post office. The letter should arrive in Cambridge in the morning and its appearance on the breakfast table would be sure to please her mother and father. They would take it as a signal of a return to more normal times when their letters to each other used to cross regularly in the post. They would see it as validation that they had done the right thing in colluding with Sir Edward to plan this trip to Hill House. Hettie smiled as she buckled her satchel. They were probably right.

Getting to her feet, she took a turn around the library. She found instructional guides on the propagation of flowers and the flora and fauna of different lands nestled against studies of philosophy and art. There were many novels and collections of short stories and, where the depth of the shelves allowed it, framed photographs sat in front of the books as well as on tables and sideboards. Posed studio portraits jostled for space amongst casual and candid snaps in rooms around the house and out in the gardens and grounds, rather like her own juvenile efforts in the album down at Sir Charles' cottage. Hettie looked closely at the fashions and the photographic techniques. The images in their silver frames captured the life of the Mandevilles across the last seventy or so years. And so many of the faces were familiar to her. She recognised Sir Edward, of course, and his lovely wife, Alice. There were many photographs of them with Daphne and their three sons, one older than Daphne and two younger.

Hettie picked up a frame holding a photograph of Sir Edward's sister, Charlotte, and her husband Paul. She had met Paul when he was a patient at Hill House during the war, and long before he and Charlotte had married and welcomed Lula. Paul had been terribly badly wounded and even after treatment was left with scars running the full length of one side of his face. His eyebrow and lip on the damaged side were bent out of shape and the scars had a soft blancmange-like texture. They were smooth with no hint of hair or crease as there was in the rest of his face. As a child, she had never been unnerved by his scars. Her grandfather had explained that every person was a product of their history. Whether external or internal, the signs of a lived life should be welcomed and celebrated. She had always accepted the scars as a part of Paul. And Paul had always been so matter of fact about his injuries and had encouraged conversation and inquisitiveness. He was a surgeon so took a pragmatic approach to his wounds. Hettie had always been entertained by listening to him talk about his injuries in his American accent, which had seemed incredibly exotic.

Hettie placed the frame back on the shelf. It would be interesting to take a series of photographs of Doctor Paul Kenmore. The lines and scars and the altered layout of his mouth and eyebrow would make an incredible study. Perhaps one day she might send him a letter and ask whether he would mind being the subject of a sitting. It wouldn't have to be for sale to a publication, it could simply be to capture his face. Of course, if he was willing to agree to it, she knew at least half a dozen editors who would want to publish an article on him. The men badly wounded in that conflict were so often hidden away, their scars obscured behind metal masks or scarves and considered too awful to look upon since they were a constant reminder of that atrocious war. But people should be reminded. How was it possible to learn without confronting the past? Either collectively or on a personal level.

Hettie studied Paul's face again. It was half damaged and half unblemished, but all of it was handsome. And, as her grandfather had explained, it told his story, his history. And it seemed that there was a lesson in it for her. How was she to ever come to terms with what had happened to Saul if she couldn't bring herself to think about it? If she continued to push any memory of him away and attempted to forget what had happened, was she not betraying his memory? His ending was not his story. If that's all she could recall, then was she not giving power to the person who had taken his life? Saul deserved more than that.

In the last few days at Hill House, she'd had to put her grief to one side to get on with her work. She hadn't forgotten Saul, but already she knew that time away could give her the space to remember him with light and with the love she'd had for him. Because she had loved him. Like she might have loved a brother. She pictured his face. His smile and his laugh. The way he was always in a rush everywhere. The person who had murdered that good, sweet boy did not deserve the hold they had over his memory. It shadowed what his life had been when Saul Besser had been a bright shining light.

Hettie closed her eyes. Seeing Saul's face again, she smiled. When she had finished at Hill House, she would travel to London to see Mr and Mrs Besser and their daughters. It was the right thing to do, and it was what she wanted to do.

TWENTY-THREE

When the clock in the hall chimed five times, Hettie collected her things and returned to her room. She had barely hung her coat on the back of the door and placed her satchel beside the dressing table, when there came a knock at the door.

'Come in,' Hettie called, kicking off her shoes and wiggling her toes in her socks.

The door opened slowly. 'Is now still a good time?' Daphne asked.

'Of course,' Hettie said.

Daphne smiled as she entered the room and closed the door behind her. She placed a parcel wrapped in brown paper on the chest of drawers beside the wardrobe. 'I collected it from the post office on my way home from school yesterday,' she said. 'Thankfully nobody saw me when I got home, and I managed to sneak up the stairs.'

'May I ask you a question?' Hettie said.

Daphne nodded.

'Is there a reason for being so secretive about this dress? Surely nobody would mind you ordering something.'

'They wouldn't,' Daphne said. 'But I just want to keep this for me. Everyone would want to know what I was doing or have an opinion – especially Lula. And this is something that is special to me. You do understand, don't you?' she said.

'I do.' Hettie smiled in a way she hoped was reassuring. She just about remembered what it was like to be young. 'Why don't you unwrap the parcel and go into the bathroom to change?'

'Thank you so much, Hettie,' Daphne said. 'I knew you would understand.' She set about untying the string from the parcel and peeling back the paper to reveal a luxuriously silver box tied with a dark blue ribbon. Hettie recognised it instantly. It was the wrapping from one of the most exclusive retailers on Bond Street. Daphne must have saved her birthday and Christmas money since the day she was born to afford a dress from such a shop. That, or her parents gave her a hefty sum as pocket money, or she'd inherited a small fortune.

'I shan't be long,' Daphne said, carrying the parcel into the bathroom. Before she closed the door, she gave Hettie a little embarrassed shrug and smile.

Hettie took her notebook from her satchel and placed it on the dressing table. What a thing it must be for a young girl to have such a luxury. At Daphne's age, she had dressed mainly in khakis so that she looked like she belonged in a trench somewhere, brandishing a trowel with archaeology students. Often, she would accompany her father on a dig and photograph the students, who had been thrilled to see themselves captured in action. Her father probably still had those photographs somewhere; she would have to ask him. He would certainly be happy to spend an evening looking over them, sharing a glass or two of his favourite Claret.

The bathroom door creaked on its hinges as it opened. Hettie looked up. Daphne stepped into the bedroom, slowly, almost apologetically. The sight of her struck Hettie momentarily dumb. Daphne's shy smile turned to a look of uncertainty. She placed her arms across her stomach.

'Is it too much?' Daphne asked.

'No,' Hettie said. 'No, not at all. You look... very stylish.'

Daphne stood before her in a jade green satin dress with a straight skirt hemmed just below the knee. The long sleeves had a slight puff to the shoulders and the neckline finished just above Daphne's bust, exposing the perfect pale flesh of her upper chest and her collar bones. Gone were the heavy skirts and sweaters and the school uniform. Daphne was no longer a young girl; she was a young woman. She looked far, far older than her sixteen years and had obviously given much thought to her choice of dress, since the jade perfectly complimented her auburn hair and picked out the green of her eyes. The satin skimmed her hips, accentuating her slim, womanly figure. The freckles dusting her nose and cheeks, and her hair tied back from her face in plaits, gave the only clue that she was still a schoolgirl.

Daphne smiled. 'Do you like it?'

'Yes. Yes, it's beautiful.'

'And is it what the fashionable women wear in London?'

'I should think so,' Hettie said. 'Yes. It looks straight out of a display in a window in Bond Street.'

Daphne smiled again. She twisted, clearly enjoying the feel of the satin against her legs.

'So, this is the dress you intend to wear for tea with your friend tomorrow?' Hettie said.

'It is,' Daphne said, her cheeks colouring slightly.

Hettie wanted to ask whether that tea would be taken at The Savoy or The Dorchester since the dress wouldn't look out of place at the most exclusive bars and restaurants in London. Instead, she said, 'They must be a very good friend for you to want to dress up so.'

'They are,' Daphne said, colour rising in her cheeks again. 'And they are very sophisticated, so I want to look just right.'

'You look perfect,' Hettie said. And she did. The dress could hardly have been more flattering if it had been made bespoke for Daphne. 'I'm sure you will have a marvellous time at your tea.'

'I hope so,' Daphne said. 'And thank you. For taking the time to give me your opinion. I should likely have gone in one of my old frocks if I hadn't got your seal of approval.'

'You don't need my approval,' Hettie said. 'Just remember that. The only approval you need in life is your own.' She stopped herself from saying more. Had Daphne been a few years older, she would not have held back with a sermon on how every woman should be allowed to live the life they wanted. But there was no harm in sowing the seed in Daphne. She was an intelligent girl and would go far if she followed her own path.

'I do love how you speak,' Daphne said, smiling. She ran her fingers down the satin covering her stomach. 'Would you mind helping me fold the dress and putting it back in the box? I'm afraid I will crease it.'

'Not at all,' Hettie said. 'You go and get changed and we'll wrap it in its tissue paper so it's perfect for tomorrow.'

Hettie watched as Daphne walked the few short steps to the bathroom. She had the body of a young woman but the bearing of a much younger girl, with her shoulders rolled slightly as though apologetic of her presence in the world. Give it a few years and her personality would catch up with her. She would grow into her body and into who she was, especially when she went away to university. Hettie smiled at the memory of her own university days. Studying English Literature with many, many likeminded fellow undergrads had been fun. In its own way, it had been an act of rebellion as she had failed to follow in the family footsteps of immersing herself in a lifelong passion for history. English Literature was a humanity, at least, which her mother and father could just about understand, but when she announced she was throwing that all aside to go to Paris to study photography, they had been at a loss to know where it had come from. They'd had no idea that the plaything that had given her so much pleasure as a child had taken such a hold on her. As much as they had wanted to support her, they didn't really know how. Thank heavens for her grandfather.

The bathroom door opened. Daphne emerged carrying the box, dressed in her school skirt and a grey jumper over her blouse.

'There she is,' Hettie said.

'Thank you so much for your time,' Daphne said.

'I've been thinking,' Hettie said, 'You mentioned the other day that your father is keen for you to go to Cambridge.'

'He is,' Daphne said with a little frown.

'And is there a particular reason you're not keen on the idea?'

Daphne wrinkled her nose. 'Not really,' she said. 'It's just that... I should like to start to make decisions for myself.'

Hettie pushed her hands into the pockets of her trousers and rocked back on her heels. 'I could show you around the place, if you'd like,' she said. 'I could arrange for us to have lunch at my old college, if you fancy the idea. It would give you a better idea of how you feel about the prospect of studying there. There would be no pressure from me. You should study where you like. But at least you will have a better feel for the place.'

Daphne's eyes widened. 'You would do that for me?'

'Of course,' Hettie said. 'And you'd be welcome to stay with my parents. It's not too bad, if you don't mind being surrounded by old pots and ancient artefacts. And I don't just mean my parents.' Hettie laughed and Daphne laughed with her.

'I would love to,' Daphne said. 'I really would love to.'

'Then that's sorted,' Hettie said. 'You just let me know

when suits and I can tell my parents. My mother and father could arrange for you to meet some of the professors in the subjects that interest you.'

'Thank you so much,' Daphne said. She laughed and shook her head. 'I am so glad that you came to stay.'

Hettie pulled back the sleeve of her cardigan and glanced at her watch. 'Do you have to rush off?' she asked.

Daphne shook her head. 'I have some homework, but I can do it after dinner.'

After helping Daphne wrap the dress back in its tissue paper, Hettie sat down and patted the side of the bed. Putting the box on the chest of drawers, Daphne sat beside her, facing the window. Hettie reached for her satchel and pulled it onto the bed. She unfastened the buckles and pulled out the bar of chocolate and bags of sweets. 'Peckish?' she asked.

'For sweets?' Daphne said. 'Always.'

'Good.' Hettie said, 'because this is for you.' She placed the bar in Daphne's hands.

'For me?' Daphne said.

'Every last bite,' Hettie said, smiling at how Daphne's response mirrored Lula's.

'Will you share it with me?' Daphne said.

'Only if you share these with me,' Hettie said. She unfurled the tops of the bags and held one out in each hand.

Daphne looked into both bags. 'May I have a coconut ice?' she asked.

'Of course,' Hettie said. 'I'll join you.'

They each took a sticky square from the bag. Hettie chewed hers slowly.

'I always think it's exotic,' Daphne said.

'The coconut?' Hettie said. 'It is rather. My grandfather had the shell of a coconut he collected on his travels in India. He kept it in his study. It was cut in two halves, and he taught me how to tap them together to make the sound of horses' hooves on cobbles.'

Daphne nodded, still chewing her square of desiccated coconut set in condensed milk. 'Your grandfather travelled abroad with my grandfather, didn't he?' Daphne said. 'I wonder whether my grandfather was with your grandfather in India.'

Hettie paused in chewing her sweet. 'It's certainly possible,' she said.

'I'd like to think they were there together,' Daphne said.

Hettie swallowed her sweet. 'So would I,' she said.

Daphne turned to her and smiled. 'They were very good friends, weren't they?'

'They were,' Hettie said. 'The best of friends.'

Daphne nodded and looked to the chocolate bar in her lap.

'There's a photograph album at the cottage,' Hettie said. 'It's silly really, but it's full of photographs I took when I spent a holiday here when I was younger even than Lula. Your mother and father are in some of the photographs. And your aunt. There are even some of our grandfathers together. I could show the album to you, if you'd like.'

'I would like that,' Daphne said. 'Very much.' She paused. 'Did you always know that you wanted to be a photographer?'

'Not always,' Hettie said. 'But from when I was very young, I had the idea.'

'If I knew what I wanted to be, perhaps the conversations with my father about university would be easier to have,' Daphne said.

Hettie smiled. 'You have plenty of time to think about that. Just enjoy your studies for now. You'll know when you come upon what it is that you want to do.'

Daphne smiled again and Hettie felt she had permission to continue.

'If I say anything that upsets you. You must tell me,' she said.

Daphne shook her head. 'You haven't upset me. Lula is often sad when we speak of our grandfather, but I feel I want to know more about him. Does that sound odd?'

'Not at all,' Hettie said. 'When my grandfather... when he died, I was desperately sad for a long time. But the price we pay for love is feeling a loss keenly.' Hettie watched Daphne closely. When she didn't reply, Hettie said, 'As time passes, it's only natural to want to know more about them. About who they were beyond the person we knew.' Again, she watched Daphne closely.

'Will you help me understand my grandfather, Hettie?' Daphne said. 'I'm fascinated to find out more about the things he collected. Perhaps we could become friends as our grandfathers were. I know I'm much younger than you, but perhaps when we are older?'

Hettie put her hand on Daphne's. 'We can be friends now,' she said. 'If you want to talk, I'm never more than a telephone call away.'

Daphne turned to her. 'Thank you, Hettie,' she said. 'And thank you so much for looking at my dress for me.'

'You are very welcome,' Hettie said.

Daphne looked down at the bar of chocolate. 'Would you like a piece?' she asked.

Hettie shook her head. 'I think I'll save myself for dinner. And you should probably go and do your homework. Or I'll have Kate after me.'

'I should,' Daphne laughed. She paused.

'Was there something else you wanted to talk about?' Hettie said.

Daphne paused again before she shook her head. 'No, it's all right. I will see you at dinner, Hettie,' she said.

'You will,' Hettie said. 'And you take that chocolate and enjoy it later.'

Getting to her feet, Daphne collected her parcel.

'Thank you again, Hettie,' she said and let herself out of the room.

Hettie lay back on the bed and stared at the ceiling. It felt right to help Daphne. She was an intelligent and sensible girl. It would be a delight to welcome her to Cambridge to show her around. And she felt sure her grandfather would have approved of her helping his friend's granddaughter.

TWENTY-FOUR
APRIL 1876

'This is how you feed it through the saw,' the chap said to Charles. He had been asked by Mr MacGregor to show Charles the working of all the machinery up close.

'I see,' Charles said, shouting to be heard over the noise of the saw and the belts and pulleys.

He watched the saw move up and down. It smelled of oil and wood shavings. Truly, if he had been allowed to find his own path in life, he might go back to college to learn more about engineering and then come out to a place like this to work. With mechanics but in nature. It seemed the perfect combination.

'And then this is how it's finished,' the man said.

'Sorry,' Charles said, pointing to his ears.

The man leant in closer and shouted louder. 'I said, this is how it's finished.'

Charles nodded and watched the man work on the plank.

Because if he moved out to a place such as this, he might make this is home and—

Charles couldn't be sure what happened next. In his distracted state, it was possible that he had taken a step forward. He stumbled and reached out to support himself. For the briefest moment, his hand touched a piece of wood about to be loaded into the saw. Two men were moving it, and the rough edge dragged along Charles' hand. It was fortunate for him that the wood hadn't been in the machine otherwise the speed it moved at would have taken his hand off. As it was, the pain hit him instantly like a stab. He shoved his hand into his armpit and sucked in his cheeks to stop from yelling out.

'Everything all right?' the chap shouted. He hadn't seen Charles' stupidity, and Charles wasn't about to reveal it to him.

Charles nodded. 'Fine, thank you.' Without looking at what he had done, he shoved his hand into the pocket of his overcoat.

When the opportunity presented itself, Charles excused himself and went outside. Standing with his back to the side of the mill building, he took his hand from his pocket. It continued to pulse with pain. Unfurling his fingers slowly, he looked into his palm and found a large splinter embedded in his flesh. It could have been worse. Much worse. Bracing himself, he took hold of the end of the splinter and with one hard pull, tugged it free. He stamped his foot against the pain and threw the splinter to the ground. What a stupid thing he had done. He was lucky that it had only left a drop of blood so he wouldn't have to explain himself to anyone. Taking his handkerchief from his pocket, he clutched it in his hand and closed his fingers around the white cotton.

It wasn't until much later in the day, when he was enjoying another coffee with Mr MacGregor in his office, that Charles began to feel a little off colour.

'Everything all right?' Mr MacGregor asked. 'You look a bit... clammy.'

'I think I'm just tired,' Charles said. 'It was a long trip up from New York and I haven't had much sleep since.'

'I'm an eight-hours-a-night man myself,' Mr MacGregor said. 'No good to man nor beast on any less. Why don't you go back to your hotel, and I'll see you in the morning when you've caught up on your shut-eye? You're leaving on the midday steamboat. Is that right?'

'It is. And thank you,' Charles said. 'I'll be back early in the morning.'

On returning to the hotel when Mrs Harvey handed Charles his key, she said he was looking a bit peaky and offered to make him a cup of beef tea. He thanked her and slowly climbed the stairs. Shrugging off his overcoat, he hung it behind the door and was pleased to sink down into the armchair beside the fire. Mrs Harvey knocked on the door and he called for her to come in. She placed the cup and saucer on the small table beside him. 'That'll see you right,' she said.

Charles smiled and thanked her again.

He rested his head against the side of the chair and fell instantly asleep.

'Charles. Charles.'

He heard someone calling to him from the midst of his sleep. It seemed such an effort to open his eyes. 'Monica?' he said.

She was kneeling beside his chair, looking at him with such concern. 'Mrs Harvey asked me to bring you up a fresh beef tea,' she said. 'But you haven't touched the first one.'

'Sorry,' Charles said. 'So tired.' He tried to close his eyes again, but Monica spoke to him.

'I think you need to get into bed,' she said. 'Can you manage?'

He nodded but when he tried to stand, he stumbled. Monica caught him and very slowly helped him shuffle to the bed. He slumped down on the eiderdown, his hands hanging to his sides.

'What's happened to you?' Monica asked. She was holding his hand and looking at his palm. He looked at it too. The skin around the tiny wound had changed colour. It was pale and mottled with purple.

'A splinter,' he said.

'And did you receive any treatment?'

Charles shook his head.

'Oh, Charles,' she whispered.

She placed her hands on his shoulders and gently eased him down so that his head rested on the pillow. She crouched beside him and pulled the eiderdown over him. 'Stay here,' she said. 'I've got to go home to get a few things. But I'll be back as soon as I can.'

'Please,' he said. 'Tell your father that I can't meet him at the tavern. Say I am sorry.'

'Don't worry about that now. Try to sleep.'

Charles nodded and closed his eyes.

Charles became aware of someone in the room with him. They knelt before the fireplace. Smoke. Smoke rose above them. The scent of herbs.

'Who...?' he said. 'Who are...?'

'Shhh,' they said. They came to the side of the bed and brushed their hand across his hair. 'Sleep now.'

He woke again. Candles burned brightly in the hearth. Someone was speaking. Calling. Who were they calling? Asking for?

'Hello,' he said.

'Shhh,' they said. They came to the side of the bed and brushed their hand across his hair. 'Heal now.'

. . .

Charles woke again. It felt as though the room was full of people, but he saw no one. Except the person who had been kneeling before the fire. They now knelt beside him. Calling. Asking. 'Heal him, I call on you to heal him.' A cup was held to his lips, and he sipped the warm, sweet liquid.

TWENTY-FIVE
FEBRUARY 1937

With an hour until dinner, Hettie let herself out of her room. She looked down at herself and shook her head. On the corridor of bedrooms, a young woman was no doubt trying on her dress again from the fashionable shop on Bond Street and here she was in her slacks, brogues, cardigan and necktie. But, as her mother had always said, it would be boring if everyone was the same.

In the library, Hettie took up a newspaper from the small side table, flicked through the pages, then placed it on the arm of the chair. She felt so at ease in this room with the history of the world and the Mandevilles all around her. As well as the framed photographs, the walls of the library were decorated with paintings. A few small oval-shaped portraits framed in gold, hung on the walls in threes, connected by red ribbons. Many of the sitters wore wigs. From her knowledge of the history of fashion and her much more limited knowledge of art history, Hettie guessed that the Mandevilles in the finely painted miniatures had lived during the reign of George III or through the Regency. It was possible that they were the original residents of Hill House. Some looked sensible, some kind and some even had a look of mischief in their eyes.

Next to the chimneybreast and beside a set of the miniatures was a drawing of people in similar clothes, picnicking beneath a grand tree. The tree was so vast that it had created a sort of canopy beneath which they sat at a table laden with food. It was rendered in what looked like pencil or charcoal rather than in the vivid colours of the portraits. Another set of three portraits hung on the other side of the sketch of the tree and picnickers. Hettie looked closer to see the faces and realised they were quite unlike the other miniatures surrounding them. They were the portraits of three children: two boys and a girl. They might have been painted in a style to mimic the Regency miniatures, but they were different. The children's clothes were more modern and the faces were familiar to Hettie. They were the three Mandeville siblings born in the final decades of the last century. Their doting parents must have had the likenesses of their children captured in the manner of their ancestors to sit alongside them in their family home. The younger boy with red hair wore thick spectacles. His even younger sister had blonde ringlets and an upturned nose. The older boy had dark hair flecked with auburn. And he had about the kindest eyes Hettie had ever seen. Eyes that had been captured in another portrait in the house when the sitter had been much older and a man in the absolute prime of health and fitness. Eyes that had followed Hettie around the hallway just beyond the library door when she had visited as a young child and still watched over her now. And here he was, captured in miniature, Thomas with his younger siblings, Edward and Charlotte. But Hettie had seen that younger version of him more recently. He was the older of the two boys tussling over the bottle in the chest in the back bedroom of Sir Charles' cottage.

Hettie let out a sigh. It made complete sense. She would have seen the miniature portrait of Thomas dozens of times over the years but paid it no mind. Her memory had pulled a recollection of Thomas' childhood portrait from the depths of her mind to include in the odd daydream. If she'd had the patience to search the many photographs in the library, she would surely find the other boy from her daydream. The surly little boy. She must have seen him somewhere before. That's why she had recognised the unsettling look in his eyes. She had seen it in a photograph.

Hettie sat in the chair before the hearth. It was a relief to have found an answer to one of her strange experiences at least. She took up the newspaper. A door outside slammed. Heavy footsteps ran across tiles.

A shout disturbed the silence. 'Fire!'

Hettie threw the newspaper down. She ran from the library into the hall and found Audrey racing into the corridor beneath the stairs. She followed. Audrey grasped the handle of a metal mechanism mounted beside the door.

'Fire!' she shouted again and turned the stiff handle. Hettie grabbed the free part of the mechanism and helped Audrey. The mechanism began to make a wail. It started slowly and at a low pitch, but as they turned the handle it grew looser, and the sound increased in volume and speed. Soon a siren sounded all around the house. Footsteps thudded from upstairs with Kate following the girls down the steps. Rosemary appeared from the doorway at the back of the hall. The women and the two girls rushed to the corridor.

'Where's Bertie?' Audrey shouted over the din.

'He's out in the grounds somewhere,' Kate said, puffing as she and the girls stopped just outside the corridor.

'Where's the fire?' Hettie said. 'We'll have to tackle it ourselves.'

'Out by the gardens,' Audrey said.

Both Hettie and Audrey released their grasp on the handle.

The momentum kept it turning slowly for a few seconds more as the wailing siren slowed.

'Go and telephone the fire brigade,' Kate said to Daphne. 'Use the telephone in your father's office. And take Lula with you. Stay there until we get back. Do you understand?'

Daphne nodded. She grabbed her little cousin's hand and together they ran along the corridor. The four women all ran through the hall, out of the front door and into the cold night.

In the darkness, the blaze of the fire could be seen from the drive outside Hill House. The air was filled with the scent of smoke as they ran down the path towards the flames.

'There's sand kept in buckets in the stables,' Audrey called over her shoulder. 'And a hose we can attach to the tap in the yard. Sir Charles was always afraid there might be a fire and said we were to be prepared.'

They reached the yard and Hettie saw that the fire was just further along the path by the entrance to the walled garden. She joined Rosemary and Kate in following Audrey.

In the stables, Audrey called out for Elliot but received no reply. She pointed to the stall along from where one of the three horses chomped lazily on hay suspended in a bag on the wall. 'The full buckets are kept in there,' Audrey said. 'Grab what you can. I'll set up the hose.'

Hettie ran into the stall first and grabbed two buckets. They were far heavier than she had anticipated but she was determined to take two rather than one. Balancing herself, she walked as quickly as she could past Rosemary and Kate and out into the yard. Audrey was busy attaching the hose to an outside tap. By the time Hettie got out onto the path, the fire had grown in size. The fire blazed on a cart beside the wall and next to the gates of the walled garden. It crackled and spat showers of burning material into the sky, which twisted and blazed red in the darkness before falling to the ground all about the path. If it wasn't extinguished quickly, it may spread to take in the wooden gates. And possibly the trees that grew along the path and led down to the woodland.

Hettie dumped one of the buckets on the path. The sand would only have an effect on the fire if it was thrown at close quarters. If she stood too far back, the heavy sand would land on the ground and not on the flames. Hettie rushed to the fire, holding the handle of the bucket with one hand and with the other, she held the bottom. When she was as close as she could bear, she launched the sand onto the flames. The fire hissed and fizzed and spat showers of sand at Hettie. She ran back to where the other bucket waited. Dumping the first bucket on the ground, she collected the second and ran at the fire, launching the sand onto the flames. Once again, it spat showers of hot sand back at her. When she saw Rosemary and Kate approaching, she ran to them. She grabbed Rosemary's bucket.

'I'll take this,' she called. 'You go and get another.'

Running along the path, Hettie again threw the sand onto the flames. She returned and took Kate's bucket. She ran at the fire again before retreating a short distance. Any dent she had made in the flames was soon replaced by new sparks. She turned to run back to the stables and was relieved to see Audrey appear through the gates, pushing a metal wheel that unravelled a hose as she progressed. Hettie sprinted to help. The metal wheel clattered along the path as they pushed it. When they were within a few feet of the fire, they stopped and let out the remainder of the hose by hand. The hose behind them sat taut and fat on the ground, filled as it was with water.

'You hold onto the hose,' Audrey called over the sound of the fire. 'I'll direct the water. Just make sure there are no kinks that stop the flow.'

Hettie grasped the hose while Audrey took hold of the end. When Audrey turned the nozzle, the pressure of the water suddenly saw the hose attempt to launch itself into the air. Hettie held on tight to the thing that felt like a living creature, writhing to free itself from her grasp. Audrey directed the jet of water to the base of the fire. She moved the direction from side to side and Hettie followed her lead, making sure that Audrey was free to do what she needed to. The fire raged red, the heat meaning they had to keep some distance. There was a roar to the flames and the smell of campfires. More pieces of burning material floated into the air, twisting and landing not only on the path but on the women. Hettie watched them shower onto Audrey. Mercifully the fine fibres had burned out before they landed on her clothes.

Hettie stared into the flames as finally they began to die back. Audrey moved the nozzle, showering any flames that threatened to spring forth. Gradually, the flames stopped sprouting from the black mass on the cart. Audrey turned the nozzle, and the water turned to just a trickle as she placed the hose on the ground. Hettie followed her lead and placed the hose down on the path. She joined Audrey to look over what was left of the fire.

It seemed eerily quiet without the rush of water and the thunder of the flames. And so dark with just the moonlight, the starlight and the light from the stables. Hettie and Audrey panted, their chests rising and falling. An owl hooted. Hettie stood beside Audrey looking at the damp mess.

'It's the little cart from the yard,' Audrey said, peering into the mass, still breathing deeply. 'The children used to attach it to one of their donkeys and pull each other around.'

'What's the mess on top of it?' Hettie asked.

'It looks like hay.' Audrey got closer to the charred remnants of the cart and what little of the fuel that had fed the flames remained. She stepped back. 'What's the cart doing out here?' she said quietly to herself. 'It doesn't make any sense.'

The sound of footsteps came from behind them. Hettie looked around to see Kate and Rosemary approaching, each struggling with the weight of another bucket of sand. Audrey stood beside her. The world had turned almost to a palette of greys now that there was so little light. Even so, she could see that Audrey's face was smeared with soot. She smoothed down her hair and her white apron, leaving dark marks wherever her hands had touched.

'It's fine,' Audrey said as the two women approached.

Kate and Rosemary came to a stop and placed the buckets on the ground. Rosemary's eyes widened as she looked past her sister. 'Fine!' she said. 'Fine! What's fine about a fire coming out of nowhere—'

'It's not out of nowhere,' Audrey said, cutting across her sister. It was obvious to Hettie that Audrey was trying to stop Rosemary saying something.

'It's the curse!' Rosemary said. She gesticulated to the remains of the cart and then in the direction of the cottage. 'I told you,' she said. 'Didn't I say that messing about with things in Sir Charles' cottage could only lead to trouble.'

'Now there,' Kate said. 'Nobody is "messing" with things. Sir Charles' collection is being catalogued. It's all being done right and proper and with the—'

'I'm not blaming her,' Rosemary said pointing to Hettie. 'It's not her fault. She knows nothing of what happens there.' Her voice rose higher. 'She should have been warned. If you touch things... things happen. They—'

'Now you can stop right there,' Audrey said, cutting across her sister again. 'I go inside that cottage every day and have seen nothing.'

'It's because you don't want to see,' Rosemary said. 'And even if you did see something that was so strange that it would have the rest of the world screaming down the path and through the gate, you would still say it was nothing and carry on running your duster over the mantelshelf. All those years ago those boys saw—'

'That is enough!' Audrey said, with such a force that Hettie felt as though she too had been reprimanded. 'I left the cart there. I was putting some fresh hay down over the tender plants in the borders. So that the frost doesn't cause them to rot.'

'And how did it catch on fire?' Rosemary demanded. 'Did it set light all by itself?' she added with more than a slight note of sarcasm.

Audrey took a step closer to her sister. 'Probably someone having a cigarette and being careless with their match.'

'That's right,' Kate said. 'They likely thought it was spent and flicked it away, not knowing that it was still alight.'

'And who would be walking around here to do that?' Rosemary said.

'Could be anyone,' Audrey said. 'You know the farmhands come down here to cut through the woods as a shortcut to the village.'

'It's true,' Kate said, her voice very sensible. 'They know they shouldn't as it's private land, but we all turn a blind eye to it.' She brushed her hair back from her face. 'So, that's sorted,' she said. But as she smiled at Hettie, there came the clatter of a bell in the distance. Kate's eyes widened. 'Oh, heavens,' she said. 'The fire engine. I asked Daphne to telephone for them.'

Hettie joined the other women in watching the headlamps of a vehicle grow as it travelled at speed up the drive. In no more than a minute or so, it had come to a stop just outside the house, the light from its lamps illuminating the portico. There was soon the sound of heavy boots running along the path, guided by torches, voices calling out to each other. They had clearly been given information on the location of the fire by Daphne as soon Hettie and the other women were caught in the beams from the torches. Hettie blinked at the sudden light in the dark night.

'They're here!' a voice shouted as men ran towards them. Hettie counted at least ten. They looked so large and sounded so loud. The men came to a stop. Some of them wore a uniform of dark coat and trousers with a golden coloured helmet. There were other men dressed in more everyday clothes. Bertie and Elliot. And Rhys.

Bertie ran to Kate and put his arms around his wife, pulling her close to him.

'It's out,' Audrey said. 'We used the sand and the hose.'

'Show me,' one of the firemen said. He had gold braid at his shoulders, presumably indicating that he was in charge. 'If you wouldn't mind,' he added.

Audrey led the firemen to the cart, and they began to examine what was left of it and the fire that was still smouldering.

'Kate,' Bertie said. 'Are you all right? The shock. Is the—'

'Everything's fine,' Kate said quickly, as though she didn't want her husband to continue. 'I'm fine. We're all fine.' She let out a little laugh. 'Thanks to Audrey and Hettie. They were so brave and didn't bat an eyelid at tackling the flames.'

'It was nothing, really,' Hettie said. 'It was Audrey mainly. I just helped a little.'

'Isn't it dreadful,' Rosemary said, her eyes looking to the firemen and Audrey and then back to the small group around her, although she seemed to focus on none of them. 'Who could have done this? Was it on purpose, do you think?' Her words were directed at everyone and nobody.

'I should imagine it was an accident,' Bertie said, his arm still around Kate.

Hettie felt a presence beside her but felt unable to acknowledge it. She looked instead at Elliot. His dog was by his feet, watching the activity outside the usually quiet stable yard, as his master looked around everyone present. It seemed to Hettie as though Elliot was scrutinising them all. For what purpose, she couldn't tell. If he was looking for the person who had started the fire, then she felt sure they weren't to be found here.

'Audrey thinks it could have been started by a farmhand

carelessly throwing away a match while they were taking a short cut,' Rosemary said.

'That sounds like a likely cause,' Bertie said.

Hettie watched Bertie look to Elliot and then to Rhys beside her. Bertie's voice might have had a level of certainty to it, but the look in his eyes couldn't have been more uncertain. It seemed that he was looking to the two other men for some kind of agreement.

'It could be that, indeed,' Rhys said. 'Many a fire has been started by carelessness.'

'Indeed,' Bertie said.

Rosemary's eyes still darted about the scene. She held her right arm across her waist and with her free hand, she patted her chest. Kate left her husband's side and put her arm around Rosemary's shoulders. 'It's all over now,' she said, smiling at the younger woman. 'Come on, there's nothing to be done here. Let's go back to the house and see the girls.'

Rosemary nodded silently and let herself be turned around. As Kate led her away, Bertie said, 'If you'll excuse me, I'll have a word with the chief officer.'

'Very good,' Rhys said.

Hettie watched Bertie join Audrey and the small group of firemen who were examining the smouldering ashes, their torches directed at the remains of the fire. Again, she felt Rhys' presence beside her. Part of her wished that he would leave her side to join Bertie. Part of her wanted him to stay. All of her knew that she would have to say something as this silence could not go on indefinitely. He had no idea of the thoughts she had begun to harbour about him throughout the day and which had struck her dumb.

'Well done, Hettie,' Rhys said.

She took a deep breath. Turning to face him, she said, 'I really didn't do anything.' Lifting her eyes, she looked into his face. The crease of a frown formed between his eyebrows. He seemed to search her face.

'Can you breathe normally?' he asked.

'Yes,' Hettie said. 'Of course.'

'How close were you to the fire?' he asked, the crease deepening.

'Quite close,' she said.

'Sometimes the fumes can get into your lungs,' he said.

'I don't think they did,' Hettie said.

She felt Rhys' eyes take in the details of her face. He pushed his hand into the pocket of his trousers. He removed a handkerchief. 'It's clean,' he said, pressing it into Hettie's hands. 'Washed and pressed this morning.'

Hettie looked down at the fresh white cotton. 'Why?' she said.

'You have some soot on your face,' Rhys said.

'I don't want to make this dirty,' Hettie said. She tried to hand the handkerchief back to Rhys, but he folded his hands over hers and pressed it back towards her gently.

'It can be washed,' he said. He was so earnest and there was such concern in his voice that Hettie didn't feel she could refuse him. She pressed the handkerchief to her cheeks and as she rubbed her face, she smelled lavender mixed with the scent of something that had been in a pocket and pressed against a warm body. She closed her eyes and swallowed. When she took the handkerchief away from her face, she saw that it was smeared in black.

'I'm so sorry,' she said.

'No apology needed.' Rhys smiled. This time he accepted the handkerchief when Hettie returned it. He folded it and pushed it back into his pocket.

'I should probably go to clean up properly,' Hettie said.

'That sounds like a good idea,' Rhys said.

From over her shoulder, Hettie heard Bertie and Audrey

talking to the firemen, discussing the presence of the cart on the path and how they should dampen it still further to make sure that the fire was completely out. Hettie looked to her feet. She knew that Rhys had only ever been honest with her in everything he said. And she knew that he would be honest with her about this.

'There's something else going on here, isn't there?' she said quietly. 'With the fire and with recent events.' She lowered her voice further. 'Audrey tried to reassure Rosemary and Kate. But I know she didn't give them the full truth of what she knows.'

She watched Rhys' face for his response. He glanced to the party still by the cart. 'Come to the shed,' he said. 'Later. After your dinner. And I'll explain what I can.'

'Can't you explain now?' Hettie asked.

He glanced back to the group on the path. 'No. Later,' he said.

TWENTY-SIX

With so much activity outside, Hettie was able to slip back into the house unseen. In her bedroom, she undressed and hung her clothes on the wardrobe door. She had collected her satchel on her way up and placed it on the end of the bed. She looked at her reflection in the mirror of the dressing table. Her body was pale, as it always was. But her hands and her face above where her collar had been were smeared with smuts. She could smell the fire in her hair and on her. Pressing her fingertips to her cheeks, she traced the clearer lines where she had wiped away the grime. With Rhys' handkerchief. She closed her eyes and leant forward. Her brain was trying to fool her into thinking that any interaction with Rhys was some sort of sign that he had feelings for her when, in fact, he was simply a man who would have shown compassion to anyone who found themselves in her situation. The only reason he had asked her to go to see him in the shed later that evening was so they could talk out of the earshot of others. He would have assessed the situation and judged that it would be tactful not to upset anyone else. That was it. There was no more to be read into his actions than those of a man considering the feelings of others.

In the bathroom, Hettie filled the tub with hot water and a splash of rosewater from a bottle on a shelf beside the window. While she waited for it to run, she took up a flannel, rubbed it against the bar of soap on the sink and scrubbed at her face so that the water turned to a murky cloud. She rinsed out the flannel and continued to scrub her face until the water in the sink stayed clear.

Slipping off her brassiere and stepping out of her knickers, she sank into the water up to her chin. She laid back so that her hair was beneath the surface and only her face and knees above the water. She tried so hard to clear her mind and to not think about the mistruths people were clearly telling around the fire. She would speak to Rhys later and he would provide an explanation. Just the thought of his name made her body respond so that every inch of her felt charged. It was a part of herself that she could not control. The part that sought out and found an attraction in another human. Her desire had always been this way. Visceral. Raw. And hungry. Like the aching rumble in a stomach that would only quieten when it had its fill of what it craved.

Sitting up quickly, water cascaded down her body. Hettie pulled the plug from the hole and water slurped and gurgled as it disappeared down the drain. She stepped from the bath, grabbed a towel, and swiped roughly at her naked body. But that only intensified the feelings charging through her. Hanging the damp towel on the rail, she turned and was confronted with her reflection in the mirror above the sink. Her instinct was to cross her arms over herself. As much as she enjoyed the physicality of others, admiring her own reflection was not something she had ever been completely at ease with. With one arm across her breasts and the other hand over her privates, she studied her broad shoulders and wide hips. She was so unlike the women she photographed. With their slim waists, slender limbs and angular collar bones, clothes hung from them as though they were a perfect wire hanger on which to display a garment. The women who saw those images in magazines and who bought the clothes, aspired to look like those women she captured through her lens. But she did not aspire to be them. It would have been an exercise in futility. Nothing would have shaved the extra inches from the bones in her shoulders or her hips. Her lovers had always revelled in her strength. She had a presence that had appealed to them in the way that her form had appealed to the photographers who had used her as a model in those early days in Paris. Not for fashion but to make a statement. To make art.

Hettie let her eyes travel across her pale flesh. Most of her lovers had been unusual. With an edge that excited her in the way that her body had excited the lust in them. But was this the type of body that a man used to more normal women might desire? She closed her eyes tightly. This was no good. No good at all. Leaving her reflection behind, she returned to the bedroom. The smell of fire on her clothes hanging on the wardrobe door was almost too much to bear.

Taking fresh knickers and a clean shirt, green sweater and wide-legged tweed trousers from the wardrobe, she dressed and put a comb through her hair. After pulling on her boots, she took the clothes from the hangers and held them at arm's length away from her as she left the room and made her way down into the hall and out into the chill of the winter night. Her car was still unlocked so she placed the fire-riddled clothes in the boot. She would have them laundered when she got home at her own expense and not that of the Mandevilles.

TWENTY-SEVEN

Dinner was a strange affair. Talk of the fire was a mixture of horror, shock and intrigue. Since no damage had been done aside from the cart having been destroyed, the firemen had decided that there was no need to involve the police, and no further action was to be taken.

When Rosemary tried to guess which farmhand might have accidentally flicked a match or cigarette stub into the cart which had ignited the brittle hay, Audrey told her to hold her tongue and eat her cottage pie before it got cold.

Hettie paused with a forkful of mashed potato midway to her mouth. She studied Audrey's face but nothing gave away the fact that she had not told the truth about how the cart had come to be on the path outside the garden. Hettie had been the only one to hear Audrey's words. Had she been mistaken in what she had heard? No, she had heard it clearly. She closed her mouth around the potato and chewed slowly. She looked at Bertie who seemed to have his chair very close to Kate's. More so than usual. He regularly let his hand come to rest beside hers so that their fingers touched. Every so often Kate turned to her husband and gave him a reassuring nod.

Lula talked constantly about the excitement of the fire engine coming down the drive. Daphne responded only to nod and smile indulgently. If Hettie were to guess, she would have said that Daphne's thoughts were very much on her new dress and the tea with her friend tomorrow rather than her younger cousin's excitement. Kate explained to Lula that she had telephoned her mother, who wanted to hear all about the excitement.

Daphne suddenly emerged from her silence. She sat forward. 'They're not coming home, are they? There's no need for Papa and Mama or Aunt Charlotte and Uncle Paul to come back. We are all fine.'

Kate looked at her as though she thought the question a little odd. 'No, they are not coming home. Your father and mother are happy that everything has been dealt with correctly. Lula's mother simply wants to speak to her so that she can hear from her about the fire engine.'

Daphne sat back in her chair. 'That's good,' she said. And then, as though remembering herself when Kate looked her again, she added. 'Because Grandmama and Great-Aunt Leo wanted so much to go to a particular play at the theatre tomorrow evening and Mama and Aunt Charlotte are to join them. It would be a shame for them to miss it if everyone felt they had to come home when there is no call for it as everything is fine.'

Lula nodded, agreeing with her cousin. 'And it has been *so* much quieter without Charlie and Oscar here.' She turned to Daphne. 'Why are your brothers so noisy?' she said. 'Why are *all* boys *so* annoying?'

Hettie thought she saw Daphne blush as she batted her cousin's remark away.

A sense of normality settled across the table with Lula talking about a book she would like to borrow from the library in town and arrangements for Kate to drive her there next week.

The excitement of the fire had subsided. But not for Hettie. She still had so many questions around it and the reactions and behaviour of so many of the household.

TWENTY-EIGHT

Hettie declined the invitation to participate in that evening's post dinner activity of tackling a particularly tricky jigsaw in the billiard room. When everyone else had settled into whatever they planned to do for the rest of the evening, Hettie let herself quietly through the vestibule and out through the front door. She decided against going to her room to collect her coat as that may draw attention and lead to questions about her plans.

It was a cloudless night. Pinpoints of bright stars pricked the inky blackness and the soles of Hettie's boots crunched in the gravel. When she came level with the stable gates, she saw that the lights were on in the downstairs room, indicating that Elliot was home. She could still picture his face earlier in the evening, searching the faces of everyone standing on the path. What had he been hoping to find?

Even before she saw the shell of the cart, Hettie smelled it. A charred stench lingered in the air and grew stronger the closer she got to its source. There was enough moonlight to see that the cart had been reduced to nothing more than charred pieces of wood. The hay which had blazed so brightly had burned away to almost nothing. What was left had been further covered with sand so that the whole thing looked like nothing more than a sodden rubbish pile. It was hard to believe that only a few hours ago it had burned so fiercely, threatening to set alight the gates to the walled garden which Hettie now passed through.

Picking her way carefully along the paths between the beds of earth, she was guided by the light coming from the window of the shed. She stopped at the door and took a moment before raising her hand to knock. In the short time it took for the door to begin to open, her body was flooded with sensations, which came to rest in her chest when she saw Rhys' face. He smiled at her. Without a word, he opened the door wider for her to step inside.

A fire was lit in the hearth but, unlike the fire outside, it provided a welcoming glow. Rhys closed the door behind her. 'You've no coat,' he said. 'You must be cold. Come, sit by the fire.'

He pulled out a chair at the table. Hettie took a seat, realising that she hadn't felt the cold at all on her walk from the house.

'I thought you might appreciate something a little stronger than tea,' Rhys said.

Hettie tried not to stare at him as he took two glasses and a bottle from a shelf. He sat opposite her at the small table. Hettie focused on the glass he put before her, desperate to collect her thoughts. For a moment, Rhys didn't speak, but Hettie knew he was looking at her.

'How are you?' he asked.

'I'm fine,' Hettie said.

'Really?' Rhys asked. There was concern in his voice and Hettie didn't want to be the cause of it. Her current state of being had little to do with the fire and lay almost exclusively in the man sitting before her. Had she been in a different place and had Rhys been a different kind of man, she would have had no fear or reluctance in telling him how she felt about him to see where it might lead them. But that was not a path she could follow with Rhys. He was nothing like the people from her normal life.

Raising her eyes, Hettie looked at Rhys. He seemed so at one with his environment with his relaxed appearance in a shirt open at the neck, his hair slightly messy. He looked at her kindly, a small smile at the corner of his mouth seeming to be an invitation for her to talk.

'Really,' she said answering his question that she had left hanging for too long. 'Once I'd had a bath, I felt much better.'

'And you're sure that your breathing hasn't been affected?' Rhys asked.

'Not that I've noticed,' Hettie said.

'Good,' Rhys said. 'The damage would have been a lot worse if you and Audrey hadn't tackled the blaze. It could have spread. As it is, only the cart was damaged.'

The questions that Hettie had wanted to discuss with Rhys had left her mind since stepping foot over the threshold of the shed. But at the mention of the cart, they returned.

'Have you ever known Audrey to tell a lie?' Hettie asked.

Rhys unscrewed the cap of the bottle. He poured a little of the amber liquid into each glass. 'Never,' he said. 'Audrey is about the most honest person I have ever met.'

Hettie shifted in her seat.

'What is it?' Rhys asked.

Hettie was going to ask if she could be honest with him. Because what she was about to say might shatter his impression of Audrey. But of the many people she had met in her life, she knew that Rhys was one with whom she could be candid. 'Audrey said something,' Hettie started. 'About the cart. Which only I heard. I'm certain that it was to protect the family and her sister.' She looked to Rhys for a reaction. He watched her but didn't interrupt.

'When we first came to tackle the fire,' Hettie continued. 'Audrey said to me that she had no idea why the cart had been moved from the stable yard. But then Rosemary kept asking about the source of the fire and whether someone might have set it on purpose. She began to grow hysterical. She even mentioned that ridiculous curse. That's when Audrey said that she had moved the cart to the position just outside the gardens. She said that earlier in the day she had been placing hay on the plants in the beds to protect them from the frost. That's when she said that a passerby had probably been careless with how they had discarded a match.' Hettie stopped. Again, Rhys didn't interrupt, but the worried look that crossed his brow earlier had returned.

'The two things can't be true,' Hettie said. 'It can't be true that Audrey knew nothing about the position of the cart but then suddenly said she had moved it. And if it's not true that Audrey had positioned the cart outside the gate to the garden, then it also doesn't make sense that it was an errant match that caused the fire. Which opens so many questions about who moved the cart and how the fire started.' Hettie placed her hands on the table. 'What if it was done on purpose? What if it has something to do with this intruder that Bertie has been worried about?'

Rhys rubbed his finger across his top lip. 'Have you said anything of this to Audrey or Rosemary or Katherine?'

Hettie shook her head. 'No. That would have meant calling Audrey a liar, which I don't think she is. I can only imagine she said what she did so as not to scare her sister. But that still means the fire could have been started on purpose.'

Rhys tapped his finger to his top lip slowly. When he removed it, he seemed to consider her for a moment. 'I have something I would like to talk to you about,' he said. He picked up his glass and Hettie picked up hers. She joined him in knocking back the drink in one. The Scotch warmed Hettie's throat on the way down.

Rhys picked up the bottle to refill their glasses. Hettie watched the muscles contract in his hands. The dark hair at the base of each finger. She tried to focus on their conversation but all she could think was that his hands were so strong. She would like to take photographs of them. The shadow and contours of flesh and muscle and sinew over bone. She would like to have them touch her.

'Down the hatch,' Rhys said. Once again Hettie joined him in downing her drink.

Rhys placed his glass on the table. He added a little more Scotch to each glass. He breathed in and out deeply. On his breath out, he said, 'I think we each know parts of a puzzle that, should we share our pieces, might come some way close to making a whole picture.'

The rhythm and rhyme of what he said and how he spoke so softly stoked Hettie's feelings. But she would not be put off what had to be done. 'I think you're right,' she said.

She looked into Rhys' eyes, and he looked into hers. It was as though they were weighing the trust they could put in each other. 'I had a confidence shared with me today,' Rhys said. 'If I share that confidence with you, I know that it will go no further. And the knowledge of it will only be used for good.'

It was a statement rather than a question, but Hettie felt that it needed an answer. 'You can be sure of it,' she said.

Rhys breathed in then out again. 'The intruder,' he said. 'He is not a stranger to the Mandevilles. The intruder may not be the intruder himself. The Mandevilles have a cousin. His name is George Caxton.'

'From Caxton Hall,' Hettie said. 'I heard you and Bertie talking last night. I shouldn't have been eavesdropping, but I heard my name mentioned.'

'How much did you hear?' Rhys asked.

'Everything,' she said. 'Including what Bertie and Elliot spoke about after you left.'

There was a risk that admitting to this might turn Rhys against her, but it was a risk she had to take since the Mandevilles might be in danger from Caxton or anyone he had sent to do his bidding.

'Will you share what you heard with me?' Rhys said. 'And I can share what I was told this morning. Do you trust me enough to do that?'

Hettie didn't have to think of how to reply. 'Of course,' she said.

'As I understand it,' Rhys said, 'Caxton was banished from his family years ago. His sister will not speak his name or have it uttered in her presence.'

'I heard that Caxton is in prison,' Hettie said. 'For crimes committed against the Mandevilles. And he has some kind of grudge against them. But he can't be the intruder if he is in a prison cell. And what does he have against the Mandevilles that he would attack people and try to ruin Sir Charles?'

'From what Bertie and Elliot told me today,' Rhys said, 'George Caxon is a thief, an extortionist, a blackmailer and kidnapper. There is even talk that he has murdered more than one man. But the crimes for which he is currently in prison do not extend to taking the life of another. So far, he has been too devious to be convicted for any crime for which he would swing.' Rhys paused. 'I'm given to believe that his vendetta against the Mandevilles began when he was a small boy and was directed at Captain Mandeville. Nobody knows why, exactly. But with Captain Mandeville around, Caxton was held at bay. When Captain Mandeville joined the army and went abroad, Caxton attempted to implicate Sir Charles in a financial scandal. After Captain Mandeville died Caxton was free to turn his attention to the rest of the Mandevilles. Until his father disowned him and sent him abroad so that his younger sister inherited the Caxton estates. George Caxton was in prison overseas and is now in prison here.'

'I still don't understand how he can be the intruder if he is in prison,' Hettie said.

'It's possible he is paying someone to act on his behalf.' Rhys looked at Hettie. He seemed to be searching her face. 'I can speak to you plainly and it will go no further?' he said.

'After everything I've told you, I think you can trust me,' Hettie said.

'There is something I am not being told,' Rhys said. 'Bertie and Elliot have only said enough to get me on side and to support them in watching out for and dealing with an intruder.'

'Why haven't they brought in the police?' Hettie asked.

'There's nothing to tell. No real proof.'

'Aside from the fire,' Hettie said.

Rhys shook his head. 'They seem to want to deal with this themselves. But I know facts are being withheld from me.' He rubbed his finger along his top lip. 'Something happened,' he said, 'More recently. Bertie began to tell me about another attack on Tommy by Caxton. Tommy was away at university but came home gravely ill. Bertie said that Caxton was behind it but that's where Elliot stepped in to stop the conversation. I think Bertie trusts me more than Elliot does. I thought he might trust me, being we have the same background in the military. But it seems he is as wary of me as he is of any man.'

'I don't imagine it's personal,' Hettie said. She wanted to reassure Rhys that Elliot had said only complimentary things about him. But that seemed wrong, somehow. Sharing facts to help the Mandevilles was one thing but sharing more personal information that she had overheard felt off.

Rhys pressed his fingertips to his chin. 'This afternoon, I was called away on an errand. I was told that the landlady of The White Lion needed some help. When I arrived, she had no idea what I was talking about. Bertie and Elliot were there too, having been called away from the house for other reasons that turned out to be untrue. When we realised, we rushed outside only to see the fire engine on its way here.'

'You think the person that set the fire called you all away under false presentences?'

'After what you said about Audrey telling a falsehood about the cart, I am sure of it.'

'You can't think that Audrey is involved,' Hettie said.

'I don't,' Rhys said. 'I think she said those things to Rosemary and Kate so they weren't worried. I know she spoke to Bertie earlier and I am sure it was to tell him the truth.'

'And if it wasn't the accident that everyone believes, then someone started that fire on purpose,' Hettie said.

Rhys nodded. 'Either as a warning or because they wanted to do real damage and harm.' He shifted in his seat. 'You and I are both only being told half of the facts. Half of the truth. Whether to protect us or to protect secrets, I cannot tell. But there is one thing that is clear. There is very real danger from someone. Someone started that fire. Someone has been sneaking around the cottage.'

Hettie thought to the cigarette stub in the ashtray. If she told Rhys about that, would she have to tell him about the strange writing and her other odd experiences and the daydreams of the two boys? No, those were flights of fancy, not the facts that Rhys was searching for to come up with an answer to who was behind this.

'What is it?' Rhys said, as though he had read her thoughts.

'I was thinking things through,' Hettie said.

'You would tell me if there was anything else?' Rhys said.

'I would,' Hettie said. And she would, if there was something sensible to say. To speak of her strange experiences would only muddy the waters. Rhys was looking for help in answering questions not to be posed with new ones.

'It's not for me to tell you what to do,' Rhys said. 'But would you consider letting me walk you to and from the cottage each day?'

Ordinarily Hettie would have answered such a suggestion by saying she did not need a chaperone. She had travelled around the globe alone. She could certainly walk a few hundred yards each day without the need for an escort. But there was something in Rhys' eyes that caused her normal way of thinking to leave her.

'If it would reassure you,' she said.

'It would,' Rhys said.

Hettie picked up her glass and took a sip. In attempting not to notice the bed in the corner over Rhys' shoulder, she noticed the crate that had been his makeshift chair beside the workbench under the window.

'You got another chair,' she said. It was a ridiculous thing to say in amongst the talk of kidnap and intruders.

'It was in the old storehouse,' Rhys said. 'I brought it over after your last visit, in case you wanted to call again.'

Hettie almost choked on a mouthful of Scotch. The thought that she should call on him made it sound as though they were in a Jane Austen novel. Rhys might be the model of military chivalry but her approach to an evening was far less traditional. What would Rhys say if he knew about her past and how she would ordinarily behave if she called on someone she felt a pull to?

'It's rather warm in here,' she said, pressing the back of her fingers to her cheeks.

'As it was designed to be.'

'Pardon me?'

'To heat the glasshouses on the other side of the wall.'

'Of course.' Hettie took another drink. She glanced at Rhys' hand around his glass. At his strong fingers and the tendons and muscles beneath his flesh. She finished her Scotch with one more mouthful. 'I should go,' she said, getting to her feet. 'I didn't let anyone know I was leaving the house. They might be worried if they go looking for me and can't find me.'

'Why would they go looking for you?' Rhys asked. It was a straightforward question but rather than giving a straightforward answer, all Hettie could say was, 'I don't know. They just might.'

'In which case, it is better that you go back. They have enough to worry about without adding to it unnecessarily. And especially as all you are doing is taking a drink with me.'

Hettie pushed the chair in under the table. There it was again. His mannered way of speaking. His gentlemanliness. Something about it only made her want him more. Turning from the table, she took the few steps to the door. Rhys had clearly risen too as he was behind her. 'You've no coat,' he said. He was speaking to the back of her head since she had not turned around.

'I'm fine,' Hettie said.

'Would you allow me to walk you back to the house?' Rhys asked. He was so close that Hettie could feel his breath on the back of her neck.

'There's no need,' she said.

'Will you let me walk you to the end of the path, at least?' Rhys asked. 'I can watch from there to make sure you get to the house with no trouble.'

'Really, there is no need,' Hettie repeated. It seemed that with every response, her voice was growing quieter.

'Please,' Rhys said. 'If only to keep my mind at rest that you are safe.'

Finally, Hettie relented. 'All right.'

She stepped aside and Rhys opened the door. The cold of the winter's night rushed inside.

'Are you sure you won't take my coat?' Rhys asked.

Hettie shook her head. Crossing her arms in front of her chest, she said, 'It's only a short walk.'

Rhys followed her outside and pulled the door to behind them. He walked beside her down the path. Hettie did not speak and neither did Rhys. The white moonlight lit their way and everything in the garden – the earth in the empty beds, the grass, the wires and canes waiting for the spring and regrowth – were all just shades of grey.

Rhys kept close as they walked side by side down the narrow path. He was so close that Hettie could feel his warmth. She swallowed and kept her eyes resolutely on the path before her.

As promised, at the gate, Rhys came to a stop. Hettie turned to face him. As with the garden, he was picked out in shades of grey. Shadows clung to the lines and contours of his face. Hettie had never seen him look more attractive.

'And you will you let me walk you to the cottage in the morning?' Rhys asked.

'If it will put your mind at rest,' Hettie said.

'It will.' Rhys smiled. 'What time?'

'Around nine,' Hettie said. 'After breakfast.'

'Very good,' Rhys said. 'I'll be outside the front door.'

'Thank you,' Hettie said.

They stood for a moment.

'I should let you go,' Rhys said.

'You should,' Hettie said.

'Until tomorrow then,' Rhys said.

'Until tomorrow.'

Hettie walked briskly along the path, all the while knowing that Rhys' eyes were following her progress. At any other time, she would have railed at a man wanting to look out for her when she had only ever looked out for herself. But she wanted him to see her. To watch her. She could try to convince herself that it was simply because she was reassured by his presence in the face of the intruder. But that wouldn't have been even half the truth. She wanted him to see her. And to want her. But she had no idea what type of person he would find attractive. She hoped that there was something in her that would be of interest to him.

Hettie paused when she came to the door of Hill House. She turned back. Anything beyond the stable yard was in darkness. But Rhys watched her still. She could feel it.

Voices came from the billiard room when Hettie opened and then softly closed the front door. She managed to go up to her room without disturbance. After closing the door behind her, she kicked off her boots but left the lights off when she stood in the window. In darkness, she pressed her head to the glass. Moonlight vaguely lit the land to the front of Hill House. Almost without realising, she turned to look down the path that ran parallel to the house, in the direction of first the stable yard, and then the walled gardens.

What a gentle man Rhys was. What a kind and considerate man. With his old-fashioned way of speaking. With that soft Welsh accent. That dark hair. Those dark eyes. Those strong hands.

Hettie kept her forehead pressed to the glass. For the first time, it seemed that it was not predominantly a person's body that interested her. With previous lovers, she had enjoyed conversations. She had been interested in the workings of their brains. But conversation had always been a prelude or a postscript to sex. What she wanted from Rhys went beyond that. She wanted to know him. Who was he as a person? He had been in the cavalry. He had fought in the war. He would have seen and survived all manner of horrors. Had he been brave? She was sure he had. He was the type of man who would have put the safety of others before his own safety. And would have worn his bravery lightly so that it seemed he did not wear it at all. As Thomas Mandeville had. Perhaps that was why she found Rhys so appealing. He and Thomas Mandeville were of a type. It made sense that since she had always had an affection for Thomas Mandeville that her interest should be piqued by a man who shared his qualities. But whereas she had seen Thomas as a much older brother, how she saw Rhys was very different. In the way that Rhys was very, very different to her last lover.

There he was, elbowing his way into her thoughts again. Gray. What she had felt for him – if indeed she had *felt* anything – was an obsession. Not with his mind or his personality. But with his body. She could have come to terms with what they had done in bed even though it had gone far beyond what she had ever done before. She had been a willing participant in their exploration of each other's bodies. It had been thrilling. It was only with hindsight that she burned with shame. She had allowed herself to fall under some kind of spell, becoming enamoured with what they could do to each other, with the pleasure she got from it and how hungry she had been for it. Pleasure was nothing to be ashamed of. Her body was hers to do with as she wished. But what she could not reconcile was Gray's betrayal. She might only have known previous lovers on a superficial level, but at least there had always been mutual respect. Gray had lied to her. About his job. About where he lived. What else might he have lied to her about? She knew nothing about him. Nothing. After meeting him in Pagani's, all he had revealed was his name – if indeed his name really was Gray – his job, that he liked to dance and drink whisky and smoke Astines. Beyond his job, he had never spoken of anything. The small talk they had shared centred on who he had driven in his employer's car. But it had all been a fabrication. The only thing she could be sure that she knew of him truthfully, was his body.

Hettie closed her eyes. She could convince herself that she had only fallen for Rhys as he was the opposite of Gray. But it was more than that. She felt an attraction to him on such a deep and profound level. Thinking of him, she felt herself smile. Was she imagining that he had stood closer to her that evening than he had before? Was he looking at her differently? Had he been more concerned about her safety following the fire than would have been usual as he had more feelings for her than were usual? Or was it an overwhelming case of wishful thinking?

Heat flushed Hettie's body and her face. She put her fingertips to her cheek and became aware of a movement on the roof of the portico. Sliding the window up, she leant out. There, sitting on the portico, looking up at her as though it were as natural as anything, was Stella, her eyes shining bright in the darkness.

'Hello, you,' Hettie said softly, her belly on the ledge as she leant out further. 'Are you keeping an eye on me?' she asked with a laugh.

Stella cocked her head to one side. Before Hettie knew what was happening, the cat had leapt from the roof to the ledge. It stood beside her and rubbed its chin on her arm. Hettie retreated inside the room. She rested her hands on the ledge and looked at Stella who still sat there. She really oughtn't to encourage it... 'Come on,' she said softly, stepping aside. 'It's cold out there. I'm sure nobody will mind.'

Stella jumped from the ledge into the room, the pads of her paws drumming gently on the carpet. She leapt onto the bed and after circling a couple of times, settled into a curl beside where Hettie slept. Hettie laughed gently. 'As long as you are out in the morning,' she said softly as she began to undress and place her clothes on the stool at the dressing table. She pulled her pyjamas gently from beneath her pillow to avoid waking Stella who was purring contentedly. She stepped into the thick cotton night clothes, crawled into bed and shivered against the cool sheets. She placed her hand on Stella's side and felt it gently rise and fall. Closing her eyes, she was presented with an image of the fire burning fiercely. It wound around the thought of an intruder sent by George Caxton, the image of an Astine stub in an ashtray, two small boys tussling in the back bedroom of the cottage, handwriting in her notebook. The thoughts circled each other, looping around and beginning again. In her half consciousness, Hettie kicked out and felt a movement beside her. Opening her eyes, she found that Stella had moved in closer so that she was curled into Hettie, her face resting on Hettie's shoulder. Hettie stroked Stella's soft fur, welcoming the warmth. Gradually, she began to slip into sleep to the rhythmic and reassuring sound of Stella purring in her ear.

TWENTY-NINE
APRIL 1876

Charles woke feeling as though he didn't know where he was. He looked around. He was in the room. In Harvey's Hotel. He let his mind wander back. He had returned from the mill as he was feeling unwell. There had been some beef tea and Monica had said that she would look after him. He took his pocket watch from the nightstand. It was three o'clock in the morning. His clothes were folded neatly on the chest of drawers in the window. He lifted his eiderdown and looked down at himself. He was wearing his night shirt but had no idea how he had undressed.

'Charles,' a voice said gently.

Charles looked to the armchair beside the hearth. 'Monica?' he said.

Getting to her feet, she stepped into the light created by the fire. 'How are you?' Monica asked quietly.

'I'm fine,' he said, resting on his elbows. 'Why...?'

'You were ill, and I looked after you.'

He looked down at himself.

'Don't worry,' she said. 'I put your nightshirt on you before I removed your trousers, I saw nothing.'

'Thank you,' he said, glad for the darkness making it less likely she would see him blush. 'I was ill?' he said. 'There was beef tea, wasn't there?'

Monica stepped a little closer to the bed and nodded.

The air in the room smelt like herbs. A memory came back to him. 'You've been here all night,' he said. 'But I don't remember much of it.'

He looked up into Monica's face. A tear glinted in her eye. 'Hey now,' he said. 'What's wrong?'

Monica shook her head. 'I'm just glad you are well.'

Pushing back the covers, Charles placed his feet on the floor. He felt a little unsteady as he stood. 'Was I very ill?' he asked.

'For a while,' Monica said.

'I don't understand.'

She touched his hand. 'I'll explain it all tomorrow when you are fully better.'

Her green eyes gazed at him. Her hand still touched his and he wrapped his fingers around hers.

'Thank you,' he said.

Without speaking, Monica leant forward and kissed him on the cheek. 'I can leave if you would rather,' she said. 'So that you can rest.'

He held her hand tighter. 'I would much rather you didn't,' he said. He leant in and kissed her. At first his lips just brushed her lips. When she responded, he dared to go further. He put his arms around her and held her to him. She put her hands in his hair, pulling him closer to her. Her lips were soft. So very soft. When they parted, they continued to look at each other.

'You are leaving tomorrow evening,' Monica said.

Charles nodded.

'I told you last night that I am always honest about my feelings.'

Charles nodded again.

'I've never felt about anyone the way I feel about you,' Monica said. 'My soul wants you. I want you.'

Charles swallowed. 'I feel the same. We've only just met, but I feel the same.'

They kissed again and when they parted, they were both breathless.

'I've never... before,' Charles said.

'Neither have I,' Monica said.

THIRTY

FEBRUARY 1937

It was already eight o'clock when Hettie woke. She sat up, stretched and smiled at the fire that had been lit in her room. She lifted the blanket on the bed and looked beneath it before hanging over the side of the bed.

'Stella,' she whispered. 'Stella. Puss, puss, puss!'

There was no sign of the cat. She must have snuck out of the open door when Rosemary crept in to make up the fire. Hettie grimaced. There was nothing she could do about it now. She would apologise if the cat was found in the house and had made a mischief of itself.

Hettie forced herself to get out of the warm sheets. There was still time for breakfast, if she hurried. But she didn't want to hurry. She took up a pillow and plumped it. She wanted to savour the hour before she was due to meet Rhys. She held the pillow to her stomach. Rhys. Such a Celtic name for such a Welsh man. She placed the pillow back on the bed and took up the blanket. She shook it out, folded it and placed it neatly at the foot of the bed.

They had shared a confidence last night about the possible intruder. But in the cold light of day, she wondered whether events might have seemed worse late at night than they really were. If there was an intruder responsible for poking around the cottage and even setting fires, he would be caught, since most of the household seemed to be on the lookout for him. And if Bertie and Elliot and even Audrey were colluding to keep secrets it was only to protect other members of the household. Bertie was certainly being very protective of Kate, and if Rosemary got the mere hint that something was amiss she would likely go into a spin. With Rhys on the side of Bertie, Elliot and Audrey, there would surely be no more trouble. And if there was, Rhys would be there to see off the intruder.

'I'm sorry you missed breakfast,' Kate said when Hettie entered the kitchen at just after a quarter to nine. Kate was at the sink beside Audrey, washing the dishes, with Lula helping Rosemary to clear the table.

Audrey turned to Hettie. 'I could put some eggs and bacon on for you,' she said, pushing her spectacles up her nose with her shoulder.

'I'm fine, really,' Hettie said. She could hardly expect Audrey to prepare her a breakfast when she had spent the last half an hour bathing and dressing. She was ready to leave, with her overcoat buttoned up and her satchel across her body. 'I'll get something at the cottage.'

'You're working today?' Kate asked. 'At the weekend?'

'I'm a bit behind,' Hettie said. 'I'd like to get on with everything that needs to be done.'

'Rather you than me,' Rosemary said with a glance at Hettie while she still scrubbed the table.

'Whisht!' Audrey said to her sister.

Lula, who seemed never to miss a thing, looked to the women. 'What is it?' she said.

'Nothing,' Kate said. 'I think Rosemary is saying that if she had the chance to take the day off, she would. That's right, isn't it, Rosemary?'

Rosemary made a grunting sound in reply.

'Will you be joining us for dinner this evening?' Kate asked.

'I plan to,' Hettie said.

'Audrey's making a hotpot,' Kate said. 'It's one of our favourites. You wouldn't want to miss it. And Daphne should be back from her visit to Miriam by then. Mind, I don't know how hungry she'll be after a fancy afternoon tea! She's that excited that she excused herself after eating barely a mouthful of breakfast.'

A piece of cutlery clattered to the floor. 'I'm sorry,' Lula said, stooping to collect the teaspoon and placing it back on the table.

'No harm done,' Kate said.

'Might I be excused?' Lula asked.

'Of course,' Kate said. 'How will you spend the day with Daphne away at Miriam's? Would you like to try another jigsaw? I'd be happy to help.'

'Thank you,' Lula said quietly. 'But I have some homework. I think I'll stay in my room and work on it. If that's all right with you.'

'Of course it is,' Kate said. 'But you just come to find me if you want some company.'

Lula nodded. She left the kitchen without looking again at any of the women. When her footsteps had disappeared along the corridor, Kate took a step away from the sink. She folded the tea towel in half and held it to her stomach. 'Poor mite,' she said. 'She's not herself today at all.'

Rosemary paused in scrubbing the tabletop. 'I'm not surprised. With that fire last night. It's that curse, I tell you—'

Audrey slammed a pan down in the water so that soap suds splashed from the sink. 'What have I told you?' she said to her sister. 'Do not talk like that in front of Lula. Filling her head with your nonsense and frightening the poor girl. Hasn't she had enough to cope with recently?'

'There was a fire, wasn't there?' Rosemary said, her voice rising. 'And nobody knows why it was set, do they? Tell me I'm not right?'

The sisters glared at each other.

'Hey now,' Kate said, her voice calm. 'Let's not be cross with each other. It was an accident. Hasn't Bertie told us that? And didn't the fire brigade say as much? We all did a grand job putting it out and that should be an end to it.' She shook out the tea towel. Taking a plate from the draining board, she began to dry it. 'I just think Lula is feeling a bit left out. You know how she looks up to Daphne. And how she follows her everywhere. I think she's starting to feel a bit lost with her cousin going out for the day.'

Audrey and Rosemary still stared at each other. It was Rosemary who spoke first. 'Sorry,' she said. 'I didn't think. I wouldn't say anything on purpose to upset Lula.'

'We know that,' Kate said. 'I think we should just try to be a little bit more careful with her today, that's all.'

Audrey turned back to the sink. 'You could make her some fairy cakes this afternoon,' she said. 'You know how they are her favourite.'

Rosemary took up the cloth and began to scrub the table again. 'I'll do that. Make her feel a bit better.'

Kate looked from one sister to the other before looking at Hettie and shrugging. It was clear that Kate was used to acting as referee for the sisters' bickering.

Up in the hallway, Hettie paused to check her reflection in the mirror above the fireplace. She checked the clock at the back of the hall. It was still before ten to nine. She looked towards the vestibule and front door. She didn't want to appear too keen.

Turning back to the mirror, the sight that met her gave her heart a jolt. She spun around. 'Lula!' she said. 'Whatever are you doing standing behind me?'

She was silenced by Lula pressing a finger to her lips before beckoning for Hettie to follow her. Hettie glanced at the clock again. She had a few minutes to spare.

Hettie joined Lula in the morning room. Lula stepped back into the hall and looked around. When she stepped back inside, she closed the door behind her. She looked up at Hettie with such seriousness in her face.

'What is it?' Hettie asked.

Again, Lula pressed her finger to her lips. She took Hettie's hand and led her to the far side of the room. When she spoke, it was still in little more than a whisper. 'Can I ask you something?' Lula said.

'Of course,' Hettie said, keeping her voice soft.

Lula still held Hettie's hand. 'Would you keep a secret if a friend asked you to?' she said.

Something inside Hettie told her to tread carefully. 'Has someone asked you to keep a secret?'

Lula's nose wrinkled. 'Not exactly.' She paused for a moment. 'Our grandfathers were friends, weren't they?'

'They were,' Hettie said. 'They were very good friends.'

'Are you my friend, Hatshepsut?'

Hettie smiled. 'Of course I'm your friend,' she said, squeezing Lula's hand.

'And we can talk about things?'

'Of course,' Hettie said. 'Did you want to talk about something now?'

Lula shook her head. 'Are you going to the cottage?'

'I am,' Hettie said. 'And are you going to do your homework?'

Lula nodded.

Hettie smiled at the little girl again. As Kate had said,

Lula was out of sorts since Daphne was heading out for the day without her. Lula had no doubt begun to think about a future without her cousin in it as much. 'I hope your day goes well,' Hettie said. 'I'd like to hear all about it at dinner tonight.'

Lula looked up at her with her big blue eyes. 'Thank you, Hatshepsut, I'd like that.'

Hettie gave Lula's hand a final squeeze. 'I'll see you later then, Lula.'

Together, they left the morning room and Lula only released Hettie's hand when she started to climb the stairs to her room. Hettie watched Lula until she disappeared at the top of the landing. What a dear little thing she was. And what a hard lesson it was that she was learning about people moving on and the feeling of being left behind. At least Lula was surrounded by a family and household that loved her and would help her through the transition in her young life. Besides, Daphne would be home from her tea with her friend later and Lula would feel a little less lost.

The long-cased clock chimed nine times. Hettie adjusted the strap of her satchel and straightened her coat. Heading to the front door, she gave herself a passing glance in the mirror.

'Good morning,' Rhys said when Hettie stepped outside. He stood beneath the portico, resting against the wall beside the door. As with every other day since her arrival, frost clung to the land of Hill House. And as with every other day, Rhys wore no coat over his blue sweater.

Hettie dug her hands into the pockets of her overcoat. 'I hope I haven't kept you waiting,' she said.

Rhys pushed away from the wall. 'Not at all. I only just got here.' He held his palm out to the path. 'Should we?' he asked.

Hettie nodded. She walked beside Rhys for a few steps before she said, 'Do you really not feel the cold?'

Their footsteps crunched in the gravel for a few moments

before she felt Rhys lean in a little closer. 'Do you want to know a secret?' he said.

Hettie tried not to grin. 'I don't know, do I?'

'It's a Gansey,' Rhys said.

Hettie glanced at Rhys. 'A what-sey?' she said.

Rhys laughed. 'A Gansey. It's a type of sweater that fishermen wear. They're knitted in a special way that keeps out the wind and the cold when the fishermen are at sea. My grandmother's family come from the coast and my great-aunts thought a man in the military could make use of the properties of a Gansey, so they knitted me a couple over the years.'

'Which is why you have no need for an overcoat?' Hettie said.

'Not often,' Rhys said. 'Ganseys aside, I run rather hot at the best of times.'

Hettie stared at her boots. It had been an innocent statement. Rhys could have no idea that his words had set light to the kindling already smouldering inside her. She needed to say something. Something to dampen her thoughts. 'You're the second person this morning to ask me to keep a secret,' she said.

'Oh?' Rhys said. 'Who was the other?'

'Lula.' Hettie paused. It dawned on her that Lula hadn't actually told her what the secret was. Instead, they had spoken about their grandfathers and how Lula would spend the day. 'I think she's a bit distracted with Daphne going to take tea with a friend today. She's feeling lost.'

Hettie could hear the smile in Rhys' voice when he said, 'Lula is a sweet little thing. Serious beyond her years sometimes. She must know everything I am doing when I work around the house. Oftentimes she insists on helping me. She will surely be a little lost without her cousin around.'

Hettie looked down at their boots walking side by side in the gravel. Rhys' boots were clean and polished but worn and used, with a life etched into the lines in the leather. Hers were almost new, bought on a rare trip to a department store with her mother just after Christmas.

'Have you had any further thoughts on what happened yesterday?' Hettie asked.

'The fire?' Rhys said.

Hettie nodded.

'George Caxton could be behind it,' Rhys said. 'It's possible that he has sent someone to cause trouble just for the sake of it. Until he is free and can make trouble himself.'

'Do you really think that a member of the Mandevilles' own family would be capable of harming them?'

There was a moment before Rhys said, 'I have seen much in my life. I know man to be capable of terrible acts on man, family or no. My concern is that, if there is an intruder, they felt bold enough to start a fire. But there are many of us looking out now and I am reassured that Bertie and Elliot felt able to share some of what they know with me, if not all. There are things kept hidden in all of us.'

Rhys stopped walking and Hettie came to a stop beside him. He looked down at her. 'I am not a man for skirting around a subject,' he said. 'And I have tried not to upset you since you arrived. I know of the events of last autumn. I know about your friend who was killed. If this is too panful a subject, I will go no further.'

Hettie let her focus drop from Rhys' eyes to the cable knit of his sweater. She hadn't spoken of what had happened that day in November to anyone other than to the police on that same day and to answer the questions of Saul's family. For four months, what she had experienced had lived only within her. She looked up at Rhys. There was such kindness in his dark eyes. 'My friend was called Saul,' she said. 'He was so young. So talented. And I miss him every day.'

Rhys still looked at her. 'What happened to Saul was not at

your hands. It was not your fault.' He spoke the words so gently that Hettie wanted to believe him.

'You are being very kind,' she said.

'I've had some experience of loss,' Rhys said. 'I know it does not feel like it now, but with time, you will begin to find a way to live with what has happened.' He paused as though to let his words sink in. 'Would you like to continue?' he asked.

Hettie nodded. She walked beside Rhys with just the sound of their footsteps and birds calling to each other from high in the trees. She focused on their boots. It seemed easy to walk beside Rhys without the need for words.

When they reached the gate of the cottage, Hettie pushed it open and stepped through.

Rhys remained on the pavement. 'Will you be all right?' he asked.

Hettie nodded. 'I have my work to keep me busy.'

'Very good,' Rhys said. 'Will you allow me to walk you back to the house when you have finished for the day?'

'I'd like that,' Hettie said. 'I usually finish when the light begins to fade, just after two o'clock.'

'Then you can expect me by then,' Rhys said. 'If you don't mind, I'll go round to the back alleyway and check all is right.'

'I don't mind at all,' Hettie said.

'You know where you can find me if you need me,' Rhys said. 'Until this afternoon, then.'

'Yes,' Hettie said. 'Until this afternoon.'

Hettie closed the gate. The latch clicked and she watched Rhys walk along the pavement and take the path round to the back of the cottage. Digging in her overcoat pocket, she pulled out the key and opened the door. It had barely closed when she ran up the stairs and pushed open the door to the back bedroom. She held the curtain away from the window. She watched Rhys place his hands on the top of the gate and give it a good shove. It didn't budge. Hettie watched his fingers slip from the wood. She watched him walk further along the alley, past the cottage next door, looking to the ground as though checking the cobbled path. Hettie stared at his thick, dark hair, from the novel angle of above, which was just as good as every other angle she had seen him from. She was so busy staring at Rhys that she hardly registered that he had turned and was heading back towards the gate. He stopped and looked up. Hettie dropped the curtain and stood with her back pressed to the wall beside the chest on legs. She put her palm across her eyes. Had he seen her? Quite possibly. She was behaving like a young girl in the grips of an infatuation. She placed her free hand on the top of the chest to balance herself. She was running the very real risk of making a fool of herself. But she couldn't seem to help it.

Staying pressed to the wall, Hettie kept her hand on the wooden chest. Unlike yesterday when she had opened its lid, she felt nothing and saw nothing. No images of a young Thomas bickering with an even younger boy, whose eyes seemed familiar, but she was unsure why. No imagined presence beside the fireplace that had terrified the boys and made them flee from the room. She had clearly slept better.

Down in the hall, Hettie hung her coat on one of the hooks at the bottom of the stairs. Taking her satchel through to the parlour, she placed it on the table beside her miniature studio and found that she was not alone.

'How the devil did you get in here?' she said to Stella, who was curled up on the chair before the hearth. The cat didn't move, even when Hettie stroked its ears. 'Did you sneak in when Audrey was setting the fires this morning? Naughty puss.'

She stroked the cat's ears again before turning her attention to the table. Her camera case sat on the floor beside the desk, her tripod was open and ready for her to place a camera on top, and her miniature, three-sided backdrop waited for the first object of the day to be placed before it. Hettie adjusted the angles of the hinges. Try as hard as she might, she couldn't stop thinking about Rhys' hands constructing this just for her. In his shed at the back of the garden. With the table – that now had two chairs should she want to call on him – and the workbench beneath the window. And the bed in the back corner...

No. No. No. She couldn't let her thoughts take her where they wanted to go, otherwise she would be no good for any work.

Focus, Hettie.

Job in hand, Hettie.

Sir Charles' collection, Hettie.

Picking up where she had left off, she crouched before the desk, opened the door and eased out the brown leatherbound ledgers. She placed them on the table and lifted the cover of the first book. And stopped. Where she had been hoping to find a record of Sir Charles' purchases for his collection, she found a page of newspaper cuttings. She turned the page and found a page from a magazine with accompanying photographs. Each page she turned led to another article and more photographs. And beside each article was a handwritten note of the publication from which it had been cut, along with the date. Each page held the record of a political rally or a march or a meeting across the last three years. Hettie sat heavily in a chair at the table. It was a scrapbook of sorts. A scrapbook of all the articles she had written since her very first commission. It charted her history as a photojournalist in a way she had never seen. But why? It was marvellous, but why had Sir Charles done this? She put her hand to her hair and laughed. There was a perfect and unintentional symmetry: Sir Charles had taken an interest in her work, which was her passion, and she was here to help catalogue Sir Charles' collection – the result of his passion.

Hettie got to her feet. She flipped the lid of her leather bag and removed her camera and a film. If she had known Sir Charles had been interested in her work, she would have visited him to discuss it. And she would have thanked him.

Hettie rolled the film onto the spools. She secured the camera on the tripod and with great care, took a vase down from the shelf. It was decorated with a cobalt blue mythical beast with wings and jagged spines. She placed it before the backdrop and adjusted it to best capture its detail. This would be her thanks to Sir Charles; to help his family understand his collection. Even though he would never know her gratitude, she would gladly play her part in helping this become his legacy.

Hettie continued to photograph items from the collection all morning, making the most of the sun that had made an appearance and burned through the icy fog. It had turned into a bright crisp winter's day with the perfect sharp light for photography. As well as Sir Charles' collection, Hettie took photographs of the parlour; how the furniture was arranged, the books on the shelves, the collection in its entirety rather than individually. At some point in the future, someone may want a reference for how Sir Charles had left everything.

Hettie did the same in the kitchen, taking photographs of the room as a whole before photographing the contents of the shelves, the layout of the furniture, even Sir Charles' supply of food and everyday crockery in the cupboard. After she had taken a photograph of the tinned fish on one of the shelves, she felt a familiar nudge at her ankles.

'Is that a hint?' she said to Stella. 'Did you see me at the fish shelf?' The cat closed its eyes and rubbed its head against Hettie's shins. 'You win,' Hettie smiled. Placing her camera on the table, she set about preparing Stella a meal of sardines with a bowl of water. She found a packet of crackers in a tin and a jar of potted beef, so sat at the table to join Stella for an early lunch.

Stella finished first and after washing her face with her paws, left Hettie alone to clear away their dishes. Hettie placed their crockery in the sink and had just turned on the taps when a crash came from the parlour. 'Not this again,' she said under her breath. She wiped her hands on the tea towel.

Hettie had been expecting to find the parlour empty. But the sight that met her made her laugh and then grimace. Stella sat on the rug before the shelves with a book open on the floor beside her. At least there was a reason for the noise this time. But it also came with the knowledge that Stella had been exploring the shelves and worry for what she might knock off next.

'Oh, puss,' Hettie said. 'I think I might have to put you out. These aren't my things. They are precious, and I can't have you damaging them.'

Stella looked down at the book. Worried that she might be about to use it as a plaything, Hettie stooped to collect it from the floor. It was a book bound in red fabric, with a cracked spine. It had fallen open at two pages illustrated by photographs of a large wooden structure – 'MacGregor's Sawmill – and the view of a paddle steamer at the jetty, dwellings, a shop and perhaps a hotel, all surrounded by trees. It had fallen open at the photographs of Simpson's Bay Settlement. Hettie looked from the book to Stella. It was the book she had looked at on her first visit to the cottage, and which had fallen to the floor and created the first noise she had heard. Hettie placed her hand on the space in the bookshelf where the book had been. Perhaps the shelf at that point was not level so the book was in the habit of slipping off. She ran her hand over the shelf, it seemed perfectly flat. She placed the book on the table.

'I'm sorry,' she said to Stella. She bent to scoop the cat into her arms, but Stella was too quick. She trotted out of the parlour and into the hall. Through the bannisters, Hettie saw her make her way up the stairs. Hettie followed and was halfway up when Stella disappeared into the back bedroom. Imagining the fate that might befall one of the delicate items, Hettie ran up the remainder of the stairs.

Unlike every other time Stella had taken up residence in a room, she was not curled on a chair, eyes closed, ready for sleep. Instead, she sat in front of the chest as she had sat beside the book on the floor in the parlour.

'Puss,' Hettie said. 'Puss, you really do have to go outside.' Hettie had taken just one step inside the room when Stella got to her feet. She curled around one of the legs of the chest. 'No,' Hettie said. 'You mustn't touch anything.' She dropped to her knees and tried to entice the cat with some encouraging noises. It did no good, Stella proceeded to wrap herself around another of the chest's legs and rubbed her chin against the carved wood.

Hettie got to her feet. She had been a fool to let Stella stay inside the cottage. She had encouraged her. The cat was getting bolder. Who knew what she might do next? Use the legs of the chest as a scratching post? Jump onto a shelf so that the beautiful butterfly incense burner smashed to the floor. Stella retreated further beneath the chest. Hettie knelt on the floor and reached for her, but Stella pressed against the back wall so that Hettie's fingers barely brushed her fur. She tried again and for the first time, Stella let out a hiss. It came as such a surprise that Hettie snatched her hand away from the cat and in doing so, banged her elbow with some force against one of the legs. The chest wobbled. Hettie heard a noise from inside. The bottle. Had she dislodged the bottle?

Still on her knees, panic churned in Hettie's stomach. She put the heels of her hands to the lid of the chest, pushed it open and looked inside. She breathed a heavy sigh. The bottle had moved so that it was half on its red cushion and half off. But mercifully it was still in one piece, its contents intact. Hettie paused for a moment and let her head hang forward as she took another breath. For something from Sir Charles' cottage to be damaged because of her actions was too awful to contemplate. She reached inside and put her fingers beneath the bottle so that she would gently ease it back onto its cushion. But the moment her fingertips touched the glass, a charge shot up her arm. It was cold. Bitterly cold, as though she had taken hold of a shard of ice. And with the sensation came an image. As bright and as vivid as the ice travelling up her arm.

Bertie, Elliot and Kate were sitting at a table. In a kitchen unfamiliar to Hettie but at the same time familiar. They spoke. Each looking so very serious.

'Does she know, do you think?' Kate asked.

'I shouldn't think so,' Bertie said. 'And I can't see how she is a special one. Why hasn't Tommy been called back if she is? I've never known one not to have a connection to someone in the household while they are here.'

'But do you sense she is one?' Kate asked.

Bertie nodded. 'I do. But I don't know why. And I can't see that the gift has passed from Tommy to anyone else. It just doesn't make sense to me.'

Elliot finished smoking a cigarette. He ground the stub out in an ashtray. 'She is one, you can be sure of that.'

'Then who is helping her?' Kate asked.

'That, I don't know,' Elliot said.

'Do you know why she is here?' Kate said. 'What she has been brought to do?'

Elliot drummed his fingertips on the table and shook his head. 'Not specifically.'

Kate looked from her husband to Elliot. 'Do you think we should try to get Louisa to come somehow? Or at the very least ask Mrs Hart to come back from London to help us?'

Bertie scooped his fringe from his face. 'We can't keep calling on them. We have to learn how to deal with these situations ourselves. Mrs Hart is getting older and should be allowed to rest. And you know that every time we call on Louisa, we are putting members of the family at great risk.'

'He's right,' Elliot said. 'We must face this ourselves.'

As suddenly as the scene had appeared, it disappeared. Now Hettie was in a restaurant. It was loud and lively and filled with voices and the sound of glasses chinking. She was sitting at a table with her friends. They were laughing and talking and smiling. It was Pagani's. She would have known it anywhere. Her friend was wearing the hat that had been admired by so many and that she had received for her birthday. That was last June. Hettie remembered it so well. She looked past her friend to the bar where a man stood. He was alone. The barman served him a large whisky. Neat. He smoked a cigarette. He stared at their table. He was oblivious to Hettie watching him. He wasn't watching them. He was scrutinising them. He was glaring. He was sneering. As though he detested them. He ground his cigarette out in the ashtray on the bar and immediately lit another with a match from a matchbook the barman handed to him. Not once did Gray take his eyes from the party at Hettie's table.

Hettie snatched her hand away from the bottle. She ran from the room and down the stairs. Without thinking about where she was going, she pushed open the door to the kitchen and ran inside. With one hand around her waist and the other clasping her forehead, she paced to the window and back again, to the window and back again. She stopped but had to restart immediately. She gripped her hair. What was happening?

Still holding herself, she left the kitchen and paced the length of the hall. To the front door and back. To the front door and back again. Had Bertie, Kate and Elliot been talking about her? If they had, what did any of it mean? She stopped and gripped her hair again. Of course, they weren't talking about her, because none of what she had just seen and heard had actually happened. Something was happening to her that made her see things. What was it about that room and that bottle that had created that image? Perhaps the question should be what was happening inside her so that she had these waking dreams of people from Hill House and Gray. Gray! Why? Why was he here, plaguing her thoughts again? Plaguing her imagination. The events of that evening last June that she had summoned were accurate. She had been at Pagani's on Great Portland Street with her friends. There had been much admiration of the new hat. There had been quite a few bottles of Chianti. But Gray hadn't been there. She hadn't met him until the end of September when he had approached the table and said that after seeing her, he had been compelled to act spontaneously. If he had been at Pagani's in June, he would have made himself known to her, wouldn't he? Especially as he had been watching her and her party so intently. But the look in his eyes wasn't the flirtatious look that he'd had when he first approached her in September. What could have changed between June and September? Because standing at the bar, he glared at her as though he hated her.

Hettie ran into the parlour. She peered into the ashtray on the mantelshelf. There was a single Astine stub in there. What had she been expecting? Another to have appeared? She didn't have the chance to answer her own question as the sound of a door closing came from outside. Through the parlour window, she watched people walking down the path of the cottage next door. Bertie, Kate and Elliot. They walked together to the gate and left the garden.

Hettie sat heavily in a chair. She rested her elbows on the table and held her head in her hands. The kitchen in her dream had seemed familiar as it mirrored the kitchen in this cottage. She sat up and tried to steady her breath. Four breaths in, four breaths out. Four breaths in. Four breaths out. Logic. Logic was what she needed to focus on. She could not see through walls, so she had not seen Bertie, Kate and Elliot. They had been in the cottage next door. Hadn't she thought only a few days ago of how noise travelled in an odd way in old houses? If Bertie, Kate and Elliot had been in the cottage next door talking, the sound could have travelled to her. Perhaps the unexplained noises since her arrival had been made by Bertie or Kate next door. Whatever was happening with these waking dreams had taken the overheard words and made them into a nonsensical conversation. Dreams rarely made sense, even those that occurred at their rightful time at night. And nothing the three had said made any sense to Hettie. Talking about the 'one,' whatever that meant. And special visitors. It was gobbledygook. As was the dream about Gray. He had been pushing himself into her thoughts whenever the opportunity presented itself. Hadn't she always hated situations without resolution? Whatever had happened between them would never be resolved.

Four breaths in.
Four breaths out.
Four breaths in.
Four breaths out.

Finally, logic elbowed its way in to take the place of panic. She very obviously wasn't herself. Her parents had made her go to see the doctor when she returned from London. He had treated her from the day she was born and explained that he thought the events in her life had led to nervous exhaustion. He prescribed a course of pills that she had not taken. Perhaps she should have taken them. If she had a broken bone, she would have welcomed a cast and a sling. Perhaps when she returned to Cambridge, she would go to see Doctor Kendal and ask whether waking dreams or hallucinations were a symptom of nervous exhaustion. If so, she might give in and take the pills.

Back in the kitchen, Hettie took a glass from the cupboard, filled it at the tap, and took a long sip of water. Cold raced to her brain. It felt just like the sensation she had experienced when she touched the bottle in the chest. The water came directly from the freezing pipes outside. Perhaps there was a draught in the back bedroom that had sent the icy blast up her arm. Perhaps her dreams were a reaction to the cold. She would ask Doctor Kendal whether that was a possibility too.

Hettie took up the dish brush and washed the crockery that she had abandoned on her wild goose chase up the stairs. Taking up the coal scuttles in the kitchen and then the parlour, she made up the fires, before returning to the kitchen to wash her hands. She collected her camera from the table where she had left it before lunch. She wound the film on and was deciding what to photograph next when she was joined in the kitchen by Stella. The cat headed for the saucer of water on the floor. She seemed unbothered by what had passed upstairs. Hettie placed her camera back on the table. She bent and rubbed her fingers together, making encouraging noises. 'Sorry,' she said to Stella. 'I don't think the book falling from the shelf was your fault and I didn't intend to scare you upstairs.'

Stella stopped drinking. She spent a moment cleaning her face and then rubbed the side of her face against Hettie's hand. 'Friends?' Hettie said. Stella rubbed her face on Hettie's hand again.

A knock at the front door made Hettie stand up. 'Are you expecting visitors?' she said to the cat. She hadn't quite left the room when Stella jumped onto the chair before the fire and made herself very comfortable.

Hettie opened the front door and a different set of emotions from fear and confusion charged at her, fairly knocking the wind from her.

'Rhys?' she said.

'Hettie.' He smiled. His intonation rose at the end of her name as though mirroring her use of his name as a question. 'It's two o'clock,' he said. 'If it's not a good time, I can come back later to walk you to the house.'

'No,' Hettie said, one hand holding the door open, the other still on the lock. 'I mean yes, it's a good time. Sorry.' She shook her head. 'I got a little sidetracked.'

'It's been a busy morning then?' Rhys said.

'Very. Sorry,' she said, opening the door wider. 'Please, come in.'

Rhys wiped his boots on the doormat and stepped into the hallway. He brought the cold in with him, and it made Hettie shudder.

'You are full of apologies this afternoon,' Rhys said.

'Sorry, yes,' Hettie said. 'I've been a little distracted. I haven't achieved all that I wanted to today.'

'There's always tomorrow,' Rhys said.

Hettie had her back to Rhys as she closed the door but was sure she could feel him watching her. 'I haven't packed up for the day,' she said.

'I am in no rush.' Rhys said. 'I can wait in the kitchen if you would rather have me out from under your feet.'

'No, it's all right,' Hettie said. 'Please, go through to the parlour.'

She followed Rhys along the short passageway. She stared at the collar of his white shirt beneath his sweater. His Gansey. She stared at the space where his dark hair ended, and the shirt began. At the bare flesh between the two.

Rhys came to a stop just inside the parlour. He turned to her. 'How have things been today?' he asked.

'Sorry?' Hettie said.

'Any sign of an intruder?' he asked.

'Sorry,' Hettie said. 'No, no intruder.'

'Are you sure nothing untoward has happened today?' Rhys said. 'You do seem a little distracted.'

'I am,' she said. 'A bit.'

'But you are all right?' Rhys said.

'I am.' Hettie said the words with conviction. She didn't

want to worry Rhys unnecessarily. As far as events at Hill House were concerned – the possible intruder and the fire – there was nothing for him to be concerned about. The events that had left her a little off kilter were the events in her mind.

'I see you've found Sir Charles' collection of cuttings,' Rhys said.

'You know about them?' Hettie asked.

Rhys opened the top book and looked down at the first page. 'Sir Charles watched your career keenly,' he said. 'He was interested in your work highlighting injustice. As a member of parliament, it was of great interest to him. And I think he felt that as your grandfather had passed, he wanted to take on his friend's role in some way by making this collection for you. He knew how interested I was in politics, so he shared them with me.'

'I had no idea,' Hettie said.

'It was his intention to talk to you about it at some time,' Rhys said. 'But it was not to be. Life sometimes interferes with our plans. It is a lesson to us all. We none of us know how long we may have or what is to come. Every day should be lived, and every opportunity acted upon.'

Hettie's thoughts turned to the kind man who had held her hand when she had been admitted to his conservatory. And his kind son on the other side, holding her other hand. She swallowed.

'I'm sorry,' Rhys said. 'It wasn't my intention to upset you.'

Rhys' dark eyes looked at her with such kindness.

'I'm not upset,' Hettie said. 'So much has happened in the last few days and I don't... I...'

'You can be sure of one thing,' Rhys said. 'You are loved by this family. Your whole family is loved by this family. And if you can be helped through the trying time you have faced recently, then know that every member of this household will be there to aid you.' He closed the book and pointed to the frame. 'How is that working for you?' he asked.

'Very well,' Hettie said, relieved to talk about something other than herself.

'Do you need me to make any adjustments to it? Or is there anything else that I can make that would be of use?'

'It's perfect,' Hettie said. 'Would you like me to show you how I use it?'

Rhys rubbed his chin between his thumb and forefinger. 'And that wouldn't be giving away any trade secrets?' he asked.

Hettie laughed. 'Not at all. There are loads of us up to this photography lark. One more let into the secrets of our dark arts won't bring our profession crashing down.'

Rhys laughed. His eyes shone. 'Then I would very much like to see how all of this works.' He circled his finger over the tripod and the frame and Hettie's leather bag on the rug.

'I'll be just a minute,' Hettie said.

She collected her camera from the kitchen and paused in the entrance to the parlour. Between the gap in the door and the frame, she watched Rhys examining the tripod, testing the components to see how it worked. All she could do was watch his dark hair. The way he bent forward with his hands on his thighs, examining the tripod. The presence of that man in the parlour made her calm, even if standing beside him, or the simple act of thinking of him, set her pulse charging. There was a depth to him. He had lived a life. He would have witnessed events in his time in the military that she couldn't comprehend. If he ever wanted to talk of it, she would love to write a piece on him. And she would love to take a photograph of him. Just as he was in that moment. Unposed. With his fringe slightly in his eyes as he leant over. The concentration on his face.

Hettie blinked and captured the image behind her eyelids that she would take of him. But she couldn't imagine a time when she would ask to write about his experiences. The thought of causing him even a moment of pain at remembering, or embarrassment at declining her request, wasn't something she could bear. He had lived through and seen so much and yet remained a kind soul. She wanted to protect that.

Rhys adjusted the height of the tripod and then returned it to the exact position in which she had left it. That man knew nothing of what he was doing to her. He was oblivious to how he made her feel. How she was being so reserved that she didn't declare herself and take him to that bed in the shed warmed by the fire. But even more than that, he had no idea that he was helping her find her way back to herself – because that's what he was doing. In his presence she felt more herself than she had in months. Lust aside, she was connecting with her photography again. Thanks to the frame he had fashioned for her and his kind and considered words.

Taking a deep breath Hettie stepped into the parlour.

Still bent over and with his hands still on his thighs, Rhys said, 'This is a fine bit of engineering.'

Hettie placed her camera on the table. 'It is,' she said. 'I spent a lot on it but quality costs.'

'Indeed, it does,' Rhys said, straightening up. He glanced at the red cloth book on the table. 'I didn't have you down as interested in the logging business in Canada.'

'I have many interests,' Hettie said.

Rhys raised his eyebrows, and his dark eyes shone again. 'It's appropriate in many ways,' he said.

'How so?' Hettie asked.

'Sir Charles travelled to that part of Canada. That's when he took an interest in its industries. As I understand it, his father had investments there. As did your grandfather's father. Your grandfather and Doctor Kenmore's father travelled with Sir Charles on that first trip.'

'Doctor Kenmore's father?' Hettie said. 'I had no idea.'

'They went before Sir Charles started his officer training at

Sandhurst. He used to regale me with of tales of their adventures on trains across America and scrapes in Mexico and Argentina. That's where your grandfather helped Sir Charles begin this collection.'

'I would be so interested to hear those stories,' Hettie said. She thought to the globe in her father's study and the old pins sticking from its surface. 'I know my grandfather travelled widely as a young man but not what he did.'

'Then one day, we will sit down with a bottle of wine, and I will tell you all that Sir Charles told me.'

'I'd like that,' Hettie said. She took up her camera. 'Would you like me to show you how I make use of the frame?'

'I would, very much,' Rhys said. He stepped away from the tripod and Hettie took his place. She put the camera on the table so she could check that each leg of the tripod was firmly locked. Taking up the camera again, she attached it to the plate. Once she was sure everything was secure, she turned to Rhys. He watched her intently. Hettie took a foo dog down from the shelf closest to her. She placed it on the table within the frame and adjusted the hinges to make the white fabric taut.

Hettie stepped back. 'Would you like to take a look?' she asked.

Rhys manoeuvred past Hettie. With the camera set up, there was very little space between the table and shelves. She was so very close to him. 'You look through there,' she said.

Rhys leant forward and looked into the view finder.

Hettie switched on the lamp behind them so he could experience her full set up. 'You can adjust the shutter speed by turning the dials at the front,' she said. 'Give it a go if you'd like to.'

'That won't spoil the way you have everything arranged?' Rhys asked.

'I can reset it,' Hettie said. 'I do it all the time. Touch

anything you like; I have to adjust it each time I take a photograph.'

Taking her at her word, Rhys began to explore the mechanisms of the camera. When he had finished, he turned to her and smiled. 'What is this ornament I'm looking at?' he asked.

'It's a dog of foo,' Hettie said. 'They were protectors of ancient Chinese emperors. They're not really dogs at all; they're lions.'

Rhys stood up straight. 'And his partner is on the shelf,' he said.

'They always come in pairs,' Hettie said. She turned to the shelf and took the pair for the dog positioned before the frame. When she turned back, Rhys was standing directly before her.

'See,' she said, quietly as he stood so close to her. 'It's a match.' She handed the ceramic to Rhys and her fingers touched his warm hands.

'I see,' Rhys said, his voice as quiet as Hettie's. 'They have each found their partner for eternity. And the strength lies in that partnership. Together they form a protective bond.'

Hettie swallowed. 'Something like that.'

Rhys placed the dog before the frame and beside its partner. He took a moment to consider the ceramics before he turned back to Hettie. 'Thank you for sharing your work with me,' he said.

'It was my pleasure,' Hettie said.

They were so close that when Hettie moved her hand, it touched Rhys' hand again. When she made to take it away, he brushed her finger with his thumb.

Still, they looked at each other and Hettie felt like Rhys was searching her soul. She took his hand, and he closed his fingers around hers. His breathing seemed to come a little faster than it had. Matching hers. His eyes moved as though taking in the details of her face.

'Hettie...' he started. But whatever Rhys had been about to

say, disappeared with a knock on the window. Their hands slipped from each other's. Hettie joined Rhys in looking through the window. There, staring at them, was Lula. When she saw them turn to her, she pressed her hands to the glass.

'Whatever can the child be doing?' Rhys said. 'She is outside and without a coat.'

Hettie raced into the hall with Rhys beside her. She opened the front door. Lula stood on the doorstep, shivering. Hettie put her arm around the small girl's shoulders. 'Whatever are you doing here?' Hettie said, attempting to usher Lula into the cottage.

Lula resisted. 'I can't,' she said. 'You must come.'

Lula's voice quivered. Her teeth chattered. But it seemed to Hettie that the cause was more than just the cold. From her wide eyes searching both Hettie and Rhys, Lula was quite clearly terrified.

'Come,' Lula implored again. 'Please.'

'Step inside for a moment,' Rhys said. 'You can surely tell us what is to do just as easily by the warmth of the fire as standing out in the cold.'

Lula allowed Hettie to guide her into the parlour while Rhys closed the front door. All the while, Hettie felt Lula shake almost uncontrollably. Once before the warmth of the hearth, Lula looked up at Hettie and Rhys. 'The secret,' she said. 'I cannot keep it. It's not right. You must come.'

Lula looked from Hettie to Rhys. Rhys got down onto his haunches. 'What secret is this?' he asked gently.

Lula looked to Hettie. 'The bad man,' Lula said. 'The bad man is here.'

Hettie felt her blood run cold. 'What bad man, darling?'

Tears sprang to Lula's eyes and her lips began to tremble. 'He's been coming. I've seen him. I wanted to tell you this morning, but I couldn't.' Tears spilled down her cheeks.

Hettie took Lula's hands in hers. They were freezing. She

rubbed Lula's soft skin as she said, 'You are not in any trouble, if that's what you are worried about. Just tell us. It must be terribly important for you to come here without your coat.'

Lula nodded. Her eyes wet with tears, she said, 'He was here the night of the fire.'

Hettie sensed Rhys tense beside her. 'Who, Lula?' he said. 'Who is this man?'

Lula shook her head. 'I don't know. But he frightens me.'

Hettie held Lula's hands tighter. 'You are with us now; you don't need to be frightened anymore.'

'Where is he?' Rhys said. His voice was calm, gently coaxing.

'He is with Daphne.'

It took all Hettie's self-control not to squeeze Lula's hands still further. The ferocity would have given away her panic. She glanced at Rhys. The look on his face held a mirror up to hers.

'Where are they?' Rhys said. His tone was still gentle but there was a strain in his voice.

Lula shook her head. 'Daphne will be so cross with me,' she said. 'She doesn't know that I followed her when she went with the man a few nights ago. I heard them say that she wasn't going to Miriam's today as Miriam's mother is ill. Daphne had Bertie drive her in the car today. But she only pretended to go inside the house. Really, she slipped away. I heard her and the man arrange to meet. And then the bad man kissed her.'

The blood froze in Hettie's veins. The new dress that had been bought with the intention of making Daphne appear so much older. Her coyness and blushing. The lies told so she could meet whoever this man was. These were all terrible, terrible omens. 'Tell us where they are, Lula,' Hettie said as gently as she could. 'I promise with all my heart that you won't be in trouble. You will be helping Daphne very, very much.'

Lula looked from Hettie to Rhys one last time. 'At the

boathouse,' she said. 'Daphne is meeting the man at the boathouse.'

Hettie and Rhys ran from the cottage. Rhys ripped off his sweater and placed it over Lula. In just his shirt, he had her jump onto his back. He ran with her like she weighed nothing, his sweater hanging from her slight frame as though it were a dress for a much older child. Hettie kept pace with him as they ran out onto the pavement, through the gates of Hill House and up the drive. Neither spoke. All their energy, they put into running as fast as they could. If their unspoken words had found a voice, Hettie knew that they would both have said the same thing; if Daphne was with the intruder, then she was in grave danger. As they ran, all Hettie could think was that precious young girl, on the cusp of becoming a woman, was rushing into a peril she could not have imagined.

THIRTY-ONE

Outside the doors of Hill House, Rhys crouched to let Lula down from his back. He took the girl's hands in his.

'Now, little one,' he said. 'You run inside and find Bertie or Kate. If you can't find them, go to Audrey and Rosemary. Tell them to telephone the police to come right away to the boathouse. Tell them that Rhys has asked you to do this, and they will know why.'

'Have I got Daphne into terrible trouble?' Lula asked, her lips trembling again.

'No, Daphne is in no trouble at all,' Rhys said.

'Then why must the police be telephoned?'

Rhys took a breath. 'Why, you said so yourself that the man who Daphne is meeting is not a nice man. I want to get the police to come and speak to him. Maybe see him off. Now, you run inside as fast as ever you can and alert the first grown-up you see. You can do that, can't you?'

Lula nodded.

Rhys smiled at her. 'There, you are ever such a clever child. Now go! Run!' He released Lula's hands, and she made directly for the front door.

Hettie watched Lula disappear inside. 'Shouldn't one of us go with her to explain what is happening?'

'Whoever she tells will certainly know that this has to do with the intruder,' Rhys said. 'We don't know what is happening down at the lake. It's best we go together. You and I can run faster than anyone else in that house.'

Without another word, they set off, down the path, past the stable yard and the walled garden. They were soon running on the gravel path between the fields and woodland. Where the trees ended and gave out onto the edge of the lake, Rhys put out his arm to slow Hettie. They stopped just a hundred or so feet from the boathouse with its jetty jutting out on stilts over the lake, the winter sun sparkling on the waves.

'We can have no idea what we will see,' Rhys said in little more than a whisper. 'Would you like me to go in first?'

'I'd like to do whatever is best for Daphne,' Hettie said.

'Follow me,' Rhys said. 'Lula may have somehow got it all wrong. If we are lucky, they are sitting inside talking and this is not the intruder.'

'I hope that's the case,' Hettie whispered.

'As do I,' Rhys said. He pressed his finger to his lips. 'Stay silent for now,' he said.

Hettie followed Rhys and slid down the grassy bank onto the sand surrounding the lake. Waves lapped at the shore and Rhys indicated for her to crouch slightly to make the most of the cover provided by the bank. They had barely gone ten feet when a cry came from the boathouse. It was a cry of fear. They stopped. 'Daphne,' Hettie whispered.

Rhys beckoned for her to continue. He picked up his pace, and Hettie matched him. Just short of the boathouse, a cry came again. It was followed by angry words in a deep male voice. Hettie was ready to run through the door of the boathouse to tackle whatever was happening inside. Again, Rhys put his hand out to stop her. He shook his head and pointed to a spot on the wooden panelled wall beside the single window. She stood in the spot where he pointed, her back to the wooden wall, attempting to make herself as invisible as possible. Rhys made his way towards the window. He stood to one side. Slowly, very slowly, he moved so that he could see through the very edge of the window. He immediately dipped away and stood with his back to the wall beside Hettie.

Another cry came from inside. A scuffle and a male shout.

The look in Rhys' eyes made Hettie want to scream.

'We've got to go in,' he said. 'Are you sure you can do this?'

Hettie nodded. 'I'm sure.'

Rhys took her hand and gave it a squeeze. 'Follow my lead as much as you can. If you sense that you are in any danger at all then please, I beg you, run.'

'I will,' Hettie said.

Staying close to the wall, they skirted the side of the boathouse until they came to the door. The only other doors were those that opened at the far end to give boats access to the lake.

'I'll try the lock,' Rhys whispered.

Hettie watched Rhys attempt to push the door. It didn't move. He took hold of either side of the frame, leant back and with great force kicked the door. The ancient wood around the lock cracked and splintered and the door flew open. Rhys ran inside and Hettie followed him.

The sound of a scuffle came from the far end of the building, beyond two boats covered by tarpaulins. 'Stay back,' a man shouted.

Hettie couldn't see anybody. Rhys began to push his way past the boats that crowded the small space.

'Stay back,' the man shouted again. 'I've got a knife.'

Rhys came to a stop and Hettie stopped behind him. There came the sound of muffled cries, but Hettie still couldn't see anyone. She wanted to run past Rhys to get to Daphne. But she had to trust that Rhys knew what he was doing. They stood halfway into the room, between one of the boats and the wall. There was a movement at the far end. The first thing Hettie saw was the green of Daphne's dress, but she couldn't see Daphne's face. All she could see were flashes of green. The man had his back to them. He wore a dark suit and a dark overcoat and clearly had hold of Daphne. Daphne began to struggle. Her arms flailed. Her hair hung loose about her. The man began to drag her, and Hettie saw that the green dress was ripped up the sides. Daphne struggled again and twisted around so that for a moment she was visible from the front. The dress was further ripped, exposing her under things and naked stomach and legs. Hettie made to run to her, but Rhys put his hand out to block her path. 'He might really have a knife,' he said.

Daphne lashed out. The man was determined to hold onto her. 'Stay still, you bitch,' he shouted, but Daphne managed to spin around so that she faced Hettie and Rhys. The man's hand was forced over her mouth, his other arm clamped around her, attempting to keep her arms to her sides. Kohl and lipstick were smeared across Daphne's face. The look of absolute fear and pleading in her eyes set every nerve in Hettie's body into action. She clasped her hands into fists and at the same time mouthed the words. 'It will be all right, Daphne. It will be all right.'

'She's just a child,' Rhys suddenly shouted. 'What do you want with her?'

'What do you think I want with her?' The man said. There was as a sneer in his voice.

Hettie felt as though her heart stopped in her chest. Everything was confused. Everything was wrong.

Still with his hand across Daphne's mouth, the man began to drag her towards the doors leading out to the jetty, her bare feet sliding across the floor. He was no longer able to hide his face. As she saw his features, Hettie nearly lost her footing.

'Gray...'

'There she is,' Gray said, his tone goading. He paused in dragging Daphne, as though wanting to bask in the recognition. 'Hello, Hettie. Well, isn't it a great pleasure to see you? I might embrace you, but as you can see, I rather have my hands full.'

Daphne made a noise and Gray clasped her mouth tighter, forcing her head back. 'Shut up!' he said.

Hettie looked to Daphne and then back to Gray. 'Why are you doing this?' she said.

'Why not?' Gray laughed. He looked to the side of Daphne's face. He kissed her on the cheek. She tried to pull away and he grasped her even tighter. 'Why wouldn't I want to enjoy some nice fresh flesh?' he said. 'I would have had it, too, if you two hadn't come barging in. The photographer and the groundsman. What a match made in heaven. Oh,' he said. 'Didn't you know I've been watching you both?' He looked up to the ceiling in an exaggerated way. 'Oh, that's right, you did. Fixing that bolt on the back gate and locking the door tight all the time. No more popping inside to watch you doze before the fire.'

'The Astine,' Hettie said. There was more of a tremble in her voice than she wanted.

'In the ashtray?' Gray said. 'I hoped you'd find it. I couldn't be certain you'd taken the hint with the matchbook – you are a bit slow, after all. I rather liked leaving the Astine. Like a calling card, don't you think? I hoped it would bring you pleasant memories of our time together. Because I've barely given you a moment's thought since I left that last time. I did think setting that fire last night and sending you all into a spin might be a step too far. I hadn't planned it, but it was too good an opportunity to miss! And what a flap you all got into about the mystery intruder. Although Hettie never minded me intruding on her before.'

Gray stared at her but Hettie would not give him the satisfaction of looking away.

'She couldn't wait for me to knock at the door of that dreadful flat above the delicatessen,' Gray said. 'Any time, day or night, she was ready. And very, *very* willing.'

Gray looked to Rhys. 'You do know I've had her, don't you?' He formed his mouth into a surprised sort of fashion. 'Now our Hettie here is *very* adventurous. The things she let me do to her. It would make you blush. I've known chorus girls more prudish than Hettie! They would never have let me do those things to them over and over and over again.' As he repeated the words, he looked Hettie directly in the eye.

Hettie felt Rhys tense beside her. The veins in his hands stood proud as he balled them into fists. He glared at Gray but still he said nothing.

Gray turned back to Rhys. 'You know, my meeting Hettie wasn't an accident. I had been following her for months. All in the name of surveillance, you understand. She was making rather a nuisance of herself with the activities of the Union. We couldn't let her carry on without punishment.' He laughed. 'The silly woman had no idea. She thought we met by chance. That the stars aligned that night at that restaurant. Did you have no idea that I had been watching you for months?' he said to Hettie. 'Did you think it was love at first sight?' His voice dripped with sarcasm. But she had to take it. Because for as long as he directed his bile at her, he wasn't hurting Daphne.

'We knew you liked *those* kind of clubs. A few in our number recognised you from your time in Berlin.' Gray paused and stared at Hettie, his eyebrows raised. 'Cat got your tongue,' he said. He grasped Daphne tighter, making her cry out.

'We've got to do something,' Hettie whispered to Rhys.

'The longer we can keep him talking the more likely it is we will get reinforcements.'

'Hey, hey, now, what are you two gossiping about?' Gray turned his attention once again to Hettie. 'So, you can talk to him but not me? That's rude, don't you think?'

Oh, she wanted to be rude to him all right. She wanted to grab him by the throat and brutalise him as he was brutalising Daphne. 'Why are you doing this?' she said, gripping the tarpaulin covering the boat closest to her.

'Come on, Hettie,' Gray said. 'Be a little more original, can't you?'

Hettie gripped the tarpaulin tighter. She hated the sound of her name coming from his mouth.

'Haven't any of you guessed?' Gray said, looking from Hettie to Rhys. 'Why are you all so dim? My father said this whole family and household is unhinged. He saw it when he was at your precious cottage when he was a boy. He said he saw either a ghost or an odd woman standing in the corner of a room waiting to scare people. He was convinced you had locked a woman away up there. Perhaps a mad aunt! The Mandevilles are all stupid. As is anyone who calls them a friend. Which includes your grandfather, Hettie.' Gray's tone changed. There was a dark edge when he said, 'My father had it all sorted out. With what he had set in place that buffoon Charles Mandeville would have been ruined. But your grandfather had to get involved. He scuppered my father's plans by advising Mandeville. And thanks to them dripping poison over at Caxton Hall, my father was banished from his family without a penny to his name. The Mandevilles are behind this. The fault for everything I have done lays at their feet.'

'Caxton has no children,' Rhys said.

'It speaks!' Gray said. 'And you can see me, can't you? So I exist. Sex does occur outside of marriage, if you didn't know. As does conception.' He pulled Daphne closer. Tears dripped down her face. 'I would do this one for free. But her,' he said, nodding dismissively to Hettie, 'the Union had to pay me handsomely to bed that one.'

It was all Hettie could do not to tear the tarpaulin from the boat and charge at Gray. Anything she might have once felt for him was turned to hatred. He would use Daphne as a pawn, as he had used her. She sensed Rhys beside her. She looked into Daphne's terrified eyes. Her legs shook. Her arms shook. Her hands gripping the tarpaulin shook.

The sound of a car engine came from outside. 'Ah,' Gray said. 'I see the cavalry has arrived.' He took a step towards the ramp leading down to the doors to the lake, dragging Daphne with him. He kicked the doors. A chain rattled and a padlock fell to the floor. The doors flew open. A small boat with a motor bobbed on the water outside. 'You didn't think I would come without an escape plan, did you?' he said.

Gray manhandled Daphne again, attempting to bundle her into the boat. She kicked out and her screams tore at Hettie's heart.

'He has no knife,' Rhys said. Without another word, he ran between the boats. He launched his body into Gray. Gray stood no chance against the bigger man. He lost his grip on Daphne and they both tumbled to the floor.

'Get up, Daphne,' Hettie shouted. 'Run!'

She wanted to go to Daphne, but Rhys might need help to contain Gray who was lashing out while Rhys attempted to pin him to the floor.

Clasping her ripped dress, Daphne ran down the side of the far boat. The sound of the car grew louder. Rhys fought with Gray. Rhys pressed down on Gray's chest as Gray lashed out trying to land punches.

'Bastard!' Gray shouted.

Rhys managed to grip Gray's wrists and pin them to the floor. Gray kicked out and shouted again. Hettie ran to Rhys and saw Gray reach for the padlock, no doubt to use as a weapon. His fingers had almost touched it when Hettie brought her boot down on his wrist. There was a crunch and Gray screamed out.

'You bitch!' he yelled.

Hettie kicked the padlock away. Her heart punched at her ribs as the door at the back opened. Bertie and Elliot called to them. Hettie looked around. Audrey was there. She put her arms around Daphne and led her away.

Grabbing Gray by the scruff of the neck, Rhys pulled him to his feet. He kept hold of the back of Gray's collar, holding his wrists tightly. Gray made a sound as though Rhys grasping his wrists had hurt him. But Rhys didn't loosen his hold. Hettie stepped aside. Rhys pushed Gray towards Bertie and Elliot. They waited in the door blocking any escape Gray might try to make. But as Rhys shoved him, Gray managed to stop for a moment when he was level with Hettie. He leant in as close as he could to her.

'Shame about your little Jew boy,' he said.

He smirked and nodded. Hettie shook. She pulled her arm back. She brought it forward and punched Gray square in the face. There was a crunch. She punched him a second and a third time. She would have done it again had someone not taken hold of her arm to stop her.

THIRTY-TWO

All that afternoon, Hill House was full of police officers questioning every member of the household. Hettie sat in the dining room at the makeshift desk the police inspector had made of the long table. She was asked to recall all the details of that afternoon and all the events that she suspected may have involved Gray in the last few days. She was questioned on her relationship with him. She held nothing back. If he was to be brought to justice for what he had done to Daphne and what he might have done had he not been found, then the police needed to know everything. She saw raised eyebrows from the younger constables taking notes, but it didn't stop her.

Daphne had been taken to hospital to be checked over and Kate had gone with her.

The kitchen was busy with Audrey and Rosemary providing a running tea for the police constables and everyone in the house. Lula had been left in their care. Fortunately, she had stayed with Rosemary and Kate when the other adults jumped in the car and drove to the boathouse, so she had been saved witnessing what had happened to her cousin. At every opportunity she was showered with praise for raising the alarm about the intruder so that he had been caught and could do no more harm. She had been reassured that Daphne was well.

Hettie helped in the kitchen. She boiled the kettle and sliced bread for sandwiches. At every lull in activity, she paced the length of the basement corridor, from the door to the outside to the steps leading up to the staff passageway and back again. On a couple of occasions, she burst into the empty butler's pantry to punch and kick a heavy door. When the news finally came that Daphne was fine apart from a few scratches and bruising, Hettie excused herself. She stumbled up the back staff stairs, through the hidden door and along the first-floor corridor to her room. She collapsed onto the bed. She clutched her knees to her chest and rocked as she sobbed.

In the early evening, a car pulled up on the drive. Hettie watched from her bedroom window as members of the Mandeville family spilled out into the light cast on the gravel from the downstairs windows. The children had been kept in London with their grandmother and great-aunt, so it was Sir Edward, Alice, Doctor Kenmore and Charlotte who rushed inside.

The activity in the house made so many memories flood back to Hettie; of the night the police officers knocked on the door of the delicatessen on Leman Street; of the police questioning of the events of that afternoon; of a desperate family concerned with the welfare of their child. But the Mandevilles had been spared the devastation of the Bessers: Daphne had been saved.

Gray's final words to her as he was taken from the boathouse repeated over and over in her head. It was hard enough to hear that he had played her. That she had been foolish and naïve and had let her lust rule her head. Every single one of the times they had spent together had seen a pay packet at the end for him. The thought that she had wanted him in her darkest hours made her want to be sick. He had been in the pay of the fascists to collect information on her activities. The most he could ever have gleaned from their conversations was that she attended meetings and rallies of all political sides to capture them on film. As a journalist, she at least had been sensible enough not to give specific details of her assignments. But the thought that made her want to scream out was the possibility that – since he was one of the fascists himself – he had been in Aldgate that day in November. Had he in some way been involved in Saul's death? It had been the only question she asked the police inspector when he finished interviewing her.

'I shouldn't think so,' the inspector said. 'Men like Graham Caxton always want the last word. I should imagine he said it to get precisely this reaction from you. It was his parting shot. But rest assured, we will report it to our colleagues in London to see whether they want to investigate further.'

Just after the arrival of the family, Hettie undressed and crawled into bed. When Rosemary was sent up to say dinner was ready and the family very much wanted her to join them, she refused, saying she had a terrible headache and if they didn't mind, she needed to go to bed to sleep it off. She would rather not be disturbed for the evening.

Hettie lay in bed, staring at the ceiling. She knew that it was only delaying the inevitable. The family would want to see her in the morning, and she would have to replay the events of the day. She had heard a whispered conversation outside her door earlier when two women she recognised as Alice and Charlotte had been tempted to knock so that they could thank her for the part she had played in saving Daphne. It was only when a male voice intervened that they decided against it. Doctor Kenmore told his wife and sister-in-law that Hettie should be left alone. She would speak to them when she was good and ready.

Hettie watched the headlights of a car trail bright stripes across the ceiling. They were accompanied by the crunch of gravel. She hadn't even known Gray's name was Graham. She hadn't known he had been following her. She hadn't known that he was linked to the Mandevilles through George Caxton. She hadn't known he was one of Mosley's men. According to the police inspector, he had been attempting to disrupt her activities in photographing the rallies. The fascists had been watching her for years. Gray had wheedled his way into her bed so that he could find out information from her. But the death of Saul had put a stop to it. She was too risky to be around since the police were sniffing about the delicatessen on Leman Street.

Hettie continued to stare at the ceiling. She knew it was more than that for Gray. He might have been in the pay of Mosley, but he had the added benefit of her connection to the Mandevilles through her grandfather. How pleased he must have been when he was the one to hoodwink her. How gleeful.

And how Rhys must hate her now since her tawdry past had been exposed for all the world to see. What kind of woman would find her pleasure in a man like Gray?

Hettie curled her knees into her chest and pulled the blanket over her head. But almost immediately, she pushed it away and sat up. She looked at her watch on the nightstand. It wasn't even a quarter past eight. There was no chance that sleep would come. Pushing the covers away, she dressed in her sweater and trousers. After pulling on her socks and boots, she opened the bedroom door. She made her way to the secret door on the landing and descended the stone steps by the light of the unshaded bulbs.

In the basement corridor, she passed the kitchen and heard the chatter of Audrey, Rosemary and Kate. Letting herself out of the door at the very end, she stood for a moment on the steps. A light from inside illuminated the small area. There, right there, just in front of the first step had been the matchbook from Pagani's. She had failed to recognise it and link it to Gray. Unlike the Astine, which she had linked to him and then dismissed as her imagination. Hettie put her hand to her forehead and gripped her hair. Had she made the connections and told someone, perhaps he would have been caught before he could lure Daphne away and attack her.

At the top of the stairs, Hettie turned left, guided along the path by the moon. Shadows crossed the light coming from curtained windows. The Mandevilles who had returned from London were in those rooms, talking, worrying about what had happened to Daphne. They would be questioning whether they were to blame. It was the way when someone was hurt. Questions, questions. Questions with no answers. Could I have done something differently? If only I hadn't done that. If only I had been there.

Passing the conservatory, Hettie couldn't bear to look up, in case saw herself reflected.

Walking down the side of the house, she wrapped her arms about her. Frost had already begun to form on the grass. Her breath hung as a cloud in the air. She hadn't given enough thought to leaving the house in the cold with no clue to where she was going. She hadn't given enough thought to anything today.

At the front of the house, she walked in the shadows, avoiding the rectangles of light from the windows in the gravel. An owl called in the trees. She glanced up. When she looked down, she saw a cloud of breath beside the portico. Her own breath caught in her chest. Her muscles twitched, ready to flee, until she remembered with relief that it couldn't be Gray.

A figure in darkness pushed away from the wall. It wasn't until they stepped onto the drive that Hettie saw who it was. Her breath caught in her chest again.

'Hettie,' Rhys said.

She shook her head. 'No,' she said. 'No.'

Rhys took another step towards her. 'What do you mean "no"?'

'I can't,' Hettie said.

Rhys took another step so that he stood directly before her. She wanted to run but her legs refused to move.

'Come to the shed,' Rhys said, his voice low.

Hettie shook her head.

'Please,' he said.

Hettie stared at the ground.

'You would be doing me a great favour,' Rhys said. 'I've waited out here in the hope of seeing you. Even my Gansey is not keeping me warm.' There was a sad laugh in his voice. Hettie looked up. Rhys was staring down at her. 'Will you come with me?' he asked.

Hettie walked beside Rhys past the stables. She could feel him beside her. Feel his presence. His life had spilled into hers. But it was hopeless. She felt her lip begin to tremble. Pretending to brush her hair away from her face, she wiped the corner of her left eye.

In the walled garden, frost glittered on the earth. An orange light glowed from the window of the shed. Rhys held the door open, and Hettie stepped through. Once inside, she stood in the shadow beside the door.

'Come to the fire to warm up,' Rhys said.

Hettie stepped closer but kept her arms wrapped around her. She stared into the flames.

Rhys stood beside her. His shoulder touched hers and she closed her eyes.

'It's been quite the day,' Rhys said. 'How are you, Hettie?' he asked.

She shook her head.

'I wish I could take back what you had to go through today,' he said. 'I wish I could have stopped him before...'

Hettie felt the tear fall onto her hand. She swiped it away. Before she could wrap her arm about herself again, she felt her hand taken.

'But you are frozen,' Rhys said. Holding her hand in his, he brought it up to his chest and pressed it to him.

The pace of Hettie's breathing increased. Rhys' hand was on her hand. His flesh on her flesh. She turned to him. He put his arms around her. She leant into him, and he held her, one hand on her lower back, the other between her shoulder blades. The gentle pressure of his palm pressed her to him. She closed her eyes, her cheek against his shoulder, her arms around his waist. Her face grew warm from the fire and her closeness to Rhys. Her breasts pressed to his chest, separated only by layers of yarn. She felt the heave of his chest. He held her closer still. Hettie moved her face so that her lips came to rest beside his cheek, his stubble on her flesh. Blood rushed to the surface of her skin. It rushed through her body. Her mouth dried. She wanted him. He pulled her closer, one hand still on the small of her back, the other between her shoulders. So tender. She wanted him. But she shouldn't. She was here because of what had happened to Daphne. Because of what Gray had done. What he had said. And now all she could do was want this man. To feel him with her.

Hettie pulled her arms from around Rhys. She took a step back.

'Hettie?' Rhys said.

Without looking at him, she turned around.

'Only he is responsible for what he did,' Rhys said.

Blood rushed to the surface of Hettie's skin again. But it felt different. She spun around. 'Do not pity me!' she said. 'Do not make excuses for me.'

'There are none to make,' Rhys said.

'No?' Hettie said. The single word sounded like an accusation. 'If I hadn't been here, he wouldn't have done those things to Daphne. If I hadn't let him do those things to me, he wouldn't have tried to do them to her. He was playing it out to goad me, can't you see?'

'You are not responsible for his actions.'

Hettie clasped her forehead. She paced from the fire to the door. 'I should have seen it. There were clues. He made it bloody obvious. But only to me. With that cigarette and the matches. I was too busy, too wrapped up in myself.' She stopped and stared at Rhys. 'What sixteen-year-old girl buys a dress like that to wear to tea with a friend? And Lula! She tried to tell me this morning and I didn't listen. I should have seen it. The danger. I should have seen it.'

'Only he is responsible for what he did.'

'Oh, you're right,' Hettie said, aware that her words dripped with sarcasm. 'He's responsible for what he did. Which makes me responsible for what I did, doesn't it? What a fool I have been. What a fool I have made of myself.' She forced herself to look at Rhys. And the instant she did, she laughed. It was a harsh laugh and directed at herself. Because in that moment, she wanted only to grab Rhys and feel his skin against hers. To give herself to release. 'I have made it worse. My being here has made it worse. Don't you see? He might have set fires or any number of things in the name of his father. But attacking Daphne... That was personal. Because he knows what kind of a woman I am. What I like. What I do. Don't you understand? I have sex with people. I enjoy it. He knows the kind of life I lead. And he used it against me. And against the Mandevilles.'

'Hettie—' Rhys started but she silenced him by holding up her hand.

'I have to go,' she said. As she made to leave, Rhys took a step towards her, he held out his hand as though to comfort her.

'Don't touch me!' she said. 'Don't ever touch me.'

Hettie grabbed the handle of the door and pulled it open. The cold welcomed her into the night as she ran through the garden. Whether Rhys followed she didn't know, as she didn't look back. Her breath came thick and hot as she ran down the path and raced past the stables. But at the side of the house, she came to a stop. She couldn't go charging inside and disturbing the Mandevilles and their household. She was supposed to be in her room. She had no right to disturb them more that her presence already had. They wanted to thank her for saving Daphne when she had no right to be thanked for anything.

Easing down the side of the house she opened the door of her car and got inside. She held her head in her hands, gripping her scalp. She kicked out so that her boots slammed down on the pedals. She fumbled for the keys, which were in the ignition. She could drive away now. Drive back to Cambridge. But that would make her a coward. It would be the coward's way out to flee and not face up to what had happened. She clenched her fists. And then unfurled her fingers and brought her hands crashing down on the steering wheel. Once, twice, three times. She clutched her face and kicked out again. She pulled her hands away from her face and stared out at the dark trees. Everything, everything tangled into an impossible mess. Saul, Gray, Daphne, Rhys. Her breath stuck in her chest. She tried to take a breath, and it stuck again. She clutched the steering wheel. Tears fell on her hands. A sob made her gasp. And then another sob. And another. And another.

THIRTY-THREE

Rising before the house was awake, Hettie dressed in darkness. Rather than take the grand staircase down into the hall, she left the landing through the secret door. Without turning on any light, she gripped the wooden bannisters and used it to guide her way down to the ground floor. She pressed her hands to the walls to feel her way along the network of passages until she came to the shallow set of steps leading down.

Doors stood open in the basement kitchen and the moonlight coming in through the windows was enough for her to see her way along to the door at the end. She opened it carefully and closed it gently behind her.

Climbing the steps to the path at the back of the house, she looked up to see that no lights were on in any room, since it wasn't even five o'clock.

Picking her way around the house, she paused to look into the conservatory. If she saw her reflection, so be it. She was too tired to care. Everything inside the glasshouse was dark – the plants, the leaves, the ivy trailing up to the ceiling. It was difficult to believe that it had been only a couple of days since she had looked into the conservatory and remembered that happy time as a small child when she had been in the company of her grandfather, Sir Charles and Thomas. She dug her hands into the pockets of her overcoat and caried on around the path, walking slowly down the drive.

The police had asked that they not disturb anything in the cottage. It had been too late in the day to conduct a search for anything that might incriminate Gray after they had questioned everyone, and they would return in the morning.

Hettie stood at the gate and looked to the windows. The lamp was still on in the parlour, as she had left it. The police hadn't specifically said that it was forbidden for anyone to go inside. And she had no intention of touching anything Gray might have. Pushing open the gate, Hettie took the key from her pocket and turned it in the lock.

It was darker inside than she had known it and colder, since the fires had all died out. She dared not make too much noise. Since the family had come home, Bertie and Kate had returned to their cottage next door.

Hettie navigated her way through the hall to the parlour. Standing just inside the room, she stopped to take in the details. The frame on the table with the dog of foo standing before it. Her camera on its tripod. Her large leather bag open on the rug, her satchel beside it. Just before the knock on the window had sent them running from the room, she and Rhys had stood behind that tripod, she had held his hand, and he hadn't recoiled. Last night he had held her. He had tried to console her, and she had thrown it back at him with her hysterics. What must he think of her now?

Hettie glanced at the ashtray on the mantelshelf. There was no doubt in her mind that Gray had been in the cottage at the same time as her. Rather than attack her, he wanted to terrorize her with the thought that he had been in the room with her while she was unconscious in sleep and could have done anything to her if he chose. And if he had done it once, he would do it again.

Hettie wanted to take a brush and scrub her flesh and mind, scouring away every trace of Gray. But as hard as she tried, she would never be free of the memory of his hands on her. Of what he had done to Daphne. And the question mark over whether he had been involved in Saul's death.

Hettie sat in a chair at the table. She should leave and go back to the house. She should hide away in her room until she was allowed to pack her equipment and leave. It would be best that someone else come to catalogue Sir Charles' collection. Hettie placed her hand on the cover of her notebook. She had catalogued the parlour, at least. And had taken contextual photographs of the downstairs. Opening the book, she flicked through the notes on the ceramics. She would affix the photographs once they had been developed. She came to the double page blank except for the lines she had scribbled while she slept.

Thomas knew
Gray is not a stranger

The meaning behind the words was still unclear. What was Thomas to Gray apart from the son of the man Gray's father had attempted to ruin? They were related through George Caxton.

And then it hit her.

The other boy in her daydream. The younger boy who had tried to grab the bottle and was stopped by Thomas. She had recognised the horrible look in the younger child's eyes because it was the same as the look in Gray's eyes. And there were other similarities in the face. That younger child had been Gray's father, George Caxton. Had the event in the bedroom upstairs contributed to that hatred George Caxton felt towards Thomas and the Mandevilles?

Hettie shook her head. Her mind was running away with her. She flicked over the page. And stopped. The double page behind the strange message had been blank. She knew it as she had turned to the pages further on to continue her cataloguing. But there, in the same hand as the first message, was a second:

Elliot
Bottle
It is his

As Hettie read the final word, she felt her senses come alive. She felt it in her skin, her scalp, the fire in her cheeks. Someone was watching her. But she knew if she looked up, she would be alone. Even though she wasn't alone. The presence was here again. At her shoulder. Was it the same presence that had frightened George Caxton and Thomas? Had it somehow manifested into a physical being when George tried to grab the bottle?

The pages in the notebook fluttered as though blown by a breeze. Hettie pushed the chair away from the table. The pages blew again. They came to rest open at the original message. 'Thomas knew'. What did he know? Had he known his cousin intended to steal the bottle? The pages fluttered again. Hettie stared at the words. The presence moved. It stood in the doorway. Watching. Waiting. Hettie flicked the pages to read the new message.

Elliot
Bottle
It is his

Staring at the words, Hettie felt she had to say something. 'The bottle is Elliot's?' she said. 'The bottle in the chest?'

The pages fluttered as though in response.

'Do you want me to take it to him?'

The pages fluttered again.

Hettie put her hand across her mouth. None of this made sense. But so many things didn't make sense anymore. Who was she to deny this was happening? The police had said not to disturb anything in the cottage that might implicate Gray. But that bottle had nothing to do with him, other than his father had tried to steal it.

Hettie looked to the door. There was nothing to see. But she felt it. Still watching. Still waiting. Pushing back the chair, she got to her feet. She passed into the hall and felt the presence behind her. Like a shadow, it followed her up the stairs, onto the dark landing and into the back bedroom. She should be scared. But she wasn't.

The moonlight through the open curtains helped Hettie see. The lid of the chest beside the bed was open, just as she had left it after following Stella into the room, before she had heard the voices next door and saw the scene in the kitchen play out, as she had seen Gray watching her in the restaurant months before they had even met.

The presence moved. It stopped just behind Hettie. She saw it like a shadow from the corner of her eye. She crossed the room and stood before the chest. There, sitting on its cushion, was the bottle containing the twigs, the leaves, the dried flowers, and the two locks of hair. Lifting the bottle gently from its cushion, she felt the presence behind her, watching. She placed the bottle on the soft eiderdown. Removing a slip from one of the pillows, she placed the bottle inside and wrapped the slip around it to create a protective case.

Holding the bottle flat so as not to disturb the contents, Hettie turned towards the door. The presence moved. It stood beside the fireplace. Hettie stopped. She looked – really looked – but could see nothing. Until she blinked. In the second her eyes closed she saw a young woman with long dark hair held back from her face in a single plait. She wore a working dress with a thick pinafore over the top, woollen stockings and heavy boots. But it was her face that Hettie saw brightly. The young woman was beautiful. So natural, with green eyes and pale skin. She smiled at Hettie. Hettie opened her eyes and the woman disappeared.

THIRTY-FOUR

It wasn't even seven o'clock when Hettie knocked at the door of the stables. She clutched her satchel to her. Inside was her precious cargo, wedged in place by her notebook.

Footsteps came from inside. A bolt slid across. The door opened. Elliot looked her up and down. He stepped aside. Hettie followed him along the cobbles, past stalls where horses snuffled at bags suspended from the walls. The warmth of their bodies heated the air, joining the sweet smell of hay. Hettie followed Elliot into a room at the very end with an old dresser, an armchair, a small table and chairs, and many shelves and racks full of saddles and equipment Hettie imagined was for horses. Elliot's Jack Russell was curled up on a rug before the fire.

'Tea?' Elliot said.

'Thank you,' Hettie said.

Elliot nodded to one of the chairs at the table and Hettie sat down, placing her satchel gently on the floor.

She watched Elliot go about the business of preparing the tea, using water from a kettle suspended over the flames. He took two chipped mugs down from the mantelshelf and poured the scalding water onto tea leaves in a pot. He didn't speak and his manner didn't invite conversation. He sat down at the table and poured milk from a jug into each mug. He poured the tea and pushed a mug across the table to Hettie.

'The police who questioned that bastard said he was bragging. He's just like his father.' Elliot's lip raised to reveal his eye tooth. 'Just like George Caxton to get an actress in trouble and then deny any connection to the child until he was old enough to be of use to him.'

Taken aback by the sudden statement, Hettie said, 'How do you know all this?'

Elliot stood. He took a tin down from the mantelshelf. He sat again, removed the lid, and took out a cigarette paper and a pinch of tobacco. As he rolled the cigarette, he said, 'I drink with one of the constables.' He licked the edge of the paper, ran his fingertips along the cigarette and placed it between his lips. He took a lighter from the inside pocket of his jacket hanging from his chair and lit the cigarette. He drew the smoke deep into his lungs before blowing it out. 'Caxton finally agreed to let the son visit him in prison three year ago. He's been priming him since then to do the business that he can't as he's inside. Them both joining the fascists was an easy way for them to hide in a gang.' Elliot took another deep draw on his cigarette. 'Your grandfather was a good man. Without him and his advice and loyalty, this place would have been lost.'

Hettie looked down into her tea. 'I had no idea until yesterday.'

'Heroes often hide their good deeds. Only cowards shout about themselves.' Elliot took another draw on his cigarette.

It felt to Hettie that there was a finality to Elliot's words as though he was bringing their conversation to a close. He hadn't even asked why she had come to his door in the early morning. She took a sip of the strong tea, trying to find the words to explain why she was about to hand him a bottle full of dried foliage.

'Was there summat in particular you wanted?' Elliot said.

Hettie shifted in her seat. 'I have something,' she said. 'That I think might belong to you.'

Elliot looked up from his tea. With one eyebrow raised, he said, 'Oh?'

She thought again about how to present the information. 'Have you ever been to Sir Charles' cottage?' she asked.

Elliot ground his cigarette out in an ashtray. He paused before he said, 'He used to come here when he wanted to talk to me. The cottage was too fancy for me to want to go in often.' His words were always spare, but there was something sombre in his response.

'I'm so sorry,' Hettie said. 'I didn't mean to upset you.'

Elliot got to his feet. He stared into the fire. 'Say what you came to say,' he said.

Hettie collected her satchel from the floor. Placing it on the table, she carefully removed the bottle still wrapped in the slip. Making sure to keep it level she unravelled the fabric. She placed the slip on the table and rested the bottle on it. 'I think this belongs to you,' she said.

Elliot turned from the fire to the table. When he saw the bottle, he took a step back, his eyes wide. 'Where did you get that?' he said.

'I'm sorry,' Hettie said. 'If you'd rather I took it—'

'No!' Elliot said. And then, more kindly, he added, 'Where did you get it?'

'From Sir Charles' cottage. It was kept in a chest. I think it must have been very precious as it was kept so safely.'

Elliot sunk into his chair, never once taking his eyes from the bottle. 'I hoped all these years, but I didn't dare to dream.'

Hettie watched him. He seemed a changed man. Uncertain rather than surly. 'So, it is yours?' Hettie said.

Elliot nodded slowly, staring at the bottle. 'And it was in Sir Charles' possession, you say? You're sure of that?'

'It was in his cottage with all the things he held so dear,' Hettie said.

Elliot breathed out sharply. 'She said it would be brought to me,' he said. 'She said whoever brought it could be trusted.' Finally, he looked at Hettie, with something akin to a smile. 'You are indeed special. You are indeed one.'

They were the words she had heard from Bertie and Kate's cottage. 'I don't know what that means,' she said.

Elliot nodded. 'Know that this house needed you as much as you needed it. And know that there will never be a person more grateful to you than I.'

Hettie tried to find the meaning in his words. She shrugged and smiled.

Elliot rose from his chair. He collected a wooden box from the mantelshelf. Retaking his seat, he placed the box on the table. He removed the lid, put it to one side and pushed the box to Hettie so that it sat beside the slip. Hettie looked inside. She looked up at Elliot and she saw a softness in his eyes she had never seen before.

She looked again at the contents of the box. It was an exact replica. She looked from the bottle in the box to the bottle on the slip.

'My mother made them,' Elliot said. 'One for me. And one for my father.'

Hettie raced through the new facts. 'Did he know?' she said.

Elliot shook his head. 'No. It was best. It was my mother's decision not to find him and tell him. He had a life that was important to live. But my mother told me that I would find out the identity of my father after he passed. I missed out on nothing growing up. My mother loved me more fiercely than a thousand fathers ever could.' He paused. 'But I couldn't be prouder to be the son of such a man. I see now why my mother encouraged me to join his regiment and was so pleased I became his batman. He had no idea.'

'What will you do now?' Hettie asked.

Elliot opened his tobacco tin and began to roll another cigarette. 'Nothing,' he said, licking the paper. 'I am content with my life and want nothing more.'

'I won't tell anyone,' Hettie said.

Elliot lit his cigarette. 'I know,' he said. 'Which is why you were chosen.' Getting up, he went to the dresser beside the fireplace. He opened a drawer and removed an envelope. Returning to the table, he handed it to Hettie. 'This is for you,' he said, taking a draw of his cigarette. 'My mother told me to hand it to whoever came to me to tell me about my father. I have been its custodian these forty years and now I pass it to you.'

Hettie took the envelope from Elliot. 'What should I do with it?' she said.

'Read it,' he said. 'But me and the dog will leave you in peace to do that.' He stubbed out his hardly smoked cigarette. Taking his jacket from the chair he pulled it on. He bent down and roused the dog by placing his hand before the dog's nose. It's tail wagged. Getting to its feet, the dog stretched and stood beside Elliot. Elliot took a cap from a hook beside the door. He placed it on his head and adjusted it. 'Help yourself to more tea, if you want it.' He gestured to the dog, and it trotted behind him out of the stables.

Hettie watched them go. For a moment she had been given an insight into a softer side of Elliot, before the brusque Yorkshire man she had known since childhood returned. No wonder he had been distraught at Sir Charles' passing. If he'd had even the vaguest hope that Sir Charles was his father, he would have been bereft at the thought he had lost him and lost the chance to know if it was true.

Hettie turned the envelope over in her hands. The paper was old and a little mottled in one corner. She slid her finger beneath the flap at the back and pulled out a single sheet of paper. Placing the envelope aside, she unfolded the letter. Her hands began to shake. She knew the handwriting. It was the handwriting of the two messages in her notebook. She steadied the page.

My dearest friend,

I hope you will not mind my addressing you in such a familiar way. But if you are reading this letter then you are very familiar to me.

There is a world beyond the world in which you live. You will realise this from how I have made myself known to you. I hope you are not afraid or unsettled by how I have come to you. That would never be my intention.

As I write this, I do not know you by name, but I know that we need each other. And the act of your reading my words means you have performed the greatest service to me. It is my time to return that.

I was blessed to find my soul love. It was when we were both young and free. We were together for hardly a moment in the history of time, but it was the greatest moment of my life, and the result was the greatest gift of my life.

There is not space enough on this page to explain how I know of your current situation. The universe has more mysteries than words can explain. What I want to say is that you will know when you find your soul love. And when you do, let your instincts guide you. They will not betray you. Don't always think. Feel your way through life.

Know that your loved ones who have left watch over you. They are by your side and love you. Those that went when it was their time and those that went before their time. All of them want what is best for you.

I thank you with all my heart.

Your friend forever,
Monica

Hettie let her eyes drift over the words. Monica. Elliot's mother. She let her mind take her to where it wanted to go. It was Monica who had written the words in her notebook. Monica whose presence she had felt in the cottage. Monica who she had seen for just a moment behind her closed eyelids. Hettie closed her eyes again. She saw her grandfather and Saul. Listening to Monica's words, she allowed herself to believe they were watching over her. They wanted what was best for her. And what was best for her was just a short walk down the path.

Hettie folded the letter and slipped it carefully back inside the envelope. She placed the envelope between the pages of her notebook and pushed it into her satchel. She was on her feet when she saw a familiar movement through in the stables. By the time she arrived at the furthest stall, Stella had been in to investigate and was on her way out.

'How are you, puss?' Hettie asked. She bent to stroke the cat's ears. Stella allowed it for a few seconds before she was on her way again, tail in the air, heading for Elliot's room at the end of the stables.

THIRTY-FIVE
APRIL 1876

Charles had to visit MacGregor's Mill on his final morning in Simpson's Bay. Plans had been made and he couldn't let anyone down. He had kissed Monica goodbye in the early hours of the morning after walking her home. She had to be back to feed the animals. She had said she would be there to see him off on the steamboat at midday.

Through the morning, Charles sat in a series of meetings where staff explained their jobs within the business. It was unnecessary to have that level of detail, but they seemed keen to share the information and were proud of the work they did.

All Charles could think of was the events of the early hours. He had snatched memories of Monica taking care of him in some way, but what was real and what had been a dream as she had nursed him through a fever was unclear. He had made such a quick and complete recovery that it was difficult to believe he had been ill at all.

What was in no doubt was what they had done when he had woken from his fever. The thought made heat rise to his cheeks. How could he possibly leave her today? He wanted to stay and show Monica how much he loved her, over and over again. Because he did love her. They had told each other so many times as they explored each other's bodies. Nature had taken over and they seemed instinctively to know what to do to prove their love.

Again, heat rose to Charles' cheeks. What kind of man would he be if, within the space of just a few hours, he lay with her then left her?

At just after eleven o'clock, Charles shook hands with Mr MacGregor and Ewan, telling them that his cousin would be in contact soon. He headed for the water's edge and paced up and down. By half past eleven, he had convinced himself that he would go to the farm to tell Monica that he was going to stay, if she would have him.

He turned and his heart leapt. Monica had just passed the cabinetmakers on her way to the jetty. She saw him look to her and indicated for him to follow her.

Charles followed Monica down a narrow pathway which led away from the town and onto a path into the woods. She guided him off the path into a dense copse of trees, and out of sight of anyone passing by. She waited and he caught up with her. He dropped his suitcase and put his arms around her. They held each other and kissed as they had kissed in the early hours.

He pulled away reluctantly and looked down at Monica. 'I'm staying,' he said.

She shook her head. 'No, you're not,' she said.

Still with his arms around her Charles said, 'Why not?'

Before Monica answered, she kissed him again. 'We were only ever meant to be together for a brief time,' she said. 'You have a whole life in a different part of the world, and you need to return to it.'

'I don't.' Charles objected.

Monica smiled at him. 'Live a great life,' she said. 'Do great things. You are so full of compassion, and you can put that to use.'

'I could put it use here,' Charles said.

'No, you couldn't,' she said. 'I will love you forever, but you need to go back to your life.'

It seemed to Charles that Monica would not see the situation his way. 'It's dishonourable to leave you after... after what we have done.'

'Honour has nothing to do with it,' she said.

When he tried to object again she silenced him by putting her finger to his lips.

'I have something for you,' Monica said. She took a step away from him so that his arms slipped from around her.

She knelt and moved snow around with her hands uncovering an object. 'I hid it here earlier,' she said. Getting to her feet, Monica held the object out to Charles. 'This is to protect you,' she said. She transferred a bottle into Charles' hands. It had a cork in one end and contained what looked like twigs and small flowers and foliage.

'I'm not sure I understand,' he said.

'There will be times in your life that you need protection,' Monica said. 'Search for the branches or leaves of the rowan, hawthorn and juniper if you ever need help. If you have this bottle with you, then I will always be with you. And I will protect you with a ferocity others can only imagine.'

Finally, Charles gave voice to the thought that had followed him through the morning. 'You saved my life last night, didn't you? How... how did you...?'

Monica smiled at him. 'I am my mother's daughter, and she taught me well. As her mother taught her and her mother before her. Nature can tell us what to do if we listen.'

Charles looked down at the bottle. 'There's no point in my arguing with you, is there?'

Monica shook her head. 'No.

Charles closed his hands around the bottle. 'I will treasure this forever. And I will treasure the memories of our time together. You have no idea what you mean to me.'

'Yes,' Monica said, 'I do.'

Charles bent to open his case. He wrapped the bottle inside his nightshirt. As he closed the case, the whistle signalling the steamboat's arrival sounded.

Getting to his feet Charles looked down into Monica's green eyes.

They kissed.

It was a kiss that would last a lifetime.

THIRTY-SIX
FEBRUARY 1937

Hettie stood before the shed in the walled garden. She knocked on the door. When it opened, she looked to the ground. She was forming an apology to Rhys for all she had said and done. But before she could speak, Rhys said, 'Morning. I'm glad it's you.'

It wasn't the welcome Hettie had been expecting. Neither was she expecting to see a smile when she looked up at Rhys. 'Are you coming in, then?' he said.

Stepping inside the shed, she could see that he had been busy making something at the workbench beneath the window.

'How are you this morning?' he asked.

'I've been better,' she said. 'I came to say sorry for—'

'Sorry? What do you have to be sorry for?'

'Yesterday.'

'What did you do yesterday that needs forgiveness?'

Hettie looked at Rhys as though expecting him to find an answer in her eyes.

'We all of us have a past,' Rhys said.

'Not many have one quite like mine,' Hettie said.

'I wouldn't be so sure,' Rhys said. 'I have something for you.' He turned to the workbench and collected a small wooden box.

Turning back to Hettie, he handed it to her. 'I made it last night, when I couldn't sleep,' he said. 'Aren't you going to open it?'

Hettie looked down at the exquisite box. 'It's for me?'

'Indeed, it is,' Rhys said.

Carefully she removed the small lid and looked inside. 'It's the pinch pot,' she said. 'That Sir Charles gave to you.'

'It is,' Rhys said. 'And now it's yours.'

'I couldn't,' Hettie said. She tried to hand the box back to Rhys. He refused to take it. 'But why?' Hettie said.

'Because I want you to be reminded that wherever in the world you go, I will be with you. As there are fingerprints on this pot, so you have left your fingerprints on me.' He closed his hands around Hettie's and took the box from her. Placing it on the workbench he took Hettie's hands in his again.

'Anyone who reads the newspapers knows that huge events are coming,' he said. 'And you will be there to tell the world through your reporting and your photography. It's what you were made for.'

'I'm glad you have that confidence in me,' Hettie said. She looked up and found him searching her eyes again. He leant into her. He pressed his lips to hers. All thoughts of apology left her mind. She put her hands to his hair and held him to her as they kissed. Rhys placed his hands either side of her face so that she felt the warmth through his palms. He moved his hands to her waist and pulled her to him. She felt his kiss through her whole body. She pulled away and looked to the bed at the back of the room.

Rhys shook his head. 'I have lived a whole decade longer than you. When you go back out into the world it will be as a free woman. And if you come back to me when you have done, I will still be here.' He leant into her and kissed her softly.

'I'm not sure I can wait that long,' Hettie said. She pressed her lips to his as she smiled.

'It's very tempting,' Rhys said. 'But you need to be free. And if you come back to me, you can be sure I will show you exactly how I feel about you.'

They kissed again.

And Hettie felt Rhys' kiss in her soul.

EPILOGUE
BERLIN, MAY 1945

A woman in khakis and a helmet stands on a pile of rubble that until a few days ago was an official government building. It has been two years since she secured a pass to report for an American magazine after her photo essay of an officer with facial wounds from the Great War struck a chord with that nation. She wears her PRESS armband with pride. Wherever she goes, she carries her camera bag on one side and typewriter bag on the other.

After three years reporting from the Home Front, she was desperate to get to the war front to report on actions on the continent. By rights, as a woman, she should report from behind the lines, but by design she has been at the forefront of many battles with her camera to report what she sees back to the world. Once or twice, she has been threatened with losing her official accreditation because of the risks she has taken.

A column of vehicles passes close by. She covers her face against the dust from their tyres and tracks. She has followed tanks, processions of people displaced from their homes and countries, watched gun battles and air attacks, and been present to bear witness to the atrocities some people can inflict on humankind. It has been the hardest thing of her life and the most rewarding.

She focuses her lens and takes a photograph of the rubble and a tattered red and white flag decorated with the face of an eagle. She puts the strap of her camera back around her neck and kicks dust at the flag. It is her small act of revenge.

She sits on the rubble and takes her pen from her bag. It is a silver pen given to her as a gift many years ago. She rips two pages from her notebook. She scribbles a few paragraphs to her parents. She adds a line for her good friend who is staying with them while undertaking postgraduate studies before becoming curator of their grandfather's collection of antiques and collectables.

She pushes her hand into her pocket and rubs her fingertips along the ridges in a tiny pinch pot. She pauses before she pens a second letter. It is to a man in a house hundreds of miles away. Wherever she goes, his letters find her. And his words give her strength and the courage to continue. His letters to her make her remember what it is to be decent. What it is to be alive. What it is to be human.

A LETTER FROM THE AUTHOR

Thank you so much for reading *The Mandeville Curse*. I hope you enjoyed the fourth mystery at Hill House with the Mandevilles and their new very special guest. If you want to join other readers in hearing all about my new releases and bonus content, you can sign up for my newsletter!

www.stormpublishing.co/callie-langridge

If you liked *The Mandeville Curse* and have a few moments, please do consider leaving a review. Even a short review can make all the difference in encouraging a reader to discover my books for the first time.

I loved diving back into the world of the Mandevilles. This book is particularly special to me as many of my ancestors lived in the East End of London and the fight of those people to be heard strikes a chord with me. I am also passionate about the role of women in World War II and loved exploring the build up to that time with Hettie.

Thank you again for being part of this amazing journey with me and I hope you'll stay in touch – I have so many more stories and ideas to share with you!

facebook.com/CallieLangridgeAuthor
x.com/CLangridgeWrite
instagram.com/CallieLangridge

ACKNOWLEDGEMENTS

I would like to thank Oliver and everyone at Storm for getting the Mandeville series into the world. Special thanks to Vicky and Kathryn for your continued support and your fantastic work in helping me make *The Mandeville Curse* the best it can be.

As always, this book has been helped on its way by the support of so many fellow authors. Thank you to Zoe Antoniades, Sam Hanson, Susie Lynes and John Rogers who have been on the journey with me for more years than I can remember. Thank you also to the writing pals I have gathered along the way – Clarissa Angus, Claire McGlasson, Emilie Olsson, Kate Riordan, Emma Robinson, Bev Thomas and Lisa Timoney.

I will be forever grateful to Kim, Val and Virginia for their ongoing encouragement and enthusiasm for my writing. And a very special thanks to Pete, always my cheerleader-in-chief.

Printed in Great Britain
by Amazon